BEAUTIFUL
Betrayal

NEW YORK TIMES BESTSELLING AUTHOR
LISA RENEE JONES

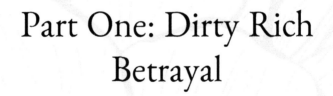

Part One: Dirty Rich Betrayal

Chapter One

Mia

With my rental idling at the gate of Grayson Bennett's beachside Hamptons mansion, I stare at the keypad. The code won't be the same. It's been a year now. He would have changed the code and yet, instead of punching the call button, my hand trembles as I reach for the numbers. I key in the code I once used often and the gate begins to creep open. I grip the steering wheel, some part of me wanting to believe that Grayson left the code in place because he hoped I'd come back. Which is ridiculous. The man betrayed me. He never loved me. He hurt me, and yet here I am, about to stand on his doorstep and ask to come inside his home and domain.

I drive the basic sedan that I picked up in the city to avoid a chopper service, and pull it around the circle drive, stopping on the opposite side of the house, where I park under my favorite willow tree. The minute I kill the engine, my heart thunders wildly in my chest. I can't believe I'm doing this, but I am. I'm here. I'm doing this. I slide my purse over my head and across my chest to allow it to rest on my jean-clad hip. I'm not backing out now.

Forcing myself to climb out of the car, I step into a gust of chilly late-October wind coming off the ocean. My light brown hair lifts, and the chill on my neck has me snuggling deeper into my light blue sweater. I inhale the fresh scent of the ocean, the taste of salt on my lips follows and so do the memories of this place, of me here with Grayson. I can't believe how emotional this feels. Why can't I just get over this man? I *am* over him. This is just me reacting to a time in my life when this man stole my every breath. It's a part of me, just as he always will be.

With that mantra in my mind, I hurry forward and rush up the stairs of the understated mansion with three steeples and wood siding. My chest pinches with the realization that the last time

I was here, Grayson had just inherited it from his late-father, a man I loved and respected. A good man with exceptional taste and standards. Raymond Bennett did nothing less than perfect, this stunning house included.

I stop at the door and reach for the bell, but my hand falls away, my lashes lowering, with the attack of memories that charge through my mind; the fight, the betrayal, the tears, so many gut-wrenching tears he didn't deserve, but there is also so much more—the history. The way he made me feel like I was his world when obviously I wasn't, but it doesn't seem to matter. I can't seem to forget him and standing here now, I can *still* smell his woodsy cologne and taste his passion and *my God.* My eyes pop open. What am I doing? I can't be here.

I should have just called.

I turn and head down the stairs, but my attempted escape comes too late. The roar of an expensive engine sounds moments before a black Porsche Boxster, Grayson's car of choice, circles the drive, and speeds toward me. I halt at the last step as he, in turn, halts the car directly in front of me. I hold my breath, preparing for the impact this man has always had on me, telling myself he won't anymore. I'm not the same person I was when we were together. I'm stronger. I'm harder. I'm more jaded.

I *won't* melt for Grayson Bennett.

He kills the engine and pops his door open, obviously not going into the garage. I'm here. He wants to know why. He unfolds himself and straightens all six feet three inches of his hard body, the wind catching in his thick, wavy dark hair, as my fingers often did in the past. He shuts his door, his unassuming, faded jeans and long-sleeved black T-shirt hugging every hard inch of a body that is just as perfect now at thirty-eight as it was at thirty-four when we met. Back when I was twenty-seven, his junior by eight years, and his wisdom and confidence inspired admiration and attraction in me.

He saunters toward me, his stride easy, but no less predatory, while oozing power and grace. He stops in front of me, towering over me despite the step down I have yet to take. He's close, so very close. My gaze sweeps the hint of gray in his neatly trimmed goatee that I like a little too much. My lashes lower, and I breathe out before I force myself to look at him, my stare colliding with his potent green eyes and even with all my inner dialogue about not reacting to him, I am. I feel every touch I've ever shared with this man right here, right now.

"Mia," he says softly, and I swear I feel his voice like a caress of his hand.

"Grayson," I say, and his name feels as right as it does wrong on my tongue. So right. So *wrong.*

"I didn't expect you," he says. "*Ever.*" There's a sudden coldness to his tone that stabs at me, a sharp bladed knife.

I'm an attorney and I'm good at my job. I maintain my control and I do it well, but I react now when I don't want to react. "This was a mistake," I say. "Forget I was here." I step around him and off the stairs, but he catches my arm and turns me to face him. Heat radiates from his hand, up my arm, and over my chest and Lord help me, my nipples are hard.

"There are many mistakes between us," he says. "Don't make coming here and backing out another one."

He's right, but that's my only thought. I can't think when he's touching me. I've never been able to think when this man touches me. "Can you not touch me, please?" I whisper.

He releases me like I've burned him when he's the one who burned me, his jaw hardening, his eyes icing. "Let's go inside," he says, motioning me forward, and I know this man. I still know him so very well. I hurt him just now. Why do I care that I hurt him? He practically took a knife and cut me open.

And yet, I do. "Grayson," I begin, not sure what I'm about to say or if I'll regret it, but he cuts me off.

"Let's go inside, Mia," he orders, anger in the depth of his voice when he rarely allows anyone to see anger, but then, this is me and I was always the one that broke through all that steel and control. Or maybe I didn't. Maybe I just thought I did because nothing was what I thought it was with Grayson.

I head up the stairs and he doesn't pull the power play of following me. That's not his style. He's at my side, and we fall into step as we walk to the porch, giving me the façade of sharing control. You don't share control with Grayson. You just think you do. That's where I went wrong with this man. I thought I was different. I believed I shared control with him. I believed I shared a lot of things with him, but I didn't. He owned me and the problem is that I wanted to be owned, but those days are over. He will never own me again.

He opens his door, and I don't know why I do it, but I look over at him and when his eyes meet mine, I do just what I said I wouldn't do. I fall into the sweltering heat of our years of history and melt for this man in a way no other man has ever made me melt. I hate him. I love him. I hate him. And as if it somehow protects me from all that he is to me, I dart inside the foyer of his home.

Chapter Two

Mia

The past, two and a half years ago

I leave the first day of my job as an associate with my head spinning. The Bennett firm is a massive operation, expanding across the world, and even outside the legal profession, which I now know is driven by the heir-apparent son. Grayson Bennett apparently wants to rule the world and he's succeeding. It's exciting to have this much opportunity after being stuck in a small firm that had a ceiling, thanks to my finances forcing me to attend a small school part-time to get my law degree. Finally, I've opened doors to a better future. Finally, I have the chance to yank my father out of poverty in Brooklyn.

Exiting the elevator, I start thinking about the case that I was put on today and how to approach winning. I need to have a plan that helps the partner I'm working under. I need to prove I can handle my own cases, the way I did at my prior firm. I hurry toward the exit and push through the glass doors on a mission. Home. Work. Research. I turn right and collide with a hard wall with such force it rattles my teeth.

"Oh my God," I gasp, as strong hands come down on my shoulders, while my hands have now settled on the broad chest of a man wearing an expensive three-piece suit. "I'm sorry. I was—" I lose that thought as I look up into his green eyes and my lips part in stunned shock. He's gorgeous. Perfect. Overwhelmingly perfect.

"No apology needed," he says softly and oh so very intimately, or maybe I'm imagining that because *come on*. What girl doesn't want this man to speak to her and only her? "In fact," he adds. "I think this is the best part of my really crappy day."

I swallow hard. "I uh—don't know how to reply to that."

The man to his right clears his throat. "We'll meet you upstairs," he says and only then do I even realize that this gorgeous man is standing in between two other men, but I don't look at them. Not when *he's* still looking at me and ignoring them. Not when his hands are still on my shoulders. The two men leave.

"Have a drink with me later," my newfound sexy stranger says, a push that is almost a command in his voice. He's older than me, thirty-five I think, while I'm twenty-seven, and he radiates the kind of confidence I need to own myself. He's no associate. He's no subordinate to anyone and I like this about him.

"I don't even know your name," I say.

One corner of his really delicious mouth curves and he says, "You will tonight. If you show up. Meet me at Morrell Wine Bar at eight. You owe me the date for running into me, but I'll buy the wine." He reaches up and strokes my cheek. "You have beautiful blue eyes, by the way." And then he leaves me there, stunned and warm all over.

When I can finally walk again, I'm not sure what to do. He has to work for Bennett. Am I allowed to date a coworker? I don't even know. I hurry toward the subway, and I try to reason with myself. He might not work for Bennett. Maybe he's just using their services. I haven't dated in a year. I've been too busy. I'm too busy now, but—there is just something about that man. He's inspiration for all I want and need to be. He owns who he is and what he is. You know this even without knowing him. I need to breathe that in, I need to have a glass of wine with that man.

Grayson

I'm packing up my office with one thing on my mind—the woman with the gorgeous blue eyes—when Eric walks in, his jacket gone, his sleeves rolled up to expose his tattooed arms. My father hates those tattoos, but to me they represent years of experience as a SEAL Team Six member while his Harvard degree is a product of a man who is both a literal savant with numbers and a mastermind behind most of our newest strategies. More so, his honesty and character make him a friend I trust.

"Your father is on a rampage," he says. "He's pissed about—well—everything."

"That usually means people get things done right next time."

"True," he says. "Though I prefer your quiet intolerance." I round the desk and he offers me a folder. "Those numbers you wanted on the building acquisition in Atlanta. They look good. I'd do it."

"Then we'll do it. Make it happen."

"After you look at the numbers. We're good because we see different things on paper. I don't want to sign off until I know what you see."

I nod. "Fair enough. I'll let you know in the morning."

"You're going to see that woman."

"I am."

"She's a new associate."

I arch a brow. "You checked?"

"Of course I checked. You're a fucking heir to a billionaire who's just made his own personal billion."

"With your help," I concede, "we've both taken a chunk of change and turned it into a whole lot more for this place and ourselves. For me, that's living up to my father's expectations. For you, it's a 'fuck you' to your father."

"And I want many more," he says. "My job is to watch your ass. I emailed you her file and then some."

"I'm not going to look at that. I'll know all I need to know when I'm with her." I start walking. I'd suspected she might work for the company, which is exactly why I booked our meet-up in my apartment building, not the offices.

"For the record," Eric calls out behind me, "on paper she's one of two things: the best thing that ever happened to you or the worst."

I stop at the door and look at him. "Sounds like the beginning of anything new." I turn and exit the office, and I don't even think about looking at that email. There is something about this woman that speaks to me. I can't explain it, but I don't want it ruined. I want it pure and I want to learn about her from her.

My car service is waiting on me and in roughly ten minutes, I'm exiting in front of my Central Park building. I hand the doorman my briefcase and tip him well enough to have him ensure my bag makes it to my apartment safely. Nix is a good man, who's been here the entire five years I have. I trust him. I always surround myself with people I trust, at every level.

I enter the bar, which is an intimate location with low hanging lights, a triangle-shaped bar, and booths lining the walls. I don't choose a booth. I head to the bar that allows me a view of the entire place and control. I also always choose control. I've barely sat down when the bartender sets my usual in front of me, an expensive whiskey they custom order for me. I'm not a man of extravagance by nature, but this whiskey is worth every dime I spend on it.

She walks in before I even take a sip, still wearing the same navy-blue suit dress that while conservative and appropriate for work, has a zipper that slides down the front. I noticed, but then I also noticed the tiny freckle on the corner of her eye. She looks around, scanning for me, and the curl of her fingers into her palms tells me she's nervous. She spots me and inhales a telling breath. Yes, she's nervous.

She walks in my direction and I watch every step, admiring her long, slender legs and the sway of her hips. I want this woman. I want her naked. I want her beneath me and I want to know who and what she is, and I have to know. I am a man with much to lose and she is too close to me and my company for me to wade blindly into anything. She stops at the seat next to me.

"Hi," she says.

"Hi," I say, finding her charming and sweet as few women strike me these days, and yet, intelligent. I see that in her eyes. "I'm glad you came."

She doesn't attempt to sit down. "I almost didn't."

"Why?"

"Because I have a lot on the line. I can't blow this job. I've been thinking about this and I need to know why you were at the Bennett building."

"Why does that matter?"

"Because I'm new there and I don't want to break any rules. So, before I sit down, I need to know if I really should."

I am a man who doesn't just like to trust people. I expect people to be honest. Because like my father, I'm honest, even when it makes my life harder. I like where she's going so far, but that doesn't mean my name won't show a side of her I won't like.

I stand up and my hands go to her waist. I turn her, placing her back to the bar, my body pinning her to it. "I appreciate your desire to follow the rules. Bennett allows inter-office relationships because I don't believe it's realistic to believe people can work together seventy hours a week, in a company this big, and never cross that line. I simply expect that they handle it professionally and let HR know."

She blinks. "I'm confused. *You* believe and expect?"

"What is your name?" I ask.

"Mia," she says, and like the good attorney she should be, she immediately circles back to her question. "I'm confused. You said—"

"I'm Grayson."

Her eyes go wide. "Grayson? As in—"

"Grayson Bennett," I supply.

"Oh my God." She pales. "Why didn't you tell me?"

"Would that have mattered?"

"*Would it have mattered?*" she asks incredulously. "Of course it would have mattered. I'm not trying to climb the ladder by climbing you."

I laugh. "Is that right?"

"Yes. It is. Please let me off the bar. I need to leave. Please, Grayson. I mean, Mr. Bennett."

I rotate us so that we're side by side, and she's no longer trapped, but my hands stay at her waist, hers on my chest when I want them all over my body. "Grayson," I say. "I hate Mr. Bennett. And I don't want you to leave, Mia. You interest me. I hope you're interested and not because of who I am."

"I am. I was, but how do I take that out of the equation?"

"I'm just a man."

"A billionaire."

"I'm just a man who wants to know you. Genuinely wants to know you and I can promise you that nothing between us will ever affect your job but neither does you walking away right now." I release her, but our legs are still touching and her hands don't leave my chest.

"I'm very confused right now." She leans back and her hands slide from my chest, but she doesn't step away. "I was interested in knowing you or I wouldn't have come here, but you being you, I need to think about this."

"I can live with that answer. Put my number in your phone. Then you can call me. You can decide what happens next."

"But you're my boss."

"Not directly. Let me have your phone."

She hesitates. I hate that she hesitates, but she reaches into her purse and hands me her phone. It rings and "Dad" comes up on her caller ID. "Sorry," she says and punches the decline button.

"You could have taken it," he says. "Fathers are important."

She tilts her head and studies me. "You're close to your father, too?"

"Very. As I was with my mother who I lost far too long ago."

She doesn't immediately respond and seems to weigh her words before she says, "I lost mine last year. I know it—it hurts. My dad is really struggling with it."

"Mine still does as well," I say, aware that it took my father well over a year to resemble anything I knew as him. "You should call your father back. You don't want him to worry."

"I'll call him in a few minutes. He knows I work long hours. See, that's just it. That's what I need you to know before I walk out of this bar. It's not because I want to. It's because I *have* to. I worked my way through school. I got accepted to two Ivy League colleges, but I couldn't go part-time or pay the tuition. I had to work for a tiny firm for two years to prove I can win cases just to get this job. And I can win. I was a good hire. I'll do a good job for you. And I can't blow that or risk being 'that' girl in the legal circles."

I let her story sink in. She could easily be someone who looks for a gravy train, but she's not and this isn't a show for her. She's not playing me. She's rejecting me, and I don't intend to let that happen. I'm still holding her phone and put my number in it, but I don't give it back to her. "I don't sleep with or date women my company employs."

"Then why am I here?"

"You interest me, now more than ever." I cup her face. "I'm going to kiss you now unless you tell me to stop."

"I don't think you should do that."

"That's not stop, Mia."

"I know," she whispers, and my mouth closes down on hers, and the moment I taste her on my tongue, I know that I want more. And when she gives a tiny little whimper and leans into me, I know she does too, but still, I pull back and press her phone into her hand.

"You have my number. Call me, but know this, Mia. The next time I kiss you, I won't stop."

Chapter Three

Mia

The present

I don't stop in the foyer that is too small not to be too close to Grayson for comfort. I quickly clear the small space and enter the open concept living area with dark wood floors, high ceilings, and dangling lights. I stop there, on the edge of a living room that no longer looks as it once did, the black couches now replaced with gray leather that matches the kitchen island to the left. I swallow hard, thinking about how hard it must have been for Grayson to take over this place, let alone decide if he should leave it as it was or change it. He loved his father deeply.

Grayson steps to my side and we both stare at the room and I wonder if he too is thinking about the funeral, and the last time we ever touched. The betrayal was gone that day, but the pain was not. "I won't say what I'm thinking," I say softly, my voice trembling ever-so-slightly.

"You don't have to. I know what you're thinking." He motions to the left. "Let's go downstairs."

Downstairs to the bar and entertainment area of the house. Downstairs, far away from the door. I wonder if he chooses this location to prevent my rapid escape, but nevertheless, this is his home. This is his decision. I nod and of course, he falls into step with me, but once we're at the winding gray and steel stairs leading downward, the path is made for one, and he does the gentlemanly thing and allows me to go first. I hesitate just a moment, but I start walking, grabbing the railing and carefully taking each step, aware of Grayson at my back in every pore of my body. Aware, too, that he didn't ask me why I'm here.

Once I'm on the lower level, there's a room with a brown sectional, a massive big-screen television to the left, and a fancy half-moon shaped bar to the right. "Let's drink," Grayson says, as he joins me, his shoulder brushing mine, and the touch is such a shock that I suck in air and cut my gaze.

I don't look at him, but I feel his stare before he moves toward the bar. I follow him, choosing a barstool opposite him as he rounds the oak countertop. "Still love your Brandy Alexanders?"

"Yes, but I better not. I'm driving back tonight. You know I don't handle my booze well." The reference to how well he knows me is out before I can stop it.

"I do know," he says, setting a glass in front of me before producing a bottle of brandy.

He then proceeds to mix my drink before filling his own glass with what I am certain is his favorite fifteen-year old scotch. He sets my glass in front of me. "But we both need a drink right about now." He picks up his glass, downs it, refills it, and then walks around the bar to stand beside me. So damn close that I can feel his body heat, and when my eyes meet his, I'm burning alive again, and yet I'm frozen in place.

"Grayson—"

"Grab your drink," he orders softly. "Let's go to the patio where you won't feel as trapped as you feel right now." He steps away from the bar and starts walking.

He knows me too well. He still knows me like no one else in this world, but it means nothing. Grayson observes people. He reads people. I pick up my drink and stand up. Grayson is to my left, opening the curtains. I join him as he opens the patio door and I step under the awning into the stone-encased private porch overlooking the ocean; the sun hidden behind clouds, a storm rumbling in the distance. I love storms over the ocean. The fireplace in the corner flickers to life and Grayson steps to my side.

I down my drink. "Now I can let it wear off before I drive." I set the glass on the table to our left that seats two and matches the one to our right, and then walk to the stone wall directly in front of us, my hands settling on the finished wooden rail above it.

I hear Grayson's glass touch the table before he steps to my side, his hands on the rail as well. "Talk to me, Mia."

I look over at him. "I came to warn you."

"What does that mean?"

"Ri is coming after you," I say.

He laughs. "Ri is always coming after me. He's been coming after me since law school when I made him look bad, and now that we both run our family empires, he's still trying to best me. He won when he got you."

I face him, and he does the same with me. "That's not even close to true. He didn't *get* me."

"He's my enemy and you left me, my bed and my company to go to him, his bed, and his company."

"That's not true. I needed a job and that's on *you.*"

"You didn't need a damn job," he bites out.

I shove fingers through my hair. "This is not why I'm here. I need you to listen to me."

"You want to tell me how the man you're fucking wants to fuck me?"

"I am not fucking Ri. Stop. Listen to me, Grayson. *I need you* to *listen to me.*"

"Like you listened to me? Because I tried really damn hard to get you to listen to me, Mia. Do you remember? Because I damn sure do."

I hug myself, backing up to rest against the concrete pillar behind me. "I listened. It wasn't enough, but you need to listen to me now. I just took a week off to look for a new job. I went to an interview at the DA's office."

"The DA's office? You won't make any money there. Why would you even consider such a thing? You're too good for that place."

"I'm tired of money. Your money. Ri's money. I want to be someplace that isn't about money and power, only I was there all of forty-five minutes and I knew that place was no different. They're all looking for power, the kind you have, which makes them hate you."

"What does that mean?"

"I was sitting in an office with an open door. There were men, four of them, I think, in the conference room across from me. They were talking about the billionaire who pretends to be ethical and perfect. Who thinks he's untouchable, but he's not. They said they have insiders in your operation. They said they're going to take you down and look like kings."

"Did they say my name?"

"No, but—"

"I don't break the law. That's not me."

"I know that. That's why I'm here. I was afraid your phones were being monitored because Grayson, it was you they were talking about. I know it. I felt it and I remember a card from a detective on Ri's desk. He's somehow setting you up."

He narrows his eyes at me. "And you're telling me, the man you say betrayed you, why?"

"You're not a criminal. And that's all I have to say." I push off the wall and try to walk past Grayson, but he shackles my arm and pulls me to him.

We stare at each other, our lower bodies pressed together, the past between us, and in this moment, it's pulling us closer, not pushing us apart. Thunder crashes above us and rain explodes from the sky, plummeting the ceiling above us and beyond the patio. Grayson tangles the fingers of one hand in my hair, while the other flattens between my shoulder blades. "You didn't really think I'd let you leave without doing this, did you?" he asks, his mouth closing down on mine.

Chapter Four

Mia

The minute Grayson's mouth is on my mouth, his body pressed to mine, I forget everything but him. It's like I can breathe again, like I've barely been living until right here, right now. I don't want to, but I still love him, and I didn't think I would ever kiss him or touch him again. He backs me up and presses me against the wide concrete pillar that divides the railings and walls, his fingers tangling into my hair, his hand slipping under my sweater, his warm palm pressing to my ribcage. It's not until that hand cups my breast that I jolt into reality.

"Stop," I say, catching his hand and pressing on his chest. "Stop. I can't do this."

He goes still but he doesn't immediately release me. God, I don't want him to release me and yet, I cannot survive the onslaught of emotions he creates in me if I don't stop now. I can't just fuck him. It's not in me. "Right," he says, his hand falling away, and pressing onto the concrete on either side of me, his body lifting away from mine. "You're with Ri."

"I'm not with Ri, and if I was with him or anyone, it wouldn't be any of your business. We're not together anymore."

"You went from me to him; you went to my enemy. Do you know how badly that cut? That's when I stopped coming after you. That's when I let you go."

"I was trying to survive. And you were cut? I was bleeding out. And do you really think I'd come to you if I was with Ri? I'm a loyal person. I never betrayed you. I wouldn't betray someone I was with."

"Unlike me, right?" he challenges. "I did not betray you. I've tried to explain."

"I'm not here to talk about this. I can't go down this path again. It still hurts and me telling you that is more than you deserve."

He stares at me, those green eyes unreadable, but his emotions are radiating off of him and pounding on me even as the rain pounds against the roof. He pushes off the pillar and walks a foot away to plant his hand on the railing and lowers his chin to his chest.

I can still feel his hand on my breast. I can still taste him and it's killing me. "I said what I came to say. I should go." But I don't move. I don't push off the pillar.

"Don't," he says, looking over at me. "Don't go."

There's torment in his voice, a guttural plea that conflicts with all he did to me. I know this, but I don't move. I squeeze my eyes shut. "I don't know why I'm still standing here." My lashes lift. "I can't stay. I have to go." I move then, I try to walk past him, but he pushes off the railing and steps in front of me.

"Eric and Davis are about to be here," he says of his best friend and business manager, and his personal attorney. "I'd like them to hear what you had to say."

"You can tell them."

"I'd like them to hear it from you."

"I need to get back."

"Stay the night and you can chopper back with me tomorrow."

"I have a rental car," I argue.

"I'll take care of it for you."

I hug myself. "I don't need or want you to take care of anything for me."

He looks skyward and then lowers his head to cast me in a turbulent stare. "You're helping me. It's the least I can do."

I inhale and let it out. "I'll get a room and drive back tomorrow."

"This house is ridiculously large. You can stay on another floor. You'll never know I'm here."

"I'll know you're here." I turn away from him and press my hands to the railing. He mimics my action and we stand there, side by side, the rain pounding fiercely.

"You always loved the rain on the ocean," he murmurs after a few moments.

I loved it when I was with him. I have good memories of loving it *with* him. "I won't let you hurt me again," I whisper.

We look at each other, a punch in the connection between us before he says, "I never meant to hurt you. I would die for you, Mia. That hasn't changed."

I cut my stare, so very confused because I believe him and that makes the way we ended illogical, at least for me, at least for my way of loving someone. I don't understand his kind of love and yet I need it so damn badly. "If I'm staying, I'll take a glass of that scotch."

I feel his eyes on me, those perfect, intelligent green eyes, before he says, "Scotch it is," and pushes off the railing. "I'll be right back."

I nod, but I don't watch him walk away. I stare out into the rain and my mind goes back to another day, back to the funeral, to sitting in the car and staring at the church. I hadn't seen Grayson in six painful months. I'd told myself that I was out of his life. I'd told myself that he wouldn't want me there, but I'd cared about his father and I still loved him. And so, I'd gotten out of that car. I'd gone inside.

Grayson's footsteps sound behind me and I turn as he sets the bottle down on a table between the two chairs facing the fireplace. He fills two glasses, mine with ice, and his without because he knows I'll want ice, and then he hands me mine. I know he's going to touch me, but I don't resist. I reach for my glass and when our hands collide, he catches mine and walks me to him.

Heat radiates up my arm from where he touches me and I know if I look at him, I'll forget why that kiss was bad when it felt so damn good. For several seconds we just stand there, rain and history suffocating us until he reaches up and brushes my cheek. The touch shocks me, and I shiver, my gaze jerking to his. "Let's sit down by the fire," he says softly.

"I'd like that."

He seems to hesitate to release my hand, but it slowly slides away and neither of us move. The wind gusts and that's enough to set us in motion. I walk around the chairs and sit down in front of the fire, sipping from the glass. "That's strong," I say as he sits down next to me and I place the glass on the table between us. "Maybe you need to drink mine. Eric and Davis aren't going to be an easy audience for me." I lean forward and hold my hands toward the fire, my elbows on my knees.

Grayson leans forward with me, only he ignores the fire. "They've both always liked you, Mia. You know that."

"They're your friends, your very good friends. They'll protect you, which is good. That's why I came. So you can throw up the armor."

"I thought I had," he says. "And then you showed up at my door." Grayson's cellphone buzzes with a text, and he pulls it from his pocket, glancing at the screen. "Eric," he says. "They're almost here." He sticks his cell back into his pocket, downs his drink, and stands up. "Let's meet them upstairs."

I nod and decide I do need that drink. I pick it up and take a big slug before setting it down. I stand up and turn to walk toward the door but Grayson steps in front of me. "Don't even think about leaving while they're here. I'll come after you, and this time I won't stop coming." He pulls me to him, his long legs pressed to mine. "We're not done, Mia. Not now. Not tonight. Not ever. We're done pretending otherwise." He kisses me, a brush of lips over lips that I feel in every part of me before he rotates us and turns me to the door, his hands on my shoulders, my back to his front as he leans in and whispers, "But be warned. I'm not going to stop the next time I kiss you."

Chapter Five

Mia

Grayson's warning twists me in knots and ultimately anger takes root. I whirl around to face him. "You don't get to say what we do or don't do. You don't get to decide if we kiss or not. You don't get to decide if we start or stop. You're not in control anymore."

"I was never in control," he says, his voice tight with returned anger. "Not with you."

"Are you kidding me? You controlled everything in the past. I was making my first real career move and your father—you, basically—owned the company. You had money and power and I came from nothing. You were this force of nature I wanted to be near. I wanted to learn from you. I wanted to be with you. You *consumed* me. I—this is not then. You're not in control this time."

His hands come down on my arms and he pulls me to him. "It sure as hell didn't feel like I was in control when you left, and I bled out both times, Mia. Both fucking times."

Both times.

He means after the funeral, which is just another knife in my chest.

"Look at us," I say. "This is who we are, Grayson. Pain and anger. Why would you want to keep me here?"

The doorbell rings and he curses, but he doesn't let me go. "Because the pain and anger are about a betrayal that never fucking happened." He tangles his fingers in my hair. "We have never fought this out honestly and completely." His mouth closes down on mine, his tongue stroking deep, and every part of me inside and out, melts into him, into us, when I don't mean to. The doorbell rings again and he tears his mouth from mine. "We're still us. We're *still us.*"

"I don't know what that means anymore."

"You will," he promises, his hands coming down on my arms once more. "Mia—"

The doorbell rings again and he grimaces. "Damn it. They aren't going away. I have to let them in."

"You do," I say. "We need to talk with them about Ri."

"Ri," he repeats tightly. "Yes. Let's talk about Ri." He releases me, a cold snap in the air as he motions me forward.

I don't like this reaction. I don't like what he thinks is between Ri and I, but I decide maybe it works right now, especially where Ri is concerned. He needs to find that hard, cold part of himself and find it now. He needs to focus on the war before him, not on me, not on us. With that thought, I launch myself across the room, hurrying up the stairs, and I half expect his hand on mine at any moment, but it doesn't happen. I've hit a nerve in him and some part of me revels in the fact that he has nerves to be hit. If he didn't care about me, he wouldn't, but I don't know why it matters. I don't want to do love his way.

I reach the upper level and I decide to offer Grayson privacy with his team to explain why I'm here, and I do so without his permission. I cross the living room and head out to the upstairs patio that oversees a rectangular infinity pool that seems to flow right into the ocean when it doesn't. I flip on the heater and ignore the round table that he often uses for meetings. Instead, I stand at the railing overlooking the pool, watching the now steady, but slower flow of raindrops hit its surface.

"Mia."

At the sound of Eric's voice, I turn to find him joining me, his light brown hair tousled, his blue eyes as intelligent as ever, but then why wouldn't they be? This is a man who's been by Grayson's side, helping him make billions, for years now. "Hi, Eric," I say, hugging myself.

"It's been a long time," he says, setting his briefcase on the table, while his snug black tee allows me a clear view of his tattoo sleeve that was once a jaguar with blue eyes, and now travels down his arm in a collage of clocks and skulls. "I haven't seen you since—" He stops himself, his lips thinning.

"The funeral," I supply. "I can't believe that's been a year now."

"I know," he says. "I can't either. I don't know how the hell Grayson lives in this place, aside from the fact that he's in the city so damn much." He shakes his head. "Enough of that, though. Davis needed Grayson to call an investor. They'll be right here."

"Good. I'm glad to have a moment with you. Maybe you'll listen before they get here because I'm not sure Grayson will. He's in trouble."

"If you're here, then he must be." He closes the space between us. "Talk to me."

"I'll tell you what I've told him." I tell him everything, the job, the interview, what I overheard at the DA's office. "They were talking about Grayson. I know they were and I saw that card on Ri's desk. Please tell me that you see that as the problem I do."

He narrows his eyes at me. "Why are you here if you're with Ri?"

"I'm not with Ri, and I'm smart enough to see the writing on the wall. He wants me to taunt Grayson. I'm a token in a game."

"And yet you went to him."

"I took a job, and I'm certain you know more about why than maybe I did before—" I stop myself. "At the time, I admit I was angry at Grayson and hurt. I just needed a place to go."

"You knew how he'd feel about you going to Ri."

"Do you know how I felt about what *he* did?" I hold up a hand. "It doesn't matter. I'm not with Ri and I'm tired of being a token in a game between two powerful men."

"You're not a token," Eric says. "You're the woman Grayson loves and that hasn't changed. You're a weapon Ri is using against him."

"I know that now," I say. "That's why I'm here. I'm not going to be a weapon against Grayson. Not now or ever."

Grayson steps onto the porch and our eyes meet, the charge between us cracking. "I never intended to be a weapon against you, Grayson. Please believe that."

Grayson lowers his lashes, the lines of his face hard and sharp. He's struggling to maintain control, and he never struggles to maintain control, because of me. Because we both know I'm not completely innocent. I did leave him and go to his enemy. I did know that would upset him. I wanted to hurt him the way he hurt me.

"I regret it," I breathe out, saying the words I should have said a long time ago, the words I'd rather say to him alone. "I regret going to him, Grayson."

His lashes lift and I don't find forgiveness or understanding. I find anger.

Chapter Six

Mia

"Mia," Davis says, stepping to Grayson's side; he's a tall man, in his late thirties, with dark brown hair and a beard to match. Today he's left his famously expensive suits behind for jeans and a T-shirt. "It's been a long time," he says warmly when he's rarely warm to anyone. "*Too* long."

I am stunned by how warm his greeting is and this tells me that Grayson never gave him reason to hate me. Grayson's angry, yes. They know he's angry, but my stomach twists with the idea that they're sympathetic to me, that they know he's guilty of *much* with me. Some part of me wants to believe he's not. I've always wanted to believe that he's not, perhaps because I had this fairytale idea of who and what we could be, what I thought we were. Maybe because my father loved my mother to the point of no return. He would have died for her. The man gave her part of his lung to try to save her life. And no, it's not a fairytale in that she died, but their love was.

Now *my* lashes lower, the pain of losing Grayson is acid in my throat. "Let's sit," Grayson says, motioning to the table, and we all listen because he's the one in charge, and not because this is his house. Because no matter how powerful the people in the room, Grayson owns the room itself, he's in control and I've always found this incredibly alluring. What I didn't do, was fear where that would lead me or what that power over me meant until he burned me. I cannot allow him to burn me again.

I walk to the table and sit down, noting the rain has now stopped, the only storm left is that between myself and Grayson. Eric sits to my right, Davis across from me, but there is only one person that consumes me. Grayson sits to my left and when we look at each other, no one else exists, a million unspoken words and so much anger between us.

Eric clears his throat. "I'll update Davis. Grayson, Mia ran through the situation with me. To make a long story short, Mia was at the DA's office for an interview."

"An interview?" Davis asks. "Why the fuck would you interview with the DA?"

"Irrelevant," Eric states. "She overheard a plan to take down Grayson."

"Grayson doesn't break the law," Davis states. "This is ridiculous."

"It's a set-up," I say. "I saw one of the detective's cards on Ri's desk. I think he's behind it all and that means he's doing what he has to in order to ensure Grayson looks guilty."

Grayson looks at Eric. "Where are we weak enough to allow this to happen?"

"You have employees worldwide, Grayson," he says. "Anyone could be paid off to plant false information, or to even go so far as to break the law. I told you. We should have dealt with Ri years ago."

"He had Mia," Grayson says. "I didn't think he'd act beyond that, but obviously, that's changed."

"I know a guy at the DA's office," Davis says. "I'll make a call. It'll cost us, but he'll get us what we need to know. If he confirms there's a problem, we're at war and we need a good criminal attorney advising us. I'm corporate and I'm good, but I want an expert."

"I'm criminal law," Grayson says. "I can handle it. I don't want anyone involved that could leak this."

"You haven't actively practiced in years," Eric argues. "And you're too close to this personally. I agree with Davis. We'll need an expert to help you insulate yourself."

"I'm a criminal lawyer," I say. "I'm actively practicing and I'm good at my job."

"You're too close to this, *and* to the enemy," Davis says, his voice hard now.

"I haven't lost a case," I say, that topic hitting a nerve between Grayson and I that has me avoiding his stare. "And I haven't resigned from Ri's company. I can get close to him and—"

Grayson gives a bitter laugh. "That's priceless, Mia. Really fucking priceless. You left me to fuck him and now you want to fuck him for me? Or fuck him because you aren't fucking me anymore." He stands up and without a word, walks into the house.

My emotions quake inside me and I can feel my hands shaking when I never shake, but this is Grayson. This is the man I still love and never stopped loving. I look between the two men he trusts the most. "I'm not with Ri. I have never been with Ri. I swear to you both."

"He's the one who needs to hear it," Eric says. "Not us."

He's right.

I stand up and follow Grayson, shutting the sliding glass door as I enter the living room.

I find him behind the island, his hand on the counter, head dipped low, my regret I'd declared gnawing at me. I'm not a person that lashes back. I really didn't lash back the way he thinks I lashed back, and for reasons he might not deserve, I really need him to know the truth. I don't leave the island between us. I round the counter and I stand beside him, facing the counter, not him.

"I've never been with Ri. I know you think I was, but I haven't been. He's tried for years. Recently I was lonely. I was *really* lonely, Grayson. I saw a picture of you with a woman and I realized that you'd moved on and I hadn't."

"I didn't fucking move on, Mia," he says turning to face me. "I was trying to survive you fucking my enemy."

I whirl around to face him as well. "I didn't, though. I didn't fuck Ri." My voice lifts as I add, "*Ever*. After seeing you with her, I finally agreed to go out with him. I tried to do what you think I already did and I had to drink wine, lots of wine, to try and actually make it happen. I mean, why wouldn't I? You and I—and you were—" I stop myself. "It doesn't matter why. I had too much wine. I fell asleep on his couch and even after seeing you with that woman, I dreamed about you, and us, and I called out your name."

"You did what?"

"I called out your name and since I was dreaming about the funeral, after the funeral, actually, the last time we were together, it wasn't in anger, but passion."

He's still, so very still, before he says, "And what did he do?"

"He was furious and then he grabbed me and tried to force himself on me. He told me he'd make me forget you."

Grayson's hands come down on my arms and he pulls me to him. "Did he force himself on you? Because if he did, I'll kill him."

He speaks those words with such guttural anger that I believe him. My hand settles on his chest, his heart racing beneath my palm.

"I gave him a knee so damn hard, I doubt he walked right for a week."

"I'm not sure that's a good enough punishment."

"He didn't touch me again. He got the point. Grayson, I should never have gone to him at all. He wanted what was yours and I knew that and even though he couldn't have me, at least, to him, you thought he did. Now, I left him and he's lashing out. I did this. I did this to you and I'm so sorry. You have to let me help. I don't want to go near that man, but I need you to understand that I'll do it for you."

"Going back to him is like sticking another knife in my heart, Mia. You will not go back to him. Do you understand me?"

"If it protects you, I will."

"You will not. That's not up for debate."

"You don't get to decide."

He turns me and pins me between himself and the counter, his powerful legs caging mine, his hands on my waist. "On this," he says. "Watch me. I'm not letting you go back to him. Even if I have to do what I should have done before and tie you to my damn bed until you listen to reason. One of my biggest regrets is not doing that a year ago, so I damn sure will do it now."

Chapter Seven

Mia

"Grayson—" I say, determined to make him listen.

"Don't," he says. "I know you still know that look and that plea on your lips makes me give in, but not this time. Not when it comes to you and Ri."

"I'm here because I caused this, because I care. You don't have to tie me to your bed. I'm staying. I'm not leaving. Please, just tell me you'll hear me out."

"Quid pro quo. I hear you out. You hear me out."

We're going down this path of the past. I can't stop it from happening. I'm not sure, if I'm honest with myself or him, that I want to stop it. "On one condition. We deal with us after him because I don't want either of us letting the past get in the way of shutting Ri down."

"Then we operate just like we did at the funeral. Nothing is off limits."

"Grayson—"

He cups my face and kisses me, a deep slide of tongue that has me biting back a moan. "God, I missed kissing you."

I missed it too, so very much, but I don't say that to him. I can't.

He rests his forehead against mine. "I need to go talk to Eric and Davis."

"Yes," I agree, pressing on his chest and forcing him to look at me, "you do. Be open-minded to what they say. I want to help."

"You have. You've motivated me to destroy him once and for all."

His voice is hard, the glint in his eye pure evil genius that actually comforts me. You don't beat Grayson Bennett when he's in this state of mind, but that also means he won't listen to reason on my influence over Ri. "I just packaged a convention center deal in Japan. There are a few legal issues on that project that are time-sensitive. I have to deal with that today. I have no choice."

"A convention center. Wow. That's huge."

"It is. It's going to double our worth."

And make Ri hate him all the more. "I'm not going anywhere, Grayson. Take care of your business. Just make sure Ri is part of that business."

He presses his hands on the island on either side of me. "You didn't cause his attack, Mia. I did. I let this misunderstanding between us go on too long, but no more." He pushes off the counter. "Do you have a bag in the car?"

"Yes. I was afraid I couldn't get to you tonight."

He studies me a long moment. "I'll get your bag." He starts to move away.

I catch his arm. "It's light. I'll get it. You go take care of business."

"Take it to my room. That's part of the deal. We put the past on hold."

My lashes lower and he cups my face. "Mia. Look at me."

I open my eyes. "My room," he says.

"Yes," I say, finding the idea that I would pretend I'd end up anywhere else a waste of energy at this point that would border on the kind of games I don't like to play. "Your room. I'm going to take a walk, though. I need to clear my head. I'll take my phone. You know my number."

His hand comes down on the island beside me again. "Yes. I know your number, just like you know the gate code to this house when no one else does. There was *never* a time when you couldn't get to me, Mia. You just didn't choose to find out until now." There is anger in his words again, in his voice. He pushes off the island and walks away and that anger is what I focus on.

He's angry, like I betrayed him, and for the first time since right after the funeral, I let myself consider the option that he's not guilty of at least one of his sins, the unforgivable one, but I shove that naiveté away. I know what happened. I swallow hard and quickly push off the island and start walking, my path leading me to my car, where I open the trunk and remove a hoodie from my suitcase. I pull it on and then head down a walkway at the side of the house that leads to the beach. Once I'm there, I walk to the edge of the water and turn and stare at the house.

This was his father's place, but we were here more weekends than his father. This is where we came after the funeral. This was where our final goodbye took place. Memories of that day charge at me and I turn away from the house and start running, the way I used to run this beach. I don't stop until I'm two miles away at the lighthouse, which I didn't just come to with Grayson. He'd bought it because I loved it so much. The sun is dimming, soon to begin fading into the horizon, the way Grayson and I faded into the horizon.

I start climbing the winding steps until I'm at the very top where Grayson and I had set-up cozy reclining chairs, side by side. I claim the one that was mine, and I painfully wonder if any other woman has been here with Grayson when I have no right. We aren't together. We haven't been together in a long time. I pull my knees to my chest and I think of his father, who is now gone. I think of the funeral, as I have so many times since he left this world. The way I did the night I pissed off Ri. It was almost a new beginning until Grayson left his phone on the bed, and I saw the number on his phone.

Grayson

I'm not a man who builds his success on other people's destruction, but I have limits, and Ri is going to find out that he's pushed me too far. I walk out onto the patio and sit down with Eric and Davis. "Go," I say, which is what I use as an invitation for them to hit me with their thoughts, of which I'm certain they have many after hearing Mia's reasons for being here.

"She's always had good instincts," Eric says. "If she believes that conversation was about you, I'm betting on her."

"Agreed," Davis says. "I trust her, and I don't trust anyone. I still think we need a criminal attorney on this."

"What we need," I say, "is an attack plan. I want Ri to go down once and for all. Make that happen and I don't care what resources, including money, it takes. Pay whoever, as much money as you have to pay them, to get the right dirt on him, to shut him down."

"Mia's already on the inside," Davis says. "She—"

"No," I say. "Mia will not go back to Ri. End of subject. What else do I need to know right here and now?"

"Reid and Carrie are headed back to Japan to take care of the challenges with the convention center takeover," Eric says, of the brokers who brought the deal together. "The other ten things on my list can wait." He eyes Davis. "We need a minute."

Davis gives him a nod and stands up. Eric waits until Davis enters the house and then leans closer. "I don't know what happened between you and Mia, but not only did it change you, it clearly hurt her. Despite that, she was there for you when your father died and she's here now. Considering the pain I still see in her eyes, I know two things: a) she still loves you, and b) she believes this threat is serious."

"I'm not discounting the threat, Eric. I said ruin him."

"You have thousands of employees, including me, counting on you. You don't have the luxury of leaving her out of this."

"Find another way," I order.

"Protect her, but keep an open mind. She could be the only person who can tear him down."

"Find another way," I repeat, and this time I stand up. "I will not have her feel as if I'm using her for my own gain or that I'm putting my well-being over hers."

He stands. "Not yours. Thousands of employees."

"And I damn sure won't risk hurting her again," I add as if he hasn't spoken. "I love you, man, and you're the brother I never had, but don't push me on this. Not on Mia." I step away from the table and head for the walkway down to the beach, with one destination in mind. The lighthouse, where I know Mia will be right now.

Chapter Eight

Mia

The past, six months ago

I pull up to the curb a few blocks from the Hamptons church and park the rental I picked up to get here from the city since I don't own a car that I'd never drive anyway. No one owns a car in Manhattan who doesn't have parking money to blow, and after growing up in a poor area of Brooklyn, I'm pretty sure I'll never feel I have that kind of money to blow. It's why I declined the car Grayson tried to buy me way back when. I didn't need it and his money was never what we were about to me. I always wanted him to know that. I always felt he *needed* to know that.

I breathe a heavy breath and kill the engine, my hands gripping the steering wheel. I want to be here for Grayson, no matter what has transpired between Grayson and I, but I don't know if I'm making this pain better or worse for him. I still love him. I don't want to make it worse, but this was not expected. A heart attack is never expected. I need Grayson to know that I wanted to be here, even if he rejects me. Even if he has someone else by his side now.

I swallow against the dryness in my throat and step out of the car, slipping the slender black purse I'm wearing over my black dress, across my chest. I shove the door shut, and damn it, my knees are wobbling. I push forward and start walking, along with a good ten other people parked nearby. I can feel eyes on me, surprised eyes that know I was with Grayson and I'm not anymore, but I don't care. I'm not here for them.

Once I reach the gorgeous white church, which ironically has three steeples just like Grayson's father's house just down the road does, I stand on the sidewalk and just stare at the door. It's almost time for the service and there are no people lingering here or there, as I'm certain there would have been earlier. I make my way up the concrete path and then travel a good twenty steps. I enter the church, and as soon as I'm inside, Eric, dressed in a black suit, is standing in front of me, as if he'd seen me approach.

"Did he tell you to send me away?"

"No," he says. "He doesn't know you're here, but he won't send you away. He needs you."

My eyes are already starting to burn. "Take me to him," I whisper.

He motions to the left, and I follow him down a hallway to a doorway where we stop. "He's alone."

I nod and he opens the door. I inhale and shut my eyes, deep breathing for a few beats. I haven't seen Grayson in six months, which feels like a century. I have so many hurt feelings with him but now is not about those feelings. I open my eyes and enter a compact prayer room to find Grayson standing in front of a cross with his back to me.

"Grayson," I say softly.

His shoulders flex, his entire body tensing before he slowly turns to face me and even today, in a black pinstripe suit, his face etched in grief for a father he loved dearly, he is beautiful. "Mia," he breathes out as if he's seeing an illusion.

"Yes. I—I wanted to be here for you and him. I hope it's okay. If it's not—"

He's across the room in a matter of two blinks and pulling me into his arms, his hand cupping my head, his mouth closing down on mine, and I'm consumed by his grief and need, by his hunger for something that is both physical and emotional. There is no part of me that holds back. No part of me that doesn't want to give him what he needs.

"Don't leave," he whispers. "I need you."

"I'm not going anywhere," I say. "I'm right here. I wanted to call sooner. I just didn't know if I would make it worse."

"I need you," is all he says, his forehead resting against mine, and he doesn't speak or move.

We just stand there holding each other, time ticking by—seconds, minutes, I'm not sure how long—until Grayson breaks the silence.

"I golfed with him that morning. I was there when it happened. I couldn't save him."

I pull back to look at him and there are tears in his eyes. I reach up and stroke away the dampness on his cheeks, more in love with this man in this moment than I ever have been. He is strong, powerful, and wealthy, and yet, he is human, he is vulnerable. "Did you get to tell him you love him?"

"Yes. Over and over. I'm not sure he heard, though."

"He knew. *He knew.*"

The door opens and Eric says, "It's time."

Grayson pulls back and looks at him. "We'll be right there."

Eric nods and exits. Grayson takes my hand. "I'm giving the eulogy."

"As it should be," I say.

He bends our elbows and pulls me close, his eyes meeting mine. "As it should be," he says. He's talking about me by his side.

"Yes," I say, without hesitation. "As it should be."

He brings our joined hands to his lips and kisses them before he guides me forward and we exit the room. Hand in hand, we enter the church, which is packed with hundreds of people and we walk down the center aisle with all eyes on us. We sit in the front row, and Leslie, his godmother, his second mother, who was his mother's best friend, reaches around and squeezes my leg, her long dark hair pulled back at the nape, her blue eyes pained. I realize then that Grayson is alone but for her. His mother has been gone for five years. Now his father is gone as well.

Grayson doesn't let go of me until it's his turn to speak. He looks at me when it's time and I cup his face. "As it should be," I whisper, and he kisses me before he stands.

I listen to the heartfelt words about a man who inspired him, a man who was hard on him, but only because he wanted the best for him, and every word is true. "He was a hard man who expected honesty and ethics. He expected that I be the best and I do it with hard work and integrity."

When Grayson is done there isn't a dry eye in the church and the minute he's seated again, he's holding onto me, his grip so tight it hurts, but I don't care. The rest of the ceremony is over quickly and it's not long before I'm in the front seat of Grayson's Porsche for the ride to the cemetery. He cranks the engine but doesn't place us in gear. "It was perfect," I whisper when we're finally alone. "And true. He was a good man."

"He asked me every time I saw him when you'd be back." He looks at me, his green eyes bloodshot. "Every time, Mia. For six months."

"I'm here now," I whisper. "I'm not leaving."

I mean it when I say it. I never wanted to leave in the first place.

He reaches for me, his fingers tangling in my hair. "We're going to the house," he says. "Do you have a problem with that?"

"On one condition," I say, my hand covering his. "We don't talk about why I left. I don't want to talk about it. I just want us to be us right now."

"We never stopped being us, Mia," he says, pulling my mouth to his and kissing me. And in that kiss, I taste the truth. He's right. We never stopped being us and while I've questioned if I knew what that meant over the past few months, I don't now. Right now, us, is what it always was before: everything.

Chapter Nine

Mia

The present

I come back to the present, back to the retired lighthouse Grayson bought to please me, back to my present location of the cozy chair we'd picked out together, but I'm not really here. I'm not fully outside the memory of the funeral, and I'm as confused as I was that weekend. When he'd seen me at the church, when he'd pulled me to him, I'd thought I'd been wrong to leave him. I'd thought I was wrong about so much and that I belonged with him.

And then there was the text message.

The message that made me leave again. The message that told me that he would always hurt me, but one look into his eyes, one touch of his hand, and I'd believed we were real and pure again. Like I do now. What am I thinking, being here? What am I trying to do to myself?

I stand up and rush toward the stairs as Grayson appears in front of me, so damn good looking, so damn perfect in so many ways. His hands settle on my waist, branding me. His touch, his presence, always claims me, even when I don't want to be claimed. And yet I always do with him. Right now, I'm lost, that familiar, woodsy, delicious scent of him mixing with the ocean air and consuming me as easily as the man himself. "Looking for me?" he asks softly, backing me up until I'm pressed to the bright blue wall of the lighthouse, a color we chose together. We did so many things together, everything together. He was my life, my love, my best friend.

I thought.

I flatten my hands on his chest, hard muscle beneath my palms, and I intend to push him away, but instead, my palms settle there, they feel as if they belong there; the ease at which I touch him, defying our breakup and his betrayal. "Your meeting was short, too short. What are you doing about Ri?"

He studies me, those green eyes far too intelligent for my own good. "You were about to run again, weren't you?"

"I never ran," I correct him. "Leaving and running are two different things. I made a decision. If I leave now, it's another decision."

"A decision to leave me over a lie someone else set up." He releases me and presses his hands to the wall, no longer touching me. "Obviously there's a bigger picture here. If there wasn't, you wouldn't have believed the lie."

"Lie? Regardless of the portions of this that you call a lie, there was more to me leaving, and you know it." I curl my fingers on his chest. "I said I didn't want to talk about this."

"Just like you didn't want to talk about it at the funeral?"

"Your father had just died, Grayson. I wasn't selfish enough to make that about me. I cared about your father. I still loved you."

"Loved?"

"If I didn't still love you, do you really think I'd be here?"

He stares at me, his eyes suddenly hard. "Then why the fuck were you with Ri?" he demands, his voice low, hard, affected.

He pushes off the wall and turns away, walking to the half wall encasing the private sitting area, his shoulders bunched beneath his T-shirt. I inhale with the bitterness in his words and the pain beneath them. He hurt me, but I hurt him back and I don't like that about me. It's my turn to push off the wall. I close the space between us, and once again we're side by side, facing the ocean, both of us gripping a railing when we could so easily be touching each other, too easily, and yet, not easy enough.

"I should never have gone to work for Ri's company. I regret it. I'm sorry."

We look at each other. "You were trying to hurt me. It worked."

"No. No, I never wanted to hurt you." I turn to face him, but he doesn't face me. "I've thought a lot about this in the last twenty-four hours, especially on the drive up here. I asked myself if I went to Ri to hurt you, but I didn't. I didn't want to hurt you. I was trying to survive."

Now he rotates to face me. "By going to him? By leaving my bed, not once but twice, and going to *him?*"

"I didn't sleep with him. Ever. And I didn't want to hurt you. I was desperate for a place to shelter that you didn't own, and Ri's world was the only place I knew you didn't own."

"You wanted away from me that damn badly?"

"No. I wanted to go back to you that badly and Ri's world was the only world that made that unacceptable. It was the only place I was strong enough to just say no, but I see now that I made a mistake. I opened the door for him to go after you. Why are you here, and not talking to Eric and Davis about Ri? You *need* to deal with him. *We* need to deal with him."

"*We?* That's a loaded word."

"I'm here for a reason," I say. "I want to help."

"You told me. I'm handling it."

"What does that even mean?" I press.

"It means that I don't go after many people, but he's pushed my limits." His jaw sets hard. "You need to know that I plan to hurt him. I plan to make sure he can't come for me, or you, again and that's not on you any more than his actions are on you."

"If you expect me to tell you not to hurt him, if this is a test of loyalty to you or him, I'm not failing that test. Because we both know it is. You *need* to hurt him because he will destroy you if he can. I've seen how he works. He's not you."

"Did you think he was? Did you think he could be?"

"Never, Grayson. I told you. I wasn't with him."

"But you went out with him."

"Long after we broke up and yet, I still said your name when I was with him. I told you. I was alone. I was alone and—"

He shackles my waist and pulls me to him, the heat of his body enveloping mine. "You didn't have to be alone. You were never supposed to be alone and neither was I."

"You're never alone."

"I am always alone without you." His forehead lowers to mine. "I stood in that church and willed you to appear." He pulls back to look at me, his hand sliding under my hair. "I couldn't breathe until you were there. That's how much a part of me you are." His lips brush mine, a feather-light touch I feel in every part of me before they part mine. We linger there a moment, breathing together, the way we haven't in so very long. "You have to feel how much I need you," he whispers, his hands sliding between my shoulder blades.

How much I need him, I think. "I'm still angry."

"I'm angry with you, too," he says, and his mouth comes down on mine, with his promise that the next time he kisses me he won't stop in the air between us but it doesn't matter.

Right now is just like after the funeral. We're here. We're alone. I have been so alone without him and I don't want to think about the past. I want to think about the here and now and him. The muscles low in my belly clench. My nipples ache. My heart melts. He turns me and presses me against the wall of the lighthouse in a small alcove between the stairs and the cutout view.

He reaches for the zipper of my hoodie and the lick of his tongue consumes me. I moan into his mouth and somehow his hand has caressed up my sweater to cup my breast. I gasp and arch into the touch, but a rumble of thunder shocks me, pulling me back to reality. I grab Grayson's hand. "Wait. Wait. Not here." I press on his chest and when he pulls back just enough to look at me, I add, "This place is special and not for one reason. I don't want to be here with you when we're like we are now."

"It *is* special, which is exactly why we need to be here, to remember who we are together. I know you don't want to talk now, but we have to talk. It's time, Mia. It's past time."

"I know," I concede, "but not before we—not tonight. I don't want to need to leave again. And I don't want this place to become about a final goodbye."

His lashes lower and he cuts his gaze, torment etched in his handsome face before he looks at me again. "Be clear, Mia," he says softly. "We will not part ways in the middle again. I want you. I *will* fight for you, but we're in or we're out. We're together or we both move on once and for all."

Chapter Ten

Mia

The past, a year and three months ago

The sky and the ocean are the same blue today, I think, my hands resting on the ledge of the cutout inside the lighthouse that sits a couple of miles down from Grayson's family home. So blue, so perfect that despite the sky and the ocean starting at different places, they meld together as one. The way I do with Grayson. I rotate and rest my elbows on the ledge, my gaze landing on Grayson where he sits in one of the cozy chairs we picked out recently for our many hours spent here. His gaze is downturned, focused on his MacBook as he goes over numbers on the newest of his nationwide expansion of his father's law firm, this one opening in Washington. He's so damn good looking, so unassuming in faded jeans and a black snug T-shirt that hugs his impressive chest, his dark wavy hair rumpled and not from the wind. Because I can't ever keep my fingers out of it.

He glances up and his green eyes meet mine, and even after nine months and almost every day since with him, I feel the punch of that connection. I feel him in every part of me. He winks the way he does often like we're sharing a private secret, which we often do, and I smile, reaching for my wine glass on the table beside him. He catches my hand and pulls me to him, kissing me before he scowls into the phone. "Negative, Eric," he says, and then releases me. "I do not like the numbers on that building. Tell Davis if he can't negotiate better than that, I'll do it myself."

My lips curve because Davis, like Eric, is one of Grayson's closest friends, but Grayson doesn't pull any punches with them. When it comes to business, he's smart, savvy, and if need be, brutal but he's always honest. The honest part is probably the thing that makes me love him beyond all else, and there is plenty of else.

"That's it," Grayson says behind me. "I'm done for the day."

I rotate to find him standing up and walking toward me with his wine glass in hand. Instantly, my stomach flutters like a schoolgirl who is about to stand next to her crush. That's what this man does to me and has since that day I ran into him. "Did you notice which wine this is?" he asks, both of us facing each other, our elbows on the railing.

"That cheap but good one that I fell in love with in Sonoma last weekend after I learned there are wines to taste and wines to drink. And that the expensive ones are barely tolerable. Yes. I did. Thank you. I still love it."

"It's a good choice," he says. "And I like that you look beyond the price tag."

Because so many people in his life see his money before they ever, if they ever, see the man. "We should go to that Italian place you love tonight." He leans over and kisses me. "Or we could order in and eat in bed in between fucking and fucking some more."

My cheeks heat and do so despite the fact that I've done about every naughty thing possible with this man. "I do love our nights in bed."

He sets his glass on the ledge next to us and then takes mine and does the same. "Then bed it is." His fingers tangle in my hair, and he drags my mouth to his. "I love you, Mia. You know that, right?"

"I love you, too."

"I mean *I really* love you."

"What's wrong?" I ask, pulling back to look at him, sensing his suddenly darker mood.

"Nothing is wrong. Nothing has been wrong since the day I met you." His mouth closes down on mine, and his tongue strokes deep, his hand settling between my shoulder blades, molding me close. It's a passionate kiss, a hungry kiss. A kiss that is all about emotion and not sex. A kiss that screams "I need you" and says so much more than even words.

It ends with me breathless and his thumb strokes away the dampness on my lips. "I have something for you." He kisses me and then walks to his chair. "Come here."

His mood is hard to read and I tilt my head to study him. "What are you up to, Grayson Bennett?"

"Come find out." His green eyes light with challenge. "If you dare." With those words, the edge I've sensed in him seems to soften.

My lips curve and I join him. "I dared," I say, stepping between him and the chair, my hands settling on his chest. "Now what?"

"Sit and close your eyes."

"Now you're making me curious."

"Good. Sit, baby. You'll like this, I promise."

"Of that, I have no doubt," I assure him because this is him and he gives me no reason to do anything but like and love each day and moment.

I sit.

"Shut your eyes," he orders.

"Eyes shut," I say, doing as commanded.

He kneels beside me or I believe he does. My eyes are, of course, shut. "What if I was to blindfold you?"

My eyes open and meet his sea-green stare. "Is that what you're going to do?"

"Would it be a problem?"

"Of course not. I trust you. Is that what you're going to do?"

"Not until later." He sets an envelope in my lap. "Open it."

My teeth sink into my bottom lip and my curiosity is ripe. I unseal the flap and pull out a contract. "You bought the lighthouse from the man who retired it?"

"I did," he says. "Look at the name on the deed."

I scan and note the extreme price this place cost, and I know he did this for us, for me. "There's no name. I don't understand."

"I want you to fill in your name."

I shove at his chest. "No. No, I won't take this. No." I stand up and he sets the paperwork on the chair and joins me, his hands shackling my waist and pulling me to him. "I want you to have it."

"I want to be here with you. I don't want a present like this. I'm not with you for this."

"What's mine is yours, Mia."

"No. No, that is not true and all I want is you, Grayson. I don't care about the rest."

He cups my face. "I left it blank for a reason. I want your name on that deed, but I want it to be my name."

I blink. "I don't understand."

"Marry me, Mia. I need you forever."

I suck in a breath. "What?"

"I love you. I need you with me forever. Say yes."

"I—I have to sign a prenup. I don't want you to ever think-"

He kisses me, a deep slide of tongue before he says, "Is that a yes?"

"Yes. Yes, you know it is. You know I love you. You know I need you, too. Forever."

His lips, those perfect lips, curve. "Then I have something else for you." He reaches into his pocket and pulls out a satin pouch. "It was easier to carry this in this than in a box today." He removes the stunning, incredible, giant ring inside. "If you don't like it-"

"My God," I say, eyeing the emerald-cut diamond that sparkles with hints of blue. "It's gorgeous, but I think I need a security guard to wear it."

He laughs. "I'll be your security guard." He slips it on my finger. "It's a rare blue diamond. I special ordered it. I wanted you to have something no one else would have."

I look at it and then him. "Thank you."

"Thank me by spending the rest of your life with me."

"I wouldn't have it any other way." I swallow hard. "I hate that my mother isn't alive to know you."

"As do I of mine, Mia."

It's one of the things we've bonded on. The love of our parents. The loss of our mothers. Mine to cancer two years ago and his to a car accident five years ago. "Does your father know?"

"Not yet, but he loves you. He'll be happy, but Mia, he'll be harder on you at work. You need to be ready for that."

"I want to prove myself. You know I do. I can handle it."

He cups my face. "It doesn't mean he doesn't love you. Just the opposite. He's hard on me. He always has been."

I can't think about his father right now. I smile. "We're getting married."

He smiles. "Yeah, baby. We're getting married."

Chapter Eleven

Mia

The present

"We will not part ways in the middle again. I want you. I will fight for you, but we're in or we're out. We're together or we both move on once and for all."

I've told myself that I'm "out" with Grayson, right now—as much as I know I have real reasons for that choice—standing here with him, his body pressed to mine, his words in the air between us, it's not that simple. Especially not here, in the lighthouse where he proposed to me. Right here, right now, the idea of never seeing him again is unbearable.

He cups my face and tilts my gaze to his. "You aren't going to tell me you're already out?"

"No," I say. "And I should, but no. I'm not."

He strokes my cheek, studying me for a long moment before he says, "Everything I could say to the 'I should' part of that statement, I won't. Right now, I think we both just need to be us again. To just live in the moment."

"I can't do that here. There are too many memories here. Too much to question."

"If you keep saying things like that, I won't hold back what I have to say." He leans in and kisses me. "So yes. Let's leave. Let's go to the house." He doesn't wait for the confirmation that he knows he'll receive. I'm the one who didn't want to clutter all my good memories of us in this place with the way we are now.

He links the fingers of one of his hands with mine and turns toward the stairwell, leading me that direction, but he doesn't urge me in front of him, as the gentleman that he is might do another time. He goes first. A choice I understand, because I understand him. God, I really do understand this man. Being at my back would have been dominant, and while he's dominant without question, he doesn't want me to feel that he's suffocating me with that dominance. Even so, he doesn't let go of my hand the entire walk down the stairs. He holds onto me and keeps me close and the thing is, I want him to hold onto me. I want him to prove what can't be wrong. That's why I haven't let him try. I know he will fail. I know that once he does, I have to say that final goodbye and I don't know how I survive that. Not now that I'm with him again. That's why I don't want to talk right now. I just need to pretend none of the bad exists. I just need to be with Grayson, and I can't seem to find the will to fight that need.

We step onto the beach, and his arm slides around my shoulders. "What did Eric and Davis say about Ri?"

"Let's not talk about Ri," he says. "That's part of the bad and we don't want that right now, right?"

"Yes. Right."

"What were you thinking about in the lighthouse?"

"Good memories. Not bad. I was standing on the beach, looking at your house, and I just—felt like I was suffocating in everything bad and so I ran there."

"I still went there until after the funeral," he says. "Alone." He looks down at me. "I went there alone, thinking about when I went there with you."

My teeth scrape my bottom lip and I cut my stare. "*Before the funeral,*" I whisper. "You mean before the second time I left?"

"Yes, Mia," he says, "before the second time you left."

We don't look at each other, but that reality hangs in the air between us. That's when he stopped trying to tear down my walls. That's when he let me slam them down between us and keep them down. That's when he moved on. I don't like the idea of him moving on. I've never liked the idea and yet, I have no right to care. I walked away. It doesn't matter that it killed me to do it.

We reach the house and enter through the patio and the minute we're inside the living room, he turns me to him, his fingers lacing into my hair. "After the funeral because you left me not once, but twice. After the funeral, because I needed you so fucking badly and you still left. Again. After the funeral, because that's when I started to question us. That's when I decided that if what we had was real,

46

then you wouldn't have written me off without really hearing me out."

I lower my chin, trying to catch my breath, my hand flattening on his chest. "Words won't fix this."

"Mia—"

I jerk my gaze to his. "And I'm going to tell you what I admitted to myself walking with you from the lighthouse. I didn't want you to try to explain because we both know you can't, and once you can't, we're done. Some illogical part of me, and you know I'm not an illogical person, felt that if you never tried, I could keep clinging to maybe, to that possibility that what we had was real."

"It was real," he says, stepping into me, his hand flattening on my lower back, fingers tightening in my hair. "It *is* real." His mouth comes down on my mouth, and when his tongue strokes mine, I don't even consider holding back. I have craved this man forever it seems. I have needed him eternally. I sink into him and the kiss, I drink in the taste of him, the feel of him, the absolute perfection of him.

His hand slides up my back, settling between my shoulder blades, molding me to him. "I can't stop needing you, Mia. I shouldn't have tried." His mouth is back on mine before I can even fully process those words, his tongue licking into my mouth, stroking and tasting me the way I do him. And he tastes of those words, of need and hunger, of regret and passion. Suddenly I can't get close enough to him, I can't get enough of him.

My hands slide under his T-shirt, a raw need clawing at me. I need and need and need some more. I shove at his shirt and he pulls it over his head, but my hands never leave his perfect body, which he spends hours in the gym making that perfect. I kiss his chest and he drags my sweater over my head, his hands settling on my face, even before it hits the ground. His lips are on mine. We're wild and hungry, and he scoops me up and starts walking. That's when reality hits me.

"Stop!"

He halts, his lashes lowering, and I can see him reaching for restraint. "What are we doing, Mia?" he asks softly.

"Not the bedroom." He stands there a few beats and then starts walking again. "Grayson."

He doesn't reply. He doesn't stop again until he's laying me down on the bed we once shared, and he's on top of me. "This is our bed. That lighthouse is our lighthouse. We're these things, and we need *us* right now. So yes, Mia. In the bed, *our* bed, where I plan to fuck you and make love to you as many times as humanly possible this very weekend and the rest of our lives if I have my way. If you have a problem with that, I need to know now."

Chapter Twelve

Mia

My reasons for not wanting to be in this bed fade with his declaration that it's ours, and that he wants me in it for the rest of our lives. "The only problem I have right this minute is that you aren't kissing me."

He leans in, his lips a breath from mine, but he doesn't kiss me. "Why didn't you want to be here with me?"

"Ask me later. Kiss me now."

"No. You think I've had someone else here, in our bed." It's not a question.

"I don't have the right to ask."

"Is that why you didn't want to be here?"

"Yes," I whisper, my hand settling on his cheek. "But I know—"

"I never brought a woman here or to my place in the city. Just you, Mia. But I can't tell you that I didn't try to fuck you out of my system. I needed to fuck the images of you with Ri out of my head."

"I *wasn't* with Ri."

"I know that now, but I didn't then. It doesn't matter who it was. The idea of you with someone else drove me crazy. It still does."

"I wasn't with anyone else," I dare to confess, when a part of me doesn't believe he deserves that confession and another feels I owe it to him.

He pulls back to study me. "What?"

"Never. I didn't. Not once. And I told myself that it was because I was busy, trying to build my career, but—"

"But what, Mia?"

"I just wasn't ever ready to let go. I didn't *want* to leave you. But I had to."

"No, baby. You didn't, but I get that you really felt that you did. It hurts, but I get it." His mouth comes down on mine, and I feel as

49

if he's breathing me in. I know I am with him. No. I'm drinking him in, arching into the sweet weight of him on top of me. We kiss with desperation, like two people who need each other to survive, and right now, I don't know how I have survived without him. He rolls us to our sides facing each other, his fingers catching the hook of my bra and just that fast, he's pulling it away, and his hand replaces the silk. His mouth is back on mine and sensations consume me, so many sensations colliding with emotion and need.

"Are you still on the pill?" he asks.

"Yes. I just—I am."

"Good. For now." He kisses me, a quick brush of lips over lips. "I need you naked. I need to feel you next to me." He rolls me to my back and with that "for now" in the air, he moves and resettles with his lips to my stomach and this is not an accidental connection. My heart squeezes with the certainty that he's reminding me of how many times he told me he wanted a little girl just like me. It affects me. We had so many plans. We were best friends. We were so many things that happened so very quickly and easily, and then it was gone.

He pulls down my pants, and all too quickly my sneakers and everything else are gone. I'm naked and not just my body. I am so very naked with this man and always have been. But as for my body, I'm not alone for long. He strips away his clothes, and I lift to my elbows to admire all that sinewy, perfect muscle before he reaches down, grabs my legs and pulls me to him. The minute my backside is on the edge of the bed, he goes down on a knee. I sit up and cup his face. "Not now. Now I need—I need—"

He cups my head and pulls my mouth to his, kissing me with a long stroke of his tongue before he says, "And I need to taste you."

"Not now. I'm not leaving. We have time. I need—you. Here with me."

His eyes soften but he still leans in and licks my clit, and then suckles. I'm all but undone by the sensation because one thing I know and know well is how good this man is with his tongue. But he doesn't ignore my request. He pushes off the floor, and in a heartbeat, he's kissing me and I don't even know how we end up in the center of the bed, our naked bodies entwined. We just are and it's wonderful and right in ways nothing has been in so very long.

He lifts my leg to his thigh and presses his thick erection inside me, filling me in ways that go beyond our bodies; driving deep, his hand on my backside, pulling me into him, pushing into me, but then we don't move. Then we just lay there, intimately connected, lost in the moment and each other. "Is this what you wanted?"

"Yes," I say. "This is what I wanted."

"I didn't think I'd ever have you here, like this, with me again."

"Me either," I whisper, my fingers curling on his jaw. "Grayson," I say for no reason other than I need his name on my lips. I need everything with this man.

He kisses me, a fast, deep, passionate kiss. "I missed the hell out of you, Mia. So *fucking* much. I don't think you really understand how much."

This moment, right here, right now, is one of our raw, honest, perfect moments that has always made his betrayal hard to accept. I need that honesty in my life and with him and I don't even think about denying him my truth. "I missed you, too. More than you know, Grayson."

He squeezes my backside and drives into me again. I pant with the sensations that rip through my body, my hand going to his shoulder. "Nothing was right without you," he says. "Nothing, Mia." He kisses me, and I sink into the connection, pressing into him, into his thrust, into the hard warmth of his entire body. Needing to be close. Needing the things that separated us not to exist.

Our lips part and his mouth is on my breast, lips suckling my nipple, my sex clenching around his shaft with the sensation, a soft whimper escaping my lips. And then he's kissing my neck and whispering in my ear, "I love you, Mia."

And I say it. I have to say it. "I love you, too."

He pulls back to look at me. "Say it again."

"I love you."

He cups my face and forces my gaze to his. "Don't forget that. I'm not going to this time." He doesn't give me time to respond. His mouth crashes down on mine and in a fury of heat, we snap and tumble into that wild, animalistic place that allows nothing but give and take. We're all over each other. We're saying, grinding, pumping, touching, kissing. I don't want it to end and yet I need that next place we're trying to find, I need all that I can take and give with this man, and there is no holding back. I am there, on the edge, and tumbling right over, far too quickly. I stiffen and then my body quakes, arching into Grayson's, my fingers digging into his back. A low guttural sound escapes his lips as he buries his face in my neck and shudders into release right along with me. Because that's just one of the things about us I remember. We're really good at doing things together.

We collapse into the mattress, into each other and for a long time we just hold each other. I'm not sure how long we stay like this. I just know that it can't be long enough. Finally, though, Grayson rolls me to my back and grabs tissues that he offers me, but when he pulls out, he doesn't move. He stays right there with me, his elbows planted on either side of me.

"We need to have a serious conversation, Mia," he says softly.

"I know. I know we do."

"Good. So which will it be? Pizza or Chinese?"

Tension uncoils in my belly and becomes laughter. "Pizza. I haven't had this pizza in—"

"Too long," he says softly, brushing his thumb down my cheek. "Too long, Mia." He kisses me. "I'll order." He lifts away from me and I am instantly cold where I was hot moments before. He sits down beside me and grabs his phone from the nightstand.

I listen as he orders our usual, remembering my preferences like I'd never left him. When he's done, he sits his phone on the nightstand and leans over me. "I'll be right back." He kisses me and then in all his beautiful nakedness, he stands up and walks to the bathroom.

I sit up and take in the room that I haven't really looked at in years, finding it as remarkable and unchanged as the chemistry between me and Grayson. It's a traditional room, the bed an oversized king in black, with thick posts on each corner, and furnishings to match. A sitting room to the left with black leather furnishings and—

Grayson's phone buzzes with a text and my stomach clenches. I throw away the blanket and sit up, staring at it on the nightstand. This is where it ended last time. In this bed, in this room, with a text message I'd accidentally read, but I don't want it to end again, not this time.

I don't want it to end.

I don't want to say goodbye to Grayson.

Chapter Thirteen

Mia

The past, six months ago

Grayson and I don't speak on the drive from the cemetery to the Long Island mansion that is our destination. When we arrive, he doesn't reach for the panel to key in the code. His hands grip the steering wheel, and I know why. While his father was rarely here in the Hamptons, this was his house. Now it's Grayson's, and I feel the punch in my heart with this knowledge.

"Fuck," he whispers, and when I reach for him, he pulls me to him and kisses me, like I'm breathing life into him, like I'm why he can move forward.

He releases me and rolls down the window, keying in the code. The gate opens and he maneuvers us past it and down the half-moon-shaped drive. We park in the garage, and when he kills the engine, we just sit there in the tiny space, neither of us wanting to move. "He was never here and yet somehow walking into this house, without him being here, makes this all so damn real."

"Because it's a piece of him. It's a part of your life you shared with him. What are you doing about his apartment in the city?"

"I made arrangements. I have a service packing up everything and putting it in storage. I can't go through it now. I need time and I need to sell the place." He laughs bitterly. "He'd be furious if I left it sitting there, creating a useless tax bill."

"He really would," I say, giving him a sad smile. "I can help you go through everything."

He looks over at me. "I need you to help me, Mia."

"Then I will."

He lowers his chin to his chest and draws a deep breath before he opens the door and gets out. By the time I'm out of the car, his fingers are tunneling into my hair and he's pulling me against him. Somehow the door gets shut and I'm against it. And right there, in the garage, next to his father's Mercedes, we're all over each other. It's like an explosion of everything all at once; anger, passion, love, pain, heartache of so many varieties.

My skirt is at my waist, his hand on my bare backside, fingers under the strip of satin running down the center. My hands are under his jacket, at his waistband. He shrugs out of the confines of his jacket and then it happens. We fuck. His pants are shoved down and my panties never come off, but they too, are just shoved away. My leg is at his hip and he presses inside me and I gasp, even as he shackles my backside and lifts me off the ground. My back is against the Porsche, and in a crazy, frenzied rush we pump, grind, and just plain fuck. Only fucking isn't even the right word. We need. We take. He needs more than I do and I just need to help him sate the pain.

When it's over, he all but collapses on top of me, but still, he's so damn strong that he holds me up. He carries me just like that, into the house, and to a small bathroom off the garage entrance, and once I'm on the sink and we're put back together, he cups my face. "Let's go to the lighthouse," he whispers.

I look down at my high heels. "I need to get rid of these."

"Your things are still in the closet."

My lashes lower, a punch of emotion in my chest. My things. He kept my things. He strokes my cheek. "Where they belong, Mia." He doesn't give me time to argue, taking my hand and guiding me through the house, but I wouldn't argue anyway. With this man is where I've belonged since the moment I met him. Every moment apart has felt wrong, and I refused to let myself think about why I left. I won't. Not now. I wish never.

We enter his bedroom, our bedroom until I left because we were here every weekend, and he doesn't stop until we're standing in an enormous, fancy, dressing room closet. He stands me in front of my row of clothes, him at my back, his hands on my shoulders. I stare at my things, at the way they hang next to his, and emotions assail me.

Grayson releases me and we dress, our eyes holding almost the entire time, neither of us looking at our naked bodies. Once we're both in sweats and sneakers, as well as hoodies, we head to the beach.

Hand and hand, we walk to the lighthouse and side by side, in a lounge chair we share, we watch the sun set over the ocean. When finally we speak, it's of his father. We talk about him, just him.

Grayson and I spend two days holed up in the mansion. We don't leave. We don't talk about us. Not the broken part of us. We do a lot of remembering the good parts of us. We make love. God, how we make love. We speak in those unspoken ways and I don't ever want to leave him again. But Saturday night arrives, and with it, the reality of a return to the city and my job with Ri's company with it. Grayson and I are in the bed, both in sweats and tees, and I'm lying on his chest while we watch Tombstone, one of his dad's favorite movies, when he suddenly hits mute and rolls us to lay face to face.

"We're out of time. I don't want this hanging over us tomorrow. I have to go back to the city tomorrow night."

"Me, too."

"We go back together."

"Yes," I say. I don't even hesitate. "Together." He strokes hair from my face and I can sense he needs to say more, but I suspect he just doesn't have that in him right now. "Are you hungry?"

"Yes. You?"

"Yes. Pizza or Chinese?"

"Pizza. You know I love the pizza we get here."

"Yes, Mia. I do know you love it."

He says it like it's so much more than pizza. And it is. The way he knows me is everything. He reaches across from me and grabs his phone. He orders the pizza, drops the phone on the bed, and then stands up and heads to the bathroom. His phone buzzes with one of the million text messages he's gotten this weekend and I look down, and I don't mean to, but I read the message.

I pant out a breath and sit up, holding my stomach, tears welling in my eyes. My God. I'm such a fool. I have to leave. I scoot off the bed and Grayson's phone starts ringing. I grab my sneakers off the floor and call out, "Your cell is ringing," before I disappear into the hallway. I collapse against the wall and swipe at my tears. I hate him. I love him so damn much. I have to get out of here. I dart for the living room, grab my purse and exit beachside, where I start running what will be miles of beach to reach a spot where I can catch an Uber. It's time to leave Grayson and our lighthouse behind.

Chapter Fourteen

Mia

"Hey, baby, did my phone buzz?"

I glance up to find Grayson standing in the bathroom doorway, now wearing sweats, his perfect chest naked, and shaving cream all over his face. "Yes," I say. "It vibrated on the nightstand. Why are you shaving?"

"Your face is all red."

I reach up and touch my cheek where the sting of his whiskers remains for the first time in far too long while he rakes his gaze over my naked body. "And if you don't get dressed, you're about to have shaving cream all over you." He winks. "Check the message for me, will you?" He disappears into the bathroom. "Read it out to me!" he calls out.

I inhale and let my breath out, ticking through all the reasons why I am not going to leave.

He left his phone behind last time and now. He didn't feel like he had anything to hide then or now. He's shaving for me. He was always thinking of me. When I went to him at the funeral, we felt real and honest, like we do now. When I'm with him, despite every piece of evidence that says he's guilty, my heart says that he's innocent. If it didn't, I wouldn't be here now trying to protect him; trying to protect someone who I know to be a good, fair, honest person.

I grab his phone and I don't look for anything to cover up with, because naked says I'm willing to be vulnerable with him again. And I have to be if I'm going to stay here, and I am. Everything inside me says that I belong here. I walk into the bathroom and slide between him and the counter.

"I told you to get dressed," he reminds me. "You never did follow orders well."

"That hasn't changed and it won't." I lift his phone and read the message. "It's from Eric." I say, glancing at Grayson and then back to the screen, to add, "he says: *We aren't going to get anyone closer than Mia is to Ri to take him down. You need to be reasonable on this. We'll protect her. You have my word.*" I look up at him. "He's right. I came here to protect you. Let me protect you."

He studies me for two hard seconds and then he grabs a towel, wipes his yet to be shaved face, and tosses it. "No. Not just no. *Hell no*, Mia. I am not making you a target." He walks to the door, grabs my pink silk robe I left here a year ago and pulls it around me.

"No," he says, tying the belt for me. "This isn't a discussion."

"I was always a target, Grayson," I say, sliding my arms into the robe. "Always. He wanted to hurt you. He used me and I let him. *I hate* that I let him. I don't know how to undo that but to go after him for you."

"You're not going to go after anyone. That's what I do. Not you, Mia. *Not* you."

I reject that idea immediately. "You don't go after people. That's one of the things that makes you you and not him. That's one of the reasons why I love you."

"And yet you've spent the last year with him."

"Working at his company, not with him. I didn't lie. I haven't been with anyone, I haven't been with him."

He grabs his phone and exits the bathroom. I feel the blow of his words and it hits me then that if I'm wrong, if he didn't do what he appeared guilty of doing, I'm the bitch. I'm the one that doesn't deserve him. I owe him in so many ways and I decide right then that I love him enough to accept the guilt, because he doesn't feel guilty to me.

I race after him and I exit the bedroom, a gust of wind blasting through the now open patio door. I exit into a chilly breeze to find Grayson standing at the railing facing the ocean, his upper body naked, the muscles in his back and shoulders bunched. I don't even hesitate. I go to him and the minute I'm by his side, he pulls me between him and the railing but he doesn't speak. He just looks at me.

I reach up and brush my hand over his unshaven face, the rasp of whiskers on his jawline, then along the thicker edge of his goatee. "I like having your whisker marks on my face and everywhere else. I miss seeing those marks on my body."

He pulls away the silk tie at my waist, parting my robe and then molding my naked body to his body. "I stood out here wondering if you'd just leave again, Mia. I didn't know for sure that you'd follow me out here. I can't walk out of a room and have you disappear again. If that's where this is headed, then we need to ignore the pizza, fuck again right now, and make it a final goodbye."

"Can we fuck again right here and now before the pizza gets here, and just not say goodbye?"

The buzzer that signals a front gate visitor goes off and Grayson ignores it. "I don't want the fucking pizza. I want us to make a decision about us, *but* we have a pizza at the damn gate." He releases me, grabs his phone and hits a button that opens the gate on his security system app.

I yank my robe shut and his eyes meet mine, heat and anger in the depth of his stare. And then he just turns and leaves the room. It's then that I feel as if I've been punched. It's then that I realize that in the midst of finding each other again, we're closer now to losing each other for good than ever before.

I enter the bedroom and stare at the massive space, and the bed where I have slept so many times with this man wrapped around me. I miss sleeping like that, with him. I don't know how long I stand there imagining those moments with him holding me, but he doesn't come back. Time ticks by and Grayson still doesn't come back to the bedroom.

It's been too long and I hurry down the hallway and start hunting for him. I enter the living room and find the pizza box on the island in the kitchen, but he isn't there. My gaze lifts to the patio, and I know then that he's back outside, but he's chosen to exit through a location that divides us this time. I don't let that dissuade me. I cross the room and exit to find him, just as he was on the other patio, his back to me, leaning on the railing.

"I don't want this to be goodbye, Grayson. I don't know how to make sure it's not goodbye. There's so much bad now. I'm afraid there's too much bad. Are we just here to find that out?"

He inhales and pushes off the railing, turning to look at me, his hands on his hips. "I am angry, Mia. Because being with you, feeling how good it is, makes me wonder if you ever felt what I feel."

"It wouldn't feel this good if I didn't. You know I did."

"Then how can you believe that Ri could set me up with the DA and not set me up that night?" He doesn't give me time to answer. "Eric called. He has a source he's been working for a while now. He's been nickel and diming us with information about Ri, who we knew was up to something. Eric offered him an excessively large sum of cash and he delivered in a big way and fast."

"What does that mean?"

"He says that this plan to take me down has been two years in the making, before my father died, and right after we got together. The reason I believe him is that he named names, people working inside my operation and working for Ri. Two of those people were identified as problems and are already gone."

My stomach knots. "*She* was one of them, right?"

"Yes, Mia. She was one of them."

It's then that I know that Grayson didn't betray me, but instead, I've betrayed him and us.

Chapter Fifteen

Grayson

The past, a year ago

"She won't answer her phone," I say, standing at the window of Eric's office, the sun dipping beneath the skyline.

He steps to my side. "You yanked her off her case, Grayson," he says. "You didn't warn her. You didn't even talk to her first."

"I'm quite aware of what I did, and you know why. The lead counsel on the case was fired because the feds are breathing down our throats over this case and apparently for good reason."

"I get it. We had a lead counsel playing dirty with a dirty client. You didn't want Mia anywhere near that shit, but you should have warned her."

"If I'd have warned her, she'd have looked at me with those beautiful blue eyes and told me why she should stay on the case."

"Because she's got a perfect, clean record that represents us well. There's logic there." I open my mouth to lay into him and he holds up his hands. "But it's a danger to Mia. I get it. She'd still be dealing with a mobster, *defending* a mobster. She'd still end up with that reputation of aligning herself with that man."

"Not to mention my father and his damn rule. You lose your first lead case, you're out. And we're going to lose this case."

"The future mother of his grandchildren? Surely not."

"You've known my father since we were both at Harvard. You know his mentality, so yes, even Mia, who he loves, hell, more so *because* he loves her. He calls it tough love. And let's face it. If she was made an exception, that would ruin her here at the firm. She'd be my woman and nothing more, and that's not what she is or what she wants. It's not what *I* want for her."

"You gave the case to Becky. She hates Becky. They're rivals."

"I handed that decision to Mitch. He's the lead partner over the associates. I didn't take that decision from him, nor did I make it for him, but yes, I approved his choice. Becky is cutthroat and disposable. Mia is not."

"A choice that's not in your favor with Mia."

He's right. I don't want him to be, but he is. I scrub my jaw, glancing at my watch, and tick off the four hours since Mia left the office furious. It's seven now and so far the doorman hasn't seen her at the apartment, which means she has to be at her best friend Courtney's house or her father's place. "I need to find her, but I have a conference call with the Lugo Corporation in fifteen minutes."

"I can handle Lugo," Eric says. "I got it. You go."

And because this is Eric, who I trust like a brother, I take his offer. I head for the door and waste no time making my way to my private office. Once I'm inside, I step behind my desk with the intent of gathering my work to take home with me when Becky steps into my office. "I need to talk to you about the case you put me on." She shuts the door and flattens herself against it, her blouse cut low, her red hair free of the clip she normally wears it in and I don't like it any more than I do her style of sexual manipulation. "I heard you're the reason I got the lead on the Pitts case."

"Don't come into my office and shut the door without my permission. Open it."

"I need to talk about this case in private."

"I'm not your supervisor. Mitch Rivers is. Talk to him about who, where, why, and what case. I have someplace to be."

"This case is tricky." She races forward and stops in front of my desk. "The client involved is a mobster."

I do not have time for this woman right now. "If you're over your head Becky, talk to Mitch."

"I'm not over my head and I appreciate you believing in me. I can handle this case. I'm not backing out."

The phone on my desk rings. "Open the fucking door," I say, and hoping the call is from Mia and that she's back in her office, I grab the line without even looking at the extension. "Davis says he needs to see you before you leave," Eric says. "It's urgent."

I give Becky my back. "Define urgent."

"He says the feds want documents you aren't going to want to give them."

My jaw sets hard. "What documents?"

"Do you really want to talk about this on the phone?" Eric asks. "I'll be right there." I hang up and when I set the receiver back on the desk, I realize that my door is still shut but Becky is no longer in front of my desk.

I rotate to my right to find her on my side of the desk, naked from the waist up. "What the fuck are you doing?"

"Thanking you for the case." She steps into me and I grab her arms, holding her back. "Get dressed. Now." I set her back from me.

My door opens and Mia gasps. "Oh my God," she whispers, and my heart is thundering in my ears, adrenaline surging through me. "It's not what it looks like, Mia. I swear." I release Becky and the stupid bitch wraps her arms around me and presses her breasts to my chest. "Fuck. Get off me." I shove her back and rotate toward the door, but Mia is already turning away. "Mia! Fuck. Mia." Becky comes back at me, wrapping her arms around my waist. "Get the fuck off of me, Becky." I untangle her from my body and I'm around the desk in a blink, chasing after Mia, and I don't give a fuck who knows.

"Mia!" I shout watching her round a corner and damn it, I pray the elevator is shut and slow to reach her.

I race in her direction, but I'm too late. She's in the elevator and I reach the doors right before they close; just in time to see the stricken look on her face, in time to look into her eyes and see the pain, but unable to get to her. "It's not what it looks like!" I call out as the doors shut and immediately head for the stairs. I'm in the stairwell in another blink and I start the run down thirty flights. I exit to the lobby and search for Mia, but she's not there. I charge for the front door and burst onto the street and again, she's not fucking there. I head back inside and scan my surroundings before going back outside. Nothing. I grab my phone from my pocket and I dial Mia.

"Answer, baby. Answer the damn call." But she doesn't answer. I dial again. I send her a text: *It's not what it looked like. I turned my back and she undressed. I swear to God, Mia. It was not what it looked like. She flung herself at me. I love you. You're everything to me.*

I pace the lobby and call the security for our building. "If Mia gets there, I don't care what it takes, you call me, and you keep her there. There's a thousand dollars in it for you. No, five. Five thousand dollars." I hang up and anger takes over the panic.

I walk to the elevator and punch the button, dialing Eric while I wait. "Meet me in Becky's office with the security guard in three minutes." I don't give him time to respond. I hang up and step into the car.

Once I'm inside, I inhale and force out a breath, forcing myself to calm. The floors tick by and I exit, entering the office lobby, but I don't stop. I cut left and walk past the bullpen of cubicles to an office on the right where Eric and the guard are waiting. "Is she in there?" I ask.

"She is," Eric says.

I start forward, step inside and Eric and the guard flank me, then step to my side. Becky is behind her desk, her hair now neatly pulled back at her nape, a look of shock crosses her face, rocketing her to her feet. "What is this?" she demands.

"Pack up and leave," I say. "You're fired."

She blanches. "What? No. You can't fire me." Her voice lifts and takes on a desperate quality. "I'll claim sexual harassment."

I lean on the desk, my fists on the wooden surface. "If you just made me lose Mia, I'll destroy you and enjoy it. Hell, I'll destroy you and enjoy it just for making her feel what she's feeling right now. So you want to sue me? Bring it the fuck on, but get out."

Chapter Sixteen

Mia

The past, a year ago

I don't know how I make it out of the office building without crying. I don't even know how I get blocks away on foot. I search the area around me and I don't even know where I am. A cab with a light on drives by and I chase after him. He stops. For once a New York City cab driver actually stops for me. I climb inside. "Just drive," I say. "Just drive and there's a big tip in it for you. And ignore me back here." The minute the car starts moving, the inevitable happens. I burst into tears, a fierce, body-quaking explosion. I cry and cry and I don't even try to hold back.

"Big tip," I call out when the driver looks back at me. "Just drive." My phone starts ringing again and I know it's Grayson. Of course it's Grayson. He's busted. He's so very busted. I don't look at my phone. I want to throw it out of the window. I have nowhere to go. I can't go home. It's his home that was clearly never mine. That's what I get for moving in with a man at three months and then accepting a proposal at nine months. "Out—out of the city," I sob to the driver. "A hotel. Queens or Brooklyn. I don't care which. Just take me. A hundred dollars on top of your fare."

I sink back against the cushion and look at my gorgeous special ring that seemed to have so much thought behind it. It meant something. Now it doesn't. It doesn't mean anything. I squeeze my eyes shut and the image of Becky pressed to Grayson, no, her *breasts* pressed against Grayson, twists me in knots. He fired me from the case and gave it to her. Now I know why. My phone rings again and I grab it, stare at Grayson's number and turn it off. It's off. *We're* off. We're over forever.

I start to cry all over again and curl up against the door behind the driver's seat. I lose time inside the tears until finally, the driver stops. "Holiday Inn, sweetheart," the driver says. "That's as good as it gets right now. I'm done driving."

I open my purse, glance at the meter and toss him cash; I always have cash because Grayson always worries I might need it. Or he did. Those days are over. Maybe he didn't worry at all. I exit the car and try to pull myself together. I have to walk into this hotel and get a room without blubbering. I shut the cab door and it races away. I glance around and the airplane overhead tells me I'm close to the airport. Maybe I'll just fly away and go somewhere. It's not like I have a job now. Grayson owns that, too. I think I let him own everything I am and that was okay when I thought I had everything he was, but I was wrong. I didn't have all of him. I had nothing and I have nothing.

I swipe at my cheeks and walk into the hotel lobby. I actually hold it together. I'm proud of myself. I grab my key and once I make it into the room, I'm done holding it together. I melt down right there at the door. I sink to the floor. I lie there. Time passes and passes and I just don't stop hurting. I don't even know when I come to enough to realize that I'm in the dark. I don't care, though. I dig in my purse and turn my phone back on. Grayson calls immediately and I hit "decline" and dial my friend, Courtney, because now I have to admit my hell to someone, and who better than my best friend since childhood?

"Mia!" she says. "Grayson is looking for you. He's worried sick. What's happening?"

"I need you to come to me. I need you."

"Are you okay?"

"I'm not dying or anything, even if I feel like it. Just come."

"Where are you?" she asks, urgently.

"I don't know. Hold on." I push to my feet and flip on a light.

"You don't know?!" she asks incredulously. "Were you kidnapped? Do we need the police? Are you okay?"

"If only those things were true." I sit down on the king-sized bed with a stupid orange comforter, when orange happens to be Grayson's favorite color. Or not. I don't know what is real anymore. "I'm in a Holiday Inn in Queens. I just told the cab driver to take me wherever." I give her the address.

"I got it. Mia, *what* is going on?"

"Just come here and do not, and I mean *do not*, tell Grayson where I am or you aren't a friend." I hang up and walk to the window, pulling open the basic cream-colored curtains to spy the "liquor" sign. I'm not a drinker, but I need to be sedated right now.

I glance down and realize I've smartly settled my purse over my chest and it rests at my hip. Smartly, because I'm really barely hanging on right now. I find the key to the room on the floor by the door and grab it, sticking it in my purse. A short walk down the hallway and I'm exiting onto a street in what looks like a crappy neighborhood, but hey, I grew up in a crappy neighborhood. I'm just fine in this one. I cross the street, enter the store and walk to the counter. "Where's the cheapest bubbly you have?"

The lady behind the counter, who has dark hair speckled with gray and seems to be missing a front tooth, looks me up and down. "You don't look like you need cheap. That's an expensive purse at your hip which means your outfit is expensive, too."

"Yeah, well, I'd tell you I had a rich guy that fucked around on me and now I'm alone, but I bought these clothes and the purse on my own. And you bet your ass they're expensive. I worked for them, not him, because I don't need his damn money. It was never about his money."

"Wow, honey. Fridge. Far right. Buy two. Spumante. It tastes good when everything else tastes bad."

"How much?"

"Ten dollars a bottle."

I yank a hundred out of my purse and stick it on the counter. "Keep the change. He's buying the booze."

She hands me a paper bag and two plastic cups. "One for now and one for later," she says.

A few minutes later, I enter my room, struggle to get the stupid bottle to pop and then sit down on the loveseat against the wall where I guzzle the bubbly right from the bottle. My phone starts ringing, on the nightstand where I apparently left it, and I take my bottle with me to check it just in case it's Courtney. It's not. It's Eric.

I answer. "What do you want, Eric?"

"He didn't do it, Mia. He's devastated. He's freaking out. It was a set-up. He was—"

"Stop. Just stop. You're his best friend. You're like brothers. You'd say anything to protect him."

"I would, but I'm not. He didn't do this. He *loves* you. He needs you."

"I'm not coming back. I'll send the ring. I'll send my credit cards he gave me. I don't want his money. I don't want him or that job either."

"Mia, be reasonable."

"Reasonable?! Did you really just say that to me? Go away and take him with you."

"Mia. *Mia.*" Suddenly, I'm not talking to Eric anymore and it's not him saying my name.

At the sound of Grayson's voice, I can't breathe. I hurt so badly. So very badly. "Go away," I whisper, but I'm not even sure he can hear me. I hang up and throw my phone. I start to cry again and I don't stop until my phone rings like ten times in a row.

"Courtney," I whisper and I force myself to get up, kicking off my heels to pad across the carpet. My phone confirms Courtney has called four times. I call her back.

"Which room?" she asks.

I open my door and look at the number. "331."

"I'm on my way up."

I flip the lock to prop the door open and walk to the sofa, where I sit down. I've downed another drink and I'm starting to feel the blessed buzz when Courtney appears in the doorway, her blonde hair in disarray, her red dress ripped. "What happened?"

"Don't ask." She shuts the door and drops her purse on the floor. "He called me. He says—"

"I walked in on him with Becky's naked breasts pressed against him."

"He says she—"

"Don't. Don't you too. I saw it. Do you not understand that I saw it?" My phone rings in my hand and I toss it. "Just help me plan the rest of my life without him."

"Right now. We're going to order pizza, you need food because that bottle is half empty and you don't drink. As in, you get drunk at half a glass."

Her phone rings in her hand and she glances down at it. She answers the line. "Yes. She's—"

"Are you talking to him?" I demand.

She stands up and holds up her hand. "Mia."

"You are. I can't believe you took his call. Hang up."

"Hold on," she says into her phone and punches a button. "She's on speaker."

"Mia, I didn't do this," Grayson says. "I swear on my mother, my father, and to God."

"Stop talking, Grayson, because you see, I'm stupid. I listen to you. I want to believe you. Or I did. I trusted you. I would have died for you. No more. *No more!*"

"Baby, I'll do anything—"

"To get your baby-making machine back? So you can look perfect and have your heir? No. I'm not her. I'm taking off the ring and Courtney will bring it to you. Maybe you can put it on her. She can be—"

"Stop, Mia," Courtney says. "Stop."

"He fired me off my case and put her on it, Courtney!" I shout. "Did he tell you that?"

She pales. "What?"

"Yes. Fired me and then fucked her. Or fucked me and fucked her. I don't know. Hang up."

"Mia!" Grayson calls out. "Listen to me. I—"

My stomach rolls and I rush to the bathroom and end up on my knees at the toilet. I heave and I am so sick I want to die. When I finally fall back on the tile, Courtney kneels beside me. "Honey, I hung up. I didn't know about the case. That's—"

"Damning?"

"Yeah. It kind of is."

I curl up in a ball and let the ring in my hand settle on the tile. "Take it to him and try to get my things. I need to be alone."

"I'll deal with all of that tomorrow. I'm staying with you tonight, but let's go to my place."

"He'll find me there."

"Well, we have a friend who's a realtor. I'll see if she can get you into a place tomorrow, but you need to be somewhere where you can deal with paperwork. Let's go back to the city."

I sit up and pull my knees to my chest. "Right. Because I need a home and a new job."

Because I don't live or work with Grayson anymore.

Chapter Seventeen

Mia

The present

I'm still standing on the patio of Grayson's Hamptons home, in nothing but a silk robe I bought when he was mine and I was his. I'm staring at him and he's staring at me, and there are steps and space between us that reach beyond the physical. The night we broke up is right here with us, a wedge that won't collapse. Images of Becky pressed against him pound at my mind, driven home by that damn text message I'd read the night of his father's funeral. It zaps that blame I'd put on myself. It says that I'm not the one who betrayed us. It says *he* did. It's the message that could catch him in a lie. I don't want him to lie, but I need to know if he will. Emotions rush at me hard and fast. I need the truth once and for all, but I can't do this in this robe. I can't be that vulnerable.

I rotate and exit the patio, hurrying through the living room and I don't stop until I'm in the bedroom. I hunt down my clothes and sneakers, scoop them up and retreat to the closet. I've just managed to fully dress when Grayson appears in the doorway, and he too now wears a T-shirt with his sweats and sneakers. "Leaving again, Mia?"

"Not yet, but you're right. If I leave this time, it will be for good. Tell me," I order, my voice cracking. "When did you start fucking her?"

He curses and runs his hand through his hair, his dark waves left in disarray as his hands settle on his waist. "Really, Mia? That's where we're still at right now?"

"Tell me," I order again. "Just say it all. *Say it all.*"

He is in front of me in a snap, pulling me to him, his body absorbing mine and not gently. "There is no *when*, Mia. I was not, and *have not* been with Becky. She came into my office. She shut the door. I told her to leave. The phone rang. I thought it was you. I was hoping it was you since you'd shut me out over pulling you off the case. I turned my back and took the call. It was Eric with a problem. When I turned around, she'd stripped and rounded my desk. She flung herself at me and then you opened the door. I don't know how the hell it was planned that well, but it was planned."

"Mitch," I say, my throat going dry, my hand flattening on his chest, heat rushing up my arm. "He called me and told me that there was a blowup on the case and that it was critical I get to your office right then."

"And you took Mitch's call, but not mine?"

"I was furious with you, Grayson." I twist out of his arms and move to the opposite side of the dresser that sits in the middle of the closet. "You pulled me off the case and didn't talk to me about it in advance. *Me*. The woman lying naked next to you in bed every night"—I hold up a hand—"but that's another subject. Mitch still works for you. Mitch clearly made sure I saw you and Becky together, which means he's working against you."

"Becky and I were not together, Mia. Holy hell, woman. What do I have to do to get you to understand that?"

"You can't," I say, emotions welling in my throat. "You can't."

"Then why are we even here right now?"

"Right. Why? I'll leave." I round the dresser, but he catches my arm and pulls me to him.

"Are you really going to do this to us over a lie?"

"Ask why I left after the funeral?"

"I take it that's a yes. A lie that isn't mine destroys us."

"I read your text message that day. You went to the bathroom and it was under my arm on the bed and I read it: *Grayson, I saw Mia with you. I didn't want to come up to you and start a war. Thinking of you. Love, Becky.*"

He blanches and I've never seen Grayson blanch. "First, Becky never had my number. I have no clue how she would get it. I have no relationship with her. And the day of the funeral, the whole weekend of the funeral, I had hundreds of messages and barely glanced at any of them. I was focused on my father and you." He releases me and reaches for his phone, snagging it from his pocket. "She signed it Becky?"

"Yes," I whisper, hugging myself.

He types in the name in the search bar and pulls up the message. "And there it is," he says, his lips thinning. "That little bitch. I didn't read it or respond to it." He hands me his phone. "I didn't respond to most of the messages I got that day. You know how this goes. People use everything, including death, as an excuse to try to get a piece of me. I didn't have it in me to deal with any of that. I didn't respond to anything for days after you left and I didn't try to catch up. You can see her message and all the rest that are unread and without response."

I blanch, shocked by the idea of such a complete shutdown. "None of them?"

"I wouldn't even talk to Eric for a week after my father died and you left. Leslie had to come knocking on the door because I didn't respond to her either. And when I did come out of the haze, anyone that mattered had already found another way to talk to me. The last thing I wanted to do was read the damn messages. Go through my phone, Mia. There is no interaction between me and another woman. Nothing. Because there is no other woman."

I start to shake and I drop his phone without meaning to, but neither of us reach for it. "You really didn't do it?"

"No, baby. How could I want anyone but you? We were, we *are*, in love and it's a passionate love." He pulls me to him. "The kind of love most people never find." He strokes hair from my face. "Tell me you believe me."

Air lodges in my throat and I press a hand over my mouth, holding back a sob. I hurt him. I hurt him in a way that's unforgivable. "I left you the night of the funeral. I'm such a horrible bitch."

"No," he says, pulling my hand from my face, his fingers tangling in my hair, tilting my gaze to his. "There were devious people at play here. People who meant to break us up to hurt me. And I promise you, Mia, they will pay for the pain they caused you, caused *us*."

"I left you after your father died. You can't forgive me for that. How can you even consider trying?"

"We were fighting when this happened. And it was a big fight. You already felt betrayed. I'm not blind to my part of this. I made mistakes that made this possible."

"Yes. I was angry. And yes, there are reasons we were fighting. The case you pulled me off of. The timing. It was everything at once. It was—it was more than Becky and things we need to talk

73

about, but those things weren't me leaving you after your father died. I betrayed us."

"No, baby. You didn't. I did. I let us be that vulnerable. I did things that day that I didn't explain. I allowed us to be that exposed and it won't ever happen again. I'll protect us. I'll protect you. And Ri will pay in blood for what he's done."

Anger quakes in his voice and Grayson is not a man who allows such emotions to control him. Anger that I know is not all about Ri and what he perceives his role to be in our breakup. It's about me leaving him, me walking away. No matter what he says otherwise, we've betrayed each other in ways that have led us to where we are now. We can't just kiss and make up. We have to fight through the emotional storm to follow. We have to fight for each other.

"We're going to be okay," he promises, and I wonder if he's trying to convince me or him, or both of us. It doesn't matter though. I want him to be right. I want him to be right so badly that when his mouth comes down on mine, I am instantly clinging to him the way I would a ledge for dear life. I can't let go or I'll cease to exist. I won't let go. Not this time. Not ever. No matter how fierce that storm becomes. No matter how brutal the fight I know is to come.

Chapter Eighteen

Mia

"Stop kissing me like it's goodbye, Mia," Grayson orders, pressing me against the closet wall in between a row of his clothes and mine. His fingers tangle roughly in my hair. "There is no goodbye. Not this time. Not ever again. You're mine and just to be clear, I'm yours. I was *always* yours."

"We can't pretend it didn't happen. Things happened. Those things change us."

He kisses me, a deep, drugging kiss. "Do we taste different to you?" His hand slides down my back and he cups my backside, molding my hips to his hips, his erection pressed to my belly. "Do we feel different? How do we feel, Mia?"

"Perfect," I whisper. "But we aren't perfect. We can't pretend that we are." Emotions overwhelm me, the idea that I left him after his father died cutting me into a million little pieces. "Grayson—"

"We're back together. That's what matters. We can talk, fight, fuck, and repeat to get past this, but we have that opportunity for one reason and one reason only. We're here. We're together."

"We're together," I whisper, my hands sliding under his shirt, palms pressing against his taut flesh in an effort to confirm those words that don't yet feel real.

"I don't want to be without you again," he says, his voice low, raspy, affected, as his mouth closes down on mine and the minute our tongues connect, we're desperate all over again. Our hands are everywhere and clothes are shoved, pulled, and pushed until we're standing there in the closet, naked, and it's still not enough.

Grayson pulls my leg to his hip and his thick erection presses along the wet seam of my sex. I moan with need and satisfaction because he's here, we're here, doing this. He presses inside me and lifts me at the same time. It's just like beside the car the day of the funeral. He's holding me and his hands squeeze my ass, pulling me away from the wall and down on top of him even as he's pushing into me. I hold onto his shoulders, my nails digging in, my lips finding his as his hand settles between my shoulder blades. And when we can't kiss for the force of our passion, I bury my face in his neck, inhaling that delicious woodsy scent of him that I want to roll around in, get drunk on.

It's as if we both feel like we have to hold onto each other, to get closer to survive and perhaps that's where this leads; we do have to hold onto each other, we do have to get closer to survive all the damaged places we've been and now we cannot fully escape. I don't want this to end, and yet when my back hits the wall again and he drives into me, I welcome the tumble into bliss that follows. I welcome the shudder of his body around mine. I revel in the deep, guttural groan that escapes his lips in pleasure with me and no one else. Our bodies tremble and ease, seconds ticking before Grayson eases back and says, "How about that pizza?"

I laugh, "Yes. Please. I'm officially starving."

He kisses me, a quick brush of our mouths before he settles me on the ground, but when we would pull on our clothes, he cups my face and tilts my gaze to his. "We're together, Mia. Everything will work out."

"I want it, too. I really did hurt without you, Grayson."

"Me too, baby. Me, too." He strokes my hair. "Let's eat in the kitchen where we can heat up the pizza and talk. *Really* talk. I owe you a few more explanations."

He means about why he fired me off my case the day we broke up and I dread this conversation. I'm not even sure I can have it now. I don't want to fight with him and yet I know we need to clear the air. I know I've avoided conversations that I shouldn't have avoided. I think he feels the same thing, the dread, the wish that we could just go back to where we started. I sense it in the air, I see it in his eyes. He doesn't want to fight, but we have to have tough conversations. We have to deal with this.

As soon as we're both back in our sweats, tees, and sneakers, Grayson takes my hand and leads me forward, out of the bedroom. Once we're on the stairs, he bends our elbows, pulling me next to him. "Talk, fight, fuck," he says softly, and the new ball of dread in my belly softens when we enter the kitchen and seem to fall into old habits. He kisses my hand before he releases me to place the pizza in the oven. "Do you remember the first time we ate this pizza?" he asks, turning up the temperature.

Do I remember?

So very well.

"How can I forget our first date?" I ask, settling onto a barstool. "It was a week after our meeting for drinks, and I still hadn't called you on Friday night, so you took matters into your own hands."

"I had no choice," he says, joining me to sit on the barstool next to me, both of us facing each other, his hand settling on my knee. "I wasn't letting you run from me."

"I wasn't running."

"You were, Mia. You were running scared. I saw it in your eyes."

I cut my stare and think back to that night, to where I was in my head when I met Grayson because it feels a lot like where I am with him now. And I know Grayson. I know that's the point in this conversation. He knows that, and he wants me to tap into that memory, into those feelings, and the way he freed me from them. No. The way *we* freed me from them.

Grayson cups my head, and kisses me. "How about some wine, baby?"

"Yes. Please. Do you have that one—"

"Of course I have that one. It's what you like." He stands up and crosses the room to another bar at the end of the kitchen while I let my mind go where he wants it to go. To our first real date:

It's seven on Friday night and the cubicles beyond my office door are all empty. I gather my work and slide it into my briefcase. My cellphone rings and I grab it to find my father calling. "Hey, dad."

"You still at work?"

"I am. You?"

"Not tonight. I'm headed to a baseball game with my new foreman, Cameron, and then we're going to the casino in Connecticut."

"The casino? You don't like to gamble."

"That's what they make penny slots for," he says. "And I need a break. I'm burning it at both ends. What about you? The new job burning you out?"

"No," I say. "I love it. It's—interesting." As is the boss, who I keep thinking about way too much, but thankfully haven't seen again since our bar meet-up.

"We need to meet up for dinner. I know the job is new, but come to Brooklyn, honey. I need to hug my daughter. How about next weekend?"

"I'd like that. We'll make it work."

We chat a minute more, then disconnect and I'm bothered by the call. My father gambling? That makes no sense, but that home builders show he went to a few months back did earn him lots of new woodworking business. Maybe his money situation has eased up. I need to talk to him next weekend, but it must have if he's taking time off.

Relieved by this idea, I grab my briefcase and head for my door. I'm about to exit when Grayson steps in front of me and I do what I did once before. I smash right into him. I gasp and he catches my waist. "I do like the way you keep running into me," he says, those green eyes piercing mine. "You haven't called."

I should step back. I should push away from him. "No, and I won't." I inhale and try to step back.

He holds onto me. "Do you want me to let you go?"

"That's a trick question," I answer honestly.

"Explain, Mia."

"If you weren't my boss—"

"I'm not your boss, Mia. I'm just a man who can't stop thinking about you. Have dinner with me."

"I can't."

"You want to."

"Yes," I agree.

"Then you can," he counters.

"I can't get by the fact that you're Grayson Bennett."

"To most people, that's not a problem."

"I'm not most people," I say. "I told you that."

He stares at me several beats and then his hand falls away. "I'll see you soon, Mia." He backs out of the office and disappears.

I sink against my wall just inside the doorway and try to catch my breath, but my God, my entire body is on fire. He's just so damn—perfect. The way he looks. The way he smells. The way he feels. Those green eyes. I breathe out and force myself to move.

I exit my office and scan for Grayson but he's nowhere around, and a punch of disappointment grinds through me. He's my boss, no matter how he tries to frame it otherwise. I can't go out with him. I can't even sleep with him. It sucks. I hurry forward and enter the elevator, my body humming a tune that Grayson wrote. I need a workout. A long, hard workout. And chocolate. It's not Grayson Bennett, but it will do. My weekend plans set, I exit the building and start walking. I've made it one block, with one to go to reach the subway, when a black Porsche pulls up next to me.

The window rolls down. "Get in," a male voice calls out and I suck in air when I realize it's Grayson. It's a moment of decision. I know this. I should say no. I try.

I walk to the window and lean in. "I'm not getting in."

"No one else knows what happens between us unless we make that decision together. It's just you and me tonight, Mia."

Just me and him. I don't know why those words, all of them spoken together, hit all the right notes, but they do. "I don't want to regret this," I say, in a last bid for resistance.

"And if you walk away, will you regret that? Because I can tell you, I will."

I tell myself he's a man that already controls my job. I can't allow him to become the man who controls my heart and yet, I don't know what happens. I just—I get in the car.

Grayson sits back down next to me and hands me my glass of wine. "What are you thinking, Mia?"

"About you showing up in your fancy sports car and telling me to get in." I reach up and stroke his cheek, the rasp of his whiskers on my fingers. "And then you brought me here, to your mansion in the Hamptons, in a chopper. But we had pizza as your way to prove to me that you were just a man. That we weren't worlds apart."

"We were never worlds apart," he says. "From the day we met, we were a team."

"And yet you fired me off that case without talking to me first," I say, the words spilling out of my mouth of their own accord. "I don't understand how that made us a team. It made you the man in control of my heart and my career."

"And so instead of fighting with me, instead of giving me a chance to explain, repent, regret, make it up to you, you used Becky as an excuse to run."

"I didn't run." I try to stand up.

He catches my arm. "What are you doing right now?"

Chapter Nineteen

Mia

"What am I doing right now?" I demand, still on the barstool with Grayson holding onto my arm. "Giving myself room to fight. I don't want to be trapped in my seat right now."

He studies me for several unreadable seconds and then lets me go, but there's something in the way he does it, in the way he withdraws beyond the physical that keeps me in my seat. "I'm not even thinking about leaving. I wish I never had. I wish I could turn back the clock and get back our lost time."

He doesn't immediately respond. He doesn't agree. He doesn't offer me the forgiveness I don't deserve for leaving, and some part of me really needs to be forgiven, perhaps because I feel he never really will. Which makes the fact that he's the one who stands up now and walks away, appropriate. He offers me his back and presses his hands onto the counter opposite the island by the sink. I've hurt him again, and in turn, I've pushed him away when I want him close. I stand up and quickly slide between him and the sink, but he doesn't move. He doesn't touch me. "Is that how it is, Mia?" he asks. "I suffocate you? I make you feel trapped?"

My hand settles on his chest. "No. God no. You always made me feel safe in too many ways to name. In *us*. In the rest of the world. In my desire to go bigger and further. You made me feel so many things, good things that I have missed. I just—"

"You just what?" he demands, his voice low, taut, and still he doesn't touch me.

"I felt like that safe feeling was a lie. I was so hurt when I left that I think it's hard to let down my guard again."

"I didn't cheat on you, Mia. I don't deserve to have you put up that kind of guard again."

"I know, but I pulled up a guard to protect myself and now I have to pull that wall down. I *am* pulling it down. The problem is that when I pull it down, what's left is me leaving you over a lie that wasn't yours. That makes us unsteady."

"To me, unsteady was when we were apart. Steady is here, now. Together."

"It is, but you own your world in a way that most do not. You own my world and *me* when I'm with you. With my heart on the line, that's more than scary. It's terrifying."

"And you own mine, Mia. You *are* my world."

He says the words with deep, guttural passion, but he still doesn't touch me. "I think it's hard to feel like your equal," I admit, just wanting to say it, to get it all out once and for all.

"When have I ever made you feel less than me?" He pushes off the counter, his hands settling at his hips, withdrawing even further. "I talked to you about everything. I trusted you with everything. I needed you with me through it all."

"But you have to know that there are few human beings on this planet that can stand next to you and not compare themselves and judge themselves unworthy. I always wanted to deserve to be by your side. I wanted to have more depth to what I offer when you do ask my opinion."

"And you thought you didn't? Aside from being beautiful and intelligent, Mia, you, like my father, have a moral compass that keeps mine in line. He loved that about you just like I do. You keep me solid."

"You don't need me for that. Your father carved right and wrong into your very being. I want to be more than that for you and for me. That was something I was working toward when we broke up and it felt good. I need my own successes, so when you pulled me from that case without talking to me, I felt—owned, in the wrong way."

"Mia—"

I hold up a hand. "Before you respond, I need to say a little more. The way you handled pulling me from that account was wrong, but I had insecurities that probably made me handle it just as wrong. Had Becky not pressed her damn naked breasts against you that day, I would have talked it out with you. That's what I'm doing now. I'm talking it out with you. Not running."

"I was protecting you," he says. "That is what the man who loves you should do."

"If I was at risk of your father firing me to set an example, I should be making the decision about taking that risk."

"It was more than that. I get that you were next in line, but we pulled the lead counsel because he was in bed with the mob. That's how we ended up defending a dirty mobster we thought wasn't dirty. You didn't see all of the facts and when I did, I pulled a favor with the judge. I asked to have the opportunity to pull you. He made me do it on the spot. It was then or never and I didn't want you on the feds' or the mob's radar. The end. That wasn't happening. I love you too damn much for that."

"You should have told me you were making the call. I don't know a woman who would be upset that her man was trying to protect her. I just don't get why you didn't talk to me. That isn't us. Not the us I knew."

"I had to make a snap decision and I know you, Mia. You would've said you could take the heat off with the feds."

"I could have. I'm squeaky clean. I would have if it protected you and the firm."

"That's what I mean. You would have tried to protect me. I would have pulled you, and the fact that I ignored your pleas would have made it worse."

"No. It would not have because I wouldn't have felt betrayed. Just pissed." I step to him again and press my hand to his chest. "Don't do that to me again because we will need a weekend and a rubber room for the war that will ensue."

"If I ever have to make a snap decision to protect you, Mia, I'll make it and I'd expect you to do the same in reverse." He shackles my arm and pulls me to him. "Like you came here to protect me. That's what we do. We protect each other. That's what you would have tried to do."

I reach up and brush my fingers over his jaw. "Yes. We protect each other, but next time, you don't get to go around me."

"You're right, but just know this, baby. When I look into your eyes and you ask for something, it's hard as hell to deny you." The buzzer on the oven goes off.

"Even pizza? Because I'm really hungry."

He cups my face, and he's not focused on pizza. "If you hold back, if you get ready for me to leave you, then you've already left me again. Or just never came back. All in, Mia, or all out."

"All in," I say, despite the fact that I am unreasonably afraid of being hurt. He didn't betray me. I betrayed him. I hurt him. I need to be vulnerable. I owe him that. And I have to trust him not to hurt me, the way I should have trusted him a year ago.

"How about that pizza?" Grayson asks, kissing me. "It's been far too long since we shared one together."

"Pizza with you sounds like everything."

Tension eases from his body, and the hard lines of his handsome face soften. He's back. He's here with me and relief washes over me. I need him. I need him in ways I tried to deny and failed every time.

He walks to the oven and pulls out the pizza and I turn to watch him return. He sets it on the island counter. "How's your dad?" he asks, flipping open the lid.

My eyes go wide. "Going out of town this weekend and I don't have my phone. What if he calls?" I dart away toward the bedroom and hunt down my purse and my phone. Once I've located it, I check my missed calls and go cold. Ri has called not once but three times.

I glance at my text messages and there's one there from him as well: *Mia. We should talk. Immediately. Call me.*

Chapter Twenty

Mia

I've barely read the message from Ri when Grayson appears in the closet doorway. "Is everything okay?"

I don't even consider anything but honesty with Grayson.. "I have missed calls from Ri." I offer him my phone. "And a text message."

He steps forward and takes it, glancing at the message. "Fuck Ri. Let's go eat our pizza." He grabs me and starts to walk with my phone still in his hand.

I catch his arm and dig my heels in. "Wait."

"You are not working for him if that's what you're about to say," he says, rotating to face me. "You don't need him, his job, or his money. You have me."

"I know that, but until we hear more from your team about whatever he's up to, I think we need to hear what he has to say. Just let me do some information-grabbing."

"I've had about all of you with Ri that I care to handle, Mia."

His voice vibrates with anger, the kind of anger I deserve considering I left him over a lie that wasn't his. The kind of anger that tells me he's affected by my leaving, *we're* affected, no matter how much we both just want to go back to the old, untainted us.

"I can't take back what I did," I say, "but I can make it work for you and us. I'm protecting you, and as you said, that's what we do. We protect each other. It's a call. That's all, and you already know he's up to trouble. Let me find out what I can with you right here with me."

His lashes lower, his expression all hard lines and angles, seconds ticking by before he looks at me and says, "Make the call. Get it over with." He looks down at my phone and I swear there is this moment when he realizes he's holding it captive as if he didn't even know he'd done it. And that's not Grayson.

I push to my toes and kiss him and it feels really good to have him right here where I can do that. "Getting it over with now," I say, settling on my feet and taking my phone from him. Grayson leans on the dresser in the center of the closet, his back pressed to the wooden surface. I do the same next to him, making sure my legs are aligned with his, making sure he knows that I'm right here with him.

Only then do I hit the callback button for Ri. He answers on the first ring.

"Mia," he says.

"Ri."

"I called you an hour ago."

"I didn't hear it ring," I reply, glancing at Grayson with a question in my eyes. Can he hear?

He gives a nod.

"Word is that you're looking for a job," Ri snaps.

I don't play coy, which is another form of a lie and I hate lies. "You've been an ass to me since that incident, Ri. I haven't been feeling exactly secure."

"It's against your employment contract to hunt for a job without offering notice first," he replies, no denial of the incident or his treatment of me since. "That bonus I gave you when you signed on. I could strip it."

I glance at Grayson who smirks, because obviously money isn't exactly a good threat to use against me right about now. I assume I'll move in with him again. I assume I'll have a job with him should I so choose. I assume we'll get married, but—what if those things don't apply? Grayson must see the questions in my eyes because he steps in front of me, his legs caging me. His eyes hold mine and there is pure possessive heat in his stare, and with it, a promise that I am his and he is mine.

"Mia?" Ri snaps.

I force myself to focus on the call and Ri's threat, which may or may not mean he knows I'm back with Grayson. Ri is sneaky. He'd test me. He'd trick me. "I'm just trying to digest what you just said to me. Come on, Ri. You know how awkward it's been and that's personal, not professional. Only it's become professional because I now fear for my job."

He inhales sharply. "I gave you a job. I gave you a sign-on bonus. I waited for you to get over him. Why the fuck can't you just forget him like he has you? He's all over the papers with that model."

That cuts and I look down, afraid I won't control my reaction to Ri as well if I look into Grayson's eyes right now. I left him. He thought I was with Ri. He hasn't lied to me about being with other women. "I have won every case I've taken since joining the firm, two of which went to trial, the rest I settled otherwise. I've done a good job for you and if that's not enough, I need to find another job, and you need to consider this my official notice, which I'll follow up in writing."

He's silent a beat. "We should meet. Now. Tonight."

"I'm not meeting you, Ri. Not unless it's at the office Monday morning."

"Jesus, woman. You're still so fucking hung up on Grayson that you can't see how good I could be for you. He's gone. Leave him in the grave where he belongs."

In the grave. I don't like those words and my gaze jerks to Grayson's, anger burning in the depth of his stare. "Did you hire me for my skills or because I was Grayson's scorned woman?"

"I wouldn't have hired you if you didn't have skills, and it's not my fault that Grayson was stupid enough to fuck around and lose you, personally and professionally. We need to meet."

"Monday morning," I say. "If that's not good enough, fire me."

"You have another job offer," he assumes. "That's why you're pushing back."

"I don't have another job, but I can't take the way you're treating me. It's been an eyeopener. I finally woke up and saw the writing on the wall. I'm not a token in a game you and Grayson are playing. I want to do my job and do it well."

He's silent several beats. "Monday morning. Seven a.m. in my office." He hangs up.

Grayson takes the phone from me and sets it on the dresser behind me. His hands shackle my waist. "I have never wanted to cause someone harm until Ri. He's using that model, who I didn't fuck, by the way, to push your buttons. To push mine."

"I know," I whisper.

"But it still upset you."

"The idea of you with someone else—yeah. That's what even got me to the point of that date with Ri that resulted in a knee."

"Just like Becky sent you to his doorstep," he says as if that's a fact before he pushes off the dresser, withdrawing.

"No," I say quickly. "That's not what happened. That's not even close to what happened."

His jaw clenches. "Do you intend to meet with him Monday morning?"

"I think, under the circumstances, with him going after you, that's a decision we should make together."

"You going anywhere near Ri again is not a smart decision for us, Mia." He turns and walks out of the closet, leaving me trying to catch my breath.

There it is and it didn't take long. Already, we're there, peeling back the layers that reveal his resentment over my stupid actions and he's justified. I quickly follow him, ready to fight for the man I love. I find him in the bedroom, sitting in an oversized black leather chair in the corner of the room, a chair where we have fucked many times. A chair where I've fallen asleep in his arms while we talked afterward. I cross and sink down next to him, but he doesn't turn to look at me.

"I need to know how you ended up with him, Mia." He looks at me, those green eyes turbulent, and yet unreadable. "I didn't think I needed to know, but I do."

Chapter Twenty-One

Mia

I don't deny Grayson his request. If he wants to know how I ended up working for Ri, I'll tell him. I want him to know. I *need* him to know. I move out of the chair we're sharing and sit on the ottoman in front of him. And I go back in time, taking him there with me...

Two weeks and seven pounds lost since Grayson and I split, I stand at the window of my new apartment, watching rain pound the Manhattan streets. I should be relieved to have this place, considering it came fully furnished, with a one-year lease, and a fabulous price, but it's just so damn empty, like I am right now. I miss Grayson so much and every time he calls I just want to talk to him, but I miss him too much to do that right now. I'll believe anything he says. I need to believe he's innocent, but every time I travel down that rabbit hole, I wake up from a nightmare involving him and Becky's stupid naked breasts.

My cellphone rings and I walk to the basic wooden kitchen table in the corner of the loft-style space and grab my phone to find my father calling. "Honey, you haven't been out to see me in weeks."

"I know. Sorry. It's been crazy."

"You and your billionaire fiancé are up to fun things, I hope. Are you two in the city by chance? I had to come in for business."

"I'm here. Where are you?"

He gives me a location which isn't far from here. I suggest the coffee shop on the corner because I figure inviting him here would shock him. I have to tell him about Grayson. We hang up and my cellphone rings with Grayson's number. God. I want to take the call. I want to just hear his voice. I hit the answer button. "Mia, baby. Please. Mia, I need to see you. This is killing me."

I start to cry. Damn it, I can't cry before I see my father. "I shouldn't have answered." I hang up. I want to call back. He calls back. I hit decline and set my phone down, rubbing my palms down my jeans. Don't pick it back up. Don't talk to him. *His voice, that rough masculine timbre, God, I love his voice so much. It's just perfect, the way I thought he was.*

I grab my black Chanel trench coat, which I bought myself with my first bonus check from the Bennett firm, earned fair and square with hard work. Once I've pulled it on, I settle my purse strap on my shoulder and pick up my phone as it rings again. I'm about to turn it off when a text buzzes and I dare to read it: Mia, I love you. I can't even breathe without you. Come home.

Home? *I type in my first text response to him through all of this.* I never had a home with you. I just thought I did. And that hurts. You hurt me. You can't fix it.

I turn off my phone and stare down at my naked ring finger. I inhale and stick my phone in my pocket. I hurry out of my new apartment, that will never be home but at least it's mine, and rush down the narrow stairs leading to the street. It's not a fancy building, but it's in a safe area. I've barely settled at my table when my father walks in. I wave at him and he heads in my direction, and in jeans and a T-shirt that hug a fit body, his brown hair still thick at fifty-five, he's still a catch, but today he looks weary... definitely weary.

I stand when he approaches and he gives me a hug. "I need some caffeine. Give me a quick minute."

I nod and he walks to the counter, scrubbing his jaw as he does. Weary. Stressed. Worried. Those words go through my head over and over until he's sitting in front of me. "What's going on with my daughter?"

"What's wrong?"

He narrows his eyes on me. "You always could read me, heck you read everyone. That's why you're a damn good attorney."

"Yes. What's wrong?"

"I took a loan to grow the business that I'm struggling to pay back. I went to the bank to try to get a loan to pay back the loan. As crazy as that sounds. No go on that. It sucks. The business is growing, but these homebuilders pay at ninety days. I just don't have the cash flow to float the money, which is a common problem for growing companies."

"I'll help. How much are the payments?"

"No. I'm not having that rich fiancé of yours thinking your father is taking advantage. That's not happening."

"Dad, I'll help. Not Grayson." I have it on the tip of my tongue to tell him about the breakup, but something holds me back. "How much?"

His phone buzzes with a text. He grabs it and looks at it. "That's the bank. They want to see me again. You won't need to help. This has to be good news." He squeezes my hand. "Sorry to run off."

"Can you call me afterward?"

"Yes, but don't worry. All is well. This is good news."

He doesn't believe it's good news. I see it in his face. I watch him leave and there is a knot that expands in my belly. I press my hands to my face. I wasted a week crying and I just started sending out resumes. I need a job. "Mia."

I look up to find Ri, or rather Riley Montgomery, standing above me. He's rich. He's powerful. He went to school with Grayson and hates him, yet they cross paths too often and Grayson believes this is no coincidence. "What are you doing here, Ri?"

"I got your address off a resume floating around, but you didn't answer your door. I walked in for coffee and here you are." He motions to the seat. "Can I join you?"

No, I think. "Why?"

He sits down, his dark hair a rumpled mess that somehow still looks planned on him. Everything about this man, including his good looks, feels planned. He's the tall, good-looking, and today he's in expensive jeans and a T-shirt that probably cost a few hundred bucks. That's how he operates. He flaunts his money, while Grayson does not.

"I want to hire you," he says. "I'll up your pay with Bennett by twenty-five percent and give you a fifty-thousand-dollar sign-on bonus."

"Why?"

"You're a star in the making, and if Grayson managed to lose you, I'm happy to sweep in and take advantage. We're growing. We're expanding nationally. We need talent."

"Expanding nationally. Like Bennett. How very Grayson of you."

"I assure you, Mia, that nothing about me resembles Grayson. You have twenty-four hours to decide."

"I'm not fucking you. I'm not doing anything to hurt Grayson."

He laughs. "Do you want that in your employment contract?"

"No. I don't want the job."

He smirks. "Think about it." He slides a card in front of me. "My personal cell is on there. It's a good offer. And if Grayson is really gone from your life, if you've left him behind, why wouldn't you take it?" He stands up and starts walking.

I watch him exit the coffee shop and there is no part of me even slightly tempted to take his offer. I grab my phone, turn it on and text my father: Call me after your meeting.

Feeling the need to do something, to get out of this chair, I leave Ri's card on the table, push to my feet and hurry out of the coffee shop, my path taking me back to my building. I don't let myself read the text messages from Grayson. Once I'm back inside my apartment, I sit down at the kitchen table and start working on resumes again. I have a few interviews. I have money saved because Grayson never let me spend any of my earnings. He was good to me, but now I feel like a kept woman. Isn't that how it works? A rich guy takes care of you and then you look the other way? Except I didn't want his money. I wanted him.

I start working, sending out resume after resume with custom cover letters, and I try repeatedly to reach my father with no luck. It's several hours later when there is a knock on the door. My heart starts to race. Did Grayson find me? I will myself to calm down and walk to the door. "Who is it?"

"Delivery."

"What delivery?"

An envelope slides under my door. I frown and open it to find a picture of a man with a scar down his face with a note on top:

Mia,

I thought you'd want to know the kind of person your father borrowed money from. Don't be too hard on him. This guy is good at convincing people he's legit until they default.

The job offer stands, as does the sign-on bonus.

—Ri

My throat is dry. My heart is still racing. I walk to the table and sit down and start reviewing the information in the envelope and it's terrifying. I press my fist to my forehead and then before I can stop myself, I dial Grayson. "Mia?"

I just sit there, with his voice radiating through me, that voice, that wonderful, perfect voice.

"I love you, Mia. Come home."

Home. My home with him. "You know that I have to do what I have to do to survive, right?"

"What does that mean?" he asks.

"It means I still love you, but I have to survive. I have to make decisions—"

"Mia—" I hang up and I grab the card Ri included in the folder and dial.

"Mia," he greets me.

"Email me the offer."

"And that's how I ended up with Ri," I say, finishing my story.

Grayson studies me as he has the entire time I've been talking, more stone than man, his expression unreadable. Abruptly, he stands up and I'm on my feet with him in an instant, not about to let him walk away. "Grayson—"

"Why didn't you come to me?"

"I was going to when I called, but then I had this realization."

"What realization, Mia?"

"That if I took your money, it would seem like I was using you, and too many people use you. We might have been over, but I didn't want us to end with me holding a hand out. That's not who I am and I guess I just needed you to know that I was real."

He pulls me to him. "Damn it, woman. I wouldn't have thought that. You know I care about your father. Some part of you knew, even then, that I'd do anything for you."

"Because you will doesn't mean it's right for me to ask." I swallow hard. "And everyone does. I see how people want a piece of you."

He tangles his fingers into my hair. "And what about you, Mia? What do you want?"

"You. Just you."

"Ask me what I want."

"What do you want, Grayson?"

"Everything this time, Mia. I didn't have it last time, or you wouldn't have left as easily as you did." He doesn't give me time to tell him no one could have more of me than he did, than he *does*. His mouth closes down on mine, and that chair, our perfect fucking, talking, *us* chair, is calling us.

Chapter Twenty-Two

Grayson

I pull Mia down in the chair, resting against the cushion as she settles her head onto my chest. I have not laid with this woman in my arms like this in what feels like an eternity. And so I hold her now, and damn it, I should never have let her go. I should have known that she would never betray me with Ri and her reasons for going to work for him, well, as much as I hate them, they also represent so many of the reasons I love this woman. My money is nothing to her. She's proven that every day of our lives together. She didn't even keep the ring and damn it, that gutted me, and that's exactly where my head goes. The day I'd found out she'd taken a job with Ri and the day the ring found its way back to me...

Three weeks without Mia.

It might as well be the three thousand years it feels like. I can't sleep. I can't think. I can't fucking breathe. I toss my pen down on my desk and stand up, walking to the window, staring out over the city without really seeing it. I just see Mia's pain.

"Coffee and a protein bar," Eric says from the doorway.

I turn to find him kicking the door shut and walking my direction in a pale blue pinstriped suit which he only wears on "lucky" days. It's his deal uniform. I'd normally ask what's in the pipeline when I see that suit. Right now, I don't give a shit. "Since when do you bring me coffee?" I ask.

"You need something, man, and I figure caffeine is about as close to good as I can give you right now." He stops beside me and hands me the cup, then reaches into his pocket and hands me the protein bar. "And you need to fucking eat."

I take the damn bar and stuff it in my pocket, but I don't ignore the coffee. I take a sip. "What do you have for me?" I ask, certain him and his blue suit are here on business.

"The bids on the hotel properties were accepted. We officially have locations for the Dallas and New York City Bennett Hotel launches. The firsts of many. Once we ink, I'll work on getting the Dallas law offices moved to the property."

"And we make money on the property where we run our firm," I say. *"You're brilliant, Eric. I'm quite certain your bonus will buy you a new lucky suit."*

"Try a new lucky Jaguar or ten." He inhales, his mood shifting. *"We need to talk."*

I narrow my eyes on him. *"Talk?"*

"About Mia."

Tension radiates up my spine. *"What about Mia?"*

"She took a job."

My lashes lower and I turn away. She's officially gone. She's not coming back to work here. *"Where?"*

"That's the part I'd rather leave out of this equation."

I cut him a sharp look. *"What does that mean?"*

"Ri," he says. *"She went to work for Ri."*

Those words punch me in the chest so hard that I want to punch the window, and that's not me, that's not how I operate. *"Is she fucking him?"* I ask, the anger I can't control radiating in my voice.

"I don't know, man. I wouldn't have thought she'd take a job with him. Not Ri. She knows how much he hates you."

I love you, *she'd said on the phone days ago. More like she fucking hates me.* "Leave," *I order softly.*

"Grayson—"

"Eric, man, I love you, but get out of my fucking office. I need to be alone."

"Right. I understand." He turns and heads for the door. He's just exited when Nancy, my forty-two-year-old, quiet, always smart assistant appears in the doorway, proving she's not smart right now. Otherwise, she wouldn't be about to speak to me. She shoves her black-rimmed glasses up her nose and clears her throat. *"Courtney is here. She's a—"*

"I know who she is," I snap because of course, I know Mia's best friend. I look skyward and then say, *"Send her in."*

I stay where I'm at, needing control in a way I normally assume in less obvious ways. Courtney walks into my office and shuts the door. She's wearing funeral black, her blonde hair a mess, which tells me she's a mess, which isn't like her. *"I know about Ri,"* I say.

She reaches into her purse and closes the space between us and I'm aware of her hand in that bag, waiting to deliver another blow. "She gave this to me three weeks ago to give to you and I didn't. I thought she'd take it back, but I can't hold on to a hundred-thousand-dollar ring." *She pulls her hand from the bag and hands me Mia's ring box.*

"Two hundred thousand," *I say, not because the money matters to me, but because of the impact of Mia giving it back. She never wanted my money. Fuck. She's perfect, and in this moment I know the war is lost. She's gone. I'm not getting her back.*

I take the box.

Courtney opens her mouth and shuts it. And then she turns and walks toward the door. A minute later, she's gone and the door is shut and my mind goes where I don't want it to go. The timing of the news about Mia with Ri and this ring are hard to ignore, no matter what Courtney claims about the timing. Mia's made it clear to me that she's with Ri now and I know she knows that's the end for me, for us.

"Grayson?"

I blink back to the present to find Mia looking up at me. "Yeah, baby?"

Her eyes soften and warm. "God, I missed you calling me that. I just missed you, period. Please tell me what you're thinking."

"You could have sold the ring to help your father."

"Sell my ring? I wouldn't sell my ring. It's—special. It was—"

I tangle my fingers in her hair and pull her mouth to mine. "I know you wouldn't. I doubted you, too, though. You know that, right?"

"You thought I went to Ri to hurt you."

"Yes. I found out you went to work for him the same day Courtney brought me back the ring."

"But I gave her the ring the day we broke up."

"She didn't bring it to me."

"She brought it the day you found out?"

"Yes. She did."

She sits up and climbs on top of me, her hands going to my cheeks. "That must have felt like a 'fuck you' and it wasn't. I would never—"

"I know. I should have known there was more going on than met the eye, but damn it, Mia, you should have known I wouldn't fuck around on you. We were not as strong as I thought."

"Don't say that. Please don't say that. I thought we were perfect."

I turn her over, and lay her on her back, pressing my leg between hers, and I lean over her. "So did I. Maybe that was the problem."

"I don't understand."

"We're human. We're flawed. We can't be perfect. We need to remember that this time. We need to know that it's our flaws, our imperfections, and how they come together to be perfect that makes us perfect. But we have to see the flaws and deal with them to get to perfect."

"And what were our flaws?"

"That's what we need to figure out, baby." I stroke her cheek. "That's what we need to figure out, and if we do, we'll be stronger. We'll be better this go around."

"Promise me because I suddenly feel like the room is spinning like we're uncertain."

"I promise you that there is nothing uncertain about my love for you or my intention to keep you this time."

She strokes my cheek. "I promise you that there is nothing uncertain about my love for you or my intention to keep *you* this time."

I push off the chair and take her with me, carrying her to the bed, where I plan to hold her tonight and every night going forward, but I know that means dealing with our flaws. I know that means admitting we have them.

A long time later, I lay in bed with her in front of me, holding her close, and I think of that ring. I'm going to give it back to her, but not until I know she will never take it off again, and right now, I don't know that and I don't think she does either.

Chapter Twenty-Three

Mia

I wake to a dark room, the heavy, warm feeling of Grayson holding me, and the spicy wonderful scent of him that I've missed so very much. I smile, snuggling closer to Grayson, and he tightens his grip around me, that safe feeling I told him he makes me feel in full force right now. My lashes flutter and I slip back into that half-slumber state of pure bliss where I get to enjoy who I'm with and where I am without getting out of bed. Only I don't stay awake. I'm just too relaxed and comfortable and I feel the inevitability of sleep as the world goes dark.

The next time I wake I become aware of my surroundings, there's a dull light peeking beneath the curtains and a shift of the bed behind me. "Grayson?"

"You rest, baby," he murmurs next to my ear, his breath a warm trickle on my neck. "I need to go make some phone calls."

"Do you have to go?"

"I'm not going anywhere for long," he promises. "You sleep. I'll be back here with you when you wake up." He kisses my neck and then he's gone.

I stay where I'm at, listening to him dress, and a few seconds later, he appears on this side of the bed in a pair of sweats and disappears into the bathroom. If this was a year ago, I'd go back to sleep. I'd feel safe and secure, and really, I do now—I do, at least, when Grayson's with me, but he's not. He's up. He's moving. He's leaving the room and right now, this morning, I feel like we're dealing with those flaws that he named. Flaws. I really hate that word.

I squeeze my eyes shut and replay last night's conversation with Grayson about that word. When I open my eyes, Grayson is exiting the bathroom, pulling a T-shirt over his head and by the time it's in place, he's left the room. I tell myself to go back to sleep, to just relax into the perfection of being back here with him, but I can't.

Those phone calls he needs to make are likely about Ri and I need to be a part of fixing what problems I helped create. And I did help create them. I was used in a dangerous game Ri was, *is*, playing with Grayson. I sit up and throw away the blanket, leaving myself shivering as a chill touches my naked skin. I quickly walk across the room, enter the bathroom, and a few minutes later, my teeth and hair are brushed, my face washed, and I've pulled on sweats and a tee just in case we have company.

I hurry down the hallway and as I round the corner, the deep rumble of Grayson's voice lifts in the air. I enter the living room and spy him in the connected kitchen standing behind the island with the phone on the counter, obviously on speaker as he says, "I have no idea, Eric." He looks up and his eyes light on me and then warm, his gaze sweeping over me in that familiar, always hungry way that says he wants to gobble me up. I really do love when this man wants to gobble me up.

"How the hell would Becky even get your number?" Eric asks. "You never gave that bitch your number." I am human enough to approve of this reply from Eric and I step between Grayson and the counter, my hands settling on his chest, as Eric continues with, "She left the damn state after you promised to ruin her and before we ever found out what the fuck that set-up was all about."

My eyes go wide, and Grayson shackles my waist, pulling me against him, his fingers tangling into my hair. "Betrayal," Grayson says, his lips near mine. "It was always about betrayal." I'm not sure I like that reply and how it relates to our breakup, but his mouth comes down on mine, his tongue delivering a seductive caress that I feel from head to toe. Fighting a moan, I melt right there in the kitchen, a big puddle of need and want, my hand sliding under Grayson's T-shirt, while Eric is forgotten.

That is until he says, "Grayson? Hello? Are you there?" and I realize that perhaps he's been talking and I didn't notice.

Grayson's lips part from mine, a curve to his mouth as he says, "I'm here."

"And?" Eric prods.

"And what?" Grayson asks, his lips nearing mine again, a warm trickle of his breath promising another kiss I really want and now.

Eric laughs. "Okay. You're distracted. Good morning, Mia."

Grayson and I both laugh. "Morning, Eric," I greet.

"Glad to have you back, sweetheart," he says, "but I need his attention."

I push to my toes and kiss Grayson. "And I need coffee." I dart away from Grayson and call out, "He's all yours, Eric."

"I'm all yours, Eric," Grayson mimics, pressing his hands to the island while I think about those hands on my body. He has *really* good hands.

"I hired a new hacking expert," Eric says. "He's going to dig for answers on this Ri/DA situation and look for ties between Becky and Ri that we might have missed in the past."

"And Mitch," Grayson says, as I stick a pod of coffee in the Keurig. "Mia and I think he helped setup the Becky incident. That could mean that he's on board with Ri."

"Mitch," Eric says. "Interesting. As is the idea that Ri plotted to break up you and Mia to distract you while he landed a larger blow."

That statement guts me. I helped Ri set Grayson up. How do we come back from that?

"I'll have Mitch monitored," Eric adds. "Maybe he *is* the one helping Ri set you up."

"If Ri has the DA interested in taking me down," Grayson says, "it's a lot broader than Mitch, but he might be our door to answers."

That very accurate statement is unsettling in its content, but I'm relieved that Grayson is taking this threat seriously. Ri is coming for Grayson and he's coming in a big way. I know it. I feel it. "Davis just texted me," Eric says. "He wants to meet and talk about this threat from Ri. He says he has pressing information."

"What information?" I ask urgently, forgetting my coffee and joining Grayson back at the island.

"He said it's better talked about in person," Eric explains. "Our chopper is at two, Grayson. How about noon?"

"If your chopper is at two," Grayson says, "Mia and I will fly out on our own a few hours later but, yes, twelve is fine. We'll see you then."

I turn to Grayson. "If he won't talk about it on the phone, it's something bad, right?"

"Something sensitive," he says. "Which doesn't always mean it's bad."

"But this situation—Grayson, if the DA—"

"We'll head off the problem," he says, cupping my face. "Thanks to you, Mia."

"But what if—"

The doorbell rings and we both say, "Leslie," at the same time, referencing his godmother, the woman who was his mother's best friend, and who now protects Grayson like he is her own. We both know this because she's the only person, outside of me, that he allows to enter the gates without his approval first.

"I love her," I whisper, "but I really want to talk about this Ri situation. And I really just want to be with you right now."

"She's going to be ecstatic to see you." He strokes my hair, tender in a way that defies what a hard businessman he is. "Go make her day and answer the door. I'll call Eric back and see if I can get anything else out of him." He kisses me and turns away, already walking toward the patio, which to me is telling. He's concerned and he's trying not to show it.

I force myself to walk toward the front door and I yank it open. Leslie stands there looking as elegant and pretty as ever, her dark hair shiny and perfect. Her petite frame and perfect skin defy her age, which she teasingly changes all the time, but it's older than she looks. Of that, I'm certain. Her expression is that of shock and then pleasure. "Mia!" She rushes forward and hugs me. "You're back," she says, leaning back to look at me. "You are back, right?"

"Yes," I say. "I'm back and this time for good." And I have never meant any words more than I do those.

A few minutes later, Leslie and I are in the kitchen drinking coffee, but Grayson hasn't appeared. I do my best to eagerly interact with Leslie, but I'm worried. Ri is setting Grayson up in a way that would destroy him and maybe even put him behind bars. I can't let that happen, and that means I have to use my leverage with Ri, but Grayson won't like it. He'll forbid it and that's going to be a problem.

Chapter Twenty-Four

Mia

I spend a good twenty minutes at the kitchen island chatting with Leslie with no sign of Grayson returning from the patio, which is starting to worry me. "I have cookies in the car I didn't bring in," Leslie says. "I brought them for Grayson to take back to the city."

"Your famous oatmeal raisin?" I ask eagerly.

"Of course, and you know that I love that you love them." She holds up a finger. "I'll be right back." She hurries away and my gaze slides to the patio door where I will Grayson to appear, but still, he doesn't. I finish off my coffee and set the mug in the sink, pressing my hands to the granite counter and praying desperately that I didn't find out about Ri's plan to hurt Grayson too late to stop it from becoming a major problem. I spend about three minutes reminding myself that Grayson is filthy rich, honest, and powerful. He also has thousands of attorneys surrounding him. He'll beat this.

"I'm back with the cookies!" Leslie announces, and I eagerly rotate to face her finding her holding open a Tupperware filled with cookies. "Breakfast of champions," she adds.

"Indeed it is," I say, and I welcome the distraction of a cookie for breakfast. "I really missed these and you," I declare as I finish off the scrumptious treat.

"I missed you, too," she says, her tone sobering. "He missed you, Mia. He wasn't right without you. He just wasn't. He was—"

When I might ask her to expand on that thought, she seems to shake herself, and then refocus. "You have a full Tupperware container of cookies. You and Grayson can take them back to your place and—oh—well, I mean if you're living with him again. Are you back at the apartment?"

I don't know how to reply, and a million emotions assail me. The apartment. *Our* apartment. The place I called home with Grayson.

Am I going back there? I want to. I so want to, but—the flaws. The problems. "She shouldn't have ever left," Grayson says, appearing across from me, and then rounding the island to pull me under his arm and next to him. "As far as I'm concerned," he says, looking at me, not Leslie, "with me is where she belongs."

Heat and emotions rush through me. "I'll let you two have some time," Leslie says. "Obviously this reunion is new. Make it a good one, you two." She winks and heads for the door.

Grayson and I stand there, watching her leave and the minute the door shuts, I turn in his arms and stare up at him. "You're right," I say. "I shouldn't have ever left. I regret that more every minute I'm with you again."

"Then you're coming home."

"What about our flaws?" I ask, feeling insecure when I've never felt such things with Grayson.

His hand settles on my cheek. "Baby, we're the most perfect thing in my life, but perhaps that's the flaw. My inability, *our* inabilities, to see a flaw because seeing a flaw means we make sure that we deal with it before we let it hurt us. Come home, baby. Move back into *our home*."

"Yes," I say with no hesitation. "Yes, I want to come home."

He cups my face. "That's what I wanted to hear." He kisses me. "Let's go take a shower."

"Yes, but—"

He scoops me up and starts walking toward the bedroom. "Grayson, what about the call? What did Eric say?"

"Absolutely nothing new."

"You were talking to him forever."

He enters the bedroom and crosses to the bathroom, setting me down in front of the shower. "Grayson, I'm worried. What did he say?"

He drags my tee over my head. "I was sidetracked by a call from Japan." He molds me close, unhooks my bra and kisses me. "Remember? I bought into a convention center in Tokyo."

"Right. I still can't get my head around that. That's a huge buy-in."

"Yes. It was. It kept me busy. I had to stay busy while you were gone."

And he did. He tried to fuck me out of his system. It's not a good thought, but it's also not one I can blame him for. I left. I distrusted him. He pulls his shirt over his head and turns on the shower. "We should go see it soon," he adds, dragging me into the shower.

"I'd like that," I say, as he molds me close, the spray of warm water all but blocked by his big, wonderful body. "Have you ever been to Tokyo?"

"Not with you," he replies, backing me into the corner, his fingers tangling into my hair, the thick ridge of his erection nestled between my legs. "There are so many things I want to do with you and experience with you, Mia. Things I've seen and I want you to see. Things I haven't seen and I want to see with you for the first time." His mouth closes down on mine, tongue flicking against mine, and I moan with the possessive taste of him. There is no part of me that doesn't want this man, and as much as I fear there will be a part of him that doesn't want me, that's not what I feel.

He cups my backside and squeezes, his cheek coming to rest against mine, his lips at my ear, "So many things I want to do to you." He presses inside me and his mouth crashes down on mine, and at least for now our flaws disappear. There is no Ri, there is no past, there is only the future, where I want to live forever.

Hours later, Grayson and I have both dressed, him in jeans and a T-shirt, all black, while I chose a soft emerald green blouse and faded jeans. We both pack up for the return to the city and then finally sit at the island and eat the pizza we didn't get to last night, or rather, order a fresh one to enjoy. We talk about Japan, a project he's excited about and I gobble up every detail, the way I always had in the past. He wants to take me there and there is this question in the air that we don't discuss about my future: Will I go back to work for Bennett? It's not a topic we dive into now, not when him pulling me off that case was what really left us vulnerable for a breakup. But that topic is coming and coming soon. I have to go back to work on Monday. I *will* go back to work Monday, and I *will* meet with Ri. No matter how Grayson feels about it. We're going to fight, but this time I'm not leaving when we do. This time I'm going to fight and win because it's about protecting him, something I've failed at miserably.

Grayson feels this topic in the air as well. I see it in his eyes and sense it in his mood, so much so that when Eric and Davis arrive and he stands up to let them in, he stops by my chair, tilts my head back and says, "I won't make the same mistakes again. You have my word." He kisses me and heads toward the door, and I know he's talking about pulling me off that case.

He wants me to come back to work with him, but right now we're about to find out more about the threat against Grayson. We're about to find out how hard we all have to fight. My mind goes back to that interview at the DA's office and the words of one of the men talking about Grayson: *I love taking down a rich fucker who thinks his shit doesn't stink. I'm going to get about ten promotions for burying that rich, fake do-gooder.*

I want Eric and Davis to walk in the door and tell us that this problem is over and that I can just leave Ri behind, but I know deep in my gut they won't.

Chapter Twenty-Five

Mia

I'm still behind the island when Eric and Davis, two men I know well, enter the connected living room area. Both good looking, confident, in jeans and T-shirts, which on Davis feels weird, awkward almost, but Eric is another story. Eric is an ex-Navy SEAL with a Harvard background, a brilliant financial mind, and a sleeve of tattoos down one arm. He's someone who manages to feel comfortable in every moment, while Davis prefers the edge of discomfort.

Grayson is on their heels and he immediately crosses to stand beside me, the action an assumption that the other two men will join us on the opposite side. Instead, they halt in the living area, a good distance away from us, too far for a real conversation. "We need to see you alone," Davis announces, speaking to Grayson and obviously shutting me out.

"Mia is with me," Grayson says. "That means she's with us."

"And yet she was with Ri," Davis replies, and like anyone close to Grayson, he actually has the courage to look at me when he makes that statement. "How do we know she's not being inserted now to weaken you?"

"I'm on Team Mia, for the record," Eric quickly adds.

"My job is to protect you, Grayson," Davis argues. "And beyond my job, you're a friend. I don't want you fucked any more than you already are."

"What does that mean?" I ask quickly. "Fucked how?"

"Yes," Grayson says. "What *does* that mean?"

"I really must insist that I speak to you alone," Davis says.

My temper snaps. "I didn't sleep with Ri, Davis," I state. "I was never with Ri. He gave me a job with a sign-on bonus at a time when my father was in debt to a bunch of very bad people. I wasn't going to ask Grayson for money. What kind of bitch would I be to use him for money? I couldn't do that to him or us, and when Ri tried to force a personal relationship, I started looking for a job, which is why I was at the DA's office. And in case you don't remember, Davis, I saw a naked woman pressed against the man I love, *my fiancé*. I wasn't in a good place emotionally, I was dying inside, but I still loved him. I didn't, I wouldn't, I haven't ever tried to hurt him." I press my hands to the counter. "Questions?"

Davis stares at me for several intense moments and then eyes Grayson, who says, "Can we get down to business now?"

Davis shifts his attention back to me. "You always did have a way of getting to the point. Welcome back, Mia."

Eric joins us at the island, pressing his hands on the tile. "Mia," he greets, standing directly across from me.

I slide the cookies toward him. "Leslie made them."

"Oatmeal raisin?" he asks hopefully.

"Yes," I say, looking at Davis. "None for you."

"Fuck, Mia," he says. "Have a heart, will you?"

I laugh. "No. You're a bastard. No cookie for you."

"You know I'm just protecting him," he says.

"Which," I say, "is the only reason I forgive you."

"What did you find out?" Grayson asks. "Is there a collaboration with the DA to take me down?"

"Yes," Davis says. "There is, and it's already six feet deep with layers of evidence."

An explosion of fear for Grayson rocks me, but he's calm, cool, his tone even as he asks, "Evidence of what?"

"Money laundering, racketeering, bribing judges, the list goes on and on," Davis states. "This is an elaborate set-up that might have taken years of work."

"Which brings me to Mia," Eric says.

"Me?" I ask, stiffening while Grayson's hand settles on my back, a silent show of support.

"You," he says. "I think the Becky show was supposed to break you two up. It was supposed to distract Grayson."

I pant out a breath. "I think so, too. I've been thinking that for about twelve hours straight, and believe me, it's a painful realization."

"None of us saw it," Grayson says. "Not me. Not you. Not the people around us."

"That number that texted you the day of the funeral," Eric says, "it was made from a phone that's had two users since and none were Becky. We're working on more."

"Back to the here and now," Davis says, "and my prior suggestion. We need to pick a criminal attorney, a killer that you trust and that isn't connected to the firm."

"He's right," I say, and this time I don't argue for me to handle this. This is too big for my experience and I'm too close to Grayson. "You have no idea who's working for Ri," I add. "You need someone who's a proven winner."

"Agreed," Eric chimes in and looks at Grayson. "Reid Maxwell," he says, glancing at me to explain. "He's one of the attorneys handling the Japan convention center," before he adds, "He has ties to a couple of the best criminal attorneys in the country who happen to own the same firm."

"What ties?" Grayson asks.

"His sister is married to one of them," Eric says. "He represented one of them against the DA over a misconduct case, and the misconduct was against the DA."

"Both are good choices," Davis says, "but Reese Summer is married to Cat of the Cat Does Crime column and when she gets behind him and his cases, she influences a lot of minds. I'd go with Reese. He's the best of the best and she's a bonus."

"Get me a number," Grayson says. "Where are we on finding the mole?"

"I brought in a new security team. One of my old SEAL buddies works with them. I trust him. We won't deal with Ri's influence. They're doing a sweep of our operations to find our moles nationwide. They assure me they'll have an initial evaluation here locally done in two days. They're good. We'll get results."

"How long do we have before charges are filed?" I ask.

"Uncertain," Davis said. "But my source feels it's weeks out, but not months. Weeks. That's not long."

"What else?" Grayson asks.

Davis looks at me. "The closer she is to you, the more chance Ri gets nervous and tries to speed things up." He shifts his attention to Grayson. "She needs to stay away and if you love her, you'll listen. I'm protecting you and her. Ri could smear her just to burn you deeper."

Grayson doesn't reject his words and I suddenly want to explode in protest, but not now with Eric and Davis here. Grayson looks at Eric. "What are your thoughts?"

"I'm not sure Mia being with you matters," he says. "It's all about positioning. If she stays, how do you make that work for you?"

Grayson stiffens, and I know he doesn't like that answer. "Where are we on leverage against Ri?"

"The security team I hired has a master hacker on their payroll," Eric says. "More soon."

Grayson nods. "I'll see you both in the city," he says.

Both men look like they want to argue, but they don't. They turn and leave. The minute the door shuts, Grayson pulls me to him. "I need you to go to Japan, work on that convention center project, and get out of target range until I make this go away."

And so, the war begins. The war between me and Grayson, not Grayson and Ri, because he knows what I know. I'm not a master hacker, but I'm inside Ri's operation, I'm close to him. He needs me here. "No," I say, preparing for the storm to follow as I add, "I'm not leaving."

Chapter Twenty-Six

Mia

The past, two and a half years ago

"I should not be in this car with you," I say, glancing over at Grayson as he navigates his Porsche through Manhattan traffic, the man and the car radiating sexiness and power.

"We're just going for pizza," he says, turning a corner.

"In the Hamptons," I say. "I can't go to the Hamptons with you."

"Why not?" he asks.

"All the reasons I didn't call you. All the reasons I already told you I can't see you."

"And yet you got in the car," he points out.

"I know." I swallow hard. "Grayson."

"Yes, Mia?"

"Can you stop the car?"

"At the chopper pick-up, yes."

"I'm the kind of girl who's fine with a slice of pizza at the corner pizza joint. Can we just do that before you leave?"

"We're already here." He pulls us into a parking lot for the chopper service that I knew was nearby but never gave much thought to it until now.

"And there's a pizza spot one block down. I'll even buy." I give a strained laugh. "I just got this great new job, you know?"

He kills the engine and turns to face me. "I'll bring you back tonight if you want to come back. No one is going to know we did this but you and me, Mia. I'll protect your privacy. I'll protect *you*."

"Not by helping me at work," I say quickly, rotating to face him as he does the same of me. "That's not what you mean, right?" I press. "I'm not doing this for special treatment. I don't need that. I don't want that. That wasn't what made me get in the car, in fact, it all but kept me from doing so."

"Why *did* you get into the car?"

"I—You're distracting me."

He arches a dark brow. "I'm distracting you?"

"It's not your money either, which you must have thought about."

"I thought it was my hot body," he teases.

"It's not your money," I say, unwilling to let this topic go for reasons that I can't define, yet still feel important. "Actually, I think your money is part of my reservation. Yes, I hate your money."

"And why is that, Mia?"

"You have to expect everyone wants it. You have to expect I'll want it. You won't ever be real because you won't ever believe I'll be real. Sex would be the only thing real with you, which doesn't require a trip to the Hamptons."

He leans in and cups my face, his breath a warm tease on my cheek before he kisses me, a deep, sexy slide of tongue that leaves me panting as he says, "Is that real enough for you?"

Too real, I think. There is something about Grayson that gets to me, that makes me do stupid things like getting into his car. "I need to leave."

I try to pull away from him, but he slides a hand under my hair and holds me to him. "Mia," he says softly.

"Grayson." My hand has planted itself on the hard wall of his chest. "I want you. I don't think I could hide that very well but if this is just fucking, can we just do that? Then I'll go back to work and you'll go back to being king of the world without me?"

He kisses me again, and my God, the man can kiss, and he smells all woodsy and spicy and addictive. "Don't move," he orders softly before he releases me and then exits the car. I assume he's going inside to cancel the chopper, but suddenly he's opening my door and squatting beside me.

"What are you doing?" I ask.

"Getting you out of here," he says, reaching across me for my seatbelt, his arm brushing my breast in the process, and the tightening of my nipples radiates straight to my sex.

He freezes a moment and I sense a hunger in him, which only serves to stir more hunger in me. He unclips my seatbelt and pulls me to my feet, shutting the door and then leaning me against it, his big body framing mine. His hands on my hips. "I don't bring women to the Hamptons or my apartment," he says. "And yes, I am going to fuck you, Mia, before and after you try my favorite pizza spot *in the Hamptons*." He brushes a strand of hair from my eyes. "If you come with me." He releases me and steps back, offering me his hand and a choice as he does.

I don't ask him to explain. Maybe he just wants to keep our fling private. I *am* an employee of his company. Or maybe there's more to this. I'm not sure, but when I look into his eyes, the connection we share is real and I have this sense that Grayson Bennett needs something real in his life, if only for right now. I press my hand to his and when it closes down on mine, some part of me knows that this night and this man are about to forever change me.

Grayson walks me to him and then puts us both in motion. "Have you ever been to the Hamptons?" he asks.

"No. Have you ever been to Brooklyn?"

He laughs a low, deep, sexy laugh I feel from head to toe. "I know Brooklyn better than you might think."

"You own half of it, right?"

"I do not," he says, opening the door for me to enter the building, "in fact own anything in Brooklyn."

I enter the building, where a small waiting area is my destination with a dozen empty seats and glass doors leading to, I assume, the chopper. Grayson joins me, taking my hand again, his opposite hand lifting to the solo, thirty-something man behind a counter. "Jesse." The greeting is light, genuine, and without airs.

"It'll be five minutes, Grayson," Jesse replies, casual and comfortable, even friendly, with Grayson. He doesn't act like Grayson is a billionaire with an ego.

Grayson nods to the other man and turns to face me, returning to our prior conversation. "I don't own half of Brooklyn, however, I do have a close friend, and business associate who grew up in Brooklyn a few streets from where you grew up."

"And you know this because you looked at my HR file?"

"Yes, Mia," he confirms. "I looked at your HR file."

"I guess that's fair. I googled you. I probably know more about you than you do about me now."

"You know what I allow to be known."

"Because nothing is real."

His hands come down on my hips and he pulls me to him. "Be real with me, Mia, and I'll be real with you."

"I dare you to mean those words or not," I amend, pulling back to look at him. "I don't have any expectations." It hits me that he's made me promises but I have made him none. "If this is pizza and a fuck, then it's pizza and a fuck and no one will ever know but you and me. That's as real as it gets."

He cups my face. "I can already tell you that that's not real enough, but it's a start." He kisses me and once again I'm breathless.

Our lips are still lingering together when someone clears their throat and Grayson smiles. "Let's go eat that pizza." He takes my hand and as we walk toward the exit, one word stays in my mind: Real. It's a word that matters to him. It's a word that matters to me.

A few minutes later when he helps me into the chopper and we buckle up, I go back to the word "real." There's a real possibility I'm in over my head with this man, and yet, I can't seem to care. The chopper door is still open, and I know only one thing with certainty: I'm not leaving and that's as real as it gets.

Chapter Twenty-Seven

Mia

The present

It's not long before Eric and Davis are back at the house. Somehow Eric manages to not only contact his ex-SEAL buddy who he's hired to help with the Ri situation, but he manages to get Adam to the Hamptons in rapid, nearly impossible, speed.

Adam turns out to be tall, good looking and in his mid-thirties, with dark, wavy hair. "Adam is an expert of disguise," Eric says as we all gather around the kitchen island. "That's his thing. He can get anywhere and no one will know it's him."

I wonder what Adam's thing was, but I assume for a SEAL that could just be his ability to kill and protect. It's a bit disconcerting how comforting that is right about now, but then, my gut is screaming with a warning. We're wading in knee-deep quicksand, still moving, but there's the very real possibility that we're already trapped and going under but don't know it yet. "Walker Security is a diverse, skilled group," Adam says, pulling me back into the moment as he responds to something Grayson has asked about Adam's employer. "Mia," Adam says, "I need you to tell me about the dynamic between you and Ri."

Grayson's displeasure cuts through the air and I have no doubt every person in this house feels the blade. "He wants to fuck her for obvious reasons, but as an added plus, he'd fuck me at the same time."

Tension curls in my belly. This isn't a topic I enjoy sharing, but it's necessary. "He tried to kiss me recently," I say. "I kneed him. Hard. Really hard. He's pretty bitter." I go on to run through the details of Ri finding out that I'm looking for a job and the Monday meeting.

Adam listens without much input and for the most part, Eric and Davis simply take it all in as well. They're all thoughtful, attentive, intelligent people who will all have opinions, some of which I won't agree with and some that I will. I prepare myself for the varied opinions, but Adam guides the conversation in an unexpected direction. "We already have a female from our team ready to stay at your apartment tonight," he says. "With Ri showing interest in you, Mia, I suggest we have me play the boyfriend, and I can hang out with our Mia double at your place."

"No," I say, rejecting that idea. "Ri has to think he has a chance to turn me or he'll go at Grayson ten times harder."

"Mia, damn it," Grayson says, his voice low, guttural.

I turn to him, my hand on his chest. "Hear me out. He feels like I'm a weapon. Let him keep that weapon while you knock his legs out from underneath him."

"At the risk of being pummeled," Eric says, "I agree. We'll watch her, Grayson. We'll wire her. We'll keep her with you as much as possible."

"Just make it count," I say, focused on Grayson. "Use me to take him out before he takes you out."

Grayson pulls me to him, ignoring the rest of the room. "I will. You can count on it."

He says those words so damn vehemently I want to cheer. His focus is no longer on getting me out of town. It's on ending this, on beating Ri once and for all. I push to my toes to give Grayson a quick kiss, but he cups the back of my head and slants his mouth over mine in a sultry, hot kiss that has Eric clearing his throat. "All right then. Time for us to head to the chopper service."

As in all of us, since Eric and Davis missed their original departure time. Grayson reluctantly turns his attention to the room, his gaze on Adam. "Whatever it takes, he goes down. You understand?"

"Quite well," Adam states. "Eric made that point in crystal clear terms."

"Make sure you make it to your team," Grayson replies. "Whatever it takes."

"Perhaps we should talk outside," Adam states.

"You can ride with me and Eric to the airport," Grayson states, kissing me. "Ride with Davis, baby."

I don't like the way this is going down, but I'm not going to push. Grayson doesn't like what Ri is making him become. I'll give him the space he needs to handle this without worrying about how I'll react. He'll tell me what he did later when he's ready. "What about my car?"

"I have another female agent handling it," Adam states. "We have you covered." He looks at Grayson, who motions him forward. It's clear that right now Grayson is focused and he wants action.

Grayson and Adam head toward the door. Eric stands his ground and leans on the island across from me. "Selfless, beautiful, and in love. You're what he needs. I might even fucking love you myself, that's how much I believe he needed you." He pushes off the island and follows Grayson and Adam toward the door.

Davis steps in front of me. "I don't love you, but I like you."

I laugh. "Right. You like me, but you accused me of being up to no good."

"I had to push you and then look into your eyes and see what there was to see."

"And what did you see?"

"His future wife."

Those words stay with me as we head to Davis's rental and with good reason. Grayson asked me to come home, but he didn't give me my ring back. By the time I'm in the passenger seat of the sedan, Davis is in the driver's seat. He shuts the door and then sits there a minute. "He'll ask again."

The words shock me and I turn to look at him. "What?"

"I'm a damn good attorney for a reason. I hit a nerve with the future wife thing. He'll ask again."

I inhale and shake my head, but I say nothing else. The only words that matter are the ones between me and Grayson, which are still too few. Thankfully Davis has never been a man of many words and he is, in fact, good at reading people. He leaves me to my thoughts, which include a reply to that talk about flaws that keeps bothering me.

The ride is short, though, and we pull through a private gate to park at a smaller building. The minute Davis kills the engine, Grayson is at my door, opening it, and pulling me to my feet, molding me close. "How was your talk?" I ask.

"Productive. Unfortunately, we need to meet a couple of Adam's team at the apartment when we get home."

"*Home*," I say. "I love that word."

"I'm glad you do, baby." He kisses me. "Come on." He takes my hand and guides me toward the chopper.

I have déjà vu about ten times over in the next five minutes. This place, the Sunday night return to the city, Grayson helping me into the chopper, his hand at my waist, us side by side in leather seats, familiar seats. And then, Grayson reaches over me and connects my seatbelt, and I flash back to that first Sunday again when he'd done the same thing: *Now you go home with me*, he'd said. Grayson's lips hint at a curve, his green eyes alight with memories, and he lets me know that he's thinking the same thing I am by saying, "Now you go home with me," but he adds, "Now *we* go home."

My hand goes to his jaw, and suddenly, the ring doesn't matter. What matters is what comes next. "Now we go home," I say.

Chapter Twenty-Eight

Mia

Once we land in the city, Grayson and I part ways with the rest of the men and head to his Porsche. The minute I bring it into view, I smile. "You finally got the sapphire blue you wanted," I say, "and the very idea that you denied yourself because you had a car and didn't need another, is part of your appeal. You could do everything in excess, but you don't."

"The only thing I need in excess is you, baby," he says, clicking the door lock and pulling me to him to give me a quick kiss. His voice lowers and he repeats, "Just you," in a rougher, affected voice that has me all kinds of equally affected.

"Me, too," I say. "You. Just you."

He strokes my hair and then opens the door for me. It would probably be silly to most people, but I missed little moments like this one in such a huge way. I mean, it's just a door, but it's so much more. Once Grayson has sealed me inside the Porsche and has joined me, we just sit there for a moment and stare at each other until we both start smiling. I'm going home. That's what we're both thinking. I know it. He knows it. "Come here," he orders, his hand sliding under my hair to my neck as he leans over to kiss me and whispers, "Mia."

"Grayson," I murmur.

We both smile again and I swear I'm not sure I really smiled at all this past year, not a real smile as I have with him this weekend. Grayson settles back behind the wheel and cranks the engine, all kinds of masculine perfection as he does. "I really did miss your obsession with Porsche," I declare.

He casts me a sideways look. "You love Porsche, too."

"I love you behind the wheel of a Porsche," I say. "You make the car look good."

"*You* make the car look good, baby." He winks, backs up, and soon we're on the road with only a short drive ahead of us to be home. My hot man is a billionaire and doesn't act like it in ways others with money do, but then, his father beat the word "humble" into his head.

I have the briefest flashback of the first time I met his father, an older version of Grayson, who'd stayed fit and handsome, which made the heart attack shocking. *I've been sitting in a coffee shop and he's shocked me by sitting down right in front of me.*

"*You're dating my son.*"

"*Yes,*" I say. "*I am.*"

"*But you work for the company.*"

"*Do you want me to resign?*"

"*I hear you work very hard,*" he says.

"*From Grayson?*"

"*No. Everyone.*"

"*Harder than ever now. I don't want to seem like I'm riding his coattails. I didn't want to date him for that very reason but, well, I ran into him quite literally and it just—we happened.*"

"*Are you after his money?*"

"*I hate his money,*" I say, as I had to Grayson. "*I really hate his money.*"

He arches a brow. "*Why?*"

"*Because you have to ask me that question. Because he has to ask that question of everyone around him. I didn't think we could be real for that reason. I didn't think he could be real with anyone.*"

His lips quirk. "*His mother hated my money. She* really *hated my money. Did you know that?*"

"*Grayson told me. He's told me a lot about his mother. He loved her very much.*"

"*And she loved him very much. Do you love Grayson?*"

"*Yes. Very much.*"

"*Then why are you hiding your relationship?*"

"*I can't be the girl who slept her way to the top.*"

"*Then don't be. Win and win big. No one can question you if you do that, but they will question you and create rumors about you and my son. I had to find out from Leslie. I'll tell you what I'm going to tell Grayson. Own it. Deal with it. I won't give you special treatment and neither will Grayson. I didn't give him special treatment.*"

"*I don't want special treatment.*"

"Good." He winks. *"I suspect I'll see you soon, Mia."*
He gets up and leaves.

"Mia?"

I blink and glance at Grayson who's halted us at a stoplight. "Yes?"

"Where were you right now?" Grayson asks.

"I was remembering the day your father outed us."

He laughs. "Ah, yes. You called me in a panic."

"We'd only been seeing each other for six weeks and he had me confessing love before I even told you. And he showed up at the apartment that night and told you I said I loved you."

"And then I told you that I loved you." He winks like his father had that day in the coffee shop, so like him it's scary.

"How did he have a heart attack?" I ask. "He was so fit."

"He had a heart defect they said he probably had his entire life."

"Did you get checked?"

"It's not an inherited condition."

"Still, can you please just get checked?"

He takes my hand and kisses it. "I'm fine."

His cellphone rings, forcing me to bank this topic for now as Eric's number flashes across his dash. Grayson releases me and punches the Bluetooth button. "We're three minutes away," Grayson answers.

"I'm in your lobby," he says. "Just a heads up that Adam has two men with him, one of whom is Blake Walker, one of the three Walkers who owns Walker Security. He's also considered one of the best hackers in the world, and I mean that quite literally. He's already been digging around."

"And?" I prod quickly.

"That's all I know," Eric says. "I was just given this information."

"We'll see you in a few," Grayson says and disconnects as we approach the gorgeous glass high-rise that is our destination. "If this Blake Walker can't prove I'm being set up, I don't know who can," he says, pulling us into the parking garage and it's not long until we're parked in his private space. "There has to be a trail he can follow." He opens his door to get out and I forget about Blake. Right now, I'm about to be home for the first time in a year and some part of me just needs to know that's what it still feels like—home. I want to know that we still feel like us when we walk in the door.

I don't wait for Grayson to help me out of the car. I get out and he meets me on my side. "Have you changed anything at the apartment?"

"Everything is as you left it, waiting for you to return." He strokes my hair out of my eyes, his touch sending a shiver down my spine. "Just like I was."

"I really do wish that we were doing this alone."

"We'll be alone soon. We'll be in our bed again soon." And with that promise, he laces the fingers of one of his hands with mine, and folds our elbows, aligning our hips and setting us in motion. That silly question of this feeling like home fades. Home is Grayson, not the apartment, and if this is what being flawed feels like, flawed feels pretty damn perfect.

Chapter Twenty-Nine

Mia

M ia
Eric, Davis, Adam, and two men he introduces as Blake and Asher, wait for us at the elevator on our floor. Blake and Asher are casual in jeans and Walker Security T-shirts, and they both have long hair tied at the nape, only Blake has dark hair and no obvious ink while Asher has blond hair and double tattooed sleeves.

"Let's head inside," Grayson says, motioning toward the apartment and my stomach flutters with the realization that this is it. The moment where Grayson and I come full circle.

He leads me forward and when we reach the door, he pulls me in front of him and surprises me by pressing a key into my hand. I look down to find my old pink keychain. It's my key. Emotion and heat overwhelm me to such a degree that my hand trembles as I lift it. Grayson must notice, as he covers my hand with his and helps me open the door.

Together.

We open it together.

As it should be, I think.

I step into the foyer, which is a square room with dark wood floors and ivory walls and an ivory low-to-the-ground table in the center with a couple dozen teardrop lights dangling above it. Grayson steps to my side and his arm slides around my shoulders. He ignores the rest of the crowd and walks me forward under an archway and into the stunning living room, which is a wide open space that seems to sit on the ocean during the day and at night, as is the present case, a sea of stars and city lights.

To my right is a grand piano, which Grayson has played since he was a child, while the center of the room is set with distinction by a cream-colored rug. The two couches facing each other are a deep, gorgeous blue that we'd picked together only a few months after I'd moved in. He'd wanted the house to be ours. He'd wanted me to feel this was my place, not just his. I'd just wanted him, but he'd been right. Making choices together had made me feel like this was our place and it still does.

Grayson steps behind me, his hands on my shoulders, his lips near my ear. "I have not fucked you on those couches in far too long."

I smile and my cheeks are downright flushed, I am certain, as Eric and the masses join us. Eric and Grayson share a look and without words, they decide on the dining room table, directly to our right, for our meeting which accommodates twelve and offers plenty of room. We all sit down at the long ivory table, more teardrop lights above it and us. Grayson sits in the center of me and Eric on one side, with Davis by Eric. While Blake, Asher, and Adam sit across from us.

"I'm going to hand the update over to Blake," Adam says. "Not only is he the boss, he and Asher are badass hackers, but first, Mia, is there anything our agents need to know? What is your morning routine?"

"I run at five. I leave my house at seven." My eyes go wide. "I have no clothes for work tomorrow."

"We can handle that," Adam says. "What do you need? I'll have it here in the morning."

"Everything," Grayson says. "Anyway you can make that happen, make it happen."

"We can do that," Adam says. "For the morning, though, let's keep the items limited and discreet." I give him a list that he writes down before he adds, "I'll be here at six in the morning. And that's all I need. I'll turn this over to Blake and Asher, who as I said, are expert hackers."

"Blake makes me look like an amateur," Asher says. "And I'm not amateur."

"Asher's damn good," Blake says. "But hacking is like a second skin to me. Asher is heading up the dive into your electronics, looking for those betraying you. I'm dealing with Ri."

"And?" Eric prods. "What do we know so far?"

"The electronic trail is too clean," Blake says. "Someone is wiping it, someone good."

"Which confirms that this is a well thought out, calculated hit," Grayson assumes.

"Exactly," Blake says. "But they've made mistakes and when I have more than two hours, as I just had, to find the problems, I'll find them."

"Mitch is a problem," I say. "He's one of Grayson's employees."

"We have eyes on him," Adam says.

"Physically and electronically," Asher adds.

"But you have nothing yet," I say.

Blake's piercing brown stare meets mine. "We will."

"You can't know that," I say. "I need to know what I can get from Ri that ends this for Grayson."

Grayson's hand comes down on my knee and he squeezes. "Answer that knowing that she is all that matters to me."

Blake's eyes meet Grayson's. "As is my wife, and she is an ex-FBI agent who works for Walker. I understand where you're coming from." He looks between us. "We'll wire Mia. Adam filled me in on what happened. I doubt that you will get Ri to admit to setting up Grayson. A sudden change of attitude on your part, Mia, will be suspicious, but getting him to talk trash about Grayson is helpful."

"That's not going to do much of anything," I argue. "I'm a criminal attorney, remember?"

"I'm going to give you a couple of bugs to plant in his office and around the offices in general," Blake says, eyeing Grayson. "We're going inside your offices and bugging them as well. We're starting here locally and we'll expand based on where our initial research takes us." He refocuses on me. "Things you can get that help us: electronic devices and documents."

"I don't like this," Grayson says. "Mia could be placed in danger." He looks at me. "Just go. Convince Ri everything is fine. Let him talk you into staying and then just work, close the case you're on because that's the right move for your client. Leave the rest to the professionals."

"I'll be careful," I promise. "But I can easily place a few bugs. I can do this, Grayson. Let me do this for you, for us. For your staff."

"I'm going to be a stone's throw away," Asher says. "There won't be a moment that we aren't within her reach if she needs us."

Grayson starts tapping the table and then he stands, leaving everyone at the table. I glance over my shoulder to find him crossing the living room, toward the wall of windows. He's effectively told our audience he's done with everyone but me. Blake fixes me in an unaffected stare. "We'll leave you two to hash this out. Adam will be here in the morning. I'll call personally if we find out anything new. I plan to work all night."

"As do we all," Asher chimes in.

"I have a few questions," Eric says. "Can we continue this elsewhere?"

"Yes," Davis says. "Agreed. I have questions as well."

Blake nods and we all stand up. I walk them all to the door and Eric holds back to talk to me. "You okay?"

"Only when I know he's free of this."

"Agreed. Call me if you need me." He leaves and I lock the door.

I don't linger or contemplate what to say to Grayson. I'll know when I'm with him. I exit the foyer and find him still at the window, radiating dark, hard emotions and I am determined to make the man I love feel something other than those things; I want him to feel me and us.

Chapter Thirty

Mia

R ight when I would join Grayson at the living room window, there's a knock on the front door behind me. Obviously, it's one of the men that just left, most likely Eric and most likely he left something behind. Eager to be alone with Grayson, I turn back to the door and hit the camera button beside it to find Blake Walker waiting on the other side, and my heart races with the idea that he might have received some sort of news about the plot against Grayson.

I quickly open the door and he hands me a card. "In case you need me. That has my cellphone on it."

"Right." I don't feel relief. I feel disappointment. I want news. I want answers. "Thank you," I add.

He must read my reaction. "We'll make this go away," he promises. "When you set someone up for a crime, as Ri is doing to Grayson, you commit a crime yourself. Ri will pay for his jealousy and competitiveness going too far." He speaks with a confidence that I welcome. We need someone strong behind us right now and I do believe Blake Walker and his team are good additions to our efforts to shut down Ri. I hope Grayson feels the same and I urgently want to find out.

"*Thank you,*" I repeat but this time there's force behind the words.

His eyes narrow on mine as if he's looking for the same confidence in me that he's showing in himself. "I'll update you before bed." With that, he turns away.

I quickly shut the door and lock up again, stuffing his card into my pocket before I rush toward the living room. The minute I pass through the archway, my gaze seeks out Grayson but he's no longer by the window. The patio door is open, obviously his way of inviting me to join him. I close the space between me and that door, exiting the apartment, only to have Grayson grab me from the left. In a blink, I'm against the glass door and he's pressed close.

"You will not put yourself in the middle of this," he orders, his voice rough, his handsome face all hard lines and shadows, his fingers tangling in my hair and not gently. "I agreed to you going back for one reason: It buys me time to destroy him and that's for me to do, not you. You go. You convince him you're still there to stay and that's all."

"Yes, but—"

"No buts, Mia, That's all you do. The end. Do not argue."

"Grayson," I plead, but his mouth comes down on mine and his tongue drives away my objections, each stroke a demand that I cannot turn down.

"Nothing else," he says when his lips part from mine. "Do you understand me?"

Somehow after that kiss and with his perfect body pressed close, I manage a coherent reply. "Everyone in that room believes you need me."

"And they were right. I do need you. I've been quite clear on that point, which is why I'm protecting you. Anyone who will go as far as Ri is going over jealousy could be capable of more. You could get hurt and I'm not letting that happen."

"So could you. We protect each other."

"Mia—"

"Grayson—"

"You will not fight me on this," he says. "You will not win, so don't even try."

His voice is pure steel, the heavy-handedness of his mood is out of character for him, and to such an extreme that he turns me to face the glass, forcing me to catch myself on my hands. His legs cage mine, his hands shackling my hips, his lips at my ear. "You will not win." His hand slides upward and he cups my breast. "You will do as I say."

I cup his hand where it's covering my breast, and he squeezes while I manage to process the fact that he's not himself. He's lost his father. He's lost me. He can't lose me again. That's where this is coming from and I know that I can fight with him later if need be, debate with him, and we can make decisions together, but what he needs right now is agreement. "I'm not going to do anything we don't agree on, Grayson. I won't."

"You're right." He pulls my shirt over my head. "You won't." And before I even know it's happened, my bra is unhooked too. He drags me to him, cradling my body to his harder one to rid me of my bra completely, his hands cupping my breast, fingers closing down on my nipple. "And I won't change my mind."

I moan with the sensations rocking my body, spikes of pleasure blossoming from my nipples straight to my sex. "I'm going to try, though," I pant out. "You know that."

He leans me forward again, pressing my hands to the wall by my head. "Don't try, Mia. It takes away time we can just be here, home, together." He slides to my side, his leg still at the back of my knees, caging me, the lean of my body forcing my hands to stay put.

"I was never your submissive, Grayson," I remind him. "I'm not starting now."

"No?" he demands, unsnapping my jeans, and dragging the zipper down. "Are you sure about that? I seem to remember plenty of submissive moments." He moves behind me and drags my pants down.

"Sex doesn't count," I pant out, trying to look over my shoulder, only to have him palm my backside and then give it a hard smack.

"Grayson!" I yelp. "We don't do this like that."

"Now we do," he promises, shoving my pants down further and then lifting me and I don't know how he manages it, but in about thirty seconds, I'm also naked from the waist down. He smacks my backside again, and heat rushes through me.

"Grayson," I bite out this time. "I thought you didn't spank me out of anger?"

"Tonight, I do." He leans in close, near my ear again. "Did it hurt?"

"No," I whisper. "Not hurt. You know you didn't hurt me."

"Then what's the problem?" He spanks me again and I arch into the touch.

"The problem," I hiss, "is you're mad and I'm aroused right now and I shouldn't be."

"No," he says, easing back to my side, and squeezing my cheek, his free hand on my belly, "you shouldn't be. That defeats the purpose of a spanking when I'm this mad at you." His hand slides between my legs, fingers sliding along the wet seam of my sex. "You will not come."

"I'm pretty sure that I am, in fact, going to come if your fingers stay where they're at right now and you spank me again."

He cups my sex and spanks me again. I gasp, arching into the palm now back to squeezing my ass, and then into the one cupping my sex. "Grayson," I whisper, though I have no idea what I'm asking for. "Can you please—"

His fingers slide inside me, his lips at my ear. "Please what, baby?" The words are soft, seductive, but that edge, his anger, is not gone. It's sharp. It's moody and present. It's a wedge between us and I can't take it.

"I'm just trying to protect you," I whisper. "The way I should have before."

His fingers slide out of me and he turns me to face him, those green, tormented eyes fixed on me. "Protect me by trusting me this time. Trust me that he's dangerous. Trust me to protect you and us."

"I do," I whisper. "I just—"

"Don't finish that sentence, baby. Not right now." He cups my face. "Just be here."

My hands go to his hands. "I am. I've never been anywhere but here."

His mouth crashes down on mine and the taste of him explodes on my tongue: torment, fear, pain, loss, hunger, *need*. He needs so much and he has hurt so much and I can't do anything to add to those feelings. I just don't know how to do that but I'll decide with him. That's the only way this works. He scoops me up and starts walking. I'm naked in his arms while he is fully dressed and I have this sense of being willingly vulnerable with this man. I would do anything with him and anything for him.

Chapter Thirty-One

Mia

Mia

Grayson settles me on one of the soft navy-blue couches, the cushion absorbing my weight, while Grayson's big body frames mine, even as he pulls his shirt over his head and tosses it. "You," he says, "will listen to me." He doesn't give me time to reply, by obvious intent. He kisses me, licking me into that submission we both know he can get from me if he so pleases because Grayson's subtle demand for power is not so subtle when we're naked.

One of his hands slides under my backside, while the other covers my breast. He's not even undressed yet and I'm wet, wanting, and in need of him, but I know him. I know I will not be easily sated. I know the darker side of Grayson that no one else does, and in his present mood, he'll deny me until I'm downright desperate. "Don't move," he orders when his mouth parts from mine, but *he* moves. He lifts his body off of mine and then suddenly I'm on my stomach. He's turned me over and before I can even gasp, I'm not just on my stomach, he's dragging me to my elbows and knees. "Down," he says, his hand on my back and I get it and him. He needs control right now. He feels like I'm taking it. I *have* taken it.

I sink as low as this position allows me.

He's on his knees beside me, his hand caressing a slow path up and down my spine. "God, I missed you, Mia," he says, but there's a vibration in his tone I do not like.

"Why do you say that like it pisses you off?"

"Wanting you isn't what pisses me off and you know it." He stands up and I can hear him begin to undress, while he's left me here submissive, vulnerable, and willing. Because I do know why he's angry. He's angry that I left. He's mad that I misjudged him and while he'd denied those feelings back in the Hamptons, he's not denying them now. He needs my submission now and I'll give it to him, but I always did. He has always been the one person that I would dare to do anything with. He's always been that man for me, the *only* man for me.

I trust him.

I trust him completely.

My God, how did I let myself forget that? But I know in this moment exactly how. I know the flaw, my flaw, maybe *our* flaw. He sits down behind me on the couch, but I don't wait for what comes next. I need to talk to him, I need to touch him. I sit up and twist around to straddle him and all his hard, naked perfection, his erection thick at my bottom. "I know what you wanted and needed right now, but I need to say something to you. I trust you," I say, my hands on his shoulders but he doesn't touch me.

"Are you sure about that, Mia? Because you're on my lap right now. You don't seem to even trust me like this, naked."

"No, that's what I'm telling you. When I was laying there I thought: I trust him. How did this happen? How did we get here? And then it hit me. I trust you completely. I trusted you completely and the idea that I could trust that much, and find that woman pressed against you, I just—that was such a deep wound. Don't you see?"

"No, Mia, I don't. Because what happened didn't feel like trust."

My lashes lower with his anger and I force aside a moment when I want to shut down, which was exactly where I went wrong with our breakup and exactly why I admit, "I shut down. It was the only way to protect myself. That was the flaw that was really perfection. I trusted you so completely that I didn't know how to survive the wound."

"You didn't fully trust me or you wouldn't have needed to shut down."

"I did. I swear to you, Grayson. I did."

"I don't know what to do with that, Mia. You want a reason to distrust me?"

"I loved you to the point that your betrayal felt like it would end me. I can't be with you if you're going to resent me. I can't be with you if you don't think I deserve everything again. You just—I just need you to know that maybe I loved *too* much." I try to move away but he catches me, his hand on my hip and the back of my head.

"Maybe you didn't love me enough," he says. "Maybe you didn't love me like I did you because I couldn't have left you."

"Loved?"

"You know I still love you."

"Maybe not enough." I try to move again and suddenly my stomach is not feeling well but Grayson holds me. "Let go. I feel sick. I need up."

"Stop, baby. Stop pulling away." He rests his forehead against mine. "I love you more than I love life itself. I'd say you know that, but obviously, you don't. Obviously, you *didn't*."

"I did. It was my own insecurity that got us here. I told you that back in the Hamptons."

"How do we fix that? Did I do something to create it? Because if anyone knows I'm not perfect, it's you. I let you see everything. You made me be real, remember?"

"Real is good and I don't want you to stop being real even if that means being angry, but forgive me, okay? Because we can't do this if you can't."

"I'm angry at us both for letting it happen," he says, "not just you."

"Well then, yell at me, fuck me, do whatever it takes, but stop being angry."

"No yelling," he says, dragging my mouth to his. "Lots of fucking."

Our mouths collide and our tongues stroke long and deep, a frenzied rush of kissing, touching, and him lifting me to press the soft tip of his thick erection inside me. I gasp as he pulls me down and drives into me. We stay there, connected in the most intimate of ways, breathing together, wanting together, savoring each other until a crackle of electricity seems to snap between us and we're kissing again, our bodies swaying, grinding, swaying some more.

At some point, we move from that seductive emotional bond to one that borders on pure physicality. I lean back into his thrusts while his gaze rakes over my breasts, a hungry look on his handsome face. His fingers clamp down on my nipples, and with each push and pull of my body, sensations ripple along my nerve endings, tightening my sex, and I just need to be closer to him. I lean in again and our kisses become desperate. His hand squeezes my backside and then he gives me a hard smack that has me gasping and arching into his thrust.

"Oh, God," I breathe out because the man rocks my entire world in every way.

He reacts by rolling me to my back, and thrusts and pumps, his hand under my backside, lifting me into a deeper, harder, spot that has me shattering with no warning. I am just there, right *there,* in that perfect place, and my sex clenches around him. Grayson buries his face in my neck and he groans, this deep, sexy, groan and shudders into release.

For just a moment, he all but flattens on top of me, but then he rolls us to our sides, facing each other, fingers tenderly stroking my brow. "Don't leave again," he says. "You stay. We fight. We fuck."

"Yes," I whisper. "I stay. We fight. We fuck."

"Good. Then we need to talk, and we might need to fuck again when it's over."

"About Ri?"

"Yes, baby, about Ri."

Chapter Thirty-Two

Mia

Grayson shifts us and we both sit up on the couch, and then he's standing, taking me with him. I yelp as he scoops me up again, but I don't know why I'm surprised. The man is always carrying me around, but then we've been apart for a year. What is familiar is being reintroduced and in every way, it still feels perfect. He loves to carry me around and I love when he does. A short walk later, I'm on the counter in our stunning bathroom with white tile trimmed by wood that matches the floors. Grayson walks to the bathroom door, reaches behind it and grabs a pair of pajama bottoms he pulls on, which reminds me of my robe that had once hung in the same spot.

"Remember this?" he asks, pulling that very robe from the hook.

"You never moved it?" I ask, surprised by just how much he'd kept his home my home.

He crosses to wrap the white silk around me. "It's been waiting on you, just like me," he says as I slip my arms into it.

"You tried to fuck me out of your system, though," I say, feeling the bite of that confession.

He strokes my cheek, cupping it to force my gaze to his. "Mia—"

"It's okay," I say, covering his hand. "I left. I left for a year. You're human. You needed what I wasn't here to give you."

"I needed *you*." His hands settle on my waist. "I can't change how I handled you leaving any more than you can change leaving. You were right in the living room. We need to move on. We need to look forward. I want you back here. I want you next to my side. I want you out of Ri's company."

"Me, too, on all counts. I have a case, though, a woman that I really want to help. I can't dump the case. She killed her abusive husband, but the trial date isn't for four months."

"You aren't staying there for four months." His hands move to my knees.

"I know," I say quickly. "I'm not suggesting that I do. I just hate deserting her. I'm passionate about her case. She was defending herself from a brutal attack and she shouldn't have been charged. It's wrong that she's going through this. She trusts me and if she follows me to Bennett, Ri could sue me and you."

"Ri won't be suing anyone when I'm done with him," he bites out, his voice low, tight. "Let's talk about what went wrong in that meeting tonight."

"You didn't like Blake or his team?"

"Not one of them brought up the possibility that Ri could have been having you followed and knows you've been with me this weekend."

"I'm sure that's assumed with all of the efforts to hide my present location."

"I don't like unspoken assumptions that impact your safety," he says.

"You really believe Ri is dangerous?"

"Yes. I do. If Blake's team shows up here in the morning and doesn't make me feel really damn good about you going to that meeting with Ri tomorrow, you're not going."

My hands cover his. "I know you're worried about me."

"Mia, do not fight me on this."

"I know you lost your father and I left, but I'm not leaving again. I won't be stupid. If I get a bad feeling, and you know I have good gut feelings, I'll just leave."

"If you can," he says. "That building is locked down by Ri's people, who were good enough to hide from a world class hacker like Blake Walker."

Nerves knot my belly. I'm starting to get nervous, but I have to do what I can to protect Grayson. "Okay. So what makes us feel good about me going in there tomorrow?"

"Nothing."

"Grayson," I plead. "I can buy you time. I can keep his guard down just by making him think nothing has changed. I don't have to play detective."

"We'll both know in the morning when Blake's team shows up. Fair enough?"

"As long as you haven't made up your mind already," I agree.

"I do need to buy time, a few days to let our people work," he concedes. "And I do believe you suddenly quitting would put him on edge. He'd look for trouble, but it's not worth it if it puts you in danger. Agreed?"

"You going to jail for something you didn't do is not okay. I'm willing to take risks for you."

"You are, just by walking back into that building and that's more than I want you to do."

"But you will," I press.

His jaw sets hard. "If I feel good about it in the morning." He lifts me off the counter and sets me in front of him. "How about some dinner?"

"Chinese?"

"Yes," he says. "Chinese."

"You do know I still haven't become domestic, right?" I tease. "We're going to live a life of takeout in between the meals Leslie makes us."

"I can live with a life of takeout," he assures me, his green eyes lighting with laughter that I'm pleased to see return. He kisses my temple. "Now if I can just find my phone." He turns me toward the door and smacks my backside. I yelp, but I'm smiling as I head to the bedroom, right up until the moment I reach the doorway. I stop there dead in my tracks and I stare at the room that was mine with Grayson, that is mine with Grayson *again*.

We decorated it together as well, picked out the navy headboard on the massive bed with chairs that match by the window. We love blue. We love this room. Grayson steps behind me, and his hands settle on my shoulders. "This is where you belong."

I rotate to face him. "With you is where I belong. I never felt at home at that apartment, but I tried. I thought I had to make it without you, so I tried."

"Like I tried, Mia, but in a different way. I needed our place to be a sanctuary when you returned, our home, and I promise you, I'll protect that always." His hand slides under my hair to my neck. "You fill all the empty places in this home. You fill all the empty places in me, and you're the only one who knows they exist. Because I trust you, Mia."

"Do you?" I challenge, "Because—"

"I thought you left me for Ri," he says. "As I stand here thinking about what you said in the living room, I understand it. I trusted you completely. I pulled back when I thought you betrayed me because to trust that much and be betrayed cuts deeper than any blade, but I'm not pulling back now or ever again. Me and you, forever." He leans in, kisses me and the touch of his lips, tender and yet possessive, sends a rush of heat and awareness through my body.

"You don't just belong with me," he says. "You belong *to* me, and Ri is going to know that before this is over." There is something in his voice, a lethal quality that gives me pause.

Despite my push for him to go on the attack, this is the first time I've been concerned that the remedy he plans could be worse than the crimes he's been wrongly accused of. I pull back to look at him. "What are you going to do, Grayson?"

"Whatever it takes to end Ri."

"End Ri?" I ask, because that tone again, that look in his eyes, worries me. "What does that mean?"

He lowers his mouth to mine and says, "It means he won't be at our wedding, baby." He seals that declaration with a kiss that is meant to silence my questions and it works. "And yes, I'm going to ask again. Once I know that I'm not dragging you to hell with me."

"I'll go anywhere with you," I promise.

"But I won't let you." He strokes my cheek. "Because that's love, Mia. I take care of you before me." He kisses me. "I'll order the food." He heads toward the bedroom door and I think about those words. He takes care of me over himself. I need to take care of him over myself, but the problem is, with Grayson there is loss and pain to consider. I can't make a stupid decision that leaves me dead and him destroyed. I can't sacrifice myself without taking him with me. And yet, I have to go meet with Ri tomorrow after Grayson has all but declared him a killer.

Chapter Thirty-Three

Grayson

I lay in the bed holding Mia, her back to my chest, my arm wrapped snugly around her, the electronic panels on the windows sealing out any ray of the new day surely upon us; the day Mia goes back to work with Ri. I tighten my grip on her and in this moment, I'm split between heaven and hell. Heaven is having her back here in my life, in our home, in our bed. Hell is letting her go back to work today. I don't trust Ri. And I know Mia, she's all heart and passion for those she cares about and I know damn well no matter what promise she makes me about protecting herself, she's going to be tempted to put me first. It's part of what makes her, her. It's part of what made losing her so damn painful. She loves with all her heart and you feel it as deeply as she gives it.

"You're awake," Mia says, and that voice, so sweet with the hint of a rasp, always undoes me, but then everything about this woman undoes me.

"I'm awake," I say softly, leaning in and kissing her neck. "You shouldn't be. It's still early."

She reaches for the remote and turns on the bedside light to a low glow before rolling around to face me, her hand settling on my cheek. "Please tell me you slept," she says. "Because I did. I did because I'm home with you."

My hand goes to her hip and I pull her to me. "It was the best night I've had since the last time you were home in our bed."

"You didn't sleep," she accuses, not accepting my attempt at avoidance any more than she ever did. I mean how many times in the early days of our relationship did this woman look at me when I gave her a cookie cutter answer and call me on it?

I have a brief flashback of sitting across from her sharing our first pizza and her asking me, *"Why are you thirty-five and still single if your mom and dad were so happily married?"*

"I don't believe in marriage."

She studies me a moment and then says, "I'm sorry."

I frown at the odd reply. "What?"

"Everyone thinks your kind of money makes everything better, but it really does come with complications, doesn't it?"

"Yes," I find myself admitting. "It does."

"I don't want your money or a ring. I don't want to be bought. I just want to be here, right now, in the moment. It's okay if you want to really be here with me, I don't expect anything from you, Grayson. I won't become a problem for you later." She lifts the slice of pizza in her hand. "And this is a pretty good moment. Best pizza ever."

"Grayson."

I blink Mia back into view.

"Where were you right now?" she asks.

"Still with you, baby. I was just thinking about how good you are at calling me on my bullshit, even from the very beginning. That first night over pizza."

"Mr. I don't believe in marriage because it means everyone wants my money," she says, proving she knows exactly what I'm referencing. She laughs and sobers quickly. "And for the most part, they do want your money and your success. Ri is successful and wealthy but it's not enough because it's not what you have. Honestly, once I saw the magnitude of how much people want and want and want from you, I don't know how you ever let me inside."

"You didn't give me any other choice," I say, stroking a strand of hair from her eyes. "You took me by storm, Mia, and you still do. Truthfully, it's a relief to have someone I trust, someone who really knows me. You're the only one who does."

"Eric knows you. You trust him."

"Not in the way I do you. Not with everything."

She sucks in air. "And then I left."

I pull her closer, driven by emotions only this woman drags from me. "You're here now. That's what matters, but Mia, *I cannot* lose you again. I was laying here thinking about how hard it's going to be for you to step back and let me handle this."

"I promised you—"

"I know, and I know you meant it, too, but I also know *you*, baby. You will want to protect me and you won't walk away from the chance. I can't be pissed at you for wanting to protect me."

"You were last night."

"No," I say. "You read me right. I was pissed about you leaving. I was pissed that Ri is putting us through this."

"And that I let him."

"You're human, Mia. I can forgive you if you can forgive me."

"That's the first time I think you actually said you'd forgive me."

"I forgive you. Forgive me."

"For what?" she asks.

"I did try to fuck you out of my system and I know you're going to think about that but I wasn't going to lie to you. I should have recoiled to lick my wounds. I should have fought harder."

"Okay, you can stop blaming yourself any minute now because I'm not blaming you."

"Let's make a pact right now. It's over. We're together. We're not going to place blame."

"And yet we're flawed."

"We *are* flawed, Mia, beautifully, perfectly flawed in the way all humans are flawed. Perfect is an impossible façade to maintain. Love me for my imperfections, not my perfection, because perfection isn't real, and real is what you wanted from me, right?"

"Yes," she says, her voice cracking, eyes watering. "That's exactly what I've always wanted from you."

I lean in, my hand on her head, my lips near hers. "You got it, baby. All of me, completely me. Now," I brush my lips over hers, "what are you going to do with me?"

My cellphone rings at that moment and we both groan. I try to pull away and she catches my hand and presses her cheek to mine, her lips at my ear. "Lick you all over."

Now I groan and if I could just let her make good on that promise, I would, but I can't. Not this morning. I pull back, kiss her thoroughly and roll away to grab my phone from the nightstand right as it stops ringing. I'm just checking caller ID to find Eric's number when he calls again. "Eric," I answer.

"We'll be there in half an hour. I just thought after you and Mia reunited you might need a wake-up call."

"I assure you that this is not a morning that makes me want to sleep. Stay in bed and fuck, yes, but Mia isn't going to let that happen."

Mia leans over me and calls out, "Morning, Eric," completely unfazed by the conversation—but then Eric is like a brother to her so why would she be?

Eric chuckles. "Morning, Mia," he calls out and she kisses my shoulder and rolls away, the bed shifting as she gets up and heads to the bathroom.

"I need to go," I say, realizing that I haven't finished my talk with Mia over today and time is ticking. "Mia and I need to talk before you get here."

"Understood." We disconnect and I walk into the bathroom to find the shower on and Mia inside.

I strip out of my pajama bottoms and don't even hesitate to join her. She turns to face me, naked, wet and beautiful but I'm not distracted. I pull her to me, turn her, and press her to the wall. "I will not let you go today if I don't feel good about the plan in place. You will not fight me on this. Promise me, Mia."

"I never fight with you unless we're alone and I'm not going to start now. I have no desire to end up dead. I'll listen to what you think."

"Good, and if I let you go, try baby, try with all your might to remember your promise. Let me handle Ri. Walk away so you don't end up dead. Don't think about me behind bars. I do have a shit ton of money and resources so that's not going to happen. I promise you."

"You don't know what he has on you."

"Mia—"

"I promise," she says. "I do. I don't want to screw up and lose us again."

I cup her face. "Say it again."

"I promise. I don't want to—"

I kiss her and drag her with me under the water, wishing like hell I had time to fuck her this morning and she doesn't make my willpower any stronger. Her hand wraps the thick ridge of my now rock-hard cock. "I think I need to remind you just how right here with you I am, Grayson."

"Later, baby. We're about to have a houseful of people."

"I don't think this will take long." She goes down on her knees just outside the spray, and holy fuck, her tongue licks the water off my cock and then she's suckling and licking and pumping. I don't even try to maintain my willpower. I haven't had this woman's mouth on me in far too long. My hands go to her hair and I hold on perhaps too tightly but Mia has always liked that part of me that can't hold back with her, perhaps because she knows she's the only one that does that to me.

She sucks, and now I move with her, and she's right, it doesn't take long before I shudder with release, and she suckles me until it's over. When it is, she's made her point. She's back. We're back. And damn, it's good. Too good to let that fucking little bitch Ri get in the way again. And he did get in the way of me and Mia, and for that, he will pay like I have not ever made anyone pay.

Chapter Thirty-Four

Grayson

G rayson

I finish shaving and pull on the navy-blue suit jacket with a light blue pinstripe which Mia insisted I wear because it's her favorite. I stare at it in the mirror and only then do I admit just how much I missed the hell out of all the little things, like her choosing my suit, and I'm not sure I let myself admit just how much until now when she's back. I couldn't. I'd have lost my fucking mind and I was already hanging on a ledge and bloodied as it was.

The doorbell rings and she rushes out of the closet in a pair of sweats and a T-shirt with no bra, her nipples puckering from underneath. "My hair isn't dry," she says. "Damn it, I'm behind."

"You also aren't wearing a bra, so stay the hell here. Finish up. I want to talk to Blake anyway."

She looks down at her nipples and back up at me. "Do you really think I'd go out there like this?"

I cross the room and pull her to me. "I'm feeling a little territorial this morning."

"Why? You do remember what I just did to you, right?"

"With crystal clear clarity that will distract me frequently," I assure her. "But right now, I'm deciding if you go back to Ri or not."

Her eyes go wide. "Back to Ri?" Anger flares in her eyes. "Grayson, damn it—"

I kiss her soundly on the lips. "I'm sorry, baby. I told you. I'm feeling territorial this morning. I know you were never with him. I just need to get past today and get you back home with me."

Her hand flattens over my heart. "I'll be back home with you and not soon enough for me." She pushes to her toes and kisses me. "I'll wait here until you're ready for me and if you don't feel good about today, we'll figure out what to do."

I cover her wet hair with my hand and kiss her again, but this time, it's a deep, drink-her-in kiss. "I love you, baby," I say, knowing damn well she wants to fight me over today but she knows me enough to know that now isn't the time to do that. Mia was right when she said she saves our fights for private moments, and as the doorbell rings again, we're both reminded that this isn't one of them.

"I'll come get you," I say, releasing her and heading for the other room.

By the time I'm at the front door, tension is radiating like a pulse down my spine. I open the door and Eric arches a brow at my slow response but like Mia, he and I have a history and not just with each other, with Ri, too. We all went to school together for a year before Eric changed schools and then went into the military. Now, years after leaving his family fortune behind, Eric is my best friend, confidant, and damn near a billionaire, by his own making.

I back up and allow him to enter. Adam and a brunette female in a skirt and blouse follow with Blake on their heels. Blake stops to talk to me as I shut the door. The rest of the group follows Eric into the apartment. "Who's the woman?" I ask.

"My wife, Kara, who's ex-FBI. We arranged to have her sent to Ri's office as a temp today. She's reporting to Mia's floor and I promise you this, she's lethal. I was undercover when she met me. She thought I was the enemy and she drugged me and left me flat on my ass. Not a moment I'm proud of but the point is, she knows how to get the job done."

"Or you don't," I counter.

He laughs. "Fuck, man, you had to take the shot, right?"

"Had to," I assure him.

His eyes meet mine. "As an added bonus, you know that the thing I cherish most in this world is with your woman."

"Keep talking," I say.

"We can't know that Ri didn't have Mia followed. He could know she was with you this weekend. I couldn't send Mia in there without knowing I had someone who would kill for her within reach. And Kara would."

"How much risk do you think there is to Mia?"

"I dug up enough on Ri to know that he's capable of just about anything."

"Meaning what?"

"Meaning he didn't scrub his data as far back as he should have. Five years ago, he was communicating with a mob affiliate named Rosemond, a man whose people will kill, smear, wound, and repeat for the right price, and he was doing it to win a case. You don't use someone like that guy and not have a really nasty side yourself and you don't connect yourself to Rosemond and walk away. I don't trust Ri. I don't want Mia near him, and yes, I considered telling you to pull her out of this completely."

"But you aren't. Why?"

"Pulling her abruptly doesn't just get Ri's attention and get him accelerating his efforts to take you down. It places attention on her. I'm going to tell you a story I tell very few and while some might consider it a poorly timed story, I do not, and I'll explain why after I tell it. Before Kara, I was engaged. I was undercover and so was Whitney, my fiancée. The man, the leader of a drug cartel, not only figured out I was ATF, he figured out that Whitney was everything to me. He killed her and she bled out in my arms."

His confession punches me in the chest and I turn away from him, pressing my hand on the door, a reaction I wouldn't normally allow anyone to see, but, "Fuck, Blake," I murmur, forcing myself back off that wall and to face him. "Tell me you killed him."

"That's a long, complicated story, but do you get what I'm telling you?"

"If he believes she's back with me, he'll see her as a weapon to use against me. I'm crystal clear on the point you've made. You better fucking protect her."

"I will," he replies.

I look up to find Kara standing a few feet away. "I'll protect her," she says. "I need to talk to her and help her with the wire. I need to come up with a plan of action for every possible scenario and Adam is working as a janitor in the building. He'll be right there with us."

I have to let Mia go to Ri today and it's killing me, but I'll never be captive like this again. I turn to Blake. "Make this count. Let me repeat what I told Adam, just to be clear. End him. I don't mean dead. That's too good for him. I want him to self-destruct. I want him to lose everything."

"And he will," Blake promises, "but you need to be removed from the process. It can't be about you, and my reason is this: If he's in bed with these gangsters I've connected him to and you take him down, you hurt their bank account. You don't want to cut the head off a snake to watch it grow another. You get the two of them fighting and they forget about you."

I narrow my eyes at him. "Where are you going with this?"

"We make sure Ri pisses off Rosemond. While Ri is playing defense, we make sure law enforcement raids his office on a matter related to Rosemond and just happen to find proof he set you up."

"What proof?" I ask.

"That's the hole," Blake says. "We need proof."

"Adam and Kara will place bugs in and around his office," Blake says. "But the only one who may be able to get close enough to Ri, to get real proof, is Mia. We need to know what role you want her to play."

"Mia's going to do her job and keep Ri in his happy zone. You get the damn proof yourself. That's what I'm paying you for." I start walking, pissed off that he just suggested Mia put herself on the line at all after he just told me about Whitney being murdered. "You want to meet Mia, Kara, come now."

I don't wait on her. I keep tracking forward and when I reach the bedroom she's on my heels. "Whatever you think Blake just suggested," Kara says. "He didn't."

I turn to face her. "It sounded like he wants Mia to fuck her way to finding that proof for me."

"No," Kara says. "He just asked your decision on her involvement. Everyone is not you. Everyone doesn't put their woman before themselves. That you do only makes me want to help you and protect her all the more. Blake feels the same, I promise you."

"Protect Mia above all else. I don't care if I rot in jail for crimes I didn't commit. Do you understand me?"

"Yes," Kara says. "I do. I'll protect Mia. You have my word." Her eyes lift to my shoulder and I realize then that Mia has opened the door.

Chapter Thirty-Five

Mia

*P*rotect *Mia at all costs.*

Grayson's words linger in the air as I step to his side and face the woman who's in front of him, who I assume works for Blake Walker. "And I'd ask you to protect him over me at all costs," I say, my hand going to Grayson's arm, and just being able to touch him again is like heaven on earth. "I guess," I add, "that's called love, right?" I turn to Grayson, push to my toes and kiss him.

He pulls me to his hip and stares down at me. "Most definitely love," he says, his voice low gravely, affected, and then without looking away he adds, "This is Kara, Blake's wife, and an ex-FBI agent who will be undercover as a temp in Ri's office today."

"Kara," I say, reluctantly pulling away from Grayson to turn and face her before offering her my hand. "Nice to meet you."

"A great pleasure to meet you, Mia. And right now, I need to get you wired." She indicates a roller bag she's grabbed on the heels of following me. "I have your clothes, as well. Hopefully, I chose well." She looks at Grayson. "Can Mia and I have a few minutes?"

"As long as you don't plan to corrupt her into doing something stupid," he replies dryly.

I give Grayson a gentle nudge. "I'm not that corruptible," I say.

"No," he says, "that's not the problem."

"What does that mean?"

"I'll just go on into the bedroom," Kara says, "if that's okay?"

"Of course," I say, stepping aside to allow her to enter, and even as she disappears I step in front of Grayson. "What did that mean?"

His hands come down on my arms and he drags me to him. "You have nothing to prove, you have nothing to repent with me. Don't go in there with Ri trying to make something up to me."

The words hit a nerve that I didn't know existed. He's right. I do want to make up for leaving him. I left him after his father died. "I'll be smart."

"Woman," he bites out. "That is not a reply I like. We had this conversation. You're going to want to protect me. Resist."

"You're letting me go. That must mean that Blake satisfied your expectations this morning."

"He brought up every concern I had and then some."

"And then some?"

He caresses my cheek. "They know what they're doing or I wouldn't be letting you go. You know that." He turns me to the door. "Go talk to Kara. I need you to know how to protect yourself while you're there today and I want to talk to Blake about how they're monitoring you while you're there." He smacks my backside and while that would normally send an erotic chill up my spine, it doesn't.

I suddenly want this day over with more than ever.

That gets me moving and I hurry back into the bedroom to find Kara standing by the bed where she's opened the suitcase she's used for my things, that isn't mine at all, and pulled out the three outfits she brought me. Grayson shuts the bedroom door for us behind me and I mentally choose the basic black skirt and royal blue blouse to wear today. I hate that I do it because Ri complimented me on that blouse, but today is all about making him feel that I'm team Ri without going overboard and raising suspicions.

"Let's get you dressed and wired first," Kara says, her hands settling at her hips. "I just need you right here in front of me and if you don't mind, in only your bra and panties. Sorry, I know you don't know me but I need to get this right and fast."

I laugh. "If I had those things on, that would be fine," I say, "but I don't."

She laughs. "Those are the best mornings. I brought you basic stuff, including those items, most of your bathroom toiletries, but not much else. I had to be discreet. I literally packed it in a duffle that I dropped out of your back window."

"Talk about resourceful," I say.

"But not early enough." She glances at her watch. "We're pushing it for both of us to get there."

A few minutes later, Kara's made the process quick and painless, and I'm fully dressed, working on makeup and hair in the bathroom with the supplies she's brought me. "Okay," she says, standing at the sink close to me while I work, "I need your phone. I'm going to put a collection of numbers in it. I'm first and Adam's second because we're closest in the building with you. I'm setting up a group message on your phone. Use it if you're in trouble so we all know at once."

They're worried. I'm worried. "How likely is it that Ri knows I was with Grayson this weekend?" I ask, turning to face her with Grayson's concerns on my mind.

"If he had you followed when you first split with Grayson I wouldn't assume that would continue. You stayed away from Grayson too long for him to think that you'd suddenly return. However, he's trying to take down Grayson. He could be paranoid."

The part about me staying away from Grayson feels pretty crappy. God. Why did I stay away? "Let's assume he knows and he confronts me. I don't have a story or an excuse. I need one." I press fingers to my temple. "Think, Mia." I look at her. "I have nothing."

"Tell him you invested money through Grayson but he wouldn't pay you out without seeing you and it was a packaged deal with a set end date. That way he can't check it. An agreement between you and Grayson. Be angry about it. That's your chance to be on team Ri."

"That's brilliant."

"We used it in another case so I'm not thinking on the fly. A group of us came up with it in a similar situation. That's the benefit of experience. Last thing. If you end up in trouble, go to the most public place and wait on me. The reception area. The lobby. Even an elevator instead of the stairs, but the elevator can be unpredictable for a fast escape. If you need fast, take fast, but remember there are cameras in the elevator that we've tapped into. There are no cameras in the stairwells and that's a hard area to place hidden cameras that matter. It's too many spaces in one path."

I take it all in and in a few minutes, I have my purse and briefcase on my shoulder as Kara and I walk out to the dining room where Eric, Blake, Adam, and Grayson wait. They all stand at our approach. "I'm headed to the building now," Adam says. "I just wanted to make sure you know I'm there. I wanted to make contact with you before you leave."

"Thank you," I say, and he nods and takes off for the door.

"Asher and one of our other men are in a surveillance van by the building," Blake says. "They'll be tapped into every camera in the building and any recording device Kara places will feed to them." He eyes Kara. "You need to go now."

She turns to me and her hands go to my shoulders. "Be you. Try to tune out what's going on. That's the best thing you can do. If you would normally get mad at him, get mad. Don't suddenly change with him. I'll be close."

"Thank you," I say.

"I want to be in the surveillance van," Grayson says.

"If you aren't at work today," Blake says, "that's going to be a red flag if he had her followed."

"If he had her followed, she'll be in trouble," Grayson says. "I need to be in that van."

"We came up with a story," I say. "You made me come visit you to get a payout on an investment. I'm angry about it. I'm team Ri."

Grayson's eyes narrow. He doesn't like this answer. He looks at Blake. "You better fucking protect her or I don't care how many skills you have. You will feel the pain."

"Grayson," I hiss. "Stop."

Blake looks at me. "If it were me with Kara I'd say the same thing." He looks at Grayson. "I'll protect her with my life."

"You better," he says, looking at me. "Because I don't have one without her. I can't lose her again."

It's then, in his intensity, that I know he knows something I don't know but there isn't time for me to ask. I have to get to the office and into the snake's den. I have to get to my meeting with Ri.

Chapter Thirty-Six

Grayson

The past, two years ago

I pull the Porsche to the front of the gallery where the annual children's hospital charity event is taking place with Mia in the seat next to me. "Oh my God, I'm nervous," she murmurs.

I grab her hand and kiss it. "You have no reason to be nervous."

"It's our first public outing," she argues. "And your father is going to be here. He wasn't supposed to be here."

The valets try to open the doors but I leave them locked, focused on Mia. "My father loves you."

"He and I had the coffee shop encounter. That's all. He went out of the country right after he talked to me that day. And he wasn't supposed to be here tonight," she repeats.

"You're here and on my arm. We're doing what he suggested. Owning our relationship. He was motivated to show up."

She turns to me. "The entire staff will know I'm fucking you."

I laugh. "Well since you're living with me, I think that, yes, they will assume that we're fucking."

"Are we really telling them I moved in with you?"

"Baby, we've been together six months and you haven't stayed at your place since. I'm in love with you, Mia. You're in love with me. It's time to stop hiding." The valet knocks on the window. "We need to get out. We're blocking the drive. I'll come around to get you." I hesitate. "Or we can leave. If you don't want—"

"No. I do. I don't want to hide. I'm established enough at work. I love you. Let's do this." She turns toward the door and I hit the locks. I step out of the car and hand the valet a large bill that shifts his scowl to a smile.

I round the vehicle and do the same for the guy on Mia's side and then I take her hand, walking her to me, and to the sidewalk just outside the door and behind a pillar. "You look beautiful," I say, giving her curves in a flesh tone, sparkling, knee-length gown a once-over. "Get used to spending my money. It looks good on you."

"I don't have to. You do it for both of us. You had a dozen gowns delivered, Grayson. That's excessive."

"You wouldn't shop. I didn't know what you'd like, but for the record, this was the one I wanted you to wear."

"I don't ever want you to think I care about the money."

"You can't live life with me and keep fighting the money, baby. I have it. I damn sure don't want to spend it alone."

"I know, but—"

I lean in and kiss her. "We don't argue unless we're naked, remember?"

"You win all those arguments."

"That's the idea." I wink. "Come, baby." I slide her arm to my elbow. "Let's go donate some money to charity and tell the world we're in love."

She catches my arm. "Are you sure you love me enough to do this? Because I can't risk my career if you don't really love me."

"Where did that just come from?" I cup her face. "I love you like I didn't think I could love, but if you don't love me enough to—"

"I do. You know I do."

"Then we're going now. Stop thinking so much." I pull her under my arm, sheltering her with my body and making sure she knows how completely I'm claiming her.

We enter the gallery and we're greeted at the door by a hostess who directs us toward one of the event rooms. We travel the long walkway and I slide our fingers together right as Mitch, Mia's direct supervisor, walks out of the room we're about to enter. He stops dead in his tracks, looking stunned. "What is happening?"

"I asked to meet with you for the past three days," Mia says. "I wanted to warn you."

He looks at Grayson. "I—what does this mean?"

"It means we live together, we're in love, and Mia gets no special treatment."

"I don't want it," she says. "I think I've proven I'm good at my job. I'll continue to prove that I'm good at my job."

I fix him in a stare. "You can continue to be an asshole and ignore your employee's request for a meeting for three days if you like, though that's not a behavior I personally practice. I believe you've gotten a meeting with me immediately each time you've asked."

"I have," Mitch says, glancing at me. "I'm sorry, Mia, and I'm not saying that because you're with Grayson. I was a shit to put you off." He looks at Grayson. "I'm having trouble with a case. I might need your counsel."

"Call me in the morning," I say.

Mitch nods and steps around us, "Oh my God," I whisper. "You just--"

"That had nothing to do with you, Mia," I say. "I don't approve. That's not how I operate. That's not how my father operates and he deserved to get sideswiped."

"Grayson, damn it."

I turn her to face me. "You're my woman. If he's a dick to you, he's a dick to other people. He doesn't get away with that. I expect you to tell me if there is anything that doesn't represent me the way you know I want to be represented. Earn your own way, I get that, but you're still my woman. We've talked about this. The only way to be my woman is to protect me and protecting my company is protecting me."

"I know that. You're right. We talked about this in advance."

"Okay then." I wrap my arm around her shoulder and kiss her temple. "Let's go in."

We enter the room with artwork on every wall, rows of small standing tables, and waiters maneuvering through the suits and tuxedos. We're only a few steps into the chaos, but I'm aware of all the eyes that turn in our direction as I'm certain Mia is as well. Thankfully a waiter stops in front of us, deflecting the attention sure to stir her discomfort. "Champagne?" he offers.

Mia holds up her hands but I accept two glasses. "You need this," I say, as the waiter departs.

"I might run my mouth and say who knows what if I drink this," she says, accepting the glass I hand her.

"If it makes you relax, that's a good trade-off." I hold my glass up to hers. "To us."

Her eyes warm. "To us," she says softly, the charge between us electric, the room fading away. My hand goes to her hip and I walk her closer. "We couldn't hide this, Mia. It's too damn good."

"Look who's here."

At the sound of the familiar voice, I grimace, releasing Mia to settle my hand at her back as we turn to face my old college rival. "Mia," I say, standing toe to toe with the man whose father has always been my father's business rival, his blond hair smoothed back ever so firm tonight, a silent standoff that I don't invite. He's just always fucking competing with me. "This is Riley Montgomery," I say. "You probably know him from the Montgomery firm. We went to school together."

"Call me Ri," Riley says, offering his hand to Mia and I swear I don't want to let her take it.

Mia does the expected and shakes his hand but when she would pull back he holds onto it. "You're lovely. When he's done with you, come see me. I'll help you lick your wounds."

Mia yanks her hand back. "That was inappropriate," she scolds before I can respond.

He chuckles. "I'm just an inappropriate guy."

"Try bitter. He wanted the girl who wanted me in college. I fucked her. He didn't." I look at Mia. "Just so he doesn't get the chance to tell the story and twist it on his own."

"Oh," Mia says, looking at Ri. "I'm sorry. That must have sucked."

Ri's scowl is instant. "You're sorry? You will be when he fucks you and moves on."

It's in that moment that my father joins us, stepping between Mia and Ri. "Mia, honey," he says, taking her hand. "I'm so glad to see you here and on Grayson's arm. You look stunning despite your present company." He glances at Ri. "How's your pops?"

"Opening four new offices in the next four months."

"Is he now?" he replies. "Better be careful. Too many too fast can cause grave growing pains. Good luck though." He glances at Mia. "Walk with me and talk." He settles her hand on his elbow and turns her away from me and Ri.

Ri steps closer. "Obviously your father thought you needed help."

"I'm fairly certain my father wanted to flirt with Mia, just like you tried to flirt with Mia."

He narrows his eyes on me. "You're really into her." His lips twitch. "Interesting. In this case, I'll take your sloppy seconds. Let me know when you're done." He turns and walks away and for the first time ever, Ri hits a nerve.

Mia

"He's an absolute ass," Grayson's father says, guiding me through the crowd and down a corridor where more art is displayed. "But he came by it honestly. His father is as well. He and I went to law school together and the rivalry started there."

"That's a long time to be rivals," I say. "And are you really even rivals? You're about double their size, right?"

"Thanks to Grayson, who's a believer in thinking outside the box." He stops us at a painting of a winery. "Ever been to Sonoma?"

"A few weeks ago with Grayson. It was my first time."

"And you enjoyed it?"

"It was lovely." I laugh. "I liked all the cheap wines. I guess I'm a Brooklyn girl with Brooklyn taste buds."

He laughs. "And what did Grayson think of your choices?"

"He liked them. We brought some back with us."

"*Us.* Interesting choice of words. Do you still love my son?"

I nod. "Yes, Mr. Bennett. Very much." And I don't know why but I tear up.

He reaches up and wipes away the dampness. "First. Call me Raymond. Second, why did that make you cry? Does he not love you?"

"I just—I don't know how to deal with your money. I feel like when I tell you that I love him, you'll think I love the money. I feel like when I tell him I love him, he will on some level always wonder. I mean tonight he had twelve dresses delivered because I wouldn't shop. He wants me to spend his money, but I can't." I down my champagne and set the glass on a table. "I'm telling you this for a reason because you are the only person I know who can help me."

"How is it that I can help?"

"You said your wife hated the money, so she didn't want money when she met you."

"No, she did not."

"Did you doubt her? Did you ever think she wanted the money and not you?"

"Never. Not once, but she had to get over the fear of my money, as do you, of Grayson's. If you love him you have to share his life, and who he is, and money is a part of who he is, like it or not."

"If I spend his money, how does he know it's not about the money, because it's not. God, it's so not. I do love your son."

"Because I know," Grayson steps to my side and turns me to face him. "I know," he repeats. "If I didn't know, I wouldn't be so damn in love with you." He pulls me to him and kisses me. "I'm not letting you go. Don't you let me go."

"Never," I promise.

"Well then," his father says. "Sounds like we need to plan a family day in the Hamptons."

A family day, I think. Are these two men now my family? We start strolling the corridor, and as we laugh and talk, the clear moral compass of father and son, echo within each other, stirring admiration in me. I decide, that yes, I'd like very much to call them family and I have this sudden realization that I'm not so alone anymore. I tighten my grip on Grayson's arm and when he automatically covers my hand with his, I decide he's a part of me now. I not only won't let go of him, I can't.

Chapter Thirty-Seven

Mia

The present

The room is silent for several beats after Grayson's guttural declaration from the other side of the dining room table that he can't live without me. Everyone stares at us. He stares at me. I stare at him. I just want to run into his arms and tell everyone to leave and that's what he wants, too, but that's not possible. That's not what can happen. We have to end this. He's only letting me do this to ensure Ri can't come between us again through this crazy plot to take him down.

"What now?" I force myself to ask, looking around the room.

"I for one," Kara states, "have to go." She starts walking backward. "See you soon, Mia!" she calls out and then rotates and hurries away.

Blake reaches into a bag and pulls out a blonde wig as well as a scarf. "These are for you, Mia." He closes the space between us and hands it to me. "I'll follow you out of the building and onto the subway. I'll be with you the entire time. Once you're in the tunnel, find a bathroom and dump the wig." He glances at his watch. "Do it now."

I nod and hurry to the bathroom off the foyer, pull on the wig and scarf, and barely look at the stranger in the mirror. I just want out of here. I want to get this meeting with Ri behind me and know if I've kept him oblivious to us being onto him. The minute I step back into the foyer, Blake hands me a lightweight unlined trench coat. "Put it on to hide your clothes and then dump it with the wig. Now, back to you exiting this building. Walk out like you belong here, not like you don't want to be seen."

"Got it," I say, mentally comparing it to the first day of court. You're nervous but you fake confidence until you feel it.

Grayson joins us in the foyer and steps to Blake's side, but it's me that's on his mind, me he's focused on, though he doesn't comment on the wig and like me, I think he barely notices. We both have too much else on our minds to care about my fake hair. Instead, he pulls me to him. "Remember what I told you. Just contain Ri and then do your job. Focus on your client and let us focus on Ri."

"I will," I say, my hand resting on his chest, his heart thundering beneath my palm, telling me how worried he is right now, which is why I add, "I promise."

He kisses me, a deep, drugging kiss, and then with obvious reluctance, he releases me "Let me just do this," I say, to both of them. "I go to this job every day. This is not going to be a big deal."

Eric steps into the foyer and gives me a nod, admiration and friendship in his eyes. We both love Grayson and in that there is a bond several years strong, a bond of understanding. He knows I have to protect Grayson and while I plan to keep my promise to Grayson, Eric knows me well enough to know that I'd sacrifice myself for the man I love. I turn away from Eric and I can't seem to look at Grayson again and actually walk out of the door. Right now he and I are making each other crazy and I just have to push forward and leave.

I exit the apartment into the hallway and Blake is quick to step to my side. "I'm riding down with you," he says, "but don't acknowledge me once we're in the car. There are cameras. I'll exit after you when we reach the lobby. I'll be with you all the way to the building even if you think I'm not there."

"What don't I know?" I ask, focused on my man, not myself. "Somehow Grayson is more on edge than he was before you arrived, and yet, he's letting me go to work."

"He needed to know that I take your safety seriously," Blake says. "I told him a personal story that shook him. One I'm not telling you now, but I'll summarize. He trusts me now. You can, too."

We round the corner and I punch the elevator button. "Grayson doesn't get rattled," I say. "What the heck kind of story was it?"

"A necessary one," he says. "And from my read on Grayson, he doesn't get rattled unless it's over you, which could be said of me with Kara."

The elevator opens and my chance to find out more does as well. We step inside and it begins; the day I pretend to be oblivious to all of Ri's bad deeds even as they work to destroy the man I love. The idea that I may have helped him by distracting Grayson grinds through me and by the time I exit the elevator and head for the exit, that's all I can think about.

The walk to the subway is short. I enter and hurry to the bathroom, and because it's busy, I dump my wig and coat in a bathroom stall, because that's the only way I won't be seen doing it. Once I leave my disguise behind, I rush out of the bathroom and toward the stairs leading to my train. I don't see Blake again, but I can feel his energy nearby, which is far more comforting than I realized it would be considering this is my normal route to work. It's safe, or rather it always felt as safe as you can be in New York City.

The ride is short and crowded. Once the train arrives at my stop, I exit the car, and then the tunnel, and check my watch. I have just enough time to make my normal coffee run and get to my desk and "normal" seems like a smart move today. I'm just paying for my coffee when I wonder how Blake dealt with anyone following me from my apartment, but I assume they have a plan. The fake me probably changed clothes and hair like I just did.

With my white mocha in hand, I finish my short walk to work, enter the corporate offices for the Montgomery firm and wave to the security guard Josh, as I always do. All normal things. This is a normal day, I tell myself. Just be normal. The lecture doesn't work. Nerves assail me but I refocus on this day being just like any other. As Grayson pointed out, I have a client who needs me. I'll use my energy to process her case. I step onto the elevator and end up chatting with a co-worker which while awkward at first, helps me settle into a calmer spot.

Soon, I'm inside the main offices, walking toward my own when I spy Kara. She's at a desk in the cubicle area, not far from my office, and talking to my supervisor, Kevin Murphy. All is well. I'm safe. Grayson will know that I'm safe. Ri could come at me here and never get to touch me though I doubt he'd come at me. I mean, why would he?

I enter my office, put my things away and my phone buzzes immediately. "Mia?"

At the sound of Ri's secretary's voice, my lips tighten. I punch the button on my speaker. "Yes, Tabitha?"

"Ri's confirming that you're on your way to his office?"

I curl my fingers into my palm. "I am," I say, and releasing the button, I grab my phone, stuff it in my skirt pocket and then round my desk to walk toward my door.

I'm about to exit when my boss steps in my path. "How's your case looking? I know you're passionate about this one."

Kevin's a tall, dark, and good-looking guy that might be a hottie to some, but for me, he has always had this big brother quality that feels safe and friendly. He cares about people. He loves the legal system. He's the one who's made it possible for me to pretend I don't work for Ri. "It's shaping up well," I say, "but I have to be in Ri's office now. Tabitha just called my desk to make sure I'm on the way."

"Again," he states with obvious disapproval.

"Yes. Again. You should know that he found out that I am looking for a job."

He blanches. "A job? Mia, why? You're successful here. Is it money? Do I need to fight for a raise?"

"No," I say, "but thank you. It's personal."

"It's because of Ri," he says, and it's not a question. "He's always coming at you. I knew that was going to get old for you."

"It's complicated. I'll update you on my status after I talk to him but thank you for caring."

"Caring and doing something to help are two different things. I can't help you with Ri but I wish I could. I'll try though. Let me know and I'll try." Words that could cost him his job and I won't let that happen. I do, however, let him walk away. He's better off staying away, too.

I watch him depart and Kara glances in my direction but doesn't acknowledge me. I cut down the hallway, turn a corner, and then enter Ri's private space through glass doors that lead me directly to Tabitha's desk. "He's waiting on you," she says, shoving her long red hair from her beautiful blue eyes. She's pretty, and I've often thought her to be involved with Ri, and yet he keeps coming at me, but then, really he's coming at Grayson through me.

I nod and walk around her desk and stop at Ri's door where I knock. "Come in!" he shouts.

I mentally steel myself for this encounter and enter to find him standing with his back to me at the window to the right of his massive black oval desk. "Shut the door," he says without turning.

Shut the door.

I do not want to shut the door and yet it's not an unreasonable request. I have to shut the door.

I shut the door and just like that, I'm alone with Ri. No, I'm alone with the devil himself.

Chapter Thirty-Eight

Mia

R i turns to face me the minute the door shuts, running a hand through his blond sleek hair. "Really, Mia? I helped you in a time of need and you're looking for a job?"

That sets me off and I forget fear. "*Helped me*? Are you serious? What happened to you're a fine attorney and we want to win the bidding war? What happened to me being a damn good attorney?" I walk further into the room, stopping in front of his desk between the two visitor's chairs but facing him at the window. "It was never about me now, was it? It was about fucking Grayson by fucking his woman if you could make it happen."

"His woman?"

"Oh my God, Ri. Stop. I'm talking past tense. You wanted to fuck me to fuck him and now that you know you can't, you act like a total asshole to me. You throw files on my desk. You demand updates on my cases. I don't even report directly to you. I can't believe I was this stupid." I rotate and start to walk away.

He closes the space between us and grabs my arm, whirling me around. "That's not how it is."

"Let go of me, Ri, or I swear the next knee I give you will do permanent damage and right now, I think it would be a good thing to prevent you from ever producing a mini-me."

"Did you really just say that to me?"

"Let go of me Ri. You have about thirty seconds or I *will* knee you and scream."

His jaw clenches. "Fuck, Mia." He releases me. "Happy?"

"No," I say. "I cannot be happy in the middle of this war. That's the problem but I have a client I really care about that I want to help. If you can't let me do my job then at least let me bring another attorney that I pick up to speed. You owe me that for using me like you have."

"I didn't use you. I want you. I want to be what he couldn't be for you and you know that. That's why you agreed to go out with me."

"I went to dinner with you because—it was a bad night. It was—I'd seen—"

"Grayson all over the papers with another woman. I know. I thought finally you saw the truth. He was always a ladies' man. Always, Mia. He fucked my woman in college. He fucked everyone's woman and yet, you said his fucking name in my home. You can't get over him."

"Maybe I never will," I say. "My heart is still with him. I can't change that, and you can't change it because you're like his stalker ex-girlfriend. All you care about is hurting him. You never wanted me."

His cellphone rings and he ignores it. "Stalker ex-girlfriend? Holy fuck, Mia. Did you write out that insult before coming in here?"

"You're obsessed to the point of it being scary. I don't want to be in the middle of this. Part of me wants to move to another city. I just want out."

"If I proved you wrong about Grayson—if I made you see that *you* matter, not him? Then what?"

"My God, Ri. What would happen if you did fuck me? Would you take out an announcement in *The New York Times* to make sure Grayson knew? Stop trying to fuck me already and if you can't, then let me out of my contract. Be a decent person and let me go."

He scrubs his jaw and looks away before fixing me in a stare. "You're a damn good attorney. I won't let you out of your contract. I'll back off and hope that one day you see that I have a sincere interest."

"The day you stop going after Grayson, I won't even know who you are. Maybe introduce yourself then."

"I'm not going after Grayson."

"Maybe not actively, but we both know if you get the chance, you'll take it. I don't want to be a part of that, Ri. Am I staying or are you letting me go?"

The phone on his desk buzzes and Tabitha speaks over the intercom. "Someone named RJ says it's urgent. He's on line two. Do you want it?"

Ri positively scowls. "Yeah. I want it." He looks at me. "Don't move." He stalks to his phone, grabs it, and picks up the line. "I told you not to call me at the office. I fucking meant it. I'll call you back." He hangs up and looks at me. "You have a contract, Mia. I'm not letting you out of it." His jaw sets hard. "Go back to work."

I get the sense he suddenly wants me out of his office and that it's connected to that call. I don't fight his demand. I don't have to. He doesn't know about me and Grayson. I'd know. He's just pissed at me, but he won't let me go. Not when I'm a weapon against Grayson. I open the door to exit and instinct has me turning to face his office before I push his door shut, and just in time to see him reach in his left drawer and pull out a phone and it's not the one that was normally in his pocket.

I quickly shut the door and I don't look at Tabitha. I walk past her and to my office that I enter and shut the door. The minute I'm inside, I pull my phone from my pocket and send a group text: *Someone named RJ called the office phone and Ri got pissed. He told him not to call him here. When I was leaving he didn't know I turned around and saw him open his left drawer and pull out a phone and it wasn't the one he normally had in his pocket. I think it was a burner phone and I think he was calling that RJ person.*

Blake answers immediately: *We'll get the number off the phone and tap it.*

But how? I think. Surely Ri will take that phone home tonight. I'm shocked he kept it in his desk at all but he must have a reason.

My phone buzzes again with another message from Blake: *You did good, Mia. FYI we haven't swept your office yet. Don't hold conversations that could be damaging.*

I inhale and fight the urge to call Grayson. That's what he was telling me. Don't call Grayson and Grayson can't call me or text me. He's silent and I wonder if he was listening. I wonder if there was something I said that he didn't like and it's killing me. I can't take it. I dial his number. "Mia," he breathes out into the phone.

"Did you—"

"Every word."

"You didn't—"

"You don't want in the middle of this war. I heard you. You said that to me, too."

"I was hurt and angry when I said that to you."

"You were telling the truth," he replies. "And I don't want you in the middle of it and yet, there you are today, right in the middle."

"That's not your fault."

"Yes. It is. I didn't end this a year ago when he sent Becky to my office to fuck us the way he wants to fuck you. That's right. Asher found electronic proof that Mitch and Becky were working for Ri. We no longer have to speculate. You won't be in the middle long, Mia. Of that, you can be certain."

"What does that mean?"

"A conversation better had in person."

My stomach knots. "You're not talking about us, right?"

"No, Mia, I am not talking about us. We do not end ever again. Stay out of his way today. And I'll make sure he stays out of your way from this point forward." My phone on my desk buzzes and he says, "I'll be close, baby." Grayson hangs up and the receptionist says, "Delaney Wittmore is on the line."

My client, who I need to talk to. "Put her through," I say, trying to shake off the idea that the worst thing that ever happened to Ri was for Grayson to hear that conversation which wouldn't bother me if I knew what that meant, but I don't. What is Grayson about to do and what consequences will that have for him and us? I need to see him. I need to talk to him, and yet, I cannot. I'm here, trapped inside a world that Ri controls.

I grab the phone. "Hi, Delaney."

"Mia, how are things coming along? Do we have a trial date? Is there any hope of ending this without one?"

"There's always hope." We talk a good fifteen minutes and we've just hung up when Kevin pops his head in the door.

"You're still on staff?"

"Yes," I confirm. "For now, all remains the same."

"Are you looking for a job?"

"Not anymore."

"Good. Then we have a team meeting at six. It's the only way to get past everyone's court schedule."

"Six. Yes. Okay. I'll be here."

He disappears and now I officially know that I'll be here late, after hours and exposed in a sparsely occupied office. I grab my phone and decide against a group text that might make it to Grayson and set him off. I text Kara instead: *I have to be here for a six pm staff meeting.*

She replies: *I know. I overheard Ri telling Kevin to set it up. He's behind the meeting. Stay alert and I'll stay close.*

I type, *I'll see you there and thank you, Kara,* and then set my phone down, letting this news sink in. Ri, who doesn't have any direct interaction with our team, set up this meeting. Ri wants me here late. He's up to something.

Chapter Thirty-Nine

Grayson

I don't want to be in the middle of this war.

Mia's words stay with me for the hours that follow her shouting them at Ri. I don't know how the hell I manage to go to the office, but I do. I go. I work. I get frequent, and thankfully uneventful, updates, and come early evening, Eric takes over a problem I'm managing, and Blake picks me up in the parking garage to take me back to the surveillance van.

"Nothing new," he says when I join him in the backseat of an Escalade with one of his men in the front seat. A guy named Savage with a scar down his face who looks brutal enough for me to want to introduce him to Ri. "At least not where Mia's concerned. Ri's another story. I have a lot to share." He hands me a data drive. "Everything I'm about to tell you is backed up with proof on that drive."

I pocket it. "I'm listening."

"Ri's been in bed with Rosemond, the mob affiliate I told you about since he left college. That's how he's won about every accomplishment he's had. If someone says no, he pays Rosemond and he breaks out the proverbial baseball bat. I can't prove it yet, but based on the cash withdrawals Ri is making that never show up anywhere else, I think he's being blackmailed, most likely by Rosemond. That's how he works. He does your dirty work and turns it around on you."

"And you know what you know how?"

"Data doesn't go away. When you think you've wiped it, it's not gone. The right person, and that's me, can find it. I did. Give me time, which Mia created today, and I'll put all the pieces together. Right now though, there's heat on you. You have to make a decision. Use what I found to back him off and create a standoff, or wait and risk the DA coming at you before we act."

"He's already involved the DA. Davis has a source that confirmed that with details of pending charges."

"And I have a source that confirmed that to be true but it's not where I can get to it. Not yet."

"Then we don't know what bullshit Ri gave them already and Ri can't just pull back from the DA and say he was joking to save his ass. We have to prove that I'm innocent."

"Agreed," Blake says, "but you could stop him from delivering any further blows by going at him."

"We could also shove the traitors in my operation into a hole and we won't find them until they're in trouble again."

"But we stop them and Ri from handing over damning information to the DA or planting fake information the DA finds in a raid. Right now, there is nothing in the DA's system on you."

"Per an insider at the DA's office, I assume?"

"Per their computer system that I hacked."

I arch a brow. "You hacked the DA?"

"Yes, I've also worked for the DA and hacked for the DA." He moves on. "Look, here's my concern. Rosemond. He's my concern. If he's blackmailing Ri, Ri could be trying to connect him to you and get rid of both of you at once. If he's not trying to get rid of Rosemond and you take down Ri, as I've said, you've hurt his money and you become a target."

"Mia becomes a target."

"Exactly. Mia and your company, because those things are what matter to you, in different ways, of course. We need to turn Rosemond on Ri, and get Ri focused on protecting himself from Rosemond."

"Which he could do by turning the heat on him and me with the DA. That doesn't work."

"It works if we have the proof we need to prove he set you up first."

His phone rings and he pulls it from his pocket. "Sorry, man. This is one of my men on assignment overseas. I have to take it."

I nod and he answers his call. My mind goes to my father and I try to think about what he'd do right now, even what advice he'd give me which transports me back to the last piece of advice he ever gave me. Back to the day he died and that golf course in the Hamptons:

"You're shooting like hell, son. I'd ask why but we both know why. You haven't been good since she left. You damn sure haven't been able to be here, in the Hampton's since she left."

"I've made more money for me and the company in the past six months than I have in my entire career."

"I don't give a flip about the money," he says, turning to face me, his hands settling on his hips. "I care about you and her. She loves you. You love her. Go get her."

"She's with Ri now."

"She's working for Ri. There's a difference between fucking him and working for him."

"Oh come on, pops. She thinks I fucked Becky. She's fucking Ri."

"Have you asked her?"

"She won't even talk to me." I pull the ring out of my pocket, where I've held it every day for six months. "She sent it back."

"Well, you damn sure know she didn't want your money."

"I already knew that."

He throws his golf bag in the rear of the cart and I do the same. "Make her listen."

"Becky was naked and pressed against me, dad. No words erase that."

He turns away from me and presses a hand on the rear of the cart. "Fuck." He fists his hand on his chest. "I don't—feel right, son."

"What? What does that mean?"

"I don't know. I can't seem to breathe. Call—"

He falls to his knees and I go down with him. "Dad. Fuck." I dial 911 and then it's like a tunnel consumes me. I have random moments of clarity. Me pumping my father's chest. Me shouting for help. The emergency crew. The ambulance and me riding beside my father, holding his hand. And then his final words, "Son, protect what was mine and what is yours. Do not let anyone take what is yours. Don't let anyone take who you love."

And then he'd shut his eyes and never opened them again.

"Sorry about that," Blake says, drawing me back to the present. "But, fuck. My man is in some heat right now, but then so are you. The most important thing right now is proving you're innocent. Once we get that proof, and that could be a few keystrokes from happening, then we ensure Ri pays, and that Rosemond doesn't come at you."

"You turn them on each other," I supply since that's where we're going with this conversation.

"Yes. I can make Rosemond believe Ri is setting him up even if he's not. That gets Ri fighting for his life, not trying to take yours. I'll then have a friend at the FBI offer him protection to turn evidence on Rosemond. That means Ri is out of the picture and in witness protection. But there are risks. Ri could end up dead and I need to know you know that. I'll do my best to ensure that doesn't happen. This protects you and Mia. That's my priority."

Ri could end up dead.

This protects Mia.

My father's words come back to me: *Son, protect what was mine and what is yours. Do not let anyone take what is yours. Don't let anyone take who you love.*

"Do it," I say and I feel no remorse. Mia is my first priority. My company and my employees are my second priority. Ri is nothing and I do believe that even my father, with his strict moral compass, would want him to know it.

Blake pulls us up to the high-rise where Ri's offices are and into a parking garage. A few minutes later, I'm sitting in a surveillance van watching Mia on a camera as she joins a staff meeting. Ri enters the room and instead of looking around the room and communicating to the room of twenty, his gaze lands on Mia. He can't take his eyes off her and if I sit here, watching this much longer, Rosemond might not need to kill Ri. I will. For forty-five minutes, he lectures the team about production and projections that aren't where he wants them to be. For forty-five minutes, the entire room has to know he can't keep his eyes off fucking Mia. It's almost like he knows I'm watching.

The meeting ends and Mia, like the rest of the group, stands, only when she would escape, Ri calls out her name, "Mia, my office before you leave."

That's a mistake. He has no idea what a mistake he just made because if he touches her again, I'm not staying in this van.

Chapter Forty

Mia

After ordering me to his office, Ri heads out of the conference room. My mind races and I know I'm headed into dangerous territory with him. I sense it. "Mia?" Kevin asks. "Do you need help?"

"No. Thanks. Goodnight." I rush toward the door and spy Ri already headed down the hallway. "Ri!"

He stops and turns. "My office."

"I'm running to the bathroom first," I say, needing an excuse to talk to Kara who is no longer at her desk but it's her I need. "I'll be there in three minutes."

"Make it two," he snaps, his jaw set hard, anger radiating off of him the way it had the entire meeting which was generally miserable, as he kept staring me down. In turn, Kevin scowled at him, and everyone knew it was about me.

I rush down the hallway to a bathroom nearby, step inside and enter the stall and since I don't know if this room is being recorded, I pull out my phone and text Kara: *I'm going to be in his office. Create a distraction. Get him out of there long enough for me to get the number off that phone in case he takes it home tonight. And yes, I know Grayson won't approve which is why I'm texting only you.*

Kara calls me and I answer. "You're safe to talk where you're at and no, Grayson won't approve, but you have to do it. I'll get him out of there and I'll warn you by phone when he's returning. The risk is minimal as the office is all but empty. Just get the number and get clear of the desk. Text it to us right away."

"Got it."

"Go. Now."

I hang up and I know I have to do this. I can't keep coming here. Grayson won't be able to take it. I feel it. I know it. I have to help where I can and be prepared not to come back. I stick my phone in my pocket and exit the bathroom. My path back to Ri's office is swift. Once I'm there I find Tabitha gone and the door open. I step inside. "Shut the door," he orders from behind his desk where he stands leaning on the hard surface.

"No one is out there."

"Shut the fucking door, Mia."

I remind myself that I'm wearing a wire. I have plenty of help nearby. I shut the door and lean against it. "Afraid?" he asks.

"You're acting weird."

"I know you were with Grayson this weekend."

I'm stunned despite being prepared and I react instantly. "You had me followed? Really, Ri? I've been here a year. Have you had me followed the entire time?"

"He's a competitor. It's reasonable."

"That's a yes. I can't believe you."

"*You were at his house.*"

"I don't have to explain myself, but yes, I was. He owed me money on an investment and he made me collect in person."

"For the entire weekend?"

"Yes, Ri. And now I know he and I are really over. I had to find out. I had to know."

"He fucked Becky. That was pretty over, or I thought it was. Maybe you don't give a shit what pussy he sticks his cock into as long as you have his money."

"You're a son of a bitch, Ri. I can't believe I ever came to work for you."

"Well you did, and you have a contract, and if you leave or betray me with him I'll destroy you."

His cellphone rings and my heart lurches with the hope that this is the distraction. He answers the line and scowls. "Towed? What the fuck? Stop them. Yes. I'll be right there." He rounds his desk. "My car is being towed. Do not fucking leave my office, Mia. You wait because we aren't done." He exits his office and I follow him, watching as he disappears through the glass doors.

Adrenaline shoots through me and I shut the door, rush to his desk and pull open the drawer, relieved to find the phone. I grab it, find the number, and text it to the group. I set it back in the drawer and quickly start searching drawers. I reach for the one beneath the phone and it's locked. I open his top desk drawer and find a key. Luckily it works which makes locking the drawer a joke, but thankfully Ri is funny like that.

I open the drawer and find a file that reads "Bennett" on it. I open it and want to be sick. It's all the records of the set-up, including a list of Grayson's employees being paid to help Ri. I shoot photos, lots of photos and decide I just need to take the file. This is all we need to end this. I text what photos I took to the group, shut the drawer, lock it and decide, that's it—I'm leaving. I rush out of his office and into mine because I need to seem normal. I need to seem like I just left mad, or quit. Otherwise, Ri will search his office. I grab my briefcase and computer, stick the file inside, and head for the elevator.

Still no warning about Ri which means he could come up the elevator at any moment. I don't know what areas of the office Kara can see. She might not even know where I'm standing. She might only be able to see Ri right now. I cut right and enter the stairwell, starting to run down the steps. It's a long way down but I just want out of here. I want out of this building and this office. Relief washes over me as I near the exit and I've just stepped off the final step when the door bursts open with Ri entering the stairwell.

My heart lurches. "I thought you forgot me. I was coming to make sure you were still here."

He glances at my briefcase and me and then growls, "Bullshit. You thought I'd take the elevator. And I just realized I left you in my office after you spent the weekend with Grayson."

He lunges for me and I turn to try to run but it's too little too late. He grabs my hair and all but rips it out as he yanks me around to face him. "What do you have in your bag?" He reaches for it, and I punch him, giving help time to arrive, I hope, but it does no good.

He reaches into my bag that I stupidly didn't zip and grabs the folder. "You little bitch." He drops it on the ground and shoves me against the wall. "I should have known you were still fucking him. That will never get out of this building."

"It doesn't matter. I took pictures. I sent proof to the police. Did you really think you could frame Grayson and get away with it?"

"I'll get away with it. You'll be dead and I'll tell them you were setting me up."

"Dead? You're going to kill me? Are you serious?"

"Yes, Mia. You'll die." He reaches into his pocket and pulls out his phone. "Mia will need to be dealt with tonight but not until I'm done with her. Pick her up at the normal spot." He ends the call. "We fuck first. Maybe you can talk me out of killing you."

I try to knee him but he catches my leg. "Not this time, sweetheart. This time I fuck you, you don't fuck me." He pulls out a gun. "Just in case you think you might scream. Think again." He yanks me off the wall and starts pulling me by the hair toward the door. That's when the door bursts open and Grayson appears holding a gun followed by Blake.

"Grayson," I breathe out, as the two men stand side by side, Blake directly in front of Ri, but it's Grayson Ri is looking at, his gun now pointed at him.

"Let her go, Ri, or I will shoot you," Grayson says, stepping closer. "And I'll enjoy it."

Ri holds the gun on him to my head. "We walk out together or she leaves dead. Decide."

Chapter Forty-One

Grayson

I charge at Ri in the hopes that he'll turn his gun on me, but he doesn't. He holds steady and I stop in front of Mia, not about to block Blake's shot if he so chooses to shoot the bastard before I do. Right about now, he probably wants to shoot me for taking one of his guns, but I don't give a damn. The minute I heard Mia went down the stairs and Ri decided to take the stairs instead of the elevator, I wasn't waiting for her to end up dead.

"I'll kill you, Ri," I promise. Mia's hand goes to my waist as if she just needs to touch me. I want to comfort her. I want to pull her into my arms, but I don't dare look away from Ri.

His eyes narrow on mine and I have a really fucking bad feeling he's about to pull the trigger, just to spite me, just to finally hurt me. "I love you, Grayson," Mia whispers, because yes, she feels his readiness too, but that's not the right thing for him to hear right now.

Fuck it, I'm going to kill him. My finger twitches on the trigger but a shot rings out before I shoot. Ri jolts backward and blood splatters all over my face and Mia's. I grab Mia and pull her to me. "What happened?" she asks. "What happened?!"

"Easy, baby," I say, looking over her shoulder at Ri lying across the floor, with a bullet between his eyes and blood pooling around him, thick and wide.

Blake appears by my side and takes my gun, "Thank me later. He was going to shoot and I wasn't letting you answer for that. Get her out of here." He kneels beside Ri and checks for a pulse as Adam charges in the door, "Get me an ambulance and the police," Blake shouts at him.

I cup Mia's face and tilt her eyes to mine. "You're okay?"

"He's dead, right?"

"No pulse!" Blake shouts before I can answer. "Hurry the fuck up, Adam!"

"I called. They're on the way." Adam eyes me. "Get her out of here." He opens the door as I scoop up Mia and carry her past Adam, into the garage, and then to the van where I set her on the edge of the interior.

Sirens sound in the distance and Kara runs to our side. "Is she okay?" she asks and then to Mia. "Are you okay?"

"I'm alive," Mia says, burying her head in my stomach and clinging to my waist. I cradle her head, my gaze finding Kara's. "She's shaken. Give us a few." Kara nods and hurries away while I tilt Mia's face and ease her stare to mine. "You're okay, baby. I got you. You know that, right?"

"You could have been killed. I caused this. I didn't listen to you. He knew about us and I felt like it was now or never."

"I heard everything. You were right to just get out and while I'd have preferred you never see him again, you got him to admit everything on the audio. You did good."

"He's *dead*." Her voice cracks. "I didn't do good. *He's dead.*"

"You did what he forced you to do and you tried to get out of his path." Sirens grow louder, now in the garage, closing in on us. "He was armed, Mia. Had we not called him to the garage, what happened in the stairwell might have happened in his office and we might not have gotten to you in time."

The ambulance pulls up just behind us, followed by at least one police car, and Mia grabs my shirt in reaction. "Oh God. The world knows now. The news will be blasting everywhere. My father is going to find out. Call him, please. I can't talk to him. I'll cry and he'll freak out."

I pull my phone from my pocket and kneel beside her, punching in her father's autodial that I never deleted. "Mac," I say. "It's Grayson."

"Grayson? How the hell are you?"

"Listen, sir. Mia is with me and safe, but there's been an incident at her office. She's shaken but unharmed."

"What incident? I need to talk to her. Tell her I need to talk to her."

"Sir—"

"Grayson, damn it."

I cover the phone and look at Mia. "Baby. He needs to hear your voice."

She nods and takes the phone. "Hey, dad. Yes. No. My boss. He's crazy or he was. He's dead. No. I'm fine. Just—meet us at the apartment." She looks at me. "Grayson's apartment, that's my apartment again. I hadn't had time to tell you."

"He's still on the security list," I say. "I'll have the building let him in."

She repeats my words and then hangs up right as Blake reappears. "The police are going to want to talk to you both. Just tell the truth." He looks at Mia. "You okay?"

"No, I'm not, but thank you. Grayson would have shot him, and I know what you did in that stairwell not only saved him trouble but you saved my life, Blake."

"I'm just glad I pulled the trigger before Grayson, who clearly knows how to handle a gun a little too well for my sanity today."

"My father insisted that a man with money had to know how to protect himself," I say. "And so, I do but thank you. I know you saved me a lot of grief. I would have killed him."

"It was justified," Blake says. "He was going to shoot, but it's less complicated this way."

"Then he really is dead?" Mia asks.

"He didn't have much of a chance," Blake replies. "I was taught to shoot to kill and I do. I wasn't giving him a chance to lift his gun and shoot because he would have." He eyes me. "I called Eric. He has an attorney on the way to represent you, though I see no reason this becomes a problem for you. In fact, thanks to Mia, tonight ends this for you both."

A police officer appears next to Blake, followed by a plainclothes detective, as does a tall man, in a blue suit, with a salt and pepper beard; Ridell Murphy, a ten-year veteran with the firm, and one of our best criminal defense attorneys. "Eric sent me," he says, which doesn't surprise me, as Eric respects the hell out of Ridell.

"Glad to have you with us, Ridell," I say.

"Yes," Mia agrees. "Good to see you right about now."

"I'd rather see you under different circumstances, Mia," Ridell says, and he's too much of a pro to ask how she is doing. He knows the answer: not well. Instead he and Blake take control of the questioning that comes at us hard and fast, and stretches for hours in one shape or another.

Blake repeats the same words over and over. "In my professional opinion Mia would be dead if I wouldn't have pulled that trigger when I did. We have cameras and audio for you to make your own assessments." He handles just about everything thrown our way before we can and owns it as his.

Once the police finish with us, Mia is shaking so hard that the EMS tech still on scene insists he check her out, quickly directing us to the bed inside the vehicle. I help Mia inside and when I would stay outside, and give the tech room to evaluate Mia, she isn't having it.

She pats the bed next to her and whispers, "Please."

I glance at the EMS tech, a fit, fifty-something man with gray hair, and he nods his approval.

I join Mia and sit next to her. "Joe" introduces himself and kneels next to Mia to check her vitals. "Shock," he declares after a short exam. "You really need something to calm your nerves."

"What I need is to go home," she says, looking at me. "Can we go home now?"

I reach up and brush her cheek. "Yeah, baby. We can go home." I glance at Joe. "Is she safe to go home?"

"She is, but if she doesn't stop shaking, you need to get her something to calm her nerves."

"I will," I assure him. "I have a doctor we can call if necessary."

Joe approves, and I exit the vehicle and help Mia down. Kara and Blake are waiting on us outside and an SUV pulls up next to them. Blake pats it. "Your ride. My man, Smith, is behind the wheel. He'll take you home."

Kara hands Mia a sweater. "This will warm you up and cover up any mess."

"You mean blood," Mia says. "Thank you. My father is waiting on us at the apartment. I don't want to freak him out any more than he's probably freaked out already."

She hands Mia some sort of towelettes. "Clean your face in the car."

Mia touches her face. "I wiped it off earlier. There's more blood?"

"Yeah, honey, just a little bit," Kara says and looks at me. "You, too. You have a few lingering smudges."

I nod and then Blake and I shake hands while Mia and Kara hug. "I'm here if you need me," Kara promises Mia, pulling back to look at her. "That includes to talk. That was a rough scene back there and you're going to question yourself but don't. I guided you through what to do. You asked me. You didn't act alone. Furthermore, you were trying to just get out of there. That was a good thing."

"Agreed," Blake says, and then backing up what I already expressed he adds, "He had a gun. He knew about you and Grayson. I don't want to think about you waiting for him in his office, and us not getting to you in time."

"Where do we stand on backlash from Ri's cronies?"

"That file Mia grabbed assures you have none," he says. "It proved Ri was not only trying to frame you but Rosemond also."

"Who's Rosemond?" Mia asks.

"The mob affiliate Ri was involved with," Blake explains. "Ri was his gravy train and we didn't want Rosemond lashing out at you two for hurting his bottom line. That's how those types work. Thanks to you, Mia, he won't. We scanned the data from that file which involved him and sent it to him before I handed it over to the police. He now knows that Ri was trying to take him down. You're both free and clear. Go home. Rest. I'll be around if you have questions tomorrow."

We say our goodbyes and Mia and I climb in the backseat of the SUV and I pull her close. The minute we're moving, I cup her face and lean in, kissing her with a long stroke of my tongue, emotions I've suppressed for hours, all but bleeding from me into her. "I almost lost you tonight," I whisper, pressing my cheek to hers, my lip at her ear, "I would not have survived losing you." I pull back to look at her. "I can't lose you." I press my head to hers. "I would not have let him hurt you. No one will ever come that close again. You have my word."

She pulls back, too. "You told me to get in and get out. You're not mad at me?"

"You were trying. He wouldn't let you and you were protecting me." I stroke her hair from her face. "Most importantly, you're alive, so no, I'm not mad at you." I lean in and press my lips to her ear again. "But I might need to keep you in the bed, naked, and in my arms for a few days, just to convince myself you're really okay." I stroke her hair from her face. "And to make sure you know I have you. I'm not letting go. Ever, Mia."

"Promise?"

"Promise, baby," I say, pulling her into my arms and holding onto her. She lays against my chest, and she's still trembling, quaking inside and I just want to take away the fear and trauma. The only way I know to do that is just to hold her and keep holding her for the rest of our lives. And I will, but I'll do so just a little tighter right now until she's ready for me to loosen that hold. Until she heals.

Chapter Forty-Two

Grayson

On the ride to our apartment, we meet Smith, our driver and one of Blake's men, while Mia and I clean up as much of the blood we're wearing as possible. The clean-up is successful with the exception of my white shirt splattered with blood and there's no hiding it. "My father is going to freak out when he sees the blood," Mia worries. "What was I thinking having him come here?"

I stroke her hair. "You were thinking that he's going to hear all of this on the news if he doesn't hear it from you first. You did the right thing."

"Right," she says. "I'm glad one of us remembers what I was thinking."

"We're here," Smith announces, pulling us to the front of our building and I toss all the wipes we used in a trash bag at the back of his seat. "We'll have men here at your building indefinitely," he adds, glancing back at us. "Just in case you have trouble with the press. I can also drive your father home Ms. Cavanaugh."

"Thank you," Mia says. "And call me Mia. I doubt he'll leave once he finds out what happened."

"I'll text you my number in case," Smith says. "I'll be here all night." He eyes me. "Would you like an escort to your door, sir?"

"A bodyguard will only freak out Mia's father," I say, "so unless you think we need one, we'll pass."

"Not until the press finds you," he says. "And right now, they're focused on the crime scene. You should be fine tonight."

I open the door. "Thank you, Smith."

"Yes, thank you," Mia says, and I'm encouraged by how much stronger she sounds, right up until the moment I help her out of the SUV and her knees give out.

She collapses against me and I hold onto her, the way I plan to hold onto her forever. "I got you, baby."

"I know you do," she says. "I know you do, and I can't believe I forgot that. You charged at him." Her voice cracks. "You tried to get him to point the gun at you. You knew he might shoot you."

"We protect each other, remember?"

"Don't *ever* risk your life like that again," she scolds, her voice suddenly strong, a crackle of anger beneath the surface. "Every time I think of you running at him, of what might have happened, I start to shake all over again."

I don't promise her I won't risk my life for her, because I would, I will, and I'd do it all over again to protect her. Instead, I maneuver her around me and shut the SUV door before setting us in motion toward the entrance to our building. The doorman, an older gentleman with white hair, is a new guy I don't know well. His eyes rocket to my shirt like it's a damn magnet, but he'll most likely assume I was in a fight, which isn't inaccurate. I stop and talk to him. "The press will be all over us in the morning. Be prepared."

"The press, sir?"

"Yes. The press. Don't say I didn't warn you." I urge Mia into the rotating doors, my hands on her hips, and I move with her, keeping her close.

We exit on the other side and I pull her back under my arm, guiding us to the front desk where Devon, a familiar young guard who knows us both works tonight. "Did Mia's father sign-in?" I ask.

"He did," Devon confirms, ignoring my shirt. I liked Devon before. I like him more now. He eyes Mia. "Nice to have you back, Mia."

"Thank you, Devon," she says, and I turn her away from the desk, eager to get both of us out of the public eye.

Once we're in the elevator, Mia inspects the blood all over me. "Your shirt looks horrible." She presses her hands to her face.

I pull them away. "Your father just needs to know that you're okay. Put him up in the spare bedroom and we'll all rest better."

"You never minded when he stayed."

"I only cared when you left."

"Grayson," she breathes out.

He cups my face. "I'm right here, baby. I'm not going anywhere."

The elevator halts and I kiss her, maneuvering us into the hallway as I do, and I keep us moving toward our apartment. We're almost at our door and I'm about to stop and ask her a few questions about her father when she steps in front of me, her hands on my chest, and *damn, I missed her* is all I can think of in this moment. "He can't know that I went to work for Ri for that bonus that saved him from his debt," she says. "He'll blame himself for tonight and it's not his fault. I should never have left you and no matter what, I should have to come to you. I just—I really didn't want you to think I was just coming for your money."

"We need to talk about leaving all of this behind us, but I need to know what your father knows before we walk into the apartment."

"I never told him you cheated," I say. "I just—I didn't want him to think badly of you. I never gave him real details at all."

Because on some level I know she knew I'd never cheat on her. "Then everything is between us and we'll keep it that way. Ri hated me. He went at you because of me. That will be in the news. We can't hide that from him. We shouldn't try."

"What about us being back together?"

"What about it, Mia?" I don't give her time to reply. "We're back together."

"That's right," she says, grabbing my tie. "So, don't go trying to get killed and leave me, Grayson." She turns away and I pull her to me.

"I could say the same to you. I was terrified when Ri entered that stairwell."

"I wasn't going to go back. I knew we couldn't take it. I just wanted to get what I could and get back to you."

"And you are. We'll talk later, baby. We have a lot to say. I know I do."

The door behind us opens. "Mia!"

She rotates and runs to her father, throwing her arms around him. The two of them hug and I give them a moment before I join them. Mac catches a glimpse of me over Mia's shoulder and his eyes go wide. "What the hell?" he murmurs, setting her aside to look at me. "What happened to you?"

"Let's go inside and talk," I suggest, motioning them both forward.

"Yes," he says. "Let's."

I follow them into the foyer and Mac turns, waiting on me. Mia quickly joins me, standing by my side. "Dad—"

"What the hell happened to you, Grayson?" He's a fit man, his hair streaked with gray, his green eyes intense. His worry for his daughter obvious.

"Let's sit," I suggest.

"No," Mac says. "I don't want to sit. I want answers. Both of you, talk."

"My boss hated Grayson. He—" Mia inhales. "He—"

"Tried to hurt Mia to hurt me," I supply. "I hired professional help to deal with him. One of those men shot and killed Ri tonight."

"Holy fuck. Shot and killed?" He looks at Mia. "Where were you when it happened? Because obviously, Grayson was close."

"He was—I—" She looks down. "Grayson was holding a gun to his head," she looks at her father, "because he was holding a gun to my head."

Mac blanches. "What? He was—what?" He looks at me. "Why did this happen?"

"He knew how much I loved Mia and he was jealous of my success and my relationship with her."

"You were broken up," he snaps. "Why are you even back together?"

That statement hits me wrong, almost as if he's blaming me for Ri's insanity or that he was secretly glad to get rid of me. I bite my tongue but Mia snaps, pushing away from me. "This isn't his fault. He didn't make Ri a lunatic. Ri plotted our break-up. He tried to force himself on me. He is probably behind all the trouble you had last year because he knew if he offered me a bonus to save you I'd take a job with him. And why are we even back together? Really, dad? *Really*? I *love* Grayson. I've been miserable without him and I know you know that. I don't need to hear you blame him tonight."

She rushes past him and he catches her arm, turning her to face him. "You took the job to pay off my debt?"

"Yes. I did. It was all one big set-up. Ri didn't go after me because I got back with Grayson. He went after me and Grayson last year when this all started."

Mac's hands go to Mia's shoulders. "I wasn't blaming Grayson. And right now, I'm thanking God he's back because I know he loves you."

"You said 'why are you even back together' or whatever you said," she snaps back. "I didn't like it. I'm certain Grayson didn't either."

"I know he's covered in blood because he was right there with you, willing to risk his life to save you."

"He did risk his life to save me. He dared that man in every way to shoot him, not me, and Ri hated Grayson. I'm lucky he's alive. I'm really damn lucky he's alive. If I'd have lost him tonight, I'd be ready to go, too. Don't you see that?"

"I had a moment of freak out, Mia," Mac says. "It came out wrong. I love Grayson. I have always respected him and welcomed him to our family."

I step behind Mia, and settle my hands on her shoulders, silently offering her support.

"And as for my debt," Mac continues, "I hate that you went to that man for me. That means, this is my fault."

"No," Mia says. "It's not and I didn't want to tell you because I knew you'd say that. I let Ri turn me into a weapon against Grayson that is much deeper than you can imagine."

"I'm certain Grayson doesn't blame you." He kisses her forehead and turns to me. "I *am* glad that you're back. She was never happy without you." He offers me his hand which I accept. "You're a good man," he says. "Take care of my daughter."

"I will, sir, every day of the rest of her life."

He nods and turns to Mia. "I'm going to leave because as much as I want to stay, I sense that you and Grayson need time together. Come see me soon." He hugs her and looks at me. "Both of you." He looks at Mia. "I love you, daughter." He kisses her temple and then heads for the door.

The minute it shuts, I lock it and turn to Mia who is suddenly shaking all over again, adrenaline and emotions making for a bad cocktail when mixed with shock. I grab her, scoop her up and start carrying her toward our bedroom.

Chapter Forty-Three

Grayson

I set Mia on the white tiled ledge of the sunken tub and then walk to the shower, turning on the water. Once it's warming up, I walk back to her and stroke her cheek. "Stay right here," I order. "I don't want you to fall. You're still unsteady." I try to pull away but she catches my hand.

"Grayson."

"I'll be right back, baby. I want to get you something to take the edge off."

She nods and releases me and the fact that she welcomes whatever I bring her says a lot. Mia isn't a drinker and she hates drugs of any type. I walk out of the bathroom and into the bedroom, stopping at the mini-bar in one corner, pouring her a stout drink that she'll hate, but it'll help her relax.

I return to find her shoes kicked off and I go down on a knee beside her. "Drink," I order, pressing it into her hand and when her hand shakes on the way to her mouth, I help her hold onto the glass. "Like a shot. All at once."

She swallows hard and then downs the whiskey. "Oh God. That's horrible."

"That's a twenty-five-year-old scotch that cost ten thousand dollars a bottle."

"That's a lot of money for something that tastes that bad."

I laugh. "It's good stuff. Even better with the second glass."

"It made me warm all over."

"I'd rather it be me that makes you warm all over."

"Then take that damn bloody shirt off. I can't look at it."

"Let's both just strip down and I'll get rid of our clothes." I set the glass down, stand up and take her with me.

She fumbles with my buttons and I take over, quickly pulling it over my head and then walk to the trash can, hit the lever with my foot, and stuff the shirt inside. "Better?"

"Yeah," she says. "The blood reminds me that he's dead."

And the world is a better place, but I don't say that to Mia. Ri was a killer. I saw that in his eyes tonight. He would have killed her. He would have killed again. I help her undress and then do the same. I then walk to the trash can, hit the lever on the floor and trash everything. "I'll get it out of the house after we shower," I say, grabbing her hand and leading her to the shower.

I grab the soap and waste no time making sure I get all remnants of the night off both of us. She needs it all washed away and she needs to rest. "You okay?" I ask when we're just standing there under the spray a few minutes later.

"Because you're here and I'm feeling that twenty-five-year-old whiskey. It's helping. Thank you. I can't believe I saw a man die tonight. I can't believe he was going to kill me and he was. It's—surreal in so many ways."

I stroke a strand of hair from her face. "I know, baby, but it's over and you're safe."

"My father didn't help."

"About that. What happened to not telling him about the bonus Ri gave you to help him?"

"I got angry and I probably misunderstood him, but I didn't think the man I love, who also risked his life to save me tonight, needed to be blamed."

"Come on," I say, turning off the water and grabbing a towel from over the side to wrap it around her. Once she's wrapped up well and I dry my hair and pull a towel around my waist, I lead her to the bedroom.

"Our chair," she whispers.

Our chair. I didn't sit in that damn thing the entire time she was gone. I go there willingly now, and pull her down into it with me, angling us to face each other and pulling the blanket over us. Her fingers splay on my jaw. "I'm glad Blake killed him instead of you. You would have had to live with taking a life, and we both would have known I caused it."

I roll her to her back and settle my leg between hers. "Baby, you did nothing wrong tonight. Nothing."

"Maybe I should have stayed in the office. Maybe I shouldn't have even gone back there at all. I pushed to protect you but you almost got killed tonight."

"You did protect me. You saved me, with Ri and by coming back. I'm the one who wasn't good without you. I needed you, Mia. You belong here with me, and nothing was ever going to be right again until you came back." I lean in and brush my lips over hers and it's all I can do to hold back, to remember how delicate she is tonight. I need to taste her, to feel her, to be inside her.

The instant I pull back, she lifts her head and presses her lips to mine and that's all it takes. My mouth closes down on hers, and I kiss her deeply, intensely, drinking her in, owning her because that's what I need right now. I need to feel her, to know she's here. "You're mine," I whisper, caressing a hand down her back and cupping her backside, pulling her closer. "No one will ever take you again."

"Never again," she promises, her hand on my face, and I drag her leg to my hip, the thick ridge of my erection pressing between her thighs.

"I need to be inside you, but if you—"

"Now would be good," she whispers. "*Now*, please, Grayson."

I press inside her and thrust deep, angling her to take all of me. She gasps out, "You're much, *much* better than whiskey."

I tangle my fingers in her hair and drag her gaze to mine. "Just seeing him hold that gun to your head almost killed me. I'll have nightmares about that for years to come." My mouth closes down on hers and I can't kiss her deep enough, I can't be inside her deep enough. I can't touch her enough or feel her close enough. And yet I go slow, I cradle her hips to my hips. I kiss her neck. I touch her breast and lick her nipple, suckling her until she arches into me. Until she pants out my name.

And those sounds she makes, those soft, sexy sounds drive me crazy and I press my lips to her ear. "I thought I'd never hear you make those sounds again. I thought I'd never hold you like this again. And not just tonight, Mia. I thought I lost you."

"Not for even a moment." She pulls back to look at me. "I was always here in my heart. Always."

My mouth crashes down on hers, and this time, I lose everything but the taste of her, the feel of her, the hunger I cannot sate for this woman, and God knows I tried while she was gone. I tried and failed, and I didn't even want to succeed. I have never been as lost in any other human being, including Mia, as I am lost in her now. The world fades and there is just the two of us and when she shudders in my arms, this time with pleasure, not shock or fear, I follow.

It's long minutes later, that we lay on that chair, clinging to each other, when I tilt her head back and say, "Yes, I would have killed him and I wouldn't have regretted it one day of my life or yours."

Chapter Forty-Four

Mia

I wake in our chair with Grayson curled around me, his body sheltering me the way I know he tried to do last night, the way he was trying to shelter me even when he fired me from that case, even if he went about it the wrong way. I roll around to face him and find him awake. "How are you?" he asks.

"I'm here. I'm perfect."

One of our phones buzzes somewhere in the distance. "Yours or mine?"

"Probably both. They've been going off for an hour."

"Don't we need to get them?"

"Yes, but I just couldn't make myself get up with you laying here with me." He kisses my temple. "I'll go find our phones." He throws off the blanket and walks across the room and any worry I have is momentarily lost to the sight of his perfect, naked backside.

He disappears into the bathroom and I sit up, pulling the blanket around me. "I don't remember where my purse or briefcase are," I call out.

Grayson exits the bathroom in a pair of pajama bottoms with my robe in his hands. "I don't either actually." He crosses to sit next to me and I eagerly accept the robe as he glances at his phone. "Blake, Eric, Davis, Courtney, and your father have taken turns calling."

"Courtney. Oh God. I didn't even think about calling her."

"I'm texting Courtney and your father in a group text," Grayson says, "Because I need to call Blake first." He looks at me and reads the message he's just typed: *Mac and Courtney, we were asleep. We're fine. Mia lost her phone. We have a few calls to make and then we'll call you both in a few.*

"Perfect," I say. "Hurry and call Blake. I need to pee and I don't want to go until I know what's going on."

"Go, baby. I'll be right here."

"Yeah. I better go." I stand up and race across the room and leave the door open as I hear, "Blake. What's happening?"

Of course, I can hear nothing else and by the time I exit the bathroom, Grayson is meeting me at the door, no longer on the phone. "Blake is having one of his men bring your phone and purse up to us. He had to get it cleared with the police to give it back to you."

"And?"

"And the police will want to interview us again this afternoon. Blake took the liberty of calling our attorney and offering to host the interview at his office. It's a non-event for us, outside of them going after anyone that was helping to set me up." He snags my hand. "Coffee. I need coffee." He starts walking, pulling me along, and I find myself smiling. I love coffee and Grayson, but in our kitchen, together, it's even better.

A few minutes later, we both have steaming cups in our hands and I'm using his phone to assure first Courtney, since she knows nothing at this point, and then my father that all is well when the doorbell rings. Grayson heads for the door and returns with my purse. He's barely handed it to me when my phone starts ringing. "I need to go, dad. I have to return some calls. We'll come see you soon. I love you, too."

I trade Grayson his phone for my purse and quickly pull out my phone "Kevin," I say, "my boss at Ri's firm. He's a good guy. He knew Ri was a problem and he wanted to protect me. I have to call him back, but my client called too, and she must be freaking out. She has to come first but I need some idea of what's on the news and what she's heard."

Grayson grabs the remote and turns on the small TV under the kitchen counter which offers us nothing. "The internet," he says, searching his phone and a few minutes later we both finish reading up on the press which amounts to questions about the future of Ri's firm.

I dial my client. "Mia, what the hell is going on?" she answers. "Are you okay? God, am I okay?"

"I'm fine. You'll be fine. I'm not going back to the firm. I'm—" I look at Grayson, who arches a brow. "I'm going to be with Grayson Bennett's firm. He's my—" I turn away. "We're together. I'm sure you saw that on the news. I want to take you with me but I need to be sure legally I can do that. No matter what, I'll take care of you."

"I'm in limbo. Please say that isn't so."

"I'll handle this for you one way or the other. I promise. I'll be in touch by tomorrow." I hang up and Grayson steps in front of me. "I assume I'd come back to the firm. That's okay, right?"

"I wouldn't have it any other way, but let's do this a little differently this time. You don't work for anyone but the firm. Take the cases you want but I'd really like you to work on the bigger picture with me that reaches beyond the firm. Then we can travel together." His hands come down on my arms. "If you want to. I know you want to forge your own career, but you have a brilliant mind and insight I value. You always make me think wider. I'd be lucky to have you work with me as the fourth in my team; you, me, Eric, and Davis."

"I'd like that. I would. I do love criminal law though and I have to take this case all the way. I believe in my client."

"Then you will take it all the way and you'll win. I'll get the case moved. Under the circumstances that won't be an issue. I'll make the calls right after I call a mover to get your things." He folds me against him. "You belong here with me."

"Yes," I say softly, trying not to think about that awkward moment when I didn't know what to call Grayson. "I do."

He strokes my hair from my face. "I'm your future husband," he says. "Don't forget that. I don't plan to."

All those weird feelings fade away. Of course, he's not going to ask me again the morning after we were both covered in a dead man's blood. He's not going to ask me until this is over, because he still doesn't get that I will go to hell and back with him, but I'll have a lifetime to show him that I'm here to stay. I will show him every single day.

Chapter Forty-Five

Mia

The rest of the day goes by in a whirlwind of press and chaos. The interviews with the police, however, are uneventful, at least for us. And as Grayson expected, Blake and his team are wonderful. Our team is just as wonderful, including our attorney who I barely know. By the time we leave Blake's office, Grayson has me moved back into the apartment, compliments of a big tip and a moving company. My father stops back by that evening to help us unpack. We're standing in the kitchen, while Grayson takes a few calls in his office, both of us drinking coffee. He tells me about all the new business he has, a woman he might keep seeing, and I pack up some things for him that I don't need now that I'm here.

"Mia," he says, stepping in front of me and taking my hand to shove something in it. "Thank you. I'll never put you in that position again."

I look down and stare at a check for fifty thousand dollars. "The money I owe you."

"You keep it and invest it in your business." I press it back into his hand.

"No. I'm never putting you in that position again. I won't let you make decisions for me."

"And she won't have to," Grayson says, appearing at the bottom of the stairs that lead to his office. He crosses the room to join us, standing beside me, his arm at my waist. "Mia has all the money she could ever need and so do you. Keep the money and we'll talk about how to expand your business."

"No," my father says, holding up his hands. "I never asked you for anything, Grayson. I'm not going to start now."

"But I'm offering and I had planned to offer before Mia and I broke up. We'd talked about it but you're prideful just like your daughter. We'll tread cautiously, but I have money, Mac. Your daughter is the woman I'm going to spend the rest of my life with. We're going to support your business. I want to have Eric look at your books, if you're okay with that. He's got a magical mind. Let him help you with a five-year plan and I'll invest the money."

"No, I—"

"Dad," I say, hugging him. "Let him help." I pull back to look at him. "He really wants to and I didn't ask. He did this himself. Just talk to Eric. Get excited about not struggling anymore."

He looks at Grayson. "I don't know what to say."

"Say you're going to be kinder to my football team this year."

"Damn Patriots," my father grumbles.

Grayson and I laugh. "That is a little kinder than normal," Grayson says, and the two of them head to the balcony with beers in hand to talk about those damn Patriots.

I finish unpacking because I'm home to stay.

The next morning, after much debate, Grayson and I decide that his offices don't need the press we would bring to them but we can't avoid their obsession with us. We agree to a press conference with law enforcement present that is held at Blake's offices. And once again, Grayson shelters me. He takes the heat of the questions for a solid hour before he says enough. Eric takes over from there and we hurry to a car that drives us to the airport for our escape to the Hamptons with not one, but two of Blake's men with us, just to be safe.

By the time we land in the Hamptons and we're in Grayson's Porsche that he's left at the airport, we have the legal approval for us to take over my client's case from Ri's firm. I call my client who is relieved. Next up, is a call to Kevin, my ex-boss, who I've discussed with Grayson in depth. "Mia, how the hell are you?"

"I'm good. Really good. How are you?"

"Afraid for my job. It's not good here."

"Come to work for Bennett. Grayson is going to extend you an official offer for twenty percent higher than you're being paid now."

"Sold. When do I start?"

We work out the details, talk about my client, and then plan to meet at the Bennett offices Monday morning. "I'll arrange to have her there," Kevin promises of my client and we disconnect right as we pull up to the house. "Everything is falling into place," I say, feeling a pinch of sadness. "I remember coming here and it being your father's house he just never used. Now, it's yours."

Grayson pulls us into the garage and parks. "And he'd want me to share it with you." He kills the engine and exits, and by the time I'm standing beside my door, he's there kissing me. He glances at his suit and my dress we'd worn for the press conference. "Let's change and take a walk."

"I'd like that."

A few minutes later, we're both in sweats, tees, and we head to the beach where we start walking. We talk. We talk about everything and then we do it again and as we always do, we end up at the lighthouse. Grayson follows me up the stairs, and we reach the railing just in time to watch the sun begin to lower and streak the darkening sky in orange and red.

Grayson grabs a bottle of wine, and I don't ask where it came from. We always kept wine here. We were always here. He fills two glasses and then offers me one. I sip and sigh. "So many times, I missed us here. So many times when we were here, I just wanted to stay and pretend the rest of the world didn't exist."

He sets our glasses down. "Then stay forever. Stay with me, Mia. Be with me. Be the mother of my children and we will have beautiful babies. You're my best friend, you're my other half. You're a part of me that I can't live without. You know I had to do this here. It didn't feel right anywhere else and yet you feel right in every way." He reaches into his pocket and pulls out my ring and then goes down on his knee. "Will you marry me, Mia?"

Tears prickle in my eyes, and I shake my head. "Yes, a hundred times over. Can we just go do it now, so no one can stop us?"

He stands up and slides the ring on my finger. "No one is going to stop us and you're going to have your perfect wedding, whatever you want that to be."

"The part where we say 'I do' is all I want. I don't care about the rest."

"I do already, baby."

"I do, too." And this time, when he presses me against the wall and kisses me, I don't stop him when he undresses me. I help him because this is our place, this is where I want us to get married. This is where I want our vows to be spoken. This is us.

Part Two: Love Me Forever

Chapter Forty-Six

Mia

O cean wind teased with salt washes over Grayson and I as we exit the lighthouse, our special place, and head back toward his Hamptons mansion. I glance down at my finger, where the gorgeous emerald-cut diamond with hints of blue was placed only minutes before. It's beautiful and it should never have left my finger, but it's back now. This Friday evening has brought proof that love, real love, never dies, no matter what evil tries to destroy it. But it's still painful for Grayson and me to know that I let Ri, a man who was eaten alive with jealousy over Grayson, use me as a weapon against him. Now Ri is dead.

"Does it bring back bad memories?" Grayson asks. "Because if it does, you can pick a new one."

"This is my ring," I say, stopping to turn to him. "I love this ring. You had it designed for me. No one gets to take this from me ever again."

He cups my face. "I don't want anything that will muddy up our future. Not again." He strokes an errant lock of hair behind my ear. "The ring—"

"Is perfect. I am back where *I belong*."

"Yes. Yes, you are." He motions to the house, and we turn and start walking again, his grip on my hand firm. He still feels like he could lose me again. And I get that. He quite literally just lived through a man holding a gun on me, with the intent to kill me. So did I, but that isn't where my head is right now. I'm worried about Grayson, not me, which is why my eyes land on the gorgeous mansion that is our destination, with such a heavy heart. It was his father's. When I left Grayson, we lost the chance for his father to be a part of our wedding. I loved that man. I still can't believe he's gone. And with that, my eyes burn and my mind slides back into the past. Back to the day we told him we were getting married, back before Ri tried to destroy us.

"I feel so nervous," I say as we park in the garage of the Hamptons house where Grayson's father is waiting on us. "What if he doesn't want me to be your wife? We'll be here with him. It will be awkward."

"Baby," he says, killing the engine and turning to me. "He loves you." He takes my hand and kisses it. "I love you. He sees that and frankly if I didn't, the man would call me a fool. You won him over from the moment he sat across from you and you met him." He strokes my cheek. "Let's go in."

I nod and we both reach for our doors. By the time I'm stepping out of the car, Grayson is there, pulling me to him and kissing me. God, I love this man. I love him so much and when my palm lands on his chest, his heart thundering under my hand, I know he's feeling the same thing because that's how it is with him. I feel him, and he feels me and from the day we met, we connected, inside and out. From the first time we were here in this house, I could no longer breathe without this man.

He kisses me. "Come on. Let's go share our news."

"Maybe I should take off the ring until we tell him?"

"The only time I ever want you to remove that ring is when we're saying our vows and I'm putting it back on you." He takes my hand and leads me forward, his words and actions warming me all over. Everything he does is right.

We enter the house and find his father in front of the TV watching the Yankees play. "Holy hell," he shouts at the TV. "Hit the damn ball."

I laugh at the behavior that has become familiar these past few months and somehow makes him far more human than the billionaire businessman would be otherwise. He turns to look at me. "Mia," he says, motioning me forward. "Come give me a hug."

I warm with his invitation that is also now quite familiar. He treats me like the daughter he never had and has since that night at the gallery event when we'd come out of the closet. I hurry forward and give him a hug. "Don't worry," he says. "I have a hot date tonight. I won't be here bugging you and Grayson."

I pull back to look at him. "A hot date? That sounds promising. You're finally going to start dating again?"

"A date with a whole lot of money," he says. "She's about twenty years younger than me and a client, but the money works. I'll take the money."

Grayson steps to my side and pulls me under his arm. "It's time, Dad. You need to date."

"No," he says. "Your mother was it for me."

"She wouldn't want you to be alone," Grayson says.

"She shouldn't have been so damn perfect then. How the hell can anyone follow that?" He cuts his gaze and I'm pretty sure this big, tough, amazing man is fighting tears. I think he's here this weekend because he needs Grayson.

"I understand in a way I never did before," Grayson says, his fingers flexing on my shoulder. "Mia and I are engaged."

His father looks at me. "You said yes?"

"You doubted that I would?"

"I've seen you struggle with your fear of his money," he says.

"Not his money, though yeah, at first I felt like we had a conflict of power. He had it all and I had none, but he did well. You taught him right. I've never felt that he used that against me and so that left me with my fears of him feeling like I was here for his money."

"And now?"

"And now, I want you both to know that if Grayson doesn't draft a prenup, I will. I'm never going to give him a reason to stay with me to save his money."

Grayson turns me to face him. "I will never—"

"Time and years change things," I say. "And when we reach the downs of the ups and downs, you will never think about the money and neither will I."

"Mia—" Raymond says.

"Mia," Grayson interrupts. "We're not doing a prenup."

"Both of you look at me," Raymond orders.

We both snap to his command, which is just a sign of how much respect we share for this man. "This is how this works. Mia, he needs you to know you have money if you divorce because then he knows you'll never stay for the money. Grayson, she needs you to know that money is limited, so you know she's not here for all that fucking money you have. Don't either one of you argue. It won't matter if you stay together like I did with Melanie, but it makes sure there is never a fight about money. Agree now, both of you."

"I don't want a guarantee of anything," I say.

"I don't want her to have limits," Grayson adds.

"Neither of you has a choice," his father says. "This is the complication of money. It is what it is. Do this. It worked for me and Melanie. I'll leave you both to talk about it." He grabs the remote and turns off the TV before he heads for the patio door.

I turn back to Grayson and before I can even speak, he's pulling me close. "My parents were happy, Mia. They didn't need that agreement. They were so in love, just like us."

"Then we need to listen to your father. If he says this is how we avoid conflict, we need to listen. Please. We'll let him guide us."

Grayson pulls me to him and kisses me. "Let's just plan the damn wedding, woman."

"I want nothing more, but please. Let your father guide us, Grayson. Please. I'm begging you."

He studies me long and hard before he laces his fingers with mine, and we head for the patio, where we exit to find his father waiting on us. "Well?" he prods.

"Agreed," Grayson says. "We'll let you guide us."

Relief washes over me and his father looks at me, proving that I'm always present and an individual to him, which is exactly how Grayson treats everyone. As if they matter. I nod. "Yes. We will trust your guidance."

He smiles a warm, wonderful smile and says, "Let's plan the wedding of a century."

"Penny for your thoughts," Grayson says, as we now step onto the very patio where his father had declared our future wedding the wedding of the century.

"I hate that your father won't be here for the wedding."

He strokes my hair and pulls me close, his touch, and the delicious woodsy scent of him familiar and right. I missed this man when we were apart, desperately missed him. "Me, too," he says. "Me, too, baby, but some part of me believes that he is now resting in peace, knowing we're back together. And that no matter what we face over Ri or anything else, we're facing it together."

I try not to think about what we might face over the Ri incident. Right now, I'm with Grayson, and we're engaged again. That's all that matters.

Chapter Forty-Seven

Mia

I wake Sunday morning to raindrops pitter-pattering on the bedroom window and Grayson's big strong arms wrapped around me, his woodsy scent teasing my nostrils. That scent is home to me. He is home to me and for just a moment, I think about the night I left him. I think about the woman who flung herself at him. It was such a damning moment, and yet, I should have known Grayson wasn't that man.

"You're awake," he murmurs softly, nuzzling my ear.

"Yes," I whisper, and when his hand runs over my bare arm, goosebumps lift on my skin and my nipples pucker. Just that easily, I'm alive in ways that only this man makes me alive. I'm aroused in ways only this man can make me feel.

A blink of a moment later, his hand is on my breast, his other sliding between my legs, and when he discovers just how slick and wet I am, his low, guttural murmur of, "Holy hell, woman," spreads a smile on my lips, one that becomes a moan when the extremely hard length of his erection presses inside me. His body curls around mine and even as he thrusts, I'm pressing into him.

Heat burns between us and explodes into what is almost desperation. I'm not sure if it started with Grayson or with me, but now it's ours. We own the desperation together. It's not until a long time later, when we stand under a hot shower again, that I really start to process how badly the events of the past few years impacted Grayson. He lost his mother. I left him. His father had a heart attack while he was golfing with him. Now he just watched a monster hold a gun to my head. That desperation started with him and I understand. That was all about how much he needed to feel me close. How much he needed to know I'm alive and well. It's a powerful thing to be loved so deeply.

"I love you," I say, running my fingers over the dark stubble on his jaw. "With all my heart and soul, with all that I am."

His hand slides over my wet hair. "And I love you."

"I know. I won't ever forget again."

"You don't need to keep telling me that, Mia. We're here. We're together. And we're starting fresh, new."

"I don't want to be fresh. I don't want to be new. I loved the us of the past."

"We can be both, baby." He catches my hand and holds up my finger, showing me the ring he's recently put back on it. "We can be anything we want to be together. And we will," he promises me before he kisses the diamond. "Let's go make coffee and talk about the wedding."

"Yes," I say, scolding myself for turning our morning into something heavy. "Let's go make coffee and talk about the wedding."

A few minutes later, Grayson has dressed in jeans and a T-shirt and headed into the kitchen. His departure feels abrupt and I'm concerned that there's more going on with him, or even this Ri situation than I know. I quickly dress in jeans and a T-shirt myself, apply some make-up before throwing some product in my wet hair, making quick work of drying it. In between my rushed morning routine, I exchange text messages with my father, assuring him I'm doing well. Finally, I finger comb the brown strands of my hair to find it's still damp, but my impatience to join Grayson has me leaving it this way.

Feeling that urgency, and the clawing sense of that man needing me, me and my soon-to-be frizzy hair hurry out of the bedroom and walk down a long hallway and round the corner to the grand living room that attaches to the kitchen. I find Grayson facing the marble island, hands on the surface, muscles bunched in his shoulders, his chin to his chest. I'm right. He's not good. He took care of me after the shooting. He was a rock for me, but I haven't taken care of him. That man stood there in a stairwell with Ri holding a gun to my head, afraid for me, and prepared to kill for me. How many women have a man who would kill for them? Or die for them?

I do.

I do and he's an amazing man.

With soft steps meant not to startle him, I close the space between us, shocked when this man who is always in control of his surroundings doesn't even know when I approach. I step behind him and wrap my arms around his waist. Or I intend to. Grayson catches me and pulls me in front of him, and suddenly I'm caged between him and the island, the intensity of his emotions crashing into me. "I want to keep you locked away," he says, his voice low, rough, almost guttural, "to make sure no one can ever hurt you the way he intended to hurt you."

And there it is, what I feared—*his fear*. My hand settles on his jaw. "I've told you this, but I'm going to say it again. None of us can control how long we walk this earth, but if anything ever happens to me, I've had the best damn life anyone could want for. Because of you. That's how we have to live. Every day we have to be all-in, all the way."

His forehead settles on my forehead. "I keep seeing that gun in his hand, at your head." He cups my face and tilts my gaze to his. "This isn't about me. It's about you. How are you?"

"It's not just about me, Grayson. It's about you, too."

"*How are you?*" he repeats. "How are you really?"

"Remarkably good, but you're not."

"If you're good, I'm good."

My rejection is instant. "No. No, you're not. And I'm probably not, either. I have some sort of barrier up, a wall that I've pushed all this behind. I'm not sure which is better. You with no wall or me with one that isn't allowing me to deal with this at all. I wish—" *so many things*, I think.

"You wish what, baby?" His voice is softer now, velvet meant to soothe my nerves. He is always about me and that is why I have to be about him. He needs that. He deserves that.

"I wish we could be here for weeks on end and pretend the rest of the world doesn't exist. But I also wish for our life back, completely back. I want to be in our apartment. I want to live *our life*. I want to find our routine again. There's security in those things, Grayson."

"There is," he agrees. "But when we go back, the press won't be gone. This Ri situation won't be gone. Are you sure that you're ready for that?"

"I have a deep need to be past this. I want to ride this storm and get *past it*. And your staff needs to see you. They need to know Ri and his attacks on your firm have no impact."

He skims fingers through my damp hair. "You're sure?"

"I am," I say, but again, I'm cautious not to make this just about me. "What do you want, though?"

"You. All I want is you, safe, and happy."

"You have me, safe, and happy. So, we go back?"

"Yes," he agrees. "We go back."

I kiss him and smile. "Good. I can show off my ring."

This earns me his smile and I watch the tension in his shoulders slide away. I've made him happy. And *that* is what I want.

Chapter Forty-Eight

Mia

G rayson and I sit at the island facing each other, sipping our coffee and talking about his father, with shared smiles and laughter between us. It's a magical moment in time that has successfully crushed those demons that he'd been battling upon my entry into the kitchen, and left me with the man I love. The man who cares about people. The man who is filthy rich and never acts as if he deserves it. The man who would die, and literally kill for me, and yet, I'd dared doubt him. I do not believe I will ever forgive myself for slighting our love in such a way. I'm fighting the need to ask him if he's sure he will when his cellphone buzzes with a text message.

His expression doesn't change, but I don't miss the subtle tensing of his jaw, and that's before he even he reads the message. A sign that he's expecting bullets to fly, that perhaps he doesn't think this Ri thing is over. Reluctantly it seems, he picks up his phone, reads the message, types a reply, and sets it back down.

"Blake, and his team at Walker, want to update us on the Ri investigation at his office and talk through a full security plan until this mess completely passes." He glances at his watch and then me. "It's ten now. He's sending an escort to take us to the airport at one."

I study the handsome lines of his face. "What else?"

"Nothing else."

"You're turned off. I saw it happen."

He catches my hand and kisses it. "It's going to be a week or two before we find our sweet spot back home. You know that, right?"

"You mean because of Ri and the press?" I clarify, just to be sure I know where his head is right now.

"Yes. Because of Ri and the press. You say you're okay, Mia, but there's no way you can be unaffected by what happened with Ri in that stairwell. Blake suggested you talk to a counselor."

"I don't need to see a counselor," I say, dismissing the idea quite emphatically. "I'm fine. Stop worrying." My coffee is gone, so I drink his. "But I do think we should talk about that case I'm bringing over with me. The Wittmore case."

"How can I forget Mitch Wittmore, the billionaire tech genius, being killed by his wife?"

"In self-defense," I remind him.

"I remember the details. She was a battered wife."

"Yes and I believe her. When you see the file, you will as well."

"Then what's the problem?"

"We're trying to get rid of the press. He was Mitch Wittmore. This case will bring more press, not less."

"Months from now," he says. "And we as a firm are used to that kind of press."

"If I'm to be your wife—"

"If?" he challenges.

"*Because* I'm to be your wife," I amend, "my cases will bring a different kind of attention to you, Grayson. You're a billionaire who runs a massive operation that stretches well beyond the law firm and its many offices. You have a hotel brand. Maybe even a stake in a professional football team in the near future. The interest in my cases will come with a different level of scrutiny."

He stands up and grabs the coffee pot, refilling both of our cups and then settling the hazelnut creamer we're both using between us. "And that means what to you?"

I grab the creamer and pour it into our cups. "What does it mean to you? Are you up to dealing with that?"

"You believe in this. We're fighting for what's right. Why wouldn't I be?"

I slide off the seat and step between his legs, my hands on his thighs. "I really love you, so very much."

"I really love you, too. Talk to me about the case. Why haven't they offered her a plea?"

"The ADA involved is a real asshole."

"Name?"

"Nick Reynolds."

He picks up the phone, sends a text, and then sets it down. "I asked Blake to find out what he can about him. I'll be interested to find out if he was involved in that dirt dive Ri had the DA doing on me and my businesses."

"But this case was with Ri's firm with me there until this week."

"I know. It's a long shot, but it's worth looking into. Maybe we should work this case together. I'll be the second chair."

"You? Second chair. Grayson, you're the CEO of an empire."

"And a criminal attorney, in case you forgot. Sometimes getting back to the basics reminds us about who we really are and want to be."

"You are a brilliant man with the world at his fingertips. This is beneath you."

"No. Helping someone who needs help will never be beneath me, and if it were, you know my father would turn over in his grave. But if this is about your independence—"

"No. Not at all. I would like to have you help me with the case prep, but if the press know you're a part of this, the news will explode. And if we lose, you'll look bad."

"Then let's not lose."

"I'm handling my case," I say, "but I have a proposition for you."

His perfect eyes twinkle with mischief. "You have my undivided attention."

I always do, I think. No matter what deal or project is consuming him, Grayson always makes me feel like he's one hundred percent present. "You wanted me to consider working more closely with you and the corporate side of Bennett so that we can travel and work together."

"And?"

"And what if I handle this case and then step back from a formal caseload? You've already approved me hiring Kevin, my old boss at Ri's firm. Now that Ri is gone, we legally brought over my business. Kevin can take over the rest of my caseload, or whoever you feel is appropriate. I'd love to look at the charity operation. You're not as active in charitable activity as you should be. I can have an impact. I know I can. I want to contribute."

"What happened to needing your own career and identity?"

"I don't know why this can't be that, too. And as far as needing to completely free myself of your coattails, I think we've been there, done that. I'm done feeling like I have something to prove because you're more experienced and filthy rich. And I don't care if people think I slept my way to the top anymore. I think my insecurity over those things allowed Ri to break us up. I won't make that mistake again."

His hands come down on my arms, his lashes lowering, expression tightening before he opens his eyes and fixes me in a tormented stare. "'I won't let you," he promises, his voice roughened by emotions, raw torment radiating off this brilliant, talented, *good man* because of me.

"Grayson—"

I never finish that sentence. He picks me up, throws me over his shoulder, and starts walking.

Chapter Forty-Nine

Mia

O nce we're in the bedroom, Grayson sets me down at the foot of the bed, and his hand slides under my hair, his palm hot on my neck. "Next time you run," he promises, his voice vibrating with emotion, "I swear to God, woman, you won't run fast enough. Next time, I will catch you and I will bring you home and tie you to our bed." His hand sweeps down my spine and my sex clenches, nipples puckering, this game of dominance he plays one I know well. It's about control, about those times in his life when the pressure of being Grayson Bennett pushes his buttons. In this case, when *I've* pushed his buttons.

"Then what would you do to me?" I challenge, sounding breathless, feeling breathless. "Because if you're going to tie me up, you can't just leave me there unattended."

His lips curve, his beautiful lips that can be both gentle and oh so punishing. "We both know I wouldn't leave you there." *Oh yes, we do,* I think, my only thought before his lips come down on my lips, a dark demand in the slide of his tongue that follows. I know this side of Grayson, and I know right now is not all that, unlike earlier this morning. This is all about burning fast, wicked, hot demand. He owns me right now, and I don't fight that need in him. I think—I think it's what I need, too.

He proceeds to strip us both naked, turn me over, and slide a finger along my sex, testing my readiness before he gives my backside a smack. I arch into the touch, and he drives into me. He fucks me then—rough, dirty, and an edge of urgency in every thrust of his hips that ends with us on our backs, staring at the ceiling, panting out breaths. At the same moment, we turn to face each other and my fingers curl on his jaw. "You're still angry."

"Not at you, baby." He kisses me, then pushes off the bed, bringing me a towel, and then grabs his pants, clearly avoiding this conversation.

I sit up, but I make no attempt to dress. My clothes are the least of my worries right now. I scoot to the edge of the bed and study him, only slightly distracted by his perfect abs. "Grayson," I say softly. He pulls his T-shirt over his head, his green eyes meeting mine for a piercing second before he answers my unspoken question.

"I'm fine, Mia." He sits down next to me and pulls on his boots.

"'Fine' is a word women define as 'not fine.' You know that, right?"

He stands and takes me with him.

"I'm fine," he repeats. "I promise. It's you that I'm worried about."

"I'm fine."

"So fine is okay if it's you, but not if it's me?"

"I really am fine."

"And it's my job as your future husband to make sure you stay that way. Get dressed. I want to take you to eat and make another little stop before we head to the airport."

"I thought Walker was sending men to pick us up?"

"We'll meet them at the airport." He cups my face and then gives my naked body a once over. "You're beautiful." He kisses me. "Now get dressed. I need to make a phone call." He heads to the doorway and just when he would disappear, I call out.

"Wait."

He turns and glances back at me.

"Do you know why I'm really fine right now?"

"Why?"

"Because I woke up with you. Because I'm marrying you. And because today, we've had two chances to get pregnant with our first child."

His expression softens instantly, and he's back across the room, enclosing me in his arms, molding me close. And even better, he's smiling. "You know why I'm fine?"

"Why?"

"Because you're going to be my wife and the mother of my children. And because the very fact that you might be pregnant is a good reason to rush the wedding. Now, get dressed."

He turns and walks away, but not before casting me another look and a smile. I've made him smile again. I've made him happy again. At least for now.

Chapter Fifty

Grayson

I step into the kitchen, pour the last cup of coffee, and once it's doctored to my liking, I dial Blake. "Grayson, my man," he answers on the first ring. "How's Mia?"

This is what I like about this man. He cares. And he knows what I care about. "She says she's fine."

"Fine," he says dryly. "Fine from a woman makes me say, 'oh fuck.'"

Another reason I like this man. He couldn't give a fuck that I employ him and that I have loads of cash. He does him.

"Exactly," I agree, running a hand through my hair. "I'm worried that I'm taking her back to the city too soon, but right now, that's what she wants. That's where she wants to be. Home is calling her."

"She was away from home for a long time. I say let her go home. You're one chopper ride from getting out of the city. I've seen a lot of these situations, the trauma effect, and sometimes routine and stability is the best thing for the person."

"And when does the storm hit?"

"It doesn't always happen. She's back with you. She feels stable. But that counselor I told you about is excellent. She'll come to Mia. And you. How are you holding up, man?"

"You tell me. How important is this meeting today? Where are we on ending this?"

"I just wanted to debrief you and talk through the press situation for the week."

"We held a press conference," I remind him.

"Which did nothing to shift their interest. They're all over, looking for you."

"Wonderful."

"I can just drop by later tonight if you want, bring the wifey and shit, and make it more informal."

"That works. What's happening with the investigation?"

"The Feds are involved and since I have connections, I'm getting constant updates."

Alarm bells go off in my head. "Updates on what Blake?"

"Ri is gone, but the degree to which he tried to infiltrate your company and use it for criminal activity is what matters here. Right now, we're trying to pin down every person involved. And you want us to do that. Anyone helping Ri burn you might be willing to burn you for their own gain. And I want you to talk to that attorney I told you about, Reese Summer. You just did a big deal with his brothers-in-law, Reid and Gabe."

"Right. I know who he is. I haven't met him, but I know his reputation as talented and honest. But why would I hire him, Blake? I own a law firm. A very large international law firm."

"You need a criminal attorney to deal with the Feds, and someone impartial."

"I need someone loyal," I counter, getting the idea he's not telling me everything. "And I have plenty of criminal lawyers on staff. Where are you going with this?"

"Any time the stinking Feds are involved, you want to watch your fucking ass."

"This from a man who was a Fed? And I'm back to, where are you going with this?"

"There's a reason I'm not a Fed anymore. One jealous fuck over there that hates you for your money and success, and this drags out. Reese's name alone holds power. And he doesn't work for Bennett. Ri infiltrated your operation. I like the feel of Reese being an outsider on this."

And there it is, the reasons he's pressing me to call Reese. "I'll call him," I agree tightly. "I'm taking Mia to lunch and someplace special. We'll meet your men at the airport."

"I'll keep them out of sight," he says.

I scrub the knot at the back of my neck. "I really don't want to take Mia back to this shit."

"You're not taking her back to this shit. You're taking her home, man. And it's none of my business, but it seems to me with all you've been through, you both need to be home together. What time tonight?"

"Eight."

"Eight it is. See you then. Oh fuck, I almost forgot. That ADA's name you sent me. He's dating a female ADA who's connected to this Ri thing."

"'The Ri thing.' I still can't believe the degrees this man went to try to destroy me. He infiltrated my staff, planted who knows what dirt inside my operations, and then went to the Feds."

"And that didn't turn out well for him. My job, and Reese's, will be to make sure we clean this up completely, so there are no snakes in the grass to bite you. Back to the ADA. What is this about?"

"Mia has a case he's handling. She feels like a deal, and a light one at that should have been made and instead, she and her client are headed to trial."

"We might be able to help her dig up something to turn the ADA around, but it sounds like you could request this guy hand off the case."

"I suspect that's what Mia will do, but I'll keep you posted."

We say a few more words and disconnect. I set the phone down and press my hands to the island. How damn deep did Ri get inside my operation? And how the hell did I let that happen?

"I didn't know we were planning to move the island?"

At Mia's soft, musical voice, I straighten and find her standing a few feet away, looking beautiful as hell—her long light brown hair wavy and a bit wild today. Her make-up is light, lips glossed pale pink. Eyes bright with engagement. "What are you talking about, baby?"

She closes the space between us with a sexy little shimmy to her hips.

"You," she says, stopping in front of me, "forgot to tell me that we're relocating the island. You've been pushing it all morning. We might need a contractor."

I laugh, and I'm not sure I laughed a day when we were apart. "Is that right?"

"Seems that way."

"You're crazy, woman," I say, taking her purse and setting it on the island we're presently discussing before wrapping my arm around her shoulders and folding her close. "Crazy good. And you always smell so damn good. You make me want to lick you all over."

Her hand settles on my cheek. "As good as that sounds, it has to wait."

"Why is that, exactly?"

"Are you going to tell me what's wrong, Grayson, or did you get so used to dealing with things without me that you don't need me?"

"Baby, I need you more than I need my next breath. You know that."

"Then talk to me," she prods softly. "It's the whole death thing that messes with your head, right?"

"It's a lot of things." I release her and turn to the island, and the minute my hands go down on it, I laugh and turn to her. "Maybe we do need a contractor."

She laughs, but she gives me a pleading look. "Grayson. Talk to me."

"We'll talk over lunch. How do you feel about Ed's Diner?"

"I love Ed's Diner. I really love it with you."

And just that easily, she brings me back to the simple things in life. The important things like family, like her. The way my mother did for my father. This woman needs to be my wife. It's long past due, and that's why lunch isn't our only stop this afternoon. I'm going to give us both a whole lot more than Ri and the FBI to think about when we go home.

Chapter Fifty-One

Grayson

I load up the Porsche with our luggage and then help Mia into the car. Once we're on the road, on this clear October day, I update her on my call with Walker Security. "Blake's going to swing by the apartment tonight with his wife and talk about security and the press this week."

"Oh. Well, that sounds much less daunting than a formal meeting at his place. What changed?"

"I think he thought he'd have more to tell us than he does."

She casts me a concerned look. "Is this not over, Grayson?"

"Ri infiltrated my operation. We haven't named all of those names. They're still present inside our world, capable of using our operation to do bad things. This week is going to be about flushing them out. For me, that is. You have a case to handle. I asked Blake about the ADA handling your case."

She shifts in her seat toward me. "And?"

I pull us to a halt at a stoplight. "He's dating another ADA who was working with RI to take me down."

"I still can't believe Ri convinced them you were dirty. And apparently, me with you. If I can't get that ADA off my client's case, I need to hand this case to someone else. But I don't want to do that. I'm going to raise hell until I do."

"That's my feisty woman," I say, sliding my hand down her hair. "Yes. You will."

A few minutes later, we're on the road, when Mia's father calls me, not her. After assuring him she's well, the call is short and over. Mia pretends indignance that he went around her, but I know his worry touches her. A few blocks later, we pull into one of our favorite places on the island, and I can feel my mood shift and lighten, but my determination to end this hell we're living sets firmly in my gut. We've walked through flames to get back to each other. No one is taking it from us.

Soon, Mia and I are sitting on the waterfront patio of the restaurant in an enclosed area, with heaters blasting around us, the ocean the canvas to our conversation. "It's almost the holidays," she says, once we have bubbling champagne glasses in our hands. "It's Halloween next weekend and then November."

"And you'll be home. It will be a much better year this year. Last year, Eric and I drank whiskey and ate the meal Leslie made for us before she left and went upstate to be with her family."

"I'm sure she was quite worried. That woman has done your mom proud looking after you."

"She has," I say solemnly, thinking of how damn much I missed my parents and Mia that day.

"I'm sure you watched football," she says. "In your dad's honor."

"Yes. He'd have it no other way." Emotion is about to choke me out right now and I shift the topic to what's important right here and now: her. "What about you? Were you with your father?"

"No. He had some special work project. He's been weird this past year."

Before then, I think, but I leave that alone right now. "What did you do if you weren't with him?"

"I went to a movie alone."

That news punches me so damn hard that my chin drops to my chest. "Damn it."

She catches my hand. "I'm with you this year and every year from now on. That's what matters."

"I almost called you on Thanksgiving and Christmas."

"You did?"

"Yeah, baby, but I knew I'd upset you. I didn't want to do that to you." I set my glass down. "What do you want to do for Thanksgiving this year?"

Her eyes light. "Put our tree up. And see two movies."

I laugh, and we spend the rest of our lunch talking about the holidays, but the situation with her father is bothering me. He just called me to check on her and yet he left Mia alone for the holiday. I know that hurt her and that's not like him, not the man I've come to know. He's had gambling issues in the past. I get the feeling they aren't as past as I'd hoped. And that's a dangerous path that can get you killed. That's not how I'm letting Mia lose her father. I've invested in his business but he might need to go to rehab, too, and the holidays are a volatile time that allow addictions to take hold. We need to keep him close.

Once we're done eating, and we settle back in the car, Mia is all smiles. "Where now?"

I wink. "Wait and see."

She smiles and settles her hands on her purse in her lap. "Very unfair."

"You can punish me later."

"I will," she promises, and her fingers absently stroke the Chanel logo on the front of her purse.

I have a flashback to the weekend I gave that to her. It was, in fact, our first Christmas.

Our tree is decorated to perfection with red and silver bulbs, twinkling white lights plentiful. It's beautiful, but it pales to Mia's beauty and joy this morning. Her hair is wild. Her robe is pink and fluffy. I set the giant white box with the red ribbon on her lap and watch her open it, watch the shock and joy in her eyes. And then the expected panic.

"No, Grayson," she'd said. "No. I know how much this costs."

"I know you know. Because you love Chanel."

"I don't know how you know that. I would never tell you that because that would be like me saying, hey billionaire boyfriend, buy me a ridiculously expensive purse. I wouldn't do that."

"Leslie told me."

"Oh my God, I'm going to kill her." She presses her hands to her face. "We were shopping and I told her that one day I'd make enough of my own money to treat myself. It was me talking about my goals. Not about you buying this for me."

"Do you mind that I bought it for you? I know goals matter, but I wanted to do this for you."

"It's so expensive," she says, her voice quavering with emotion.

I set the box aside and pull her to me. "Baby, I love you. And I have more money than God. I want to spend it on you. And you're going to have to get used to spending it yourself. You live with me. This is our life."

"I love you, not your money."

"I know that, or we wouldn't be who and what we are together."

"I don't know how to get comfortable with the money. I feel weird about it."

I stroke a lock of hair behind her ear. "Start by enjoying my Christmas gift to you. One of them. There's more."

"I did spend some of your money."

I arch a brow in surprise. "Did you?"

"On you. That damn credit card you gave me was burning a hole in my pocket when I found this item and I couldn't get it on my own. So, I gifted you with your own money."

"Our money, baby. Our money."

"Whatever the case, I want you to open it." She stands and rushes to the tree, returning to hand me a package.

I'm ridiculously nervous and anxious to see what this woman wanted enough to use that card when she stubbornly won't use it. I open it to find a pocket watch inside. "Read the engraving on the back." When I turn it over, I read: A great man is always willing to be little.

"It's that quote that your father—"

"Repeated often," I say, the quote by Ralph Waldo Emerson, one that my father spoke often when I was growing into the man I am today. "I know," I say, emotion welling in my chest. "Of course, I know." I set it aside and pull her to me, holding this woman that is everything to me, as close as I can. "It's about as perfect a gift as anyone has ever given me but you, you are the best gift of all."

I blink back to the present and pull the car into the driveway of the church where I was baptized. The church where my parents were married and where I said goodbye to them both. The church Mia and I were to be married in the first time we were engaged.

Chapter Fifty-Two

Mia

There are no words to describe how I feel when I realize where Grayson has taken us. It's special. It's a part of his family, *our family.*

"This is where we were supposed to get married," I say, remembering the day we'd come here to reserve the church and well aware of how much this location means to him. "It's a special place."

"It is indeed," he says, handing me my coat from the backseat. "You might need that. Hang tight and I'll come around and help you."

He grabs his own as well, a soft, sleek leather jacket that's as expensive and fine as the man himself.

Following his lead, I quickly set my purse in the backseat and reach for the door. By the time I'm stepping into the wind of a cold front blowing in, Grayson is opening my door and helping me out. The touch of his hand is firm and warmth slides up my arm, the crackle between us so much more than attraction and sex. The wind gushes again and unbidden, I shiver. Grayson, the gentleman that he always is, steps behind me, and I pop my arms inside. It's an expensive double-breasted black coat that fits a bit like a dress. I button up and tie the waist, remembering the day he'd given it to me: New Year's Eve. Only a few days after he'd given me my purse. I felt out of my league and confused. Taking the gifts went against my very core instinct. I'd feared, and on some level, I still do, that Grayson would think I could see only his money. I'd feared that he hid behind his money.

I slip back into the past, into that moment in time.

Grayson ties my belt for me and when he looks at me, the swell of emotion between us steals my breath. "Grayson," I whisper. "It's Chanel. It's extravagant."

"It matches your purse," he points out.

"I don't need gifts. I need the man beneath the money."

"It's from me to you. A gift for the woman who warms my heart. You're beautiful, inside and out." And when he says those words, his voice vibrates with so much love that I know that no matter which way my world spins, it will always stop right here with this man.

Grayson shuts my car door, jolting me back into the moment, and then steps to my side, his hand settling possessively on my lower back. We stare at the church, white with wooden shingles and a steeple, like something out of a country romance novel. His parents' perfect romance novel.

"I don't know what I was thinking," I say, stepping in front of him, wrapping my arms around his neck and letting him know how much I mean what I'm saying. "This is where your parents got married. This was where we planned to get married. We have to get married here, not at the lighthouse."

His hands settle on my waist. "We should get married at our place. We should make our future our own. I brought you here because I had something made for you before we broke up and this is the place I intended to give it to you."

"On our wedding day?"

"Yes. On our wedding day."

"Then give it to me on our new wedding day."

"I want you to have it now. You'll understand why once you see it." He reaches into his pocket and pulls out a velvet bag. "Open it."

My emotions are all over the place right now, jumping around, pummeling my belly and my chest. This gift was something he picked for me before I left him. It hurts to know that I changed our history. My hands all but tremble as I open the bag and pull out a delicate chain. I hold it up and suck in a breath with the sight of a delicate charm at the end of it that looks exactly like the church. "Oh my God, Grayson."

"Turn it over," he orders softly, his voice radiating with his own emotions.

I do as he's commanded to read the engraved message: *Grayson and Mia 8-26-18 Forever.* The day we were to be married. Tears burn my eyes and a vise closes on my chest. "This is perfect, but I wasn't. I have so many regrets, Grayson. So many regrets."

"We've talked about this," he says, cradling my face. "We both made mistakes, but we're here now. That's what matters. And I want you to keep that. But that history between us is a reminder to us both to never to take each other for granted."

"Never," I whisper, and my throat feels like wet cotton. "But I really do think we should get married here. Your parents will be our lucky charm."

"I think we need to be our own lucky charms, you to me and me to you. The lighthouse is our special place." His lips quirk. "We'll tell our wedding planner better late than never."

"Oh God. I don't know if that woman will take us back."

"I'm sure we can convince her." He motions to the church. "You want to go inside?"

"Very much. After I put on my necklace."

He helps me secure it around my neck and then hand-in-hand, we walk into the church and sit down near the front, where we talk about his mother's stories of their perfect wedding day. "I want you to have that kind of perfect day," Grayson says. "I have your dress. They delivered it the week after you left."

"I told them to cancel it," I say, remembering that call with brutal clarity. I'd barely held it together and burst into tears when I'd hung up.

"I forbid them from cancelling it. I wanted *desperately* for you to come back and wear it. You still can. Or any other dress you want. A new location. A new dress—"

"No," I say quickly. "I love that dress. It's *the* dress."

"But does it remind you of the break-up?"

"No. It reminds me of how perfect we were and are." I cover his hand with mine, thinking of something he said to me about our mistakes, about our desire to be the impossible. "I don't want to try to be perfect anymore. I want to revel in how imperfectly wonderful we are. You are the glue that holds all my broken pieces in place. You make me whole again."

He brings my hand to his lips, and when he looks into my eyes and lets me see all his broken pieces, all his pain, and whispers, "As you do me," I can almost feel the world shrinking around us. "New wedding date," he says. "August 26th, 2020."

"The same day we were to be married last year. Because we're embracing all our broken pieces," I say.

"And making us whole again."

Chapter Fifty-Three

Mia

M ia

My fairytale engagement weekend slams to a halt shortly after Grayson pulls the Porsche into the airport and parks. An SUV parks next to us, a vehicle I recognize as belonging to our security team from Walker Security. This leads me to the assumption that they've been following us. Of course, they have. They're supposed to protect us and the façade of being here and beyond the reach of the hell waiting on us back at the city is just that: a façade. The Walker staff were discreet, but they're watching us, they're protecting us from the press and who knows who else. I mean, of course, we need protection. A man I knew well just held a gun to my head and is now dead. A pinched feeling in my chest has me reaching for my door and shoving away my thoughts.

Grayson catches my arm and when I turn to look at him, his expression is tender. He strokes my hair behind my ear, and despite how familiar this action has become, his touch that incredible mix of electricity and calm that defies reason. "You okay?" he asks, his gaze searching my face.

The question is proof of just how intuitive this man is with me, how connected we have always been. It's why I was shocked when I thought he had cheated. It's why I should have known better. "Yes," I say. "Yes, I'm good. I'm engaged to you again. How can I not be good?"

"Considering the circumstances," he says, "easily. If you're having second thoughts about going back, we can stay."

"We can't stay. You have a company to run and I have new staff to help welcome."

"We can make it work," he assures me.

"No," I say firmly, taking his hand and kissing it. "As much as a part of me wants to stay, I want the bad behind us, all of the bad."

"You're sure?"

"Positive. Let's go home."

"We are home, baby. We're together."

My heart swells with his words. "Yes. Yes, we are," I agree. "But our lives we share—I want to reclaim our space."

His eyes warm. This pleases him. "Then we'll go back to the city and claim our lives."

Relieved and somehow more apprehensive than ever—yes, I'm a mess right now, apparently—I reach for the door. Smith from Walker is immediately there, opening it for me. He offers me his hand but I wave him off with a murmured, "Thank you."

He's close, big, tall, and close, with sandy brown hair under a beanie. His fatigue pants and T-shirt are also black. "How very military you look this afternoon."

"I'll take that comment as better than looking tired or stupid, but only slightly."

Considering he's a quiet, formal guy, this reply surprises me and earns him a smile. "You look manly. How's that?"

He laughs, another surprise from this man. "Better than girly, unless that's what you're shooting for of course, but I assure you I am not."

Now, I laugh and Grayson appears by my side. "I think I owe you a thank you, Smith," he says. "You made her laugh. She needs to laugh."

"I'm sure she does," Smith replies. "But this will all be over soon."

Soon, I repeat in my head, stepping free of the car door and allowing Grayson to shut it. *Not soon enough*, I silently add as another tall man with wavy hair steps to Smith's side. He's also wearing all black. Good grief, what do they think is waiting on us in the city? War?

"This is Adrian," Smith says. "He's also quite military tonight in all black, and he tells bad jokes, just not as badly as our man Savage. Close, though."

Grayson and I shake his hand. "How bad are the jokes?" Grayson asks.

"Depends on how bad the situation is," Adrian replies, and we all laugh. "For now, though," Adrian adds, "your chopper awaits, which spares you the very bad random tomato joke presently popping around in my head."

"I think I might need to hear that one," Grayson replies and then adds, "When we get to the city."

"Tomato joke on the agenda, sir," Adrian assures him.

"Grayson," Grayson tells him. "Call me Grayson."

Which doesn't surprise me, and I know considering his exposure to Grayson, it can't surprise Smith. Grayson is humble. He's not an egomaniac who believes his money and power make him better than anyone else.

Adrian gives a nod, his eyes warming with surprise. At the same time, Grayson's hand settles possessively on my lower back, a strong hand. A comforting hand that eases the nerves that seem to be battling some sort of world war in my belly. The four of us enter the small airport, the only guests present, and an attendant greets us, asking us to wait just a few moments before we'll be invited to the runway to board. "We need to take this time to prep you both," Smith says, huddling our little group in the center of pale blue cushioned waiting room chairs.

"Prep us for what?" I ask before Grayson can speak, my world war nerves slicing and dicing my insides all over again. *What* is wrong with me? I've been fine all weekend.

"We've been informed that the press has turned your street back in the city into a campground this evening," Smith replies. "Especially your apartment building."

"Apparently, they anticipated your return," Adrian replies. "We have men working with security at your building to clear our path."

Grayson glances down at me, concern etched in his handsome face. "You're ready for this?"

"I'm ready to have it over with," I say, my arms instinctively folding in front of me, a protective gesture I can't seem to avoid. "All of it."

He studies me with those keen, intelligent eyes before he seems to accept my reply and glances at Smith. "What about the airport? Are they waiting there, too?"

Smith starts talking and I don't hear a word. I don't know what happens, but suddenly in my mind's eye I'm back in the stairwell where Ri attacked me, and I'm running down the stairs, trying to get away from him. My heart begins to race and my palms are clammy. I think I might throw up. "I need to go to the bathroom," I announce, twisting away from Grayson and I don't look at him or anyone. I just need to go now.

Hurrying away, I know where I'm going and I dart left and down a hallway, struggling to open the door that should be easily opened. Finally, I'm inside the single-occupancy bathroom, and I grab the counter, forcing myself to suck in air, or trying to. The desire to throw up is muted, but my need to breathe is insistent. I'm hyperventilating, I think. I can't be sure. I've never actually hyperventilated before. My God. Why is this happening? I try to breathe in again and fail.

"Stop," I order myself and just the act of speaking the word seems to pull air into my lungs. "Stop now." I inhale harshly and this time, I make it happen: I fully fill my lungs, but I don't know how I got to this point. I was fine all weekend long. How am I not fine right now? Because I'm not. This is what Grayson feared: me suddenly losing it. I swore I wouldn't. I almost died but I didn't. So did he. I squeeze my eyes shut, and I'm back in the stairwell with Ri beside me and Grayson in front of me, willing to take a bullet for me. He could have died. My God, he could *have died*.

There's a knock on the door and I hear, "Mia?"

I jolt with Grayson's voice and straighten, willing myself to calm. Death and that man have a bad history. He doesn't need me melting down on him. Hurrying forward, I reach for the handle and my hand frustratingly trembles. I open the door and Grayson is standing there—right there, in front of me—so close I can feel the heat of his perfect body.

"Hi," I say, and just that quickly, his hand is at my waist, and he's stepping into me.

"Hi," he says, his head low, intimately near mine. "You okay, baby?"

"I'm good," I say, and it's not a lie. Now that he is here, with me, touching me, I really am remarkably, incredibly good. My hand finds his face, fingers curling on his jaw. "Let's go home."

"Let's stay a couple of more nights, just you and me, baby. In our own little world."

I want what he suggests, I want it badly, just me and this man and no one else, but going back to the city isn't just about me. It's about him. He has a company under attack because of my stupid mistakes with Ri. "Let's go home," I repeat. "And come back next weekend, knowing that we've faced our dragons, and we're the ones that set the fire."

For a moment, he hesitates, searching my face again, that worry in his eyes etching his brow, but he doesn't push. He laces the fingers of one of his hands with mine and kisses my knuckles. "Let's go home." We walk down the hallway toward the lobby again and a few minutes later we're belted into the chopper.

We're going home. That's what matters.

We're together. That's what matters.

And we're going to claim our happily ever after. I won't let it be any other way.

Chapter Fifty-Four

Grayson

In life, there are defining moments. Moments that create us. Moments that break us. Losing Mia all but broke me. Finding her again healed me. The moment I stood in that stairwell and looked into Ri's eyes, I'd seen evil. I'd seen the end of Mia and that would have been the end of me. The ultimate moment that would break me again, but forever. She survived. I survived. But I didn't believe for one moment that she didn't shatter inside.

We land in the city as the sun sets, the night allowing us the shelter of a moonless night. Storms brew in the distance, somehow off the nearby bay, while others seem to brew right here with us. I don't know what triggered Mia back in the airport, but I know my future wife, and she's sliding into a hornet's nest of emotions. I need to get her home, get her alone, and place everything else on hold.

Once we're on the ground, and in the back of a Walker-driven SUV that's driving us home, Mia pressed close to my side, I text Blake: *Move the meeting to the office tomorrow morning.*

He replies with: *I know this is a bad time, but it only gets worse if we don't prepare for what comes next.*

My jaw wants to snap. I type a reply: *You. Just you.* I've met Blake's wife. She's pleasant, but I don't want Mia to have to perform socially.

He replies quickly: *Understood, but Mia has lived through trauma, and she's another woman. If you change your mind, she might be a good ear for Mia.*

I consider his comment and regroup. I want to be Mia's security blanket, but more than anything I want her to not need one at all. I reply with: *Bring her. And thank you and her.*

"Everything okay?" Mia asks, squeezing my hand.

I lean over and brush my lips over hers. "Just coordinating with Blake. He's bringing his wife," I add, not certain if I've mentioned this to her before now. "Is that okay with you?"

"Of course. Anyone who can help us get this behind us, and get Ri's influence out of your operation, is exactly what we need."

A profoundly Mia response. She's selfless. She's giving. She's a warrior. Somehow I need her to see that feeling shaken and scared, human responses to trauma doesn't change that. "Are you hungry?"

"A little," she says, which isn't Mia. She's always hungry.

"How about our favorite Chinese place?" I ask, trying to offer her what she's craving. Normalcy. A walk down memory lane, from our past, the part we both missed.

Her lips curve. "Yes. I'd like that."

"Now, or after Blake and Kara leave?" I query.

"After they leave." Her delicate little brow furrows. "Well, unless we need to feed them?"

"They know we need time to decompress."

"Then after they leave." She smiles again. "Like old times."

"Like old times."

A few minutes later, Adrian turns right instead of left, and my cellphone rings. It's Blake. "Why am I certain I won't like this call?"

"There's a news team that just brought in cameras. Someone tipped them off that you're back. They're at every door. You're going to deal with this tomorrow morning. Don't do it tonight. I reserved the Ritz presidential suite for you. Take it, man. We'll meet you there."

A muscle in my jaw begins to tick and I glance at Mia, prepared to explain. "I heard," she says. "I don't have any work clothes with me."

Blake responds to her through me. "Kara and I can go to your place and grab what you need." I intend to repeat this to Mia, but she holds up a hand.

"I heard again." She presses her fingers to her temples and nods, before casting me a sideways look. "If it's what we need to do, it's what we need to do."

"We'll meet you at the hotel," I say, and then call out to Smith and Adrian. "The Ritz," before I speak to Blake again. "How long are we going to be stuck there?"

"I'd give it a week. We've already made arrangements to get you in and out of your offices tomorrow without challenge."

I don't ask how. I trust Blake. The problem is that my staff won't. They'll be overwhelmed. They'll be shaken. "Like I said. We'll see you at the hotel." I disconnect, and speak to Mia. "Sorry, baby. Not the homecoming you were hoping for, I know."

"But it's still the right decision. You have to be at the office tomorrow. *We* have to be at the office tomorrow. Everyone needs to see that we're good. That we're okay."

I cup her face and tilt her gaze to mine. "You, woman, are my superhero."

"Funny," she says, covering my hand with hers. "I was going to say the same about you. Room service in bed with you is my new goal for the night. I mean, how many girls get to sleep in the presidential suite with her future husband and it's not even her honeymoon yet?"

"At this moment, I believe my father would say, 'You chose well, my son. You chose well.'"

"And then he'd order us one of everything on the dessert menu," Mia says. "Because that's how he dealt with things. He always found the good stuff everywhere."

"Are you suggesting we order everything on the dessert menu?" I tease.

"Well, sir, if you want to curl a girl's toes, that's certainly an option."

"Or?"

"I'll let you figure that one out." She kisses me and laughs, and that laugh is a symphony in a firestorm. It's a promise that at least for now, she's in a better place. And it's up to me to keep her there, which I'm getting the feeling from Blake might be a larger than hoped for task. Otherwise, he wouldn't be bringing his wife as a back-up.

Which leads to the question: Is Ri so damn devious that he's still coming at me from the grave?

Chapter Fifty-Five

Mia

We arrive at the hotel and Walker is cautious, arranging our entry through a side door, where we won't be spotted. That they feel the need to do this does nothing to calm my nerves. What does calm my nerves is Grayson. We exit the backseat of the SUV and his hand is at my waist: protective, possessive, and amazingly, I feel the sizzle of his touch. That's how reactive I am to this man. I'm wearing a coat, I'm a nervous wreck, and I'm aware of him on every level.

Once we're inside the hotel, we are herded to a staff elevator and it's a quick ride before we're inside a room that is larger than many apartments. There's a living area, dining room, bedroom, and sitting area. There's even a kitchen. I know this because it's not my first time in a Ritz presidential suite with Grayson.

For now, we're in the entryway, and Grayson helps me off with my coat while Smith and Adrian crowd the hall next to us. Grayson hangs up my coat and I turn to watch him shrug out of his own, all that perfect muscle and manliness a welcome distraction. He watches me watch him, his stare burning as it meets mine, his hands catching my arms. I'm hauled forward against Grayson as Smith and Adrian are smart enough to head on into the living room.

"If you keep looking at me like that, we're going to the bedroom and shutting the door."

My teeth scrape my bottom lip and slip away, my intent is to be playful, but that's not what happens. "I love you," I whisper.

His eyes soften, worry I didn't intend to stir, bleeding into them. "I love you, too. Baby,—"

There's a knock on the door. I push to my toes and kiss him. "I'm good. Remember?"

"No. No, you're not, but we'll walk the fire together." He kisses me hard and fast. "Let's get this over with." He sets me away from him and Smith is now back in our small space.

"I'll get that," he says.

The degree at which we're being protected feels excessive, as if there's something we don't know. I need out of this tiny space and I quickly hurry down the hallway to the living room, where Adrian is standing in front of the desk off the right wall, arms folded in front of him. I pass him by and sit down on the cream-colored couch, setting my purse on the simple but expensive walnut coffee table.

Hushed voices sound in the hallway in what is obviously a discreet conversation. A conversation they want to have without me. Adrian seems to react. He sits down in the chair next to me. "There was a mama tomato, a papa tomato, and six baby tomatoes. One of the babies falls behind and the mother rushes to her child and yells, 'Catch Up!'"

I laugh despite myself. "That is the stupidest joke *ever.*"

"Then I'll assume that you haven't heard many stupid jokes."

It's in that moment that Grayson and Smith appear with Blake—a tall, good-looking man, with long dark hair tied at his nape. Also present is Kara, Blake's wife, a pretty, petite brunette who like Blake is in jeans and a Walker Security T-shirt. She was there the night Ri attacked me. She's someone I trust.

"Hi, Mia," Kara greets. "Please tell me he didn't tell you the tomato joke."

I laugh. "He did." I eye Grayson, whose green-eyed stare is fixed on my face. "You missed the world's stupidest joke."

He rounds the coffee table and sits down next to me. "You can tell me later."

"Or not," I say, giving Adrian a tease. "I don't think I can tell it as perfectly as he did."

Kara claims the chair opposite Adrian, and Blake perches on the arm. Smith leans on the desk behind Adrian. Everyone falls into an awkward silence. My teeth are back on my lip and I decide this has become a nervous thing for me. My fingers are back in my palms and I glance around the room. "What's going on?"

Grayson folds one of my hands in his bigger one. "Nothing unexpected," he assures me. "The press are nuts."

"We've been working with Eric this weekend," Blake interjects. Eric being Grayson's right-hand man, best friend, and a literal savant. Eric's involvement is good but not a surprise. They've made a fortune together. They've built trust. And Grayson has talked to him over the weekend, as he did all the key players in the company. But it's Eric who is always welcome and in the middle of all things Grayson. "That bastard's brilliant," Blake says. "Between his genius and my hacking, we'll do what we need to do to end this."

"End *this?*" I ask. "I thought Ri *was* this? And Ri is gone. Are we talking about the bad players he placed inside Grayson's operation?"

"Exactly," Blake says.

"Ri contacted the Dungeon," Blake explains, "a powerful underground operation. Fool that he is, they literally inherit part of his fortune if Grayson goes down."

I gasp and look at Grayson. "I don't even want to know what 'goes down' means."

"It's vaguely defined," Blake says. "Too vaguely for my comfort. I assume there is a broader definition we haven't managed to discover."

Bile rises in my throat. "I can't believe this is happening."

"I'm not going down," Grayson assures me. "Not by any method of defining those words."

"They had a three-month window to reach this goal," Blake explains, "which I know from hacking Ri's computer and finding the agreement which he signed. It's on file with his attorney, who's being pulled in for questioning on Monday."

"Three months." I can feel the blood drain from my face. "And they have a plan. Surely they do."

"The FBI knows what's going on," Blake assures me. "They aren't deaf, dumb, or stupid."

"And Blake is one of the best hackers alive," Kara quickly adds. "He and Eric together will find out what's planned and head off any attacks."

"Who does something like this?" Guilt stabs at me, a blade that twists and grinds. "I did this." I turn to Grayson. "I fell for everything he threw at us and I left you exposed."

"He would have found a way to come at me no matter what, baby. You know he would have."

"He's right," Blake says. "I found proof that he hired the Dungeon before he ever set Grayson up and got rid of you. That's how long this has been going on."

"Got rid of me," I whisper and my gaze is now locked on some fruit arrangement on the table. I don't really know why hotels are obsessed with fruit. I don't know why I'm thinking of fruit. I guess it's easier than where my head is going otherwise. But I go there anyway, and I don't mean to say it out loud, but I do. "He might have been better off if I'd stayed away." It's out before I can stop the words, and I don't even have to wait to know Grayson will not like this answer. I turn to him. I turn to him, and he's already turned to me and the air is charged, the nerve I've hit between us raw and real.

We're oblivious to our audience. It's just me and him. It's us. And I've weighed us down with the very baggage we're trying to leave behind.

Chapter Fifty-Six

Mia

M^{ia} Grayson catches my arms. "Don't do that," he orders, his voice gruff in a way Grayson is rarely gruff. "He wins if he tears us apart again. Listen to Blake. He had a plan even before they came at you and me together."

"Maybe breaking us up would have been enough. Maybe it would have been enough. Now, your family business, your father's heart and soul, your heart and soul, is at risk."

"Everyone who needs to know, knows," Blake says. "And the bad players, as you called them, don't know we know." Grayson sucks in a breath, his broad chest expanding and when he releases me, his hands don't return to me. I want them on my body, but they're now on his legs, his fingers pressing into hard muscle.

"Grayson is not going down," Blake continues. "The bad players are. And the most important thing you can do is act like this is behind you. We need them to think that we're oblivious. This is why we wanted to meet tonight. You and Grayson together tells the world good things will follow. Show off that rock I'm seeing on your finger. Enjoy your life. We got you. We got this."

"We do," Kara says. "We have this and you."

I nod, but I'm aware of Grayson not touching me and not looking at me in such a deep, gut-wrenching way, that that's all I have to offer. I listen as Blake covers the plan. Open security until the press dies down. Then Walker will go covert operation on us. They'll watch us. We'll communicate our steps with them, but no one will know that we're still protected.

"We'll leave you two to your night," Blake says, and he and Kara stand. Adrian does as well and Smith steps into our circle as Grayson and I push to our feet.

"We're in the next room over," Smith says. "We being me and Adrian, but we'll likely rotate in some other men. Don't go anywhere without us right now."

Grayson gives him a nod and Kara catches my attention. "Lunch this week?"

I like her. We connected easily when we first met. And I trust her. "I'd like that."

"It's a date then," she says. "I'll call you tomorrow. Oh, and we brought you a couple of suitcases full of things. Sorry. I know that's kind of an invasion of privacy."

"Thank you for doing that," I say quickly, but she's right. It is. It's weird but still appreciated.

"The bags are by the door," Blake offers.

A few more words are exchanged between everyone and Grayson walks them all to the door. And he does so in that controlled way I know well. His spine is extra straight. His stride extra measured. He's owning the moment. He's forcing his control. He's angry. He's really angry.

I sit down. I grab the cushion from beside me and hug it to me. I toss the pillow away. I cannot sit here a minute longer.

Rounding the table and couch, I walk to a large half window behind the living area and stand there. I know the minute Grayson returns, and not because of his soundless footsteps. I feel him. My skin tingles. My belly flutters. Don't ask me why, when he's angry and I'm upset, but my sex clenches. And then he's there, his hands on my body a blessed relief, turning me around to face him. "We are either forever or not at all. Decide now."

"Don't do that, Grayson."

"Do what? Ask you to marry me? Ask you to spend the rest of your life with me? Because that is all I'm guilty of right now."

"I don't want to hurt you. I don't want to be the reason you, you who are such an amazing person, suffers."

"I suffered without you. I suffered just hearing you say I might be better off without you. I can't do 'maybe' with you. If that's where we're headed, you need to tell me right now. If you weren't ready, if I pushed—"

"You didn't. God, no. You didn't."

"And yet, those words came out of your mouth. Those words I never want to hear again."

Somehow in that moment, he's the refuge I seek and everything I'm running from. He wants to protect me. I want to protect him.

I can't be his destruction, but as I stare into his green eyes, the shadows there drenched in torment, I know that I am his refuge, too. His soul fills my soul as mine does his.

A tornado of emotion rips through me, the debris of a year of heartache and hell leaving me bleeding inside in ways that I won't survive without this man. I throw my arms around him. "I'm sorry. I'm scared. I need you and love you." I pull back to look at him. "I'm sorry."

"Do you want to marry me?"

His voice is low but somehow intense, his eyes shadowed, and I feel a pinch in my chest. "I can't believe you're asking me that. More than life itself."

"Then that means there is no obstacle we don't go through together. *Understand?*"

It's not a question but a demand. "I want to be the best thing that ever happened to you, not the worst."

"You are. Ri was the problem. He still is. You didn't do this."

"I let him—"

"We let him. We've talked about all the ways we let that happen. It's behind us. If that can't happen—"

"It can. You're right. I'm not myself right now. Something happened at the airport."

His hands frame my face. "Because there can't be an earthquake without aftershocks. You were attacked, baby. You're human. You're going to feel the shock and the aftermath."

He's right. I know he's right. But it's not just me feeling the aftermath. It's him, too, and his company, and I'm terrified about just how bad those aftershocks might be when they hit. I don't say that, though. That's not what he needs to hear right now.

"And my cure is you. And Chinese food. I think we both need Chinese food."

He rewards me with a curve of his sexy lips and with it, the air shifts, our moods soften. For now, we will enjoy each other. Tomorrow, we'll fight for each other.

Chapter Fifty-Seven

Mia

Grayson and I order food and then organize the bags Blake and Kara brought us. I hang a few garments up, and decide the discomfort of having only what someone else packed us is not rooted in a lack of privacy. It's about the reasons we're here. It's about Ri. A memory of that stairwell, of Grayson standing in front of me and Ri behind me, punches at my mind, and I forcefully shove it aside. When I turn away from the closet and find Grayson setting up his side of the sink, that horrid moment is washed from my mind, at least for now.

Fifteen minutes later, we've laughed at the one razor I'm going to steal from him, and changed into our sleep clothes that are really our "before we get naked clothes." For me, that's boxers and a tank. For him, it's sweats and a T-shirt. Grayson flips on the television in the bedroom to his favorite true crime channel. We have always watched the cases and each played prosecutor or defender as we litigated it as if it were our own. Tonight, the talk is of someone being shot, it's nerve-wracking.

There's a knock at the door and Grayson heads in that direction to grab our food. I snap up the remote and change the channel to the one spot I know will be safe: Hallmark. Grayson returns and we settle onto the comfy hotel bed to prepare to chow down, as my father would say. It's not home, but it's cozy, and we're together, playing house until we're actually in our house, which is actually an apartment. Once my plate of lo mein is open and tempting my watering mouth, I sigh. "I missed this place."

He opens the egg rolls and offers me one. "When was the last time you had it?"

I happily claim a crispy eggroll. "Last year. With you." I wet my lips, suddenly dreading and somehow craving his reply to the same question. "You?"

"The same."

"Yeah?"

"Yeah," he confirms.

I am pleased with this news and warmed in ways that I shouldn't be warmed. He shouldn't have had to give up things he loved because I stupidly left. But he did. And I did. "I didn't do any of our things when we were apart. Those things made me need you too badly to survive."

"Well, I wish you would have done them then."

I tilt my head and study him. "You do?"

"Yes. Then maybe you would have hurt too badly to stay away." He takes a bite of the eggroll and gives an approving nod before indicating the TV. "Is this the one where he proposes on a horse or at an ice rink?" His eyes twinkle with mischief, absolutely no judgment in him for my channel change.

"At the lighthouse," I amend. "It's the one with the perfect proposal."

The air sizzles, and he says, "Is that right?"

"Yes. The girl finally got smart and came home." I eye the hotel. "To her man. And she doesn't even care that they're now living at the Ritz." Unbidden, there's a pinch in my chest, some tiny part of me fearing that I'll never really get back to our real home. That stupid, self-defeating part of me that I barely know as me and that keeps returning to that stairwell.

Grayson must read between my lightly spoken words, because he leans over, nuzzles my neck and whispers, "You want me to tell you how the story ends?"

I ease back to stare into those simmering green eyes. "How?"

"The heroine eats Chinese food, gets naked with her future husband, and then later marries her fiancé at the lighthouse. In the original dress she ordered for the first wedding, or any dress she wishes."

"Because he saved her dress. He held onto it because he held onto me." Heart swelling, I reach over and touch his jaw, as I add, "And she lives happily ever after, with the most incredible man any woman could ever love."

He kisses my fingers. "After they eat Chinese food, right?"

"Yes." I laugh. "After they eat Chinese food."

And so, we do. We eat. And laugh. And watch the movie, both of us betting on when the peck of a kiss Hallmark will allow, actually happens. When finally we climb into bed, it's naked. When finally we sleep, it's with his big, wonderful body wrapped around mine. And I don't let myself lay there and think about the day ahead or the reasons we're in the hotel room. I shut my eyes and think about the lighthouse, my dress, and the moment I get to say "I do."

Chapter Fifty-Eight

Mia

Mia

Morning comes with a knock of reality. Grayson and I are back together, but we can't just go home. I've never needed home quite so badly. Grayson feels it, too. I see it in the sharp lines of his handsome face, and the silent intense way he presses me into the corner of the shower and takes me hard and fast. I know this man. He's on edge, and that worries me. Just how deep in trouble are we?

Fortunately, Kara has managed to pack my favorite pale pink silk blouse, and my lucky black skirt and jacket. Lucky because I won my first case in this very outfit. I dress with one goal in mind: standing by my man and finding our path to a better place—no, our path home. Together. I walk into the living area of the suite to find coffee and pastries on the coffee table, and my man dressed to kill in a gray pin-striped suit with a light blue tie. He's also standing with Adrian and Blake and I'm pretty sure no one has heard the tomato joke because they aren't smiling.

"Morning, Mia," Blake says, while Adrian offers me a nod.

I murmur a reply but it's Grayson I'm focused on. "What's wrong?" I ask, stepping in front of him.

Blake and Adrian head for the door, and my stomach knots. "Grayson, what's wrong?"

He catches my waist and pulls me to him. "You know how much I love you, right?"

I swallow hard, my voice rasping from my throat. "*What's* wrong?"

"There was a hit piece done on me this morning."

Grayson isn't rattled by hit pieces, which is why I ask, "And?"

"The reporter, who was clearly set-up by Ri's hacker hires, has photos of me with any woman I had contact with when we were split up."

"Women that you slept with?" The question rasps like blades from my throat, painful and sharp.

"No. Actually, I didn't sleep with any of the women they put in the article. Two were clients. One I went on one date with and couldn't stop thinking about you. There wasn't a second. I now have to call the clients to apologize. Mia—"

My hand comes down on his chest. "Stop. I don't want to hear about it anymore or see it, for that matter."

"Even TMZ picked it up, baby."

I inhale and let out a breath. "Okay."

"Okay?"

"It's done, Grayson. You didn't cheat on me. And even if these women were bedmates—"

"They weren't."

"I believe you, but even if they had been your bedmates, I left you. You didn't think you'd ever be right here with me again and neither did I. Let's just go get this next week or two behind us."

"Which is why I have a proposal for you."

"You already gave me the greatest proposal of all." I hold up my ring. "Twice, and honestly, Grayson, after I let Ri beat us, sometimes I don't think I deserve to be back here with you now."

"Don't do that," he says, pulling me hard to him. "*We* let it happen. And we are not going to let it happen ever again."

"That's right," I agree. "Let's go face this down. Together."

"I want to grant an interview to a high-profile reporter. I want *us* to grant the interview. I want the world to know—"

I push to my toes and kiss him. "I don't care about what the world thinks. I care about you and I care about us."

His hand flattens on my lower back. "There was a time when you feared the world would think you slept your way to the top."

"And then there's today when I don't. No one who knows us believes that's true." I push past the knot in my belly. "Fool me once, shame on you. Fool me twice, shame on me. He doesn't get to win this time."

His hands come down on my face. "I love you."

"I know you love me. And you know I love you. It's enough, Grayson. It's more than enough. It's everything. I can handle this. Trust me not to let you down."

"Mia—"

I press my lips to his and this time his hand cups the back of my head and his tongue strokes mine, deep and sultry.

A few minutes later, we're in the hallway with Blake in front of us and Adrian behind us. Once we're all in the elevator, Blake starts handing out instructions. "The press hasn't found you here. We'll be fine exiting the side door, but once we're at your offices, all bets are off. The press is everywhere." He eyes Grayson. "Reese Summer is going to meet you here tonight."

I look between them. "Why are we meeting with a criminal law attorney that doesn't even work for our firm?"

"Because he's the best of the best and I trust him," Blake replies.

"Why do we need him?" I counter.

"We're not giving the FBI a chance to twist anything Ri has done into guilt that lands in the wrong place," Blake says. "And we want someone who has no conflict of interest and a reputation for only defending the innocent."

"The innocent?" I demand. "Grayson was attacked. He's a victim the FBI should be protecting."

Grayson slides his arm around me. "Relax, baby. We're making sure this doesn't just end. It ends our way."

I've done everything I can to block out Ri holding me at gunpoint and then dying right in front of me. But it's not his death haunting me now, it's the evil in that man that still lives on.

Chapter Fifty-Nine

Mia

M ia

Nerves I don't want to feel jump around in my belly as we load up in the black Escalade with us in the back, Adrian behind the wheel and Blake in the passenger seat. Grayson and I are side by side, his leg pressed to my leg, his hand on my knee, just beneath my skirt. His hand is warm, strong, possessive, and after fearing I'd never feel his touch again, wonderful. What's not wonderful is the prison of press and past history that seek to control this day, but the sooner we're past this awkward stuff, the better.

The drive is short, and good Lord, when we turn the corner to our destination street, the building that houses the offices of Bennett Enterprises is swarming with reporters. Adrian pulls us to a side entrance where Grayson exits and helps me out, and to my shock, we enter the building without much trouble, and with relief, we head upstairs in a service elevator. The space is small to share with three large, testosterone-loaded men, and Grayson is quick to pull me in front of him and hold me close. Tension radiates off of him and it's then that I realize just how much pressure he's under. He's literally got an empire on his shoulders, the FBI breathing down his throat, and TMZ and the gossip rags won't even allow him to just be secure with us. I need to be the person who eases his stress, not adds to it.

Adrian exits the car first and Grayson and I follow with Blake on our heels. We're now in a hallway that is a short walk to the main elevator banks. Grayson slides his arm over my shoulders. "You nervous?" he murmurs near my ear.

"I'm good," I promise, but the truth is I'm not sure he is and that has me determined to be his lighthouse in stormy waters, or at least a boat, that won't sink and keeps him from drowning.

I halt and give Grayson a look. He eyes Blake over my head. "We need a minute."

Blake and Adrian move ahead of us, which means that obviously, they feel we're now secure. I want to believe that's true, but Ri has involved other people in his hate for Grayson, bad people, that it's hard to know if we can let our guards down and when. "We're good, Grayson. You don't have to worry about me, or gossip, or Ri's attacks through other people. Go to work and do what you do, focus on the challenge which is not us."

He catches my hip and walks me to him. "Where is this coming from, Mia?"

"I know you, Grayson. I can almost feel the weight on your shoulders pressing on my own. Ri isn't done attacking you and there are people out there who would hurt you just to hurt you. Because you're rich and good-looking. I want to make you stronger—"

"You do, baby. You abso-fucking-lutely do."

He says that but it's not completely true, not right this moment, but I'm going to fix that. I have to fix that. I flatten my hand on his chest, the silk of his tie, and the thunder of his heart under my palm. "I screwed up, Grayson. You're the love of my life. I know you're mine. I know I'm yours. *You* need to know, too, and know nothing touches us ever again. Set us aside, walk in there, and work that Bennett magic and get this over with. Find the bad eggs, get them out, and let's move on."

He studies me for several long beats, and then kisses me hard on the lips, ending that kiss with my lipstick on his mouth. I laugh and wipe his mouth. "It's not your shade."

He winks and links my arm with his arm and as we start walking, the bond we share, present and strong, and I can almost feel the weight on his shoulder ease just a little bit. He's lighter now, and yet there's a razor-sharp edge to him as well. He's ready to play ball and win. And any nerves I'd had about my return here fade. Being here means being with him, passionately engaged in his life, his company, and, no—our life. This is where I belong.

We round the corner to the elevators and Grayson motions Blake forward. Adrian stays behind by the elevators. Not long afterward, I'm swarmed with warm welcomes, hugs, and lots of familiar faces. I'm instantly back home. Oh yes, indeed, I belong here. I should never have left, but I will not let regret dictate the future. I'm here to stay.

We eventually make it into the executive offices that house only a dozen people out of the thousand-plus of Bennett employees in the building, and we head to Grayson's office. It's there that I'm greeted by his secretary Nancy, who's fortyish, with black-rimmed glasses, and quite lovely in all ways.

"Mia!" She shoots up from her seat and rushes around her desk. I'm pulled into a hug, and she whispers in my ear. "Screw TMZ."

I laugh and ease back to smile at her. "I'm not upset by that. We both know it's not true and—" I show her my ring.

She squeals and eyes Grayson. "When?"

"We're working on the details, but I'd do it today if we could," he assures her.

"No eloping," Nancy scolds. "You two have waited too long for this and I want to plan the wedding of the century." She eyes Grayson. "Don't let this mess dictate how you get married. Of course, TMZ is calling you a manwhore now, and they'll be trying to chopper over your wedding later. They are such whores themselves."

Grayson's displeasure with the topic washes over his features and his jaw sets hard. I can almost feel him bristling with the control he doesn't own right now but wants back. His eyes glint hard and I watch determination fill his stare. He doesn't just want it back. He's about to take it back.

Blake rejoins us at that moment—we'd lost him back in the lobby, and he's not alone. The good-looking man with him, who has tattoos peeking from under his suit jacket, and intense blue eyes, is Eric, his best friend. My friend, too.

"Welcome back, Mia," he greets, and to my surprise, he pulls me into a hug—Eric is not a hugger—and whispers in my ear. "He wasn't whole without you."

"Nor was I," I say, feeling a bit choked up, because Eric doesn't just say things to say things. Eric isn't a fluffer or a "feel-good" kind of guy, but he's just managed to make me feel quite good. That is until he releases me and Blake motions to Grayson's door.

"We need to talk," Blake says, and now he's the intense one, and that doesn't read like good news.

Chapter Sixty

Grayson

C ontrol.

There are very few people in this world that really know how much I value and need control. Mia knows. Eric knows. Right now, I do not feel in control. At all. It's driving me mad. I catch Mia's hand and pull her ahead of me into my office, a possessive, protective action, I know, but I can't help it. I just endured my enemy holding a gun on her head, and he's not done coming at me, and us, yet.

Blake shuts the door, and we converge around my conference table. Eric tosses a file down in the center. "Statistically," he says, savant that he is, "those are the ten employees hired in the past year, most likely to be dirty. However," he adds, "statistically, the odds of you being burned by one of those people is eighty percent less likely than you being burned by someone you know and trust, someone close to you."

"Me?" Mia bristles, when Mia doesn't bristle easily. "Are you talking about me?"

"Easy, baby," I murmur. "He's not talking about you."

"Are you?" she asks, focused on Eric.

"The odds of it being you are about even with it being me, Mia," he states, "which is ten percent, statistically speaking only. Neither of us is going to burn Grayson. And you know I have an intimate understanding of being burned by those close to me."

He means his family, who own an empire of their own and treat him like a bastard—which technically he is, as his mother wasn't married to his father, but that's beside the point. They treat him horribly. "If I thought you were the bad guy here," he adds, "I'd be handing Grayson a drink and talking to him one on one."

"We'd all need a drink to tell Grayson that shit," Blake adds. "The bottom line here is that we all know Grayson is still under attack. The FBI now knows that Grayson is under attack."

"How do we know the FBI isn't a part of that?" I ask. "We know the DA's office has dirty players. If the DA's office can do it, why not the FBI?"

"We have enough documentation to cover his ass," he says, "but when you talk about someone near and dear to Grayson, you're talking a bigger exposure."

There's a knock on the door, and Davis, my second confidant to Eric, and my personal attorney walks in. "You rang?"

Blake motions him forward and Davis, a tall, regal, looking man, in his thirties, with dark hair and a short, neatly trimmed beard, joins us at the table. Once he's up to speed, the debate begins. "What about Nancy?" Davis asks. "She knows everything you do."

"No," I say. "It's not Nancy. She's loyal, and she makes as much as a seasoned attorney."

"Honestly, Grayson is so good to everyone. Why would anyone who knows him burn him?"

"You'd be surprised what people will do for a big payday," Eric says, tapping the folder on the desk. "I put together the top twenty people closest to Grayson for Blake."

"We're going to start digging," Blake confirms.

"I included my banking information and welcomed him to dig into my life," Eric adds.

"I don't have much to offer, but what's mine is Grayson's," Mia says. "And we're signing a prenup anyway."

I catch her hand, lacing her fingers under the table, at the mention of a topic that we've fought about since long before my father passed. I'd been against it and Mia for it, but my opinion had changed when my father told me that he had one with my mother, who was the love of his life. Of course, I know Mia loves me. I know she isn't after my money, but my father reminded me that life is long and hard, and I want to know she stays because she keeps loving me. So rather than cheat her in a prenup, he instructed me to be generous—to make sure that if she falls out of love, she leaves. I'm damn sure not going to let her fall out of love with me.

"I'll offer up full access to my everything," Davis interjects. "I don't work here, but I'm close to Grayson, really fucking close and a data source to all his private affairs." He eyes Blake. "I'd welcome some help ensuring I've secured his documents." He grimaces.

"Though from what I understand about this group involved, it's probably too late."

"We'll take a look at your data for breaches this afternoon," Blake offers before eyeing the table. "To be clear," he adds, "this threat has a three-month expiration. After which, no one with any skin in the game remains engaged. That's when the payout expires." He motions to Davis. "I brought him up to speed. Everyone here knows that Ri hired the Dungeon." He doesn't give anyone time to reply. "*I know,*" he adds, "that three months feels like forever, but it's not forever. That said, Eric has one additional statistic that brain bomb of his conjured up that we need to discuss. It's a conclusion I came to without his complicated brain, which means we landed at the same place in different ways and need to take notice."

My gaze sharpens on Eric. "Why do I know I'm not going to like this bomb?"

He doesn't hold back. "I believe Mia will be a target," he says.

Mia hugs herself. "Because I'm seen as the traitor."

"No," I say. "No one sees you as a traitor, Mia."

"You just had a gun held to your head," Blake corrects. "That affected you, whether you've admitted that yet or not."

"And you're newly back in Grayson's life," Eric adds. "New can mean vulnerable, but the good news in this, Mia, is that we can use that to our advantage."

"Exactly," Blake agrees. "Because we'll be watching and ready and so will you."

"She's not bait," I say, no give to my voice.

"No," Blake confirms. "But she is a target. Ri saw her as that and I guarantee you he made sure the Dungeon knew her as that as well."

"Target," I repeat. "Are you telling us she's in danger?" Blake hesitates and that control I don't have spirals furthers out of reach.

His lips press into a hard line, and he says, "We can't rule that out as a possibility."

Chapter Sixty-One

Mia

I'm a target.

Again.

I wait for the panic to rush over me, but it doesn't. There's something powerful about knowledge and being prepared, I decide, which is why I say, "At least we know this time."

"I'm taking Mia out of the country for three months," Grayson announces.

"No," I insist, turning to Grayson. "No. I'm not willing to run from this. I know this is unsettling, Grayson, but I also know you want to control this situation as much as I do."

"Which is why we're leaving the city."

"I'm exactly who we want them to target. Let's catch these assholes and get back to our life."

"This feels too obvious anyway," Davis says. "She was already a target. Any logical asshole will know we'll be watching her."

"Too obvious are words that too often get people in trouble," Blake snaps. "The enemy believes you think that and makes it work for them. Look," he leans on the table, "let's just play this cautious but not extreme, Grayson. You both can go about your normal days, as soon as the fucking press allows it, and we'll keep you and Mia safe."

"Hurting Mia is the way to hurt me," he says. "The rest, I don't give a shit about."

"Of course, you do," I say. "This is your father's brainchild that you and Eric have turned into something he'd be proud of. We're staying here and fighting for it. And I have a client who needs me right now, not to mention my excitement to define my role with the company, and just go home. I want to go home."

There's a knock on the door, and Nancy walks in, shuts the door, and leans on it. "My God. A temp came in for one of the attorneys. He was digging through the desks. He was a reporter. He's locked in the conference room. Security called the police."

Grayson stares at her for several long beats, which might seem like a non-reaction, but those of us who know him know otherwise. He's simmering hot inside, irritated by the lack of control he's experiencing and I truly believe the only reason he hasn't taken that control back is that his every move is dictated by fear for me. I don't know how to fix that, but I know I have to, we have to because shackling his instincts isn't good for him, us, or the company and its employees.

"Give every employee on staff here in the corporate offices a bonus equal to their Christmas bonus," he responds, "including yourself, Nancy. It's the least I can do for the hell you're all enduring."

She blinks and instead of greedily just accepting, she says, "That's a lot of money, Grayson."

"And this is a bloody mess. Do it. Make it happen today."

"Okay. Yes. I'll get with accounting now. Do you want to press charges?"

"I'll handle the reporter," Davis offers. "I'll be right there, Nancy."

"Thanks, Davis." She turns a questioning look on Grayson.

"Go make that payday happen," he says.

She nods and exits the office. Then, as if he's read my mind, as often it seems he does, his gaze shifts and lands on me. "You're right. We need to take our life back." His attention shifts to Blake. "This is why I just want to do an actual sit-down in-depth interview, not a quick press conference, and get this over with. We need the fascination with all things us to end."

"I don't disagree with that strategy," Blake replies, "but you need to talk to Reese Summer first."

"I don't like this idea that Grayson needs an attorney," I state. "Why does he have to defend himself from the FBI, who should be protecting him right now?"

"You're an attorney," Davis replies. "You know how well we insulate our clients."

"I get that," I say, "but it angers me that Grayson is getting hit on all sides."

"We don't have to defend if we attack first," Eric says, eyeing Blake. "You and I need to find a way to smoke out the problem. I'm up for an all-day, all-nighter if you are."

"I'm all fucking in," Blake says. "And so is my team. I suggest you bring your savant brain to our offices where we can hook it up to our resources."

Eric agrees. "Done."

"I for one, nix the interview idea," Davis interjects, swinging back to the prior topic. "Reporters are vampires. They'll take this FBI mess and twist it."

Eric scoffs. "Are you fucking serious, Davis? They're already doing that. We need to do reputation damage control, and Grayson and Mia together do that better than anyone else possibly could." He eyes Grayson. "Grayson?"

A thought hits me and I push into the conversation. "I know some people hate Grayson for being Grayson—rich and powerful and good-looking—but he's a good man. The people who work here know he's a good man. I have a hard time believing that won't come across in an interview. And I have to believe that some of those people who came here to hurt Grayson will change their minds."

"But some won't," Blake states. "We just need to make sure anything that comes at us is a sideswipe, not a permanent dent."

Meaning they need to make sure I don't end up dead. Or that's my assumption, though it seems a fairly good one right after having a gun held to my head. It's in the air, hanging there, a heavy rock that wants to smash me right in the head.

"One more thing," Blake adds. "Don't assume the attack will come from here at the offices. It could come from an unknown, outside source. Or even someone close to you in your personal life. I'll be in touch on the Summer meeting."

And with that rock thrown, the room scatters and empties, the door shutting to leave me and Grayson alone in his office.

Chapter Sixty-Two

Mia

Control.

We're back to Grayson needing control.

I can feel it in the crackle of the air, even before he catches my hand and walks me to him. "I want right now," he murmurs, his head tilted low to mine. "Many things. You know that, right?"

When this man says he wants, I want, and my nipples immediately pucker while my sex clenches. "I do know," I say, my voice low, a rasp that tells a story: I'm right here with him, affected in every way.

His hands come down on my arms. "I want to pull your skirt up and fuck you right here on the table. I want to spank you. I want to take you to some exotic place and keep you naked in bed for three fucking months." His voice is low, guttural. His hands come down on my arms and he pulls back to look at me. "But more than anything, I want to go home with you. And we are. Tonight."

"Tonight?" I ask hopefully. "Are you sure?"

"One hundred percent, baby. You're right. We need our life back and I'll be damned if I'm going to let Ri continue to take that from us, but I need you to make a deal with me."

"What deal?" I ask cautiously.

"If Blake identifies a credible threat against you, we get on a plane and hunker down somewhere until this is over. Fair enough?"

"I don't have a death wish. I can live with that, quite literally."

His cellphone buzzes with a text and he snakes it from his pocket, his jaw tensing as he reads the message. "What is it?"

He types a reply and shoves his phone back into his pocket. "That was Dean Rourke, the head of the hotel operations. The press is hounding him as well." He runs a hand over his goatee, frustration in the action when he rarely allows an outward reaction to anything.

LISA RENEE JONES

He turns away, walking to the window and pressing his hands on the bar dividing the center of the glass, looks out over the jut of buildings framed by the ocean. I do the same, but I'm looking at him, not the city. "What are you thinking?"

His glances over at me. "I have a tendency to hit hard and fast and take control."

"You? Really? Is that what you call wanting to confront the press, hide me away, and—"

"Elope and call you my wife now, when I know you deserve the wedding of a century."

I push off the window to face him and he does the same, facing me. "You want to elope?"

He catches my waist, steps into me. "The idea of waiting another minute to marry you, when the next minute is never guaranteed, makes me insane." He strokes my hair behind my ear. "But then we both know that I'm in that mode I get in where I want—"

"Control now."

"Yes, but Davis is right. The press will manipulate anything we give them. And by reacting to this new threat, I'm allowing us to be manipulated. I'm going to take a step back and slow down."

"Meaning what?"

"We're not going to do an interview."

"Won't that keep them chasing your staff?"

"I'll make the staff's time worthwhile."

"That doesn't mean they won't talk," I remind him.

"I'll take my chances. We're not going to meet with the press. We're not going to hide. We're going to go back to our normal lives, and as I know well from high profile cases, they're here today and gone tomorrow. This too shall pass."

I wrap my arms around him. "But we won't."

"No, baby." He cups my head. "We won't." He kisses me. "Why don't we go take a look at your new office?"

"Yes, please."

A few minutes later, we're just down the hall from his office, and I'm presented with a gorgeous personal space already decorated with a beautiful mahogany desk, double bookshelves, and a sitting area with brown and light blue furnishings. "I love it," I say, standing in the center. "Now I need to earn it." I glance at my watch. "I'm supposed to meet Kevin in HR at noon."

He shuts the door and crosses to set my briefcase on my desk. "About Kevin." He turns to face me.

"You don't trust him."

"I don't know him, but I don't have to look at Eric's list on possible traitors to know he'll be on it."

"I believe he's one of the good guys. He is nothing like Ri. He is someone we want here on our team but," my hand settles on his chest, "I can put him on hold."

"No. Don't. You trust him. I trust you. Just be careful." He kisses me. "And I'll leave you to work your magic. I'm going to put out about a million fires. You know where to find me." He heads for the door and I rotate to watch him reach for the knob, and God, the man is the definition of power and masculine perfection. He is everything and more, and in this moment, I remember the past, I remember how easily I let his power and money define us. I let myself feel replaceable and that was all on me. Grayson never ever made me feel such things.

"Grayson."

He turns and looks at me and when this man looks at me, his eyes soften and warmth radiates between us. "Yeah, baby?"

I close the space between us and wrap my arms around him. "I'm really glad to be back here with you."

His hand comes down on the back of my head and his forehead presses to mine. "You have no idea how happy I am that you're back."

His voice is low, rough, affected again, and it's a powerful feeling to know that you affect a man like Grayson Bennett. Despite how far we have come, I'm still trembling with the knowledge that I have that power, with the knowledge that together we have that power. He strokes my hair. "I'll show you how happy tonight." He leans in and kisses my neck and then burns me alive with the heat in his stare.

He starts to turn and I catch his arm, wiping my lipstick off his mouth. "You never choose the right shade for your coloring."

He smiles and winks before he exits my office, leaving me with his words: just be careful. He trusts me. He trusts me fully and guilt spikes in me over the past. I should have trusted him that fully. I'm not going to let him down again and I know he knows that, but I wonder if Eric and Davis, his closest friends, really know. Eric did suggest I'd be a target because our breakup makes us look weak. But we are not weak and no one will hurt Grayson through me again.

I hope they do target me.

Chapter Sixty-Three

Mia

The past...

I'm trembling as I follow my new boss, Kevin Murphy, into his office. The trembling is ridiculous and the idea of going to work for Ri is killing me, but my father and his gambling debt really left me with no option. I need the signing bonus and I'm not going to go to Grayson for money. He might have turned his back on me for another woman, but I will not be the money-grabber who goes to my billionaire ex for money. I won't do it.

"Have a seat," he says, shutting his door and motioning me toward a small round conference table, which is a bit surprising. I'd expect him to sit behind his desk in his big corner office and act above me like Ri.

I claim my seat and set my briefcase on the floor beside me. He sits down across from me. He's a good-looking man with artistic features and dark wavy hair. Mr. Tall, Dark, and Handsome really, but I notice in almost a sterile way—an attorney sizing up someone she's about to face off with, not a woman sizing up a man. He's not Grayson. I don't know if I will ever react to anyone again. Right now, it feels as if I will not.

"I'm going to be frank. I'm trying to understand what to do with Grayson Bennett's ex-fiancée."

"I'm passionate about my job and if there was ever a time I needed to prove myself, it's now. Give me a caseload and let me prove I exist outside of that relationship."

He narrows his eyes on me. "You still love him."

There's a stab in my heart. "And I always will."

"Then why are you here?"

"Sometimes love isn't enough, but be clear on one thing: I'm not going to be distracted by a new man, or a man at all. I need to do me right now. I need to work and win my cases."

He studies me a long beat before he says, "What's between you and Ri?"

"He's jealous of Grayson and hates him."

"But you don't hate Grayson?"

"No. No, I do not."

"Then why are you here?"

I'm no longer trembling. I'm starting to get angry. I lean forward, my hands pressed to the table, acutely aware of my newly naked ring finger. "To do a job."

"If you love him, working for his enemy hurts him. You must not love him."

I'm on my feet in an instant. He's right. God, he's right. I reach down and grab my bag. "I need to leave." I push my chair back. I walk to the door and just when I'm about to open the door he says, "Was this about revenge?"

I whirl on him. "Never. That's not who I am."

"Then why are you here?"

"My father has a gambling debt. Ri offered me a bonus."

"Why not go to Grayson? He's a billionaire."

"Because I would never diminish him to a payday. Ever."

I start to turn again and he says, "Stay. I have the perfect case for you."

I turn to look at him. "What perfect case?"

"A woman who set her husband on fire. She says he abused her daily and it was self-defense. The DA says it's calculated, cold blooded murder."

I won that case for that woman, who'd been horribly abused by her husband, I recall as I approach the HR offices. And so, I'd become the voice of abused women. I peek my head into Sandy Miller's office to find Kevin sitting in front of her desk and today he's in a sharp blue suit with a blue tie. Sandy is presently fumbling with paperwork, nervously navigating Kevin's good looks.

"Hello," I greet.

Kevin turns and the minute he spots me, stands up. "Good to see you," he says, and he means that literally. He and I are friends, just friends, and in that there is safety. There is never any hidden agenda and there certainly is not even an ounce of sexual tension.

Sandy, who's a pretty brunette, stands herself. "We were just about to go to his new office."

"I'll take him," I offer and motion with my head for him to follow. "Where are we going?"

"Corner blue."

Corner blue meaning the office with the blue furniture, which I know because this was my world once before. "Got it."

Meanwhile, Kevin wastes no time grabbing his briefcase and joining me in the hallway. "Thanks for the rescue."

I laugh. "Yes. You really needed a rescue from the beautiful woman fumbling all over herself. I think she was the one who needed rescuing."

He laughs now. "Is that right?"

"Yes. It's right. How are you feeling about being with Bennett?"

"Damn good. I'm grateful for this opportunity."

"I do owe you," I say.

"No," he counters quickly. "You do not owe me. You were good at your job. If you hadn't been, I'd have fired you."

I pause at his new office door. "Thank you."

"Thank you?"

"Why would I want to be anywhere I wasn't wanted?" I open the door and motion him forward.

He doesn't move. "About that."

"About what?"

"On second thought." Now he motions to the office and enters ahead of me. By the time I join him, he's set his bag on a chair, barely glanced at his gorgeous office and he's facing me expectantly. I shut the door. "What's up?"

"Grayson can't feel good about me. Not after I worked for Ri for a decade of my life."

"He trusts me. You decide if he trusts you."

"How?"

"By doing your job."

"When can I meet him?"

I have no idea why this bothers me, but I can feel myself recoil and alarm bells are going off in my head. "Focus on winning cases. As you already know from your raise, Grayson's generous with his bank account." I don't give him time to say more. "I'll meet you in the conference room down the hall to the right in half an hour. I'm handing you all but one of my case files." I turn but he halts me.

"All of your cases?"

"I'm moving to corporate." I hesitate only a moment before I say, "Don't make me sorry I brought you over. There are people who would hurt Grayson."

"I'm not one of them."

"Then make sure you have your ears and eyes open with the right team in mind."

I turn and exit his office, and my nerve endings are prickling in all the wrong ways. I head down the hallway with one destination in mind: Eric's office. When he's not there, I return to my office, shut my door and call him. "Hey, Mia. What's up?"

"I brought Kevin Murphy to take on my old cases. He was my supervisor at Ri's firm and with Ri for ten years."

"I'm aware. And?"

"And I trust him, I do, but I just got a weird vibe from him. Maybe I'm paranoid after our talk this morning, but my trust just doesn't feel good enough. Not when he might burn Grayson. Can you have Blake check him out?"

"Already done. So far he's checked out."

"Are you sure? Because I can't be the reason something bad happens to Grayson, Eric. I can't."

"You, Mia, are the good in that man's life. You are not bringing any bad on him, but you did the right thing. Better safe than sorry."

"I love him."

"And he loves you. Give Kevin a hard case. Let's see what he's made of and if he fails, fuck him."

I laugh. "As long as he doesn't do that to us."

"Such a lady. Can't even say fuck. He's not going to fuck us. Now, go get comfortable. You're here to stay." He hangs up.

I smile. He's right. I am here to stay.

I start making a list of all the things I need to do today and all the things I need to update Grayson on later when we're alone, including my feelings on Kevin Murphy.

Chapter Sixty-Four

Mia

I t's nearly noon and Kevin and I are still in the conference room, but thankfully I've just finished handing over my caseload to him. "That's it," I say. "Let me know if you have questions and welcome to the team."

"You really belong here, don't you?"

"Yes. She does."

At the sound of Grayson's voice, my gaze lifts to the doorway to find him gorgeously consuming the entryway. "Hi," I say.

"Hi," he says, his eyes twinkling with the exchange. "How about some lunch?"

"I'd like that."

"Ah hi," Kevin says awkwardly, standing up. "Nice to meet you, Grayson." He's quick to round the table to meet Grayson, extending his hand.

I'm quick to move to Grayson's side. By the time I'm there, Grayson shakes his hand. "I'm not Ri."

"And that's a good thing," Kevin replies.

"And yet you worked for him for ten years."

"Until Mia joined the team, I barely saw the man, but once she joined my group, he came around often, and harassed her just as often. I did my best to protect her."

The air crackles sharp and hard, and Grayson narrows his eyes on him. "Did you now?" Grayson is not a man to outwardly respond to anything. He's calm and cool, genius and kind, but he's not a pushover. He succeeds for a reason. He acts swiftly, powerfully, and without regret.

Kevin obviously reads that in him now because he holds up his hands. "We're friends. Mia started her first day at work by telling me she loved you and would always love you."

"And gentlemen that you are, you never saw that as a challenge."

"Grayson," I warn softly.

"I didn't, actually," Kevin replies, without hesitation. "We just never had that kind of connection. And because I need to earn your trust, I'll go on when I would otherwise find that inappropriate. My fiancée died in a car crash a few months before Mia came to work for me."

"Oh God," I murmur. "No one said anything."

"She worked for Ri," Kevin says. "She crossed Ri, threatened to report him for falsifying evidence. I believe he had her killed. I hated him. I was only there for revenge. Check it out. It will all check out."

I blanch, stunned by this confession. The air crackles for several beats before Grayson asks, "Did you get that revenge?"

"No, but I would have, and I'm not sure I should be proud of that but I wouldn't have regretted it. I asked Mia to talk to you for a reason." He turns back to the table, grabs a file from his briefcase, and offers it to Grayson, lowering his voice for our ears only, though the conference room is set apart from the offices anyway. "A list of people that I know visited our offices after they came to work for you. I know he's dead, but I wouldn't trust any of them."

Grayson accepts the file. "But I should trust you?"

"Yes, but I understand why you don't. I'll gather my things and leave." He hesitates. "If that's what you want."

I suck in a breath, waiting for Grayson's reply, heavy seconds pounding in the air, before Grayson says, "Stay." He pauses a beat and adds, "For now."

Relief washes over his features and he nods. "I'll get to work on my caseload."

Grayson inclines his chin and then fixes me in that steely green stare. "Ready?"

"I am," I say, and I don't look at Kevin.

Grayson steps back to allow me to exit and I enter the hallway. He joins me. We don't touch, not here at work and while that's my rule, I find myself wanting to break that standard now. He motions to my office and we walk in that direction.

The minute we're inside, I turn to face him and he shuts the door. "Eric told you my concern?"

"He did." He lifts the folder. "Grab your things. I want to get this to Blake, and Reese Summer has a big trial starting in two days. He asked if we could meet him for lunch and unless you really need to come back afterward, I say we work from home the rest of the day."

"Home?"

"Home, baby."

My smile is instant. "I can't wait." I hurry to my desk and start gathering my things. Grayson follows and sets the folder on the desk, tabbing through the data.

"Anything that feels important?"

"The fact these people are spread out across our various divisions is indicative of a planned attack. Which we knew. The file is simply added confirmation."

I round the desk to stand next to him. "Do you trust Kevin?"

"I will never trust a man who wants in my woman's panties."

"How very caveman of you. He does not—"

His hand slides under my hair to cup my neck and he steps into me, dragging my mouth to his. "A man knows when another man wants his woman. He wants you."

"My panties are spoken for by you and have been since the moment I met you." I grab his tie. "Note my skill at being both kinky and romantic at the same time."

"And while I appreciate your skills, I do not appreciate him. At all."

I'm suddenly concerned that he might think I want to make him jealous or pay him back. "I didn't know, Grayson. I swear to you. I've always been blinded by you. I didn't—"

"I know," he says and his mouth comes down on mine, his tongue licking long and deep, and he tastes of possession, of demand.

His hand slides under my jacket and he drags it down my shoulders, trapping my wrists behind my back. "Grayson," I murmur, not sure if I'm objecting or requesting. "We're at the office."

"And when we leave, it will be with the taste of you on my tongue." He lifts me and sets me on my new desk, and his eyes, those intense green eyes, burn with passion, with hunger, and my body wants what he offers.

"I don't think—"

"Good," he says, sliding my skirt up my thighs, and inching my knees apart. "I don't want you to think."

"We've never done this here."

"There's a cure for that." He goes down on one knee, and kisses my knee through the thigh-high hose I'm wearing. My breath is raspy, my body tingling, every nerve ending I own on fire, alive. I'm so alive with this man in a way I wasn't without him.

I want to tell him he has nothing to prove. I want to tell him he's everything and Kevin is nothing but a friend, but I know he knows. He knows. This is about more than Kevin. This is about three months that he can't control. Three months that he won't be fully in control. And what he wants and needs right now, is just that: control.

His hands slide up my thighs and when his thumbs settle on the bare skin above my thigh-highs, I suck in a breath. He strokes a lazy finger along the delicate skin and I clench against the sensations. He catches my knees and kisses them. "Relax, baby."

"What if someone comes in?"

"I locked the door."

"Oh."

"Oh," he repeats, his really wonderful lips quirking, lips that are about to be in the most intimate part of me. He eases my legs apart again and inches my skirt all the way to my hips. He leans in closer, his breath a warm whisper over my sex. My nipples pucker, my breasts are heavy. My sex is pulsing and my hands are tied. He gives my clit a lick. I lean back, catching my trapped hands on the desk. And just in time. He yanks away my panties.

I gasp and before I can fully recover from the shock, he's suckling me and I'm gasping all over again, sensations trembling through me.

His fingers slide along the slick sensitive folds of my body and—oh God—slip inside me. I'm arching into his touch, unaware of anything but his hands and mouth teasing me, driving me wild. He's punishing in the most delicious of ways with his exploration, flicking my clit with his thumb while his tongue is delving in and out, licking here and there. And those fingers, those talented fingers stretch me, stroke me, press deeper and harder, exploring every sensitive part of me. I can hear my pants, feel the rasp of my dry throat, and I want to reach for him, but he pulls me forward, drapes my legs over his shoulders, forcing me to hold myself up with my hands. It's about control and he has it. And I like when he has it.

I trust him. I can forget when he's in control. I can let go when he's in control.

Blood roars in my ears, and the sweet spots he touches ignite, cool, and repeat. I know nothing right now but his touch, his control, my need for his control, but pleasure builds and suddenly there is a tight hard clenching in my stomach that darts lower and claims that control. Grayson suckles my clit and I'm there in that blissful place of no return. I cry out and my sex spasms hard around his fingers.

My vision blacks out and pleasure rocks my body so hard I can feel it in my bones.

Unable to hold myself up, I'm falling backwards, but somehow Grayson is there, catching me and pulling my jacket back into place. I'm sitting up, cradled by his hand between my shoulder blades when he kisses me, his tongue salty against mine. "Now, I taste like you," he murmurs. "And now, my world is right again."

My hand settles on his strong jaw. "You own me, Grayson Bennett. That used to scare me, but not anymore."

He catches my hand and kisses my knuckles. "You own me, too, baby." He lifts me off the desk and sets me on the floor, righting my skirt for me, and I can feel the edge in him has eased. But it's not gone. But how can it be? We're under attack by a dead man.

Chapter Sixty-Five

Grayson

With Mia on my tongue, I do indeed feel better. The pleasures of a woman you love are too often underrated, usually by those who don't know what it means to love a woman. Lord only knows I found out just how impossible it is to replace her when I lost Mia. I needed her. I *need* her. I won't lose her again. I damn sure won't let anyone take her from me.

While Mia freshens up, I grab my briefcase, check out for the day with Nancy, and Mia and I meet in the lobby. We exit to the elevator banks to find Blake waiting on us. As usual, he's dressed in jeans and a Walker Security collared shirt that he manages to make look rich in all kinds of ways. He's a man of confidence, skill, and wealth but what I like about him besides that skill, is his values, his morals, the love he has for his wife. The way he is who he is no matter who I am or who is around.

"I'm pleased as fuck," he greets, "to report that the reporters are gone. The police pushed them back so far they just left."

I arch a brow. "Why do I believe you had something to do with that?"

"They needed something from me," Blake replies. "I told them I needed something from them. I know you legal folks know all about quid pro quo. Eric's still at our offices. He was running some number sequence and I was afraid he'd have a damn seizure if I made him stop."

Mia laughs that sweet musical laugh of hers and fuck me, I feel it in my chest. I own her? She fucking owns the hell out of me and I don't even care. That's how much I love this woman. The way my father loved my mother. "Just like old times," she murmurs. "Eric and his numbers." Her voice softens.

"And his loyalty."

She's right. Eric's a good friend. One of the only people who knows just how not good I was without Mia. One of the few people I can say would die for me, and me for him. A real friend and a man like me can't be confident anyone is a friend, except Eric. And Mia. A man appreciates the value of such things in times like these and therefore I count myself lucky as hell.

Blake motions to the hallway. "I'm still recommending we exit through the side door. We don't need any company following us to the meetup with Reese."

"I cannot wait until we can just live our life again," Mia murmurs.

My hand slides to her lower back, but I don't comment. At this point, it's not about what I say. It's about what I do and what I have to do is to make this go away, now, not months from now. The three of us make our way to the service elevator. Once we're inside, with the door shut, I hand Blake the file. "Kevin Murphy gave this to me. He claims they're all connected to Ri and dirty. All of them ex-employees of Ri's we hired."

Blake accepts the file. "We've already scouted out that group, but I'll give it a look-see. You met him?"

"I did," I confirm.

"And what's your read on him?" He eyes Mia. "I know you got some weird vibe."

"I did," she says, "and I don't know what to think. I never felt weird about him until today."

"Could be nerves," he comments.

"He told us that Ri killed his fiancée," she adds. "because she was reporting him for evidence tampering and he wanted revenge. I never heard a word about a dead fiancée that worked at Ri's firm. Granted I kept to myself but that still feels off."

"If it's true," I add. "Revenge-seekers concern me. You never know when they might find a new target."

"His fiancée did work with Ri. And she is dead. As for revenge, my fiancée before Kara was murdered," Blake says. "And I damn sure wanted revenge. Tried damn hard to get it and Kara pulled me back to sanity when my brothers could not. My question would be what was Kevin doing to seek revenge and what's his present state of mind?" He lifts the folder. "The contents of this folder, to me at least, do not constitute a plan for revenge. We need to know more."

"Do we just ask him?" Mia asks.

"I'll find out," Blake replies. "I've got this."

Another thing about Blake I like when he says, I got this, he's got this.

The elevator halts and we exit, loading up in an SUV driven by one of Blake's men with Blake in the passenger seat, and Mia and I in the backseat. "I pray I didn't bring a problem with me by hiring Kevin."

"Keep your friends close, and your enemies closer. If he's a problem, we might not have seen him coming if not for you bringing him over. If he's a friend and helping us, we'll take the help."

Blake leans around the seat. "If these people in this file," he says, indicating the folder, "are the bad eggs, then he did us a favor. And he might not have done it if you wouldn't have given him a reason to protect Grayson, like a job."

I kiss her hand. "It's all going to be over soon, baby," I say, but the worry in her eyes doesn't fade. Three months doesn't feel like soon, not to her or me. In this moment, I'm still battling with that need to just take her away somewhere for three months, where we can get lost in each other, and where she'll be safe. But I have an equal need to be right here, fighting this invisible enemy—making this go away forever. And Mia wants to be home, in our home. She's been alone too long. I didn't bring her home soon enough.

And that's what's going to happen.

We're going home.

I'm ending this one way or another, sooner not later.

And I'm going to marry her, sooner not later.

The entire idea of eloping sits heavy and insistent inside me. I want her to be my wife and I have no idea why that feels as damn urgent as it does. She's back in my life. That should be enough and yet it's not. Not even close.

Chapter Sixty-Six

Mia

Our lunch is at the restaurant and bar in the building where Reese and Cat actually live, and not far from the courthouse. Grayson and I, along with Blake, meetup with them at the hostess stand and while Blake knows them and can point them out, they're also hard to miss. Reese Summer is tall, dark, and gorgeous in a dark suit, and his wife Cat is a stunning petite blonde in a pink pantsuit. They fit in ways I can't explain. They're perfect together. I also happen to know that Cat writes the syndicated "Cat Does Crime" column that I adore, which makes my fangirl moment hard to contain but I manage, barely.

"Grayson Bennett," Reese greets, shaking his hand as the hostess looks for a properly-sized table. "Not often I represent a competitor though I understand you have done some work with my brothers-in-law, Reid and Gabe."

"I have," Grayson confirms, "And I don't see them or us as competitors.," he adds, and he means it. Like his father before him, Grayson isn't cutthroat. He's competitive, but in the right ways and in the proper context.

"Blake assured me that you'd not only say that but mean it," Reese replies. "From my research, it seems you might be one of the rare few who really are honest and sincere."

"My father set a certain expectation from the day I could walk," Grayson assures him.

"And his father was his hero," I say, catching his arm. "He still is."

"I met him once," Reese replies. "I liked him."

"As my father would say," Grayson replies. "We're warriors fighting the same battle. And in this case, I need an impartial warrior who I trust."

"I'm going to head to the bar and let you four chat and get to know each other," Blake interjects, eyeing Grayson. "I've updated Reese on everything, but if you need data or confirmation of data, I'll be here." He saunters away.

A few minutes later, Grayson and I are at a wooden table across from Reese and Cat, and in the middle of the intimate seating area. Clusters of tables sit nearby but are empty, with televisions hanging in plentiful locations. And with Cat directly across from me, I can no longer hold back my admiration. "I adore your column," I gush. "I read it religiously, even when I'm too swamped to read not much else. It's so very Sex in The City meets Criminal Minds. I love the way you question ethical choices and challenge new thinking."

"Thank you," she says. "I love what I do and," she looks between me and Grayson, "I hope you don't mind that I'm here. I work sidebar, so to speak, for Reese on a regular basis."

"Two for one," Grayson replies. "As long as I don't end up in your column."

"Oh no," Cat replies quickly. "I'd never write about you unless you wanted me to write about you and even then, I'd still have to feel good about it. I don't write what people want me to write. I write what I feel passionate about."

Reese laughs. "We met when she was following one of my cases in her column. Even then, she was challenging me, and scolding me when I didn't think out of the box."

Grayson squeezes my hand under the table and says, "I understand that completely, which is why I'm happy to have Mia joining our corporate team."

My heart warms with the words that I'd once have been too insecure to accept as sincere but not anymore. It's amazing what a year can change.

"Reese thinks out of the box on his own just fine," Cat replies. "But getting him to fold the laundry is another story."

We all laugh and the waitress arrives. We order drinks and bread. When she's gone, Reese gets to the point. "Blake told me everything and holy hell, man. I don't even know where to start. Knowing your operation's been infiltrated, I understand why you want outside counsel. And this three-month payoff deadline to bring you down that Ri set-up with this underground group—I'm back to holy hell, man. Three months living under a threat with an enemy potentially in every office is rough."

Grayson releases my hand and reaches for the whiskey the waitress sets in front of him. "From Blake," she offers, and eyes Reese. "He said you and Cat have court. He'll owe you." She glances at me. "And you don't handle your whiskey well."

We all laugh. "He's not wrong."

Grayson lifts his glass at Blake and sips before he dives back into the conversation. "My biggest concern is one of those enemies being planted with the Feds or in the DA's office."

"I'd like to say I don't believe that could happen," Reese replies, "but I've seen enough, and been around enough, to know that it can. The FBI and the DA need to be working with Blake's team to take down your attackers. I suggest we set-up a meeting and get everyone on the same page, then ask for you and Mia to be given immunity."

Grayson hands me his drink and I take a sip. "Grayson talked about doing a sit-down interview to shut down the press obsession, something in-depth."

"God no," Cat objects. "You think a sit-down interview will be controlled, even scripted with pre-approved questions, but they'll go off script. The press are monsters, but that's why I'm here. If you decide to go public, which my gut says you should not, use me. And believe me, when we heard about this situation, we talked about me helping with my column in some way."

"Before we explain that idea," Reese replies, "the bad actors don't know you know they exist, correct?"

"They do not," Grayson confirms.

"Then as far as they're concerned," Reese continues, "they can move about and plot against you freely. In theory, that allows Blake to watch them and catch them."

"Except we're dealing with an advanced hacking operation," Grayson counters. "Blake's good at what he does, but this breach is apparently widespread across operations and states."

"So if we expose the underground operation in my column," Cat says, "we might scare them off and that would let them know we're onto them, but that idea comes with negatives."

"I don't know," I say. "I mean, when Grayson suggested doing an interview, it was more about answering questions about my attack and just getting the fascination with us and me over with. If we actually expose this plot, it doesn't necessarily get rid of the bad eggs. In fact, it might encourage them to stay to avoid notice. A rapid departure might indicate guilt, but I suppose at least it suppresses any bad actors."

Cat sighs. "Yes. That could happen. It's a ridiculous catch twenty-two situation. In which case, you end up with all these dirty eggs rotting away inside your operation."

"No to exposing the plot to take me down," Grayson says, his tone steel. "That could come with consequences."

Reese narrows his eyes on him. "You're afraid they'll act hard and fast before you shut them down."

"And decisively," he says, and I know Grayson. I don't even have to ask what that means. He's afraid they'll act against me. He's afraid the hired hacks will succeed where Ri failed and kill me.

Chapter Sixty-Seven

Mia

M ia

Tomorrow isn't guaranteed.

The room fades to white noise as I remember Grayson talking about eloping. I know him and understand his urgency. This man seems to have the world—money, power, friendship and more, afraid of nothing except losing someone else he loves, and that means me. How did I ever think this man cheated on me? How? I'm such an idiot. Neither of us has dealt fully with Ri's attack. For me, I've consciously, and perhaps to more of an extreme, unconsciously, used his fear to suppress Ri's attack for both our sanity, but unbidden, I'm back there now. I fight it, I do, but I lose. I'm there. Living that hell all over again.

He lunges for me and I turn and try to run, but it's too little too late. He grabs my hair and all but rips it out as he yanks me around to face him. "What do you have in your bag?" He reaches for it, and I punch him, giving help time to arrive, I hope, but it does no good.

He reaches into my bag that I stupidly didn't zip and grabs the folder. "You little bitch." He drops it on the ground and shoves me against the wall. "I should have known you were still fucking him. That will never get out of this building."

"It doesn't matter. I took pictures. I sent proof to the police. Did you really think you could frame Grayson and get away with it?"

"I'll get away with it. You'll be dead and I'll tell them you were setting me up."

"Dead? You're going to kill me? Are you serious?"

"Yes, Mia. You'll die." He reaches into his pocket and pulls out his phone. "Mia will need to be dealt with tonight, but not until

I'm done with her. Pick her up at the normal spot." He ends the call. "We fuck first. Maybe you can talk me out of killing you."

I try to knee him, but he catches my leg. "Not this time, sweetheart. This time I fuck you, you don't fuck me." He pulls out a gun. "Just in case you think you might scream. Think again." He yanks me off the wall and starts pulling me by the hair toward the door. That's when the door bursts open and Grayson appears, holding a gun and followed by Blake.

"Grayson," I breathe out as the two men stand side by side, Blake directly in front of Ri, but it's Grayson that Ri is looking at, his gun now pointed at him.

"Let her go, Ri, or I will shoot you," Grayson says, stepping closer. "And I'll enjoy it."

Ri holds the gun on him to my head. "We walk out together or she leaves dead. Decide."

Grayson squeezes my hand and I snap back to the present to find him staring at me. And I swear the concern in his green eyes meeting mine is all it takes for me to push past a weak moment. I cover his hand with mine, silently telling him that I'm okay. And I am. I'm alive. I'm here with him. Ri doesn't get to screw that up for either of us.

Fired up, I focus on Reese. "The FBI and DA need to take this hammer off of Grayson. Blake obviously feels they might come after him or we wouldn't be sitting here with you."

"Blake's being cautious," Reese assures me, motioning for Blake to join us. "As he should be. Frankly, I'm of the opinion the FBI and DA won't be stupid enough to come after Grayson. Grayson could sue—would sue—and would win. I'm more concerned about a different type of attack. Something that hits Grayson financially, or personally."

An attack that's financial or personal. Those words hit hard. I turn to Grayson. "I'm the personal attack, I get that. What could they do to you financially?"

"I've taken precautions," Grayson assures me. "Shifted my portfolio, layered up different types of insurance."

Blake pulls up a seat. "Eric and I are working through any and every way Grayson could be targeted."

Frustration takes root. "My God, can't the FBI just take down this underground group?"

"They're as slippery as the snakes they are," Blake replies. "The attorney holding the payout Ri promised those snakes is another story. The right move is to arrest him and freeze the money. No money, no group."

"Then what are we waiting on?" I ask. "Why aren't we already making that happen?"

"For starters," Blake says, "this doesn't erase any residual damage to Grayson or his operation that might be discovered later. The FBI and the DA already know what's happening, and they're sitting back and observing for now. I need to pressure them to stop sucking their thumbs and make this arrest. That means setting up a meeting that needs to include your legal counsel."

"I'm in," Reese replies, glancing at Grayson. "Cat will get you a client agreement this afternoon. That is if that's what you want?"

"All-in," Grayson replies, but his focus is instantly back on Blake. "You said for starters," he repeats. "What else is holding you back on this?"

"I don't want to fuck you in the process of trying to stop these assholes from fucking you. Everything isn't online and documented with technology. There could be another method of payment or a backup source of payment. If there is, we could trigger a rapid attack. It's like cutting a wire on a bomb. If you cut the wrong one, you blow the hell up."

Grayson's hand tightens over mine. "Then where does that leave us?"

"The attorney in question, Brian Johnson, is attending a party tonight. I'm having a team search his house and office, but even if it's clean, even if we find nothing we don't already have—"

"You can't eliminate all risks," Grayson supplies and he doesn't hesitate to add, "Take the risk. Pressure the DA and the FBI. Make this happen. I need this over with."

Chapter Sixty-Eight

Grayson

T ake the risk.

I'm all about calculated, well-researched risk-taking, but as Blake leaves Mia and me with Cat and Reese to act on that risk, it feels more like a Vegas gamble. I'm not a Vegas gambler.

"This feels like the right move," Mia murmurs as he departs, "but I still think I could use a drink I can't handle once we get home."

And just like that, Mia charms the moment into something lighter and the tension around the table fades into laughter.

The rest of the lunch, we relax into the conversation, as best as I can relax under these circumstances, but through our meal, I decide that I'm impressed with Reese Summer. If I could buy out his firm and bring him on board, I'd do it in a heartbeat and not because he needs me to grow and thrive. Because he's one of the good guys and good guys need to align.

He and I talk about his firm, his partner, and the stock markets while Mia and Cat fall into their own deep conversation, an obvious connection between the two. Watching Mia just be Mia is a piece of my life that was sadly empty when we were apart. Her laugh charms me. Her smile heats my blood. Her presence calms me in ways I was never truly calm before her or apart from her.

She's in the middle of a sentence when her gaze lifts to the TV to her right and mounted to the ceiling. The entire table's attention follows hers to the image of a woman, with a subtitle under her photo that reads: *Wife of billionaire claims self-defense in his murder.*

Mia sets her fork down and sighs. "Nothing like your client on the TV to ruin a meal."

"Delaney Wittmore is your client?" Cat asks, glancing at Reese.

"She's her client." Excitement lifts her voice and she turns back to

Mia. "Mia, I had no idea. I'm intrigued by this case. I'm interested in following the trial in my column. When does the trial start?"

"Four months," Mia says. "But right before this Ri mess, I submitted to have the judge removed, so I don't know how that will play out."

"That's a big move," Reese comments. "Why?"

"He made an offhanded comment about Delaney killing her husband for his money, which speaks of an opinion he shouldn't openly have."

"Did she?" Cat asks.

"I wouldn't be representing her if I believed that," Mia retorts quickly, sitting up straighter. "And there are a half-dozen police reports, documented bruises on her body, and a recording she made of him threatening her mother's life that say otherwise. And while I'm not surprised that the evidence doesn't matter to the press, it should to the judge on her case."

"You really believe in her," Reese observes.

"I do," Mia assures him. "I do, or I would never bring this drama to Grayson's firm right now, in the middle of all of this, if I didn't feel this passionately about her. She was terrorized by that man."

Reese sips his drink. "Who's the judge?"

"Nickleson," she says.

Reese grimaces and grabs a piece of bread. "He's a bastard. You're smart to jump off that ship if you can. Who's the prosecutor?"

"Nick Reynolds," Mia says. "And as I'm sure you know at this point from Blake, Ri was trying to set Grayson up through the DA's office."

"I'm painfully aware of that fact," Reese confirms.

"Well," Mia continues, "we now know that Nick has a connection to Ri. The honest truth here is that this poor woman has a stacked deck from me and this firm representing her, but Ri's firm is without Ri. I don't know what that will mean for its future and she trusts me. She begged me to keep her case."

"What do you want to happen for her?" Reese asks.

"Honestly," Mia replies, "she deserves to have the charges dismissed, but people love to hate pretty women who stand to inherit a fortune. I don't feel like her odds are good."

"I know Nick," Reese says. "I don't like him, but I have had some luck with him, but that aside for a moment, Cat has been researching this case. She's been talking about it non-stop. It piqued my interest even before we sat down for this lunch. If you're willing to talk about some sort of partnership, I wouldn't want to steal the spotlight this brings your career. I do, however, want to help."

"I don't care about credit," Mia says. "I care about my client, not me." She turns to me. "Grayson?"

I stare at her, my beautiful Mia, her long dark hair around her shoulders, and I understand the question she hasn't fully vocalized. She wants me to decide for her. She wants me to tell her to hold onto the case or let it go, and fuck, I want her to let it go. Delaney was just on the television. Mia will be in the press with her, and they will push her to talk about Ri. They will push her in all kinds of ways that might affect her in ways she doesn't yet realize.

And even beyond that, the underground operation could use this to attack her and play it off as some crazy protestor. I want her to take this deal with Reese, but Reese will steal her spotlight and I made the mistake of pulling her from a case against her will once before to protect her. I won't do that again. "It's your call, Mia. It's your case."

"It's your company."

"And you're about to be my wife."

"That doesn't change the business side of this. Grayson—"

"This is your case and your decision."

"I want your opinion," she counters.

"And I want you to do what feels right to you, Mia, not me. This isn't about me."

Her lips press together. "Stubborn man," she snaps and turns back to the table, inhaling before she makes her decision. "This isn't well-timed for the firm and I'm not Delaney's best path to freedom. I haven't fully processed that fact until now. This has all happened so quickly, but sitting here right now, I know that's true. Honestly, Reese, she'd be better off with you. And this is a high-profile feather in your cap if you get her off. I believe her. I know you will as well. If you would consider taking the case—when can you meet her?"

He eyes me and then Mia. "Delaney feels comfortable with you, Mia. We should co-counsel, but I need to be upfront about a few things. I'd want to see the evidence and meet your client. Does she fully inherit?"

"Not fully," Mia says, "but a hefty sum of money."

Reese grimaces. "The family will try to take it if she's convicted or even if she takes a deal."

"They'll try to take it if she gets off free and clear," Cat murmurs.

"She and I have talked about this," Mia replies. "I think she needs to go to trial. She has a daughter she doesn't want to put through this. That in itself should tell you this isn't about the money to her."

"We need to change her mind," Reese replies, "because the family might even go after her daughter's money if she inherited. That said, though, frankly, with my present schedule, if she agrees to trial, we'll need to move the trial based on my schedule. I'm booked six months out and bringing me in after what just happened to you will be an easy sell to the courts."

"When can we do the meet and greet?" Mia asks. "I need to know what I'm doing when and so does Delaney."

"I'm due back in court this afternoon. I should be able to do coffee at seven in the morning. Can you get her here? They have a coffee and breakfast service."

Mia turns to search my face, and I don't know what she's looking for or what she finds, but she turns back to Reese and says, "Perfect. I believe she'll be better off with you, Reese. She won't need me once she meets you and Cat. I'm going to call my client now." She snakes her phone from her purse and stands up, walking toward the bar.

Relief washes over me at a decision that takes her out of emotional and physical danger, but it's immediately followed by guilt. She just gave up a career-making case, when her own success and identity has always been important to her. I get that. I understand that need. She just gave this case away for me, not for herself, and not for her client. That doesn't work for her, me, Delaney, or us as a couple.

I stand up and pursue Mia, determined to catch her before she makes that call to Delaney, but I'm not the only one pursuing her. A tall man in a leather jacket charges in her direction.

Chapter Sixty-Nine

Mia

A sudden fight-or-flight sensation has me whipping around to find a big man in a leather jacket, well over six feet and two hundred pounds of pure muscle, charging at me. My heart jumps up into my throat, and a small sound lodges right there with it. I back up and hit a stool as the man stops dead in his tracks in front of me. "Sorry." He offers an apologetic smile, lines crinkling on his sunbaked fortyish skin. "I didn't mean to startle you there."

Grayson is suddenly beside me, pulling me close. "What the hell do you want?" he demands of the man.

The man grabs something from the bar and holds it up. "Left my wallet. Panicked a bit when I realized what I'd done." He glances at me. "Again. Sorry about that, ma'am." He turns and leaves.

I breathe out in utter relief and then laugh in disbelief, pressing my hand to my forehead. "I'm losing my mind," I murmur, frustrated over my silly over-reaction.

Grayson turns me to face him, cupping my face to stare down at me. "I thought—"

"Me, too. We're both clearly not as okay after Ri as we're pretending we are. And this is exactly why Reese needs to take this case."

"No." He cups my face and tilts my gaze to his. "You believe in this woman. She needs that kind of passion defending her."

"Reese—"

"Is damn good, but he's a man. She needs a woman in her corner. And Reese isn't a fool. He knows that. He needs you, just like Delaney needs you."

"I'm clearly not myself, Grayson. I just almost screamed out in a public place over a man looking for his lost wallet. She deserves counsel that's one hundred percent focused."

"You're less than a week out from an attack, Mia. And the trial won't be for six months with Reese's schedule."

"But my role in the company—"

"Will only be proved stronger with a high-profile win under your belt."

"Unless I lose."

"You won't," he says firmly.

"I'm confused. I felt your relief when I stepped aside, Grayson."

"I won't lie and tell you that you're wrong. I did feel relief. And then I felt selfish. I knew, *I know*, I was doing the same thing I did when I pulled you off that case before our break-up."

"You didn't talk to me first. That's why that was so bad. But I got it. I understood all but that. There was danger attached to that case, a monster the feds were after, who liked to kill those close to him. Which is why I would have understood if you had talked to me."

"I'm talking to you now. You deserve your own wins, Mia. And as much as we both want to believe you don't still feel like you're in my shadow, that doesn't just go away in a year of working for someone else."

"I love you. Your success is something I'm proud of."

"And I loved my father and was proud of him, but it was hell being his son before I proved my worth. I perhaps haven't been understanding enough about how that, despite a slight shift in context, might translate to you with me. Your success is good for us and I will cheer you on every step of the way. Call Delaney and tell her you want to bring in Reese as co-counsel."

I press my hand to his handsome face, searching his gaze, looking for the pain and torment that had driven me to make this decision. "You're sure?"

"Completely."

I study him a moment more and I believe him, I do, but I also know he's worried.

"I will not hold you back, Mia," he adds as if he's reading my mind. "That's not love. That's not a partnership. If you want to do this, we both need you to do this."

His voice radiates with the passion of conviction. "All right then. This will please Delaney. And me. Thank you for supporting me."

"No thanks ever needed, baby. Call her." He kisses me and then walks away.

I turn and watch him with all his grace and male beauty saunter back to the table, a regal tiger that could pounce or purr at any moment, and my heart swells with love. He sits down facing in my direction and when his eyes meet mine, there is this punch of awareness between us, and I can almost feel our bond grow right here and now.

I smile.

He smiles.

God, I love his smile.

And I love him.

In this moment, I know that Ri won't win or beat us. We will win. Together.

Chapter Seventy

Mia

Delaney Wittmore answers on the first ring. "My God, Mia. Did you see me on the television? *Again.*" She sounds frazzled and hoarse, her tone a raspy, after-crying tone I know well. I had it often after Grayson and I broke up. A break-up that could have been avoided, while Delaney couldn't have fixed her problems with her husband. He was an abuser who would have seen her dead before he let her leave him.

"I did, actually," I say, leaning on the bar and staring at a television with yet another image of her on the screen. "But you knew this was going to happen. That's the thing, Delaney. A deal doesn't stop the press from a fascination with you. True crime rules the networks these days. You don't escape this for you or your daughter, just by taking a deal."

"Well, it doesn't matter, does it? They won't give me a deal."

"Look," I say, "if you take a deal or if you're convicted, the family will likely sue for your inheritance."

"I don't want it. I have my interior design business. I can make my own money."

"They'll sue for your daughter's inheritance."

"Can they do that?"

"They can. They will."

She's silent a moment. "I should have run away and hidden years ago, but I didn't want to do that to my daughter. And he wasn't a man to let me run away. He would have found me. What next?"

"Here's what I want us to do. I met with Reese Summer today. He's well-respected. He wins. He's ethical. I want to bring him in as part of your team. Google him. You'll understand why."

"I know who he is. I considered talking to him before you, but I really wanted a woman and when I met you, I was sold. This wouldn't change you being on my team, right?"

"Not at all. This just offers you extra support, but he needs to believe in you how I do. He wants to meet tomorrow morning. Early. He's got a trial going on right now." I don't tell her we'll have to push back the trial. I want Reese to win her over first. "Can you do it?"

"Yes. I'll be there." I give her the address and directions with the help of the bartender.

"Got it," she says. "Mia, thank you."

"Thank me by staying strong."

We disconnect and I return to the table as Reese is standing to leave. "She'll be here," I say quickly. "And I've reconsidered. I think a partnership works."

Reese smiles. "I thought you might and I'm glad you did."

He and I shake on our agreement. He and Grayson shake on their agreement. Cat and I hug. "You two are going to be magic together. I feel it."

I'm smiling when they depart and Grayson leans in and murmurs, "We're magic together."

I turn and wrap my arms around him. "You're my magic, Grayson Bennett." I kiss his jaw. "Can we go home now?"

"Yes, baby," he says, his voice thick with a low, raspy, affected quality. "Let's go home."

His arm slides around me and he sets us in motion, and I'm more relaxed than I have been since our return. That is until I find the tall, dark, and lethal-looking familiar man waiting for us at the door. Adrian is here and he's here because we still require bodyguards. We're still in danger.

"Hiya, Mama Mia," he greets, and I do laugh. He's a funny guy who I sense has a lot more to him than good looks and jokes, like killer instincts. And those killer instincts are both nerve-wracking and comforting at the same time.

"Driver's waiting on us," he says, motioning us toward the front door. "His name is Will. If you need him just call out, 'Danger, Danger Will Robinson.' His name is actually Will Axe, and that isn't a joke. We call him The Axe." He jumps right to another topic, with whiplash quickness. "Are we headed to the hotel?"

"Our apartment," Grayson says. "We'll need to get our bags—"

"We'll pack 'em up and load 'em up for you, if you wish," he offers.

Grayson confirms with me and then gives the go-ahead. Adrian motions us forward. "Willy-boy awaits." And from there, he keeps talking, and by the time we load into the Escalade, Grayson is shaking his head and laughing. "He's a character."

"Yes," I say, smiling. "He is."

The driver eyes me from the front seat. "Welcome. I'm Axe."

I laugh. "The Axe?"

He grunts. "In case you didn't notice. Adrian talks too much. Just Axe is fine."

Adrian climbs into the vehicle and leans around his seat to eye us. "Axe me anything you like."

I laugh and Grayson just shakes his head. Adrian grins and turns forward. "Home we go."

Home.

That word slides under my skin and nestles deep into my soul. It affects me emotionally on so many levels. Butterflies erupt in my belly. We're going home. *I'm* going home. My eyes meet Grayson's and warmth spreads between us. "Home," I murmur.

"Home," he repeats, tenderly stroking my cheek. "And it's been too long."

"Yes, it has," I murmur.

Grayson slides his arm around me and I snuggle in close to him. We don't speak for the short ride. We just sit there, *together.* And considering not so long ago, we didn't believe we'd be together again, it's a pretty darn perfect way to spend a ride. We've just turned onto our street when Grayson's cellphone rings. He shifts and grabs his phone, glancing at the caller ID.

"Eric," he informs me before he answers.

He greets Eric and then listens and while there is no outward reaction to whatever Eric says, the air shifts, thickens, his mood darkening. "Blake has a team for that."

He listens again and then says, "Right. Understood." He disconnects.

I shift to study him. "What was that about?"

"He's going with Blake's team on the mission tonight."

I know very well that Eric is an ex-Navy SEAL so I don't allow myself to read too much into this. "Is he missing the action?"

"He says he has a gut feeling they're going to need him tonight."

The implications of tonight's raid on the attorney's house going wrong, perhaps dangerously wrong, has me turning and sinking against the seat. The scent of trouble is in the air and it's pungent and harsh.

Chapter Seventy-One

Mia

Eric's the brother Grayson never had and while I know that he knows Eric can handle himself, he's concerned for him. He has to be. I am, too. All I know about this underground group is their quest for money at all costs, and money and greed too often lead to destruction.

We arrive at the building and Axe pulls the Escalade to a side entrance. It's not long before we're out of the vehicle with both men standing with us. Axe is blond with a square jaw, the silent type who speaks few words. While Adrian is big and tall, Axe is a monster who towers over him a good two inches, which must make him six-five, at least.

"We'll both be on night shift," Adrian informs us. "We'll be watching the building and your apartment. We're wired into the property's security camera with some additions we made ourselves."

"Because we think someone is going to come and attack us in our apartment?" I ask.

Grayson catches my hand. "They're just being cautious, baby."

Adrian points at Grayson. "Your man here pays us, and pays us well, to be paranoid little shits."

And a team of bad guys wants to take down Grayson and get a big payday, I think, but I leave it alone. Bottom line, they do think someone might come at us here, or they wouldn't be here. It was a stupid question. I shouldn't have even bothered to ask it.

Adrian motions to the door. "I'll go first. You can follow. Axe is going to stay right here."

And I just want to be inside our apartment. Adrian enters the building and Grayson steps behind me, leaning in to whisper, "Relax, baby. Once we're inside the apartment, all this will melt away."

He means we can pretend that the danger is gone, but right now, that sounds pretty darn wonderful. Adrian returns and motions us forward. The minute I'm inside the familiar lobby with shiny white marble floors with the towering ceiling, memories explode inside me and so do my nerves. I'm nervous. It's so silly. This is my building with Grayson. This is my home, but I can't deny the truth. My belly is fluttering.

I end up with both men framing me on the walk toward the elevator, with Grayson holding my hand. We pass the security desk, where a guard I don't know is on duty. Grayson leans in close, near my ear, and whispers, "I never took you off the security ledger."

My heart swells with the emotions this man stirs in me and with the reminder that he never let go of me. I thought he had. I so thought he had and I was wrong. I've never been so happy to be so wrong. We reach the elevator and the doors open. His hand is on my lower back as I enter the car before him. Once he joins me, his arm is around my shoulders, our bodies snuggly molded together. I don't look at him. I can't yet because I know that when I do, when I really look at him and talk to him, it's going to be emotional for both of us. We're in love, passionately in love, but we lost each other for a full, painful year and I know now that we are far from that pain. I'm afraid, too, and I need him to know that.

In what feels like eternal minutes we finally say goodbye to Adrian and step into our apartment, our home. A huge part of me wants to just see it again, to feel it again, but it's Grayson I really need to feel. And I'm not sure he told me everything about that call with Eric. Grayson shuts the door and locks it behind us and I turn to face him, setting my purse on the entry table.

"Eric? What don't I know?"

He shrugs out of his jacket and tosses it on the entry table. "He's not a man of many words. That's all he said."

"Are you worried?"

He closes the small space between us and his hands find my face. "I don't want to talk about Eric right now."

There's a dark edginess to him that I know all too well. This is the side of Grayson only *I* know. That part of him that manages to be demanding and fierce, and yet somehow tender. "You're worried."

"I don't want to talk about Eric right now, baby. I want to enjoy being home with you. Do you know how many times I wished for you to be here? How many times it gutted me that you weren't?"

Emotions do more than well in my chest and for the moment, they quake through my body. As this man I love, seeds deep in my soul all over again, and takes root. I've said so much to him since my return and yet not enough. There are so many things I still want to say, need to say, even. "Grayson, I—"

That's all I manage. Suddenly he is kissing me, his hand closing around a chunk of my hair, the taste of him wild hunger with a big dose of that torment I'd sensed. I moan with the deliciously intense assault, my fears for Eric and his with them, fading into passion. Only he's not really gone. That torment I taste on his lips, in his kiss, is about Eric, it's about me, and every part of this story we're writing that he can't control.

His lips part from mine and he scoops me up, carrying me through the apartment, our apartment, with the ease of a man carrying a feather, which I am not. I snuggle into his strong arms and the hard wall of his chest as he walks us through our gorgeous home. I have a fleeting glimpse of the wall of windows framing the living room, and overlooking a city of twinkling lights. He's a man on a mission, and with a destination: he's taking me to our sanctuary, to our bedroom, the place I most missed when I was gone. The place where he wraps himself around me while we sleep, and holds me in that perfect way no other man could ever hold me.

It's a massive room, with a massive bed and a wall of windows. Once we're just inside the doorway, he angles me to the wall and I flip on a dim light, then fire up the fireplace in the corner. Grayson carries me to our special spot, one of the two overstuffed chairs framing the fireplace. He stands in front of it and sets me down in front of him. Before my feet have firmly settled, Grayson's hands are under my jacket and he's dragged it down my arms again, caging them and me as he did in the office. He pulls me hard against him, our bodies flush, his lips a hot breath from mine. "You belong here," he says, and his voice is low, rough, a command, even a demand that I agree with. "Say it."

"Yes," I murmur. "I belong here. I missed being here with you so very much. Grayson, I—"

He cuts me off with his mouth, his punishing, perfect mouth, and I can taste the man I know, the man no one else knows, on my tongue. This is my dark, damaged future husband, and I am certain now that we will not be sleeping tonight.

Chapter Seventy-Two

Eric

Two brothers don't need to be in one dangerous place and yet Blake and his brother Luke—my brother, too, as we're both former SEALs—insisted on raiding Brian Johnson's house. And they did so even after Blake pinged the Dungeon communications between its members about their plan to do the exact same thing on this very night. Exactly why I'm here: to protect two brothers while protecting a man who'd become my brother in Grayson.

Dressed in all black, including a black beanie and gloves, I squat in the scrub brush outside Brian Johnson's mansion while Blake works beside me on a MacBook he pulled from the bag on his hip to disarm the security system. He's already frozen the asshole's overseas accounts. The man's got mad skills. He turned over stones Ri's attorney didn't think could be turned over, and did it in keystrokes, not milestones.

Brian Johnson is a low-life scum of an attorney with greed and ethics that rival my father's. In other words, he has a whole lot of greed and very few ethics—just the kind of guy to help Ri feed these underground monsters payoff money. I left behind my family empire for Grayson's to get away from that shit. Grayson has more morals than anyone I've ever known. I won't allow a low-life loser like Ri or Johnson to take him down.

Kill or be killed.

That's what Ri turned this into, only he might as well have become a damn zombie because he just won't fucking go the hell away. The Dungeon isn't dead though. Its members are, in fact, alive and well and they want money. The question is, why come here, now, tonight? The only thing we can figure is they feel the heat, they have some idea we're onto them, and they want to grab the money and run. Which means they know we froze Brian's accounts, which was by intent, a plan Blake and I plotted out.

We wanted them to think we knew about them, but not quite be sure. We're close to shutting this shit down, but if they come up empty-handed and find no money tonight, we believe they'll stay the course and keep after Grayson. They're working for the payout. Which brings me to the other reason I'm here: the bag of cash at my hip. There's a matching one in a safe in Brian's workplace office. I've made millions on millions working for Grayson and in the stock market. Time to pay it forward. Time to end this for him. As long as we're here before the Dungeon, they'll find their money.

Blake motions me forward, which means he's sent a text message to Savage and Luke, telling them the same. I give a nod and prepare to move forward on my own, while Savage will do the same on the other side of the property where he awaits with Luke. After a lot of fucking pressure, he and Luke finally agreed to stay back and run guard. I move forward with two goals: search and deposit, and thanks to blueprints and an old Zillow posting that offered floorplan knowledge, my destination a basement window. Savage's is a living room window on the other side of the house.

I climb a wall, drop to grassy terrain, and then settle into a squat to watch and wait. Crickets chirp and an owl hoots, but there is nothing else. If Savage is moving, that big-foot Beret is one smooth operator. Staying low, I rush to the window and remove a small flashlight I intend to use to break the window, but when I try it, just to see if it might be open, it is. I'm not sure if that makes Brian stupid or if it tells us the Dungeon has been here and gone. I hope the fuck not.

I slide the window open, use the flashlight, and scan the dark finished basement to find Savage standing in front of me. "You slow as fuck fish-face SEAL. Come the fuck on. It's all clear."

The man is a piece of work, but I'm smiling as me and my bag jump into the room, shut the window and face Savage, a small handheld light between us in his big monstrous hand. Savage is about six-five give or take an inch. And broad as hell. Either he's going to trip over himself and fuck us over or he's going to jump on top of the bad guys and they'll suffocate.

"Did we find the safe?" We know he has one from Blake hacking his data files.

"I haven't been to the office beyond a cursory glance."

"I'll head there and handle the safe. See what else you can find."

"You sure you can open his safe?"

Me and hacking safes have a history thanks to the Navy, who logically assumed a savant with a thing for numbers could crack a safe that was all about numbers. "I got this." I move through the room and leave him to do what he needs to do: find anything we might need to end this hell for Grayson and put away this asshole Brian. "Because I handled the one in his office so shitty?" I ask sarcastically, because I'd opened that safe in about thirty seconds.

"Yeah, you made that look easy, but that could have been a freak fucking luck kind of thing."

I shake my head and turn my light to low before I leave him where he stands, wasting no time crossing the room and climbing a winding set of stairs. Nearing the top, I kill the light. I hesitate before rounding the corner, listening for a change that I know won't exist. Blake and Luke are in my ear, on an earpiece. They'd warn me, but years of missions and the unexpected, taught me to expect the unexpected.

After a full minute, I move forward, guided by open windows and the burn of moonlight and stars, passing through an overly luxurious living area and down a hall to the office. Once I'm there, I walk to the sitting area next to the heavy wooden desk, sit on the couch, and lift the rug. And then I go cold.

The safe is there, but the damn thing is wired to explode.

Chapter Seventy-Three

Grayson

M y lips part Mia's and I can taste a million missed moments on my tongue, a million wants, and needs. A million demands my body craves and I want to bury them all inside her. I reach up and catch the top of her blouse just above her buttons and yank, tiny buttons flying everywhere. She gasps and already I've unhooked the front clasp of her bra. Already, my gaze is raking over the swell of her high breasts, the pucker of her pink nipples.

"Grayson," she whispers, and there was a time not so long ago that I thought I'd never hear my name on her lips again, at least not spoken with that raspy burn of a plea. And that's what my name is on her lips right now: a plea.

I know what she wants, what she needs and I need. That forbidden burn of submission she has often admitted to wanting, the need in her that answers my need for control. For her, it's the only time she allows herself to fully let go, to dare to give me that control, and fear nothing. For me, inside that control is her trusting me, her being all-in in every possible way. I'd like to say I know she is, and on most levels I do, but the bite of her leaving is fresh. Her believing I cheated is a bleeding wound, only now healing. But it is healing. That said, it's true, absolutely fucking true, that her submitting right here in our bedroom and showing me how much she trusts me, feels urgent. It feels necessary.

Cupping her hands behind her back, I yank her to me hard and fast, her naked breasts smashed to my chest. I'm about to kiss her and turn her over and spank her when she says everything I didn't know I needed to hear in a mere three words. "I was lost without you." A moment later, she pushes to her toes and presses her soft lips to mine.

Just like that, she spreads a softer, sweeter emotion through me and that dark hardness only she understands submits to her. She owns me. There was a time when I might have tried to fight such an absolute need, but there was never a chance. Not with Mia.

I tear away her jacket and toss it aside, cupping her head and slanting my mouth over her mouth, drinking her in, drugging myself with that sweetness of hers that is so damn perfect. The kind of sweetness that brings a man to his knees and I'm already there. I've been there. Her fingers tangle in the thick strands of my hair and it's as if we're swept into a far, far land, in the middle of an ocean where only we exist. Where we're drowning in each other.

It's Mia that ends that kiss, tearing her lips from mine and reaching for my tie. Impatient, I grab it and yank it out of my collar. Another time, I'd use that tie, I'd twist it around her wrists. Five minutes ago, before her confession, before her kiss, I'd been in that place where the past year fucks with my head. A place where I'd lost her and my father. I'd have done just that. I'd have used sex to take us away, to consume us, and run from the pain. Instead, I'm here, I'm present, and I don't want to be anywhere but here and present.

I've barely tossed it aside when she's fumbling with my buttons. "Why are you not naked right now?"

"You first," I murmur, turning her around and unzipping her skirt. She kicks off her heels and when my hands slide under the material, I slide it, and it alone since she's still pantyless, down her hips. She steps out of it and when I might otherwise hold her here, I don't. Not now. That's not what I want now. She rotates to face me and just her standing there willingly naked and vulnerable is enough. I don't care about control right now. And my need for that is a dangerous black hole I need to avoid.

Trust.

I have to give it to get it.

I have to remember that my walls created her fears.

I unbutton my shirt and then just tear my shirt over my head. I've barely tossed it aside and she's pressed against me, soft and warm. She presses her lips to mine again, and the minute her tongue strokes mine, that need only she stirs inside me explodes. I just plain burn for Mia, a soul-deep, feel-her-in-every-part-of-me burn for this woman. I let her taste that on my lips, feel that in my touch, I hold back nothing, and it's not long before my pants are gone. I sit down in that chair where we've made love and fucked—sometimes all in the same night, so many times—and take her with me.

She straddles me and I wrap my arm around her tiny waist, anchoring her, kissing her nipple and suckling before I lift her and press inside the wet heat of her body. She slides down against me, taking every inch of me inside her and settling snuggly against my hips. My hand splays between her shoulder blades, erasing the separation between us by molding all her soft curves to every hard part of me.

"I could live inside you," I growl softly, my mouth slanting over her mouth, my tongue stroking deep, and we sink into that deep, drugging place where there is nothing but us, nothing but our need for each other. We sink into that burn that has nothing to do with fucking, and everything to do with just how insanely deep this bond we share has become. I don't taste distrust. I don't taste our separation. I taste our future. I taste our hunger. Hers. Mine. Ours. I drink it in, I drink us in, and she does the same, our bodies swaying together. Our tongues savoring each other.

My lips caress her neck, her shoulder, her pebbled nipple. I caress every inch of soft skin I can find but it's when she murmurs, "Grayson," again, like she really was lost without me, and now she's found, that I truly unravel in the best of ways.

My fingers wrap her silky brown hair, and I bring her mouth to my mouth. "I was lost without you, too, Mia," I confess, and then I'm kissing her again, and she's kissing me, in a collision of need, an explosion of passion. The air shifts, the demand between us fierce. I pull her down onto me and thrust into her over and over until she gasps and buries her face in my neck. Her body trembles, her sex clenching around my cock. I groan with the feel of her squeezing me and shudder into release.

I collapse into the soft chair and Mia with me, and for a full minute, we just lay there, naked, our bodies tangled together. This woman is everything to me. My best friend, my confidante, the future mother of my children. She shivers and I roll her over, handing her a tissue while I grab my shirt, wrapping it around her.

We end up sitting there, me holding my shirt together around her, the fire flickering around us, the warmth between us. She presses her hand to my cheek. "Let's talk about why you wanted to elope."

Chapter Seventy-Four

Grayson

The past

I stand outside of my father's Manhattan apartment and I can't make myself go inside. How the hell am I supposed to tell him that Mia and I broke up? How the hell am I supposed to say the words that gut me? How the hell can I accept that I lost her?

The door opens and he stands there, staring at me, my father, the man who has inspired me to be just like him. His eyes narrow on me. "What happened?"

"I'm going to need a drink to answer that."

He studies me for a few probing beats and then motions me forward. "Get your ass in here, boy." He turns away and I stand there at the door, unable to enter. I waited for weeks to tell my father about this. Weeks where I hoped Mia would come back to me. I waited because I knew that the minute I tell my father, this is real. She's really gone. And she is. I have to do this.

I enter the apartment and shut the door.

I find my father in the living room on the couch, the fireplace crackling with two glasses of whiskey already poured. I try not to think about how much Mia loves this room and that fireplace. I join him and sit down, losing my tie, and reaching for the drink. I down it and my father refills the glass. "Where's Mia?" he asks, homing in on the problem, because he knows me. "She hasn't been around in a while."

"An employee took her top off, pressed herself against me, and while I was trying to get her off me, Mia walked in."

"Oh fuck," he murmurs, downing his own drink. "How long ago?"

"Three weeks." I look at him. "I didn't tell you because I was certain I'd convince her it wasn't what she thought it was."

"Was it?"

"No. Hell no. There's no one for me but Mia."

"But you haven't won her back."

"No. And I won't. I'm done trying."

"Why would you stop trying?"

"She went to work for Ri. And Ri wants her. He wants her in a bad way."

"Does he have her?"

"She went to work for him, Dad." I refill my glass.

"*Does he have her*, son?"

"Mia would never have gone to work for him if he didn't. She knows he's my enemy."

"Sounds like you want an excuse to quit fighting for her."

"That's not true," I say. "I just know when to give up. You taught me that. Don't fight a losing battle."

"Working for Ri and fucking him are two different things."

"No," I say. "If she's working for him, she's fucking him."

"Like you were fucking that woman in your office?" he challenges.

"It's not the same thing."

He arches a brow. "Why isn't it?"

"I didn't choose to have that woman pressed up against me. Mia chose that job."

"She probably thinks you chose it for her by fucking that other woman." He doesn't give me time to reply. "On a positive note, you know she's not after your money. She walked away from you and it."

"How is that positive? She walked away."

"From you and the money. And if she comes back, it's for you. Just you." He doesn't give me time to reply yet again. "Did you know that I broke up with your mother once?"

"You did? When?"

"Before we got married. She thought I was being an arrogant ass and that I picked a stunning secretary for her ass, not her skills."

"Did you?" I ask.

"Hell no. I almost didn't hire her because of her ass. I didn't want your mother to think I was chasing said ass, and still, she did. I was angry at her for thinking so little of me and I didn't go after her at first. That all but did me in. Took me six months to win her back. You know what I did?"

"What?"

"We eloped. I put a ring on her finger the minute I had the chance."

"But I've seen the wedding photos," I say. "It was a huge wedding."

"Six months after we eloped. I made damn sure your mother knew there wasn't another ass on the planet that could get my attention." He lifts his glass. "And the rest is history. Kept her for the rest of her life, and I hired ugly secretaries from that point on."

I laugh, but it's not genuine. I'm not going to get Mia back. I'm not going after her to try. She has Ri now and I hate the fucking pain of losing her.

Chapter Seventy-Five

Mia

The present

W e're still sitting there in front of the fire in our special chair, with my hand on his cheek, but Grayson is far away in his mind. "Where are you right now?"

He catches my hand in his. "Very much with you, Mia. What do you want to say to me?"

"I guess I could start with all the thoughts I've had since you brought it up."

"I'm listening," he says thoughtfully.

"I'm confused," I admit. "Part of me is thrilled that you're that eager to make me your wife."

"And the other part of you?"

"Afraid it's because it's you that doesn't trust me anymore." He opens his mouth to speak and I don't give him the chance. "This is my home. This is *our* home."

"Yes. It is."

"I should never have left."

"I shouldn't have let you leave. But we've talked about this. We have to put it behind us. It's in the past."

"No," I say. "No. It's not. We're both still terrified of the damage our break-up did to us. I'm afraid you'll wake up and hate me for leaving. You're afraid I'll leave because I already left. That part of you that has lost everyone you love will never fully trust me not to leave again."

He looks away and that cut of his gaze guts me. I start to stand and he catches my wrist, his eyes meeting mine again. "I trust you like I've never trusted anyone, even my father because you know all those inner parts of me that I show no one else. And you still love me."

My heart squeezes and I press my palm to his cheek. "And you know mine. You know I will never leave again."

"Then elope with me."

"You say that like I need to elope with you to prove that I won't leave."

His hands go to my waist and he pulls me close. "Elope with me because you can't wait any more than I can wait. That doesn't mean we can't have our big wedding. It just means we spend the holidays as husband and wife."

"I don't know if I should say yes or no. I want you to believe in me and us enough to trust that I'll still be here on the day we set that wedding date. But I also want you to know that I don't want to wait either. I want to be your wife."

"Did you know that my mother and father eloped?"

Her brows furrow. "But I saw the photos."

"That's what I said when my father told me. They'd broken up, like us, over my father's secretary."

I sit up. "What?"

He catches my hand and pulls me back down on the cushion, his hand settling on my hip, his leg twined with my leg. "He didn't cheat, baby. It was similar to what happened to us. Mom was jealous of his secretary. He was upset she didn't trust him. They were apart for six months. When they finally came back together, he wasn't giving her the chance to believe there was any woman for him but her. They eloped and then planned their wedding."

This explains so much. "Was that his idea or hers?"

"He didn't say, but I got the impression it was his."

Emotions expand in my chest, so many emotions. "You really want to do this, don't you?"

He inhales a breath and looks skyward, seeming to struggle with his own emotions, a rare thing for this man, before he levels me in a turbulent stare. "I need you to marry me now. It's not about trust. It's about needing my woman, my best friend, my life, to be my wife. It's not about you leaving, it's about you not living another day that could be your last or my last, and not being my wife. Marry me because we need to be husband and wife."

Those words hit me like a wrecking ball. He's not worried about me leaving. He knew Ri for years. He just saw him lying lifeless in a stairwell, but more so, he saw him holding a gun to my head.

Grayson tried to get Ri to shoot him to save me. He's afraid we'll end this life without ever being husband and wife. If I say yes, though, I'm giving in to that fear. I'm feeding that fear. A thought slides into my mind and I go with it. "How about a compromise?"

"Meaning what?"

"I'm not sure I want a big wedding-"

"No, baby. I want you to have your dream wedding. This isn't a this or that."

"Hear me out, please," I say, the influence his father had on this decision and his life in my mind now, feeding this idea. "There is so much press right now. Grayson Bennett's wedding will be TMZ-worthy all over again."

"I want the world to know I'm marrying you, Mia."

My heart squeezes and I press my hand to his jaw. "And I love you for that, but what I'd love is to have a ceremony on New Year's Eve at the house with the tree still up. That way your father is there in spirit."

"What about the lighthouse?"

"It'll be too cold for the lighthouse, but when everyone leaves, we can escape to be there together, our private place, alone. I can still wear my dress. It will be small and intimate and special."

He searches my face. "You really like this idea?"

"I love this idea. I can't believe we didn't think of it before now. It's still a fast turnaround with Thanksgiving only two weeks away, but it's the perfect way to start a new year together. My only negative is the three months won't be over. But it will be close and we could lock ourselves away here for the last two weeks, just you and me. And this makes this our story, not your parents' story. What do you think?"

He studies me for several more beats, his green eyes warm before he molds me to him. "Yes. Let's get married on New Year's Eve in the Hamptons house."

I smile a genuine ear-to-ear grin. "Then I want to go look at my dress. I'm actually dying to see it right now. I never saw the final dress after alterations." My brows furrow. "You haven't seen it, right? That's bad luck."

"I haven't," he assures me. "It's bagged in the upstairs spare bedroom. Go look, baby. I'll go open a bottle of wine." He stands and pulls me to my feet and kisses me before he reaches for his pants.

I smile again, excitement bubbling over as I highjack his shirt that I'm still wearing and take off for the bedroom door, and hurry through the apartment, still not taking time to enjoy the luxurious living room. It takes me about two minutes to climb the winding stairs and run down a hallway to enter the walk-in closet. I flip on the light and butterflies flutter in my belly at the sight of the garment bag. Hurrying forward, I unzip the bag. My heart in my throat, silly nerves fluttering all over in my belly for no reason at all. Once the zipper is down, I don't pull the dress fully from the bag, but I don't have to. I stare in wonder, a stunning white gown that is simple elegance accented by tiny butterflies in the lace. Butterflies that to many cultures, and to me, mean hope and a positive future but they hold another meaning to many that somehow feels all the more appropriate: resurrection. The resurrection of our love. Everything else fades away but this man and our wedding, images of me in this dress, and Grayson handsome in his tuxedo. And the tree that we've decorated together in the background, symbolic of many more years together to come.

My heart squeezes and I zip it back up, before rushing from the closet and the room in search of Grayson. I find him in the kitchen behind the shiny gray marble island, filling two wine glasses, the television over the island playing the news. It's something he always does, like a habit. He turns on the news when he's in the kitchen. It's this familiar part of our life that warms me all the more. I missed these moments when he's just being himself when we're just sharing our lives, living life.

I hurry to his side and wrap my arms around him, this man who is my Prince Charming.

"It's still the dress and you're still the man. There was never going to be another man."

"And there was never going to be another woman," he says, cupping my face. "You're home, Mia, and that home is with me. Forever."

"Forever," I whisper, and when his mouth comes down on mine, it really is like I'm finally home. I'm where I belong. With him.

He offers me one of the wine glasses and once he picks up his glass, we're about to toast when the newscaster says, "We have breaking news. There's been an explosion in a New Jersey residential home with a fire that is now threatening nearby residences. While firefighters work to stop the blaze and contain the damage, we're getting word that the home belongs to an attorney named Brian Johnson."

My heart skips a beat and bile rises in my throat. Grayson and I set down our glasses because we both know who Brian Johnson is. Without a word, Grayson snakes his phone from his pocket and dials a number. And I know why. We both know who was in that house tonight and I pray that Eric and Blake's team were out before the explosion.

Chapter Seventy-Six

Grayson

I dial Eric only to have his voicemail pick up and it's like a punch in the gut followed by a blade. Next up, I dial Blake. Again, I get his voicemail. I'm bleeding out here with the idea that something happened to Eric, and Blake and his team. I try Adrian, who answers on the first ring. "Tell me they weren't in that explosion."

"I have no idea what you're talking about and no, I haven't been drinking. I just really have no idea what you're talking about."

"The house Eric went to with your team exploded and no one is answering their fucking phones."

"Say what?"

"I said—"

"Fuck," he grunts as if my words have only now hit him. "Fuck. I'm making calls. And I'm sending Axe up to stay with you until I know what the hell is going on. Don't go anywhere." He hangs up.

"Grayson?" Mia asks, watching me as I apparently pace on the opposite side of the island I don't even remember walking to now.

I force myself to halt and will myself to calm down. "No one's answering their phones, baby. Adrian didn't even know the house had blown up." I dial Blake again.

"I've got Kara's number," Mia says. "I'm calling her."

She darts around the island and I catch her wrist. "Where are you going?"

"My phone's by the door in my purse."

"Axe is coming up. You need to put on clothes. And don't answer the door. I'll do it."

She steps close and wraps her arms around me. "It's going to be okay. This is Eric. He's a SEAL. He's a genius, quite literally."

"He's still human. He still blows up in an exploding house like the rest of us."

She kisses my jaw. "He's going to be okay. I feel it in my gut. I'm going to go try Kara and try to get you some news." She pushes away from me.

I dial Davis and he answers in one ring. "Tell me you've heard from Eric."

"Not for hours. Why?"

"He went to that attorney's house with Blake's team tonight. It exploded and he's not answering his phone. None of them are." I run my hand through my hair. "Where are you?"

"At home."

"Pull out that Glock you own and keep it with you. Don't go anywhere until I find out if you're in danger." I don't give him time to start worrying my ear off. I'm doing enough of that on my own. I disconnect and text Adrian: *Is Davis in danger as my personal attorney and close friend? He's at home. I told him to stay there.*

While I wait for his reply, I head to our bedroom, walk into the closet and throw on jeans, a basic black tee, and sneakers. Adrian finally replies with: *I have four men here with me. I sent one to Davis, just to be safe. Axe will be there with you any second.*

I'm about to exit the bedroom when Mia appears in the doorway, her dark hair still a finger-fucked mess that I created. Fifteen minutes ago, we were planning our wedding and now this.

"Kara's not answering," she says. "I'm going to get dressed."

The doorbell rings. "That's Axe." I intend to leave her to dress, but she catches my arm.

"Grayson—"

I cup her head and kiss her. "I'm okay, baby." It's one of the only lies I ever intend to tell her.

"Liar," she accuses. "But I'll forgive you under the circumstances."

I don't dispute her accusation. The doorbell rings again, and I kiss her again and untangle my arm from her grip before Axe blows down our door. I head through the apartment toward the door with a knot in my damn gut. Eric's silence is killing me and it's not a good sign. I don't even want to know what news awaits me at the front door. I pause in the foyer and step to the panel beside the door and punch the button to the camera view to find Axe standing there.

I yank open the door. "Any news?" I back up to allow his entry.

"Nothing," he says grimly, stepping inside and shutting the door, automatically locking up.

I key the security system into action and turn to Axe, who is doing the same with me. "What do you think is happening?"

"We have a silent protocol if there is even a one percent chance we could bring danger to our families. I don't think they're dead. I think they locked down."

I don't know if I'm relieved or the opposite. I scrub my jaw. "I need a drink. You need a drink?"

"None for me." He pulls back the edge of his leather jacket and shows me his weapon. "We both want me to shoot straight."

"Well, then eat me out of house and home. You have to need something. These are the men you work with."

His jaw clenches but he offers nothing more than a barely perceivable incline of his chin. We enter the living room right as Mia, dressed in leggings and a T-shirt, with sneakers, rushes into the room. "Anything?" she asks urgently.

"Any intel that might represent a breach of safety to our team or family is a mandatory silence order until that threat is cleared. Adrian and I can't even reach our team," Axe explains.

"Then we know something went wrong," Mia replies, "aside from the obvious house exploding." She gives an awkward laugh. "I guess that was a stupid statement."

"There's a difference between getting your mind around something," Axe replies, "and stupid. That wasn't stupid."

I walk to the bar and pour a whiskey for me and Axe. If he won't drink his, I will. I return to the living room where Mia has flipped on the news on the big screen and claimed the couch, while Axe is now sitting in the chair to her left. I set the whiskey in front of him and then claim a spot next to Mia.

"As much as it pains me to decline yet again what I'm certain is a fine, and expensive whiskey," Axe says, "I must. Chocolate is my only on-duty sin."

Mia perks up. "Did someone say chocolate?" She casts me a hopeful look. "Please tell me you have some?"

"We have plenty," I assure her because she loves chocolate and it just became a habit to keep it in the house. "Always."

Her eyes soften with the knowledge that any stock of chocolate is about her, not me, and she kisses my cheek before she walks to the kitchen. "We both know that whiskey isn't going to affect you." And because I'm an observer, a man who reads people fast and well, I add, "We both also know that you're a duty kind of guy, a rule-maker, and follower. Drink it. I won't hold it against you."

Mia deposits a big bowl of chocolate on the table. "I claim the Heath bars. I'll chew your arm off for these things."

Axe studies me a moment, grabs the whiskey glass, downs the bourbon, and smiles. "Damn that's good. Thank you." He then grabs a Mr. Goodbar. "I'd chew your arm off for one of these things, I love them so much."

Mia laughs and hands me a basic Hershey's. "That's all that's left for you."

She manages to tease a hint of a smile from me, that I don't expect. I down my whiskey, set my glass down, and accept the candy.

"Did you know that chocolate really does affect the stress cortisol levels during an extreme stress spike?" Mia asks. "If you eat it every day just to eat it, then it increases your stress cortisol but during stress, it lowers it."

"Well, then I better have another Goodbar," Axe says, snapping up a second candy bar.

"What's your story, Axe?" I ask.

"Ex-CIA which means I have no story." He downs his candy and grabs three more.

"Of course you have a story," Mia insists. "Do you have family?"

"No," he says.

"Where are you from?" she asks.

"All over."

Her brow furrows. "Considering you don't talk unless it's about chocolate and all Adrian does *is talk*, how do you put up with each other?"

He holds up a miniature Goodbar. "I eat candy so I won't kill him." His eyes catch on the TV before he points to the remote. "Turn that up."

I down the chocolate in my hand and grab the remote, turning up the volume as a picture of a man flashes on the screen. "In a bizarre twist," the newscaster is saying, "This man, Brian Johnson, was not home when his home exploded tonight, but he was later found dead in his car outside an event he attended tonight. The cause of death is yet to be determined."

Axe grabs his phone from his pocket and dials. "Adrian," he says. "Yeah. I just saw it on the news." He listens a minute and hangs up. "He's on his way to the lockdown location to try to get answers."

"Lockdown location?" Mia asks before I get the chance.

"If our team locked down for safety reasons," Axe explains, "that's where they'll go."

The doorbell rings and my spine stiffens, my eyes narrowing on Axe. "If Adrian isn't here, who is that?"

Axe is already on his feet, drawing his weapon.

Chapter Seventy-Seven

Grayson

"**G**rayson?" Mia asks, pushing to her feet, all doe-eyed with fear, and why wouldn't she be? Axe has a gun in his hand, charging for the door that he knows is protected by a security system. I like the guy but *damn it.*

"Not enough chocolate or whiskey clearly, baby," I reply mildly by intent. I'm not going to add to her stress with a bombastic reaction. "Stay here just to be safe." I kiss her temple and force myself to walk with measured steps toward the door when I'd rather fucking run.

Still, I manage a fast enough pace to be on Axe's heels when he enters the foyer. "There's a security camera," I say because maybe I'm wrong and he doesn't know.

He walks to the panel and I open the drawer to the hall table and remove the Glock I do more than keep on hand. I know how to use it and use it well.

Now that I'm armed and ready for trouble, Axe lowers his weapon. "It's them," he murmurs, unlocking the door.

I don't know who "them" references, which is why I don't return my weapon to that drawer. For just a moment though, I'm back on that golf course, when my invincible father tumbled to the ground. I'm leaning over him, and my father's pale face and raspy breaths have me screaming for help that never comes. It never comes because he never had a chance. He'd had what they call a "widowmaker," a massive heart attack that shreds the heart. So yes, Mia's right about Eric being a SEAL and a genius, but I know from experience that even the good ones, even the strong ones, are not invincible.

Which is exactly why when Axe opens the door, I hold my breath, waiting for the enemy that I can't defeat, the one that takes and takes and just keeps on taking: *death.* I'm not holding the gun to shoot someone. I'm holding it because I just need some damn way to feel under control. I'm waiting for bad news, and I'd welcome another enemy, one that I'd have to battle because I can fight and win any battle that isn't death.

Axe backs up and the first person that I see walk through the door is not an enemy at all. It's Rick Savage—one of the Walker men. A giant of a man with a scar that ripples down his cheek. "Don't shoot," he says, holding up his big hands. "I told Eric not to cut that wire, but you know, I'm just a surgeon, not a fucking savant, and he didn't listen."

"I didn't cut a wire at all," Eric growls, entering the foyer. "We weren't there when the damn house exploded." He eyes my gun and then me. "You've been hanging around these guys *way* too much."

I'm just processing that Eric's really here and okay, relief washing over me when Mia beats me to an outward reaction.

"Eric!" she exclaims, rushing forward and throwing her arms around him. "We thought you were dead. God, Grayson would not have survived losing you. I wouldn't survive losing you." She looks up at him. "You have no idea how relieved we are that you're here."

We.

God, I've missed being a "we" with Mia.

Mia gets to Eric, too. I see that in the softening of his facial features that are normally steel and stone. And Eric is not an emotional man. He's not a man of many words. He's also a man with a blood family that treats him like shit, but I am his family, we're his family now that Mia is back. Mia has driven home that point—she's affected him in that way she does everyone around her.

"Well then," Eric says, "I guess I better come all the way in then, shouldn't I?" He squeezes her shoulder. "And your man there needs to put away that gun before he shoots one of us."

Mia whirls on me but she says nothing. She knows I have the gun. She knows how to use it herself, but I want her to practice. I want her to become an expert. I want her to protect herself in every way possible. I seal the gun back in its drawer, and Axe and Savage head to the living room. Mia kisses my cheek and follows them, a silent understanding in her actions that I need a minute with Eric.

God, I really did miss this woman.

I close the space between me and Eric and while we don't hug, we do lock palms. And I go one step further and grab his forearm with my free hand. "You're not a damn SEAL anymore. Don't do that shit again."

"You don't have to worry about me," Eric assures me as we break the connection.

My jaw sets. "Yeah, fuck you too, man," I say, which is not a statement I usually make. That's not how I talk, that's not who I am, but that's exactly why it gets my point across.

He laughs and confirms that I am indeed accurate in that assumption. "Point made. You want to protect me. I want to protect you. But the good news is that we feel like this is over."

My brow shoots up. "You feel? Since when do you give two coins about a feeling rather than a fact?"

"Since we're backing that statement up with facts. Brian's dead. The Dungeon killed him. They ended him because they don't want him to be able to talk. They want this over. They don't need him."

"You're sure it was them?"

"Blake picked up a plate on a traffic camera near the murder. That plate belongs to someone he's identified as part of the Dungeon." The doorbell rings. "And I hope that's the half-dozen pizzas we ordered on the way over here. Savage and I haven't eaten in hours."

Now I laugh because only Eric would take it upon himself to order pizza to be delivered to my apartment and I'm damn glad he's alive to do it.

A few minutes later, Mia and I are sitting on barstools with Eric and Savage across from us, and Axe at the endcap, all of us eating pizza. "The attorney Ri enlisted in his dirty deeds is dead," Mia says. "I can't quite get my head around that."

"Good fucking riddance," Savage, says, finishing off what I think is most of a pizza with record-breaking speed. "He was a lowlife. And they got rid of him because they didn't need him anymore."

"And that means what?" Mia presses.

"Here's what we know," Eric begins, finishing off a slice. "We were smart enough to walk away when we saw the safe wired to blow."

Savage finishes that thought before Eric gets the chance. "Those Dungeon assholes showed up after we exited the house. Which we know because us smart guys were lurking in the bushes, the way all honorable men do and all. They blew themselves the fuck up, at least a few of them did. I hear those are the brand of asshole that grow like weeds, but never fear. Eric is here. He shoved a bunch of cash into that dweeb attorney's work safe and the rest of the Dungeon, the ones still alive, grabbed it and ran."

I set my slice down, my gaze sharpening on Eric, who's directly across from me. "How much money? And where did it come from?"

"Enough money," Eric replies. "They won't stay around to get busted, believe me."

"Where did it come from?"

He arches a brow. "Does it matter?"

"If it came from your bank account, not mine, then yes. It matters."

"You know I'd never spend your money without clearing it."

"Exactly," I say. "How much do I owe you?"

He shoots right back with, "It's more about how much I owe you, now isn't it?"

"You owe me nothing."

"Untrue on every level. Bottom line," he adds, "Blake's tracking the Dungeon's communications and so far, we believe this is over."

"How much money?" I ask, looking at Savage.

"A fuck-ton."

My gaze returns to Eric's. "Then I should write the check out to you as a fuck-ton?"

Mia, my little keeper of peace, delicately clears her throat and changes the subject. "When do we know if this is over? Are we on lockdown?"

"We aren't," Eric replies. "In fact, Blake and I both agree that we need to act as normal as possible."

"And then what?" Mia asks. "When are we free from this?"

I catch her hand. "Soon, baby."

Her lips thin and she looks between me and Eric. "Now or in three months?"

Savage stands up. "Axe and I are going to leave you to this. We'll be nearby if you need us."

Axe pushes to his feet and offers us a mock salute. I've apparently gotten over him and his rash pulling of the gun. Funny how everyone being alive and well smooths out a wrinkle.

"Thanks, Axe," Mia says. "Take all that chocolate if you want it."

"Chocolate?" Savage asks, perking up. "What chocolate?"

Mia points to the living room and he heads that way, with Axe scowling and following on his heels.

Eric stands as well. "I need to hit the road."

My lips press together. "Mia, baby, give me and Eric a moment."
"Not tonight, Grayson," Eric replies. "She's home. Enjoy her being home. I'll key in the security code and lock up." With that, he heads out of the kitchen.

Bristling with his dismissal, I stand up with the intent of pursuing him, but Mia is instantly on her feet, stepping in front of me, her tiny hands settling on my chest. "Fighting over money, or me naked in your bed, our bed now, again." Her blue eyes flash. "Choose now."

When she puts it that way—Eric can wait.

I scoop her up and start walking to the bedroom.

Chapter Seventy-Eight

Mia

Grayson wastes no time settling me on the bed and coming down on top of me, the sweet weight of his big body anchored above mine by his elbows. "Mia," he whispers, his voice rough with emotion.

The truth is, I'm roughened up with emotions, in a way no one else can.

I reach up, my fingers rasping over his newly formed stubble. "I can't believe I'm here."

"Me either, baby," he murmurs, and the mix of tenderness and heat in his stare steals my breath. I still have moments when I can't believe that this amazing man is affected by me. I know it's part of what got us in trouble in the past, but I can't help it. I'm his biggest fan. I will always be his biggest fan, but what I failed to see in the past, by no fault of his, is that he's mine as well. And for all his years of experience, for all his worldliness, he's damaged, and I know that I somehow speak to that damage in all the right ways.

He rolls us to our sides, facing each other. "I just wish you didn't have to feel fear. I want you to just be home and safe."

"Maybe it's over."

"Yes," he says. "Maybe it's over, but *we*, Mia, *are not* and never will we be again. And we're getting married on New Year's Eve." Just that easily, he brings us back to where this night once sparkled and shined. His mouth closes down on mine and it's then that I know he doesn't want to talk. He doesn't want to live in the danger and the trouble. He wants to live right here with me, with us, and so do I. His lips caress mine, a feather-light touch I feel in every part of me. Even when we were apart, I felt him deep in my very soul. His fingers trail over my arm, goosebumps lifting in their wake. Right now, there is no Dungeon or house explosion. There's no murder or mayhem.

There is just us.

Me.

Him.

Loving each other forever.

We undress each other and end up under the blanket, naked and facing each other, and there is a fierce emotional energy between us. And tenderness, so much tenderness. We make love in *our bed,* in *our bedroom,* and in *our apartment.* And when it's over, I fall asleep on his chest and in his arms, and despite all that is going on around us, more relaxed than I have been in years.

I wake to Grayson snuggling me from behind and nuzzling my neck. "It's time to get up, baby."

I snuggle my backside against him and hold onto his arm where it's draped around me. "Do I have to?"

"Believe me, baby, I want to keep you right here, but Delaney—"

I groan and roll over to face him. "I have to get up." But I don't. I run my fingers through his wonderfully thick dark hair. "How are you?"

"Baby, you're home. I'm perfect."

I know that's not true. I know why he was holding that gun last night despite a monster of a man named Axe working our security. He is still spinning out of control, but he doesn't give me time to press the topic or even open it up at all. He rolls out of bed—tall, dark, rippling with muscle, and perfectly naked—and takes me with him to the shower. I forget about my questions and worries for at least a little longer, because how can I not when he's sinfully demanding in the shower, under a hot stream of water? A little while later, we stand at the double sinks together, engaging in our morning routine, sneaking peeks at each other and sharing smiles. Somehow after Ri attacked us, it's all the more surreal, so very surreal.

With fifteen minutes to spare before we leave, and as used to be our routine, we end up in the kitchen sipping coffee—me in a navy-blue suit dress and him in a gray suit with a navy-blue tie that I picked for him. We flip on the news in the kitchen, scan for anything important, and find nothing. Satisfied for now, we turn it back off and relish our morning home together. Despite the "relish in each other" part of this morning, I feel the clawing of heavier topics demanding to be heard. I'm worried about Grayson. I can't get that image of him holding that gun out of my mind. I'm about to press him to talk about how he's really feeling when his cellphone rings. I sigh and lean against the island while he leans against the counter with the sink behind him and me in front of him. He murmurs, "It's Blake," before answering the call.

My nerves are instantly bouncing around and punching me in the chest and belly. I need this to be over. *We* need this Ri situation to be over, all of us. Somehow I manage to summon my best courtroom calm, and I even sip my coffee.

"Let me put you on speaker," Grayson says and then, "Mia and Blake. You're both on the line."

"Morning, Mia," Blake greets.

"Is it?" I challenge and set my mug on the counter, quickly correcting myself. "I mean, good morning. And thank you for everything you did last night."

Grayson responds to my obvious edginess by closing the space between us, his legs shackling my legs, one hand at my waist. His eyes are warm—the message in their depths promising me that whatever is right or wrong, we'll face it together.

"It *is*," Blake assures me. "Really flipping good. And just so you know. Flipping doesn't do that sentence justice, but my wife is on my ass over the F-word. It's really f-ing good. I was up all night monitoring the Dungeon, on the dark web and otherwise. They've pulled out. They have their money. They're satisfied. The FBI and CIA have them on their radar and are working to take down their operation. Apparently, they have been for a while now. Here's where the really f-ing good comes into play. The FBI is offering you and your team immunity if you allow them to use your company to take them down."

Grayson scowls. "Use my company? I don't know if I like how that sounds."

"With limits that you and your legal counsel set-up. I'm getting the deal to you to review with your team and to Reese. He'll talk to you about a counter with your terms. Be happy. They want you to make this deal. This is going to be on your terms."

"Why are they suddenly offering a deal?"

"Things change when you pit two agencies against the other. I have an ex-CIA agent on board who knows who to talk to. Once they tried to take over, the FBI changed their tune. You're free. This is all but over. Celebrate. Eat chocolate, if my guys left you any. Drink champagne. *Get married.* Adrian and Axe are sleeping off the night. You have Jacob and Smith with you today. Both are quiet,

unlike Adrian and Savage. May the force be with you and all of us."
He hangs up.

Grayson slides his phone into his pocket. "Well?" I ask, prodding for his feelings.

"I'm cautiously optimistic."

I breathe out in relief. "Then so am I."

He picks up my coffee and sips before offering it to me, turning the cup so that we drink from the same spot. His green eyes simmer with heat, sunshine on a winter's day, sunshine on every winter day I could ever live. My belly flutters with the intimate act, that somehow is just as intimate as us naked in that shower. I sip the coffee and when I'm done, his hand covers mine over the mug.

"I think you better call the wedding planner, baby, any wedding planner that has the time to help. New Year's Eve will be here before we know it."

My lips curve and all that sunshine is pouring into me, warming all those cold spots that chilled me this past year. Optimism officially wins. Today is the day our new life really begins. Because today is the day my man, and sunshine, wins.

Chapter Seventy-Nine

Mia

S mith and Jacob are both military types that stick with
formalities like "yes, ma'am" and "how are you, sir?" I'd
normally try to break through that stiffness and force them to
be the real people they are, but today, I don't. Once we're in the
back of the Escalade, I'm focused on Delaney and my case notes.
My goal right now is to bring Reese and Delaney together in a
way that sticks and then show them both a path to victory.

Grayson sits next to me, his big powerful leg pressed to mine,
and peeks at my notes with my blessing. I want him to believe
in this case, in Delaney, in me. His cellphone rings and he snags
it from his pocket to show me the caller ID that reads, Eric.

Grayson answers and after a quick few words, he hangs up.
"He heard about the offer. He wants to talk about it."

This stiffens my spine. "And?"

"He wants to know the terms, but he's cautiously optimistic."

Cautiously optimistic, I repeat in my head. I keep hearing
those words but I cling to them. I want this to be over, really
over, but I also know Grayson. He can assess the deal, he's a
talented attorney himself, but that won't be enough. He'll want
Eric and Davis, his confidants in different ways, to offer in-depth
opinions, to pass along to Reese. This agreement is nothing but
a verbal tease right now.

I force my focus back to my client notes and Grayson's gaze
catches on the controversial idea I have for Delaney's defense.
He reaches for my notepad. "Can I?"

"Of course," I say, holding my breath as he scans the notes
in more detail before those intelligent green eyes meet mine. "I
think you need to be running our criminal law division." It's
the biggest compliment I could ever get from anyone.

I'm warmed by his praise, my cheeks heating, but I force myself to remain dubious for Delaney's sake. "I hope Reese is as approving of my strategy as you are."

"If he doesn't, she doesn't need him."

His confidence in my strategy matters and not just because I'm representing his firm and him, but because I care about what happens to Delaney.

"It's true," I say of what he's read. I don't speak the details, not with Smith and Jacob in the vehicle. I trust the Walker team, but Grayson is part of Delaney's legal team and they aren't, which means they aren't privy to the knowledge he is. "That's why I'm supporting her."

"As well you should. Does she know this is your strategy?"

"No. And I'm not telling her yet."

"Why?"

"I want her to tell her story to Reese with me guiding her to my conclusion, of course."

"As you would if she were on the stand," he assumes.

"Yes. I want him to experience what I did when I first talked to her. Her desperation, her honesty, and she is honest, no matter how brutal it is for her to speak the words."

"Are you sure a public place is the best place for this meet and greet?"

"It works for Reese, so we'll make it work, but I'm really not worried. An interesting thing about Delaney—she can tell you her story with dry eyes and somehow be composed, but you feel her spiraling inside. It's like nothing I've ever seen. You'll see. I want you to sit in on this."

"Are you sure she wants me to sit in?"

"She'll have the most powerful man in the legal world in front of her. Yes. She needs to feel that support. Unless you don't want to join us?"

The Escalade pulls to the front door of Reese and Cat's building and Grayson considers that idea a moment before he surprises me by saying, "No. This is your story, and hers, that's your writing, Mia. Not mine."

"My story is our story."

"Of course it is and inside our story, we weave our individual successes, which we celebrate together. I need to run to the bank and take care of a few things. I'll leave you with the Walker team, and meet you back here at the building." His hand slides under my hair and settles on my neck and he leans in close, his breath a warm fan on my cheek. "You've got this. And we've got each other."

I know what he's doing and I'm profoundly affected by where we've been and how far we have come together. He's right. We are two pieces of one whole, held together by love, but we have to grow each piece for a lasting bond. Because we know this now, we are stronger than ever before. We will not make the same mistakes as before. We were almost perfect and from now on, we both know that we will always be almost perfect. We can't let the word "perfect" allow us to take each other for granted.

He's right. We've got each other. "Yes, we do," I say, pressing my lips to his and we share a soft caress of tongues that I feel from head to toe.

Grayson growls soft and low. "Go before I don't let you go." He motions to Jacob.

Jacob exits the vehicle from the front and he's quickly opening my door. I hesitate to exit with my attention on Grayson. "Don't you need to speak to Reese?"

"See if we can give him a ride to the courthouse."

I nod. "Will do. Wish me luck."

"You don't need it." He winks. "You have the truth and a strategy."

I smile, but as I exit to the street, it fades into a mix of the cool fall wind and my nerves over this meeting. Jacob and Blake are both waiting for me on the sidewalk. The two men have size in common, both tall and broad, but otherwise, they're polar opposites. Jacob has a buzz cut, and he's wearing a tan suit and tie and a perfectly pressed shirt, while Blake is in jeans and a T-shirt with his long dark hair tied at his nape. Blake's a handsome man, but there are shadows under his eyes, and the lines on his face are more pronounced than usual. I'm reminded of last night and immediately say, "Thank you for all you've done. I know you're tired."

He arches a brow. "You mean I look like shit?"

"No," I say quickly. "I just meant—"

"It's okay. I'm not sensitive and shit. That's Savage." He eyes Jacob. "Right, Jacob?"

"Savage is many things I can't quite name."

I laugh, thankful for the distraction that's taken the edge off my nerves. Blake points to the back door behind me. "I'll trade spots with you," he says. "I'm going to chat with Grayson."

My brows dip and my heart lurches. "Is everything okay?" I suck in a breath and wait for the bombshell that has Blake here, chasing Grayson at seven in the morning, and clearly, one he's going to reveal alone, with me out of the conversation.

Chapter Eighty

Mia

"Blake?" I press. "Is everything okay?"

"Relax," he says. "Everything is flipping wonderful." He grins. "See. I didn't say fuck." He grimaces. "Damn it. Don't tell Kara."

Now I laugh. "I promise. If you promise everything really is flipping wonderful."

He grins again. "I promise. I'm just reassuring him about this deal being *fucking wonderful*." He winks at me now, too—apparently, it's that kind of morning—before he climbs inside the Escalade with Grayson and Smith.

Jacob shuts the door behind him. "Ready?"

"As ready as I'm going to be," I say, and together we head toward the building. "What's your story?" I ask him, preferring to know something about the people who I'm trusting to save my life.

"Army," he says, "which is a simplified way of defining my past, but I'm a simple guy."

"Somehow I doubt that," I reply.

His lips quirk, but he simply holds the building door for me. I enter with him on my heels and towering above me as we make our way toward the restaurant. We're halfway there when Reese intercepts us. "Morning, Mia." He stops in front of us, his blue suit fits to perfection, and his good looks, the reason some bloggers call him Mr. Hotness. Which I imagine he can't like, considering his professional reputation. "Morning, Jacob," he adds, before his attention shifts back to me. "I use Walker often for investigative and security work," he explains. "Jacob has helped me out a number of times. And sorry, this has to be early and fast."

"I just appreciate you making time," I say. "Grayson wants to drive you to the courthouse and get a few minutes to get a feel for what you think of this immunity deal."

"In case that ride is too short, let me just say this: I'm feeling optimistic about where this is heading with this deal. And since I know terms are what you and Grayson are likely concerned about, yes, I'm certain they'll negotiate the terms. All that said, why don't you two just come over for dinner tonight? We have our daughter and I have trial prep I need to be home to manage. That's the easiest way for us to get more time to talk."

"That works for us," I say, the idea of having our own baby girl doing funny things to my belly "We'd love that."

"Perfect," Reese says, lifting his chin at Jacob. "In case you don't know, Mia, this man's wife had something to do with helping move this along."

I glance at Jacob. "Your wife?"

Jacob gives a fast nod. "She's NYPD but she has a connection at the FBI that proved helpful, even beyond Blake's deep connections. She wasn't involved in this case, but she managed to insert herself in the right places."

"Thank you to her," I say. "I'll make sure Grayson knows."

"Not necessary, ma'am," Jacob assures me. "We just like to see the good guys win."

"As do I," I say, glancing at Reese, "which is why I appreciate this meeting, Reese."

"Well then," he says. "Let's get to it while I have time."

I nod and we head toward the restaurant. "I'll wait at the entryway," Jacob says, while Reese and I step into the doorway to the hostess stand to find Delaney sitting and waiting at a side bench. She pops to her feet, a petite, pretty woman with red hair and the kind of luminous pale freckled skin that money and good genes delivers. Her black dress, boots, and matching purse are Chanel, which I know because I love Chanel and only have Chanel because Grayson buys it for me. I won't buy it for myself. That was a bonding topic for me and Delaney as it was the same for her. Her husband bought her nice things, but unlike Grayson, who does it because he loves me, hers did it to apologize or hold her captive. She was also expected to present herself as an appropriate trophy wife. I feel as if she doesn't know how to be anything but what he literally beat her into becoming. Or else.

She hurries our direction and she's nervous when she joins us. I see that in the twist of her fingers in front of her before she shakes Reese's hand. "Delaney Wittmore. Or it is now. I'm going to change it back to Adams, soon."

"Understandable," Reese replies. "Sorry to rush this, Delaney," he adds, "but I have to be in court in an hour."

"Of course," she says. "Thank you for seeing me."

Her voice is small, but her will is not or she wouldn't have lived through the abuse she endured.

The hostess seats us and I have Delaney sit across from Reese, and it's not long before we all have steamy cups filled with coffee. I don't try to direct the meeting, not quite yet. I let Reese and Delaney start things out.

"I'm interested in your case, Delaney," Reese says. "but I don't represent anyone I don't believe is innocent. Once I believe in you, I'm passionate about winning, as I know Mia is as well. I need to feel the passion she does for your case. I need you to tell me your story in your words."

Once she begins to speak, I plan to lead her to my controversial defense that really shouldn't be controversial at all. Not once the entire story is told.

"I don't think there's a reason for me to tell my story," Delaney says, which doesn't surprise me. I know where she's going: to that honest place that won me over.

Reese arches a brow. "And why is that?"

"Because you just said that you don't represent anyone you don't believe is innocent. I'm not. I killed my husband."

Chapter Eighty-One

Mia

M ia

At Delaney's declaration that she killed her husband, Reese doesn't so much as blink. He doesn't look at me, either. He stays focused on Delaney. "Why?" he asks.

"Does it matter?" Delaney challenges. "I killed him."

"Do you want to go to jail?" Reese counters.

She cuts her stare, swallows hard, and then meets his stare again. "No, but," her fingers curl into her palms where they rest on the table, "*I killed him.*"

Reese doesn't miss a beat. "Why?"

"He wouldn't stop hitting me."

I pull a folder out of my briefcase, open it, and slide a photo of her from the night of "the incident" in front of him. In the photo, Delaney's face is beaten black and blue and her eye is swollen shut. He glances down at it, shows no reaction, and then looks at her. "Tell me more."

She swallows hard. "I was—desperate—for him to stop. I reached for anything and I grabbed the fireplace—the metal thing by the fireplace. The fire poker." She presses two fingers to her temple and then powers through the words. "I hit him. I didn't mean to kill him."

"How often did he beat you?" Reese asks.

"Daily," she replies.

"Did he rape you?" Reese asks, getting right to the point.

"Daily," she repeats.

"Why didn't you leave?" Reese asks next.

"He threatened anyone and everyone I knew." She makes a choked sound. "He even threatened the grocery store bakery manager I chat with every day who has three kids. And he had the money to make people dead and not get caught."

Reese arches a brow. "Did he tell you that?"

"Every day for sixteen of our seventeen years together."

My chest and eyes pinch just looking into her tormented stare. "Who inherits if you don't?" I ask, leading her to my strategy for her defense.

"My daughter," she replies.

"Who inherits if your daughter doesn't inherit?" I ask.

"His brother."

And we're almost to the sweet spot I'm reaching for. "What's your relationship with his brother?"

"He knew everything," she explains. "He told me I had two choices. Fight back or shut up."

"Fight back how?" Reese asks, traveling exactly where I want him to travel.

"He offered to buy me a gun."

Reese's head tilts slightly. "Are you or have you ever slept with him?"

"Never."

"Are you intimate with him in any way?"

Her lips flatten. "Never."

"Are you friends?" he asks, continuing to press.

"No," she says, as she said to me as well.

"Then how," Reese says, "did you have a conversation about buying a gun with him?"

She inhales and exhales. "He saw my bruises. He caught me off guard one day or he wouldn't have. I had practice. I knew how to hide them." She gives a choked laugh. "That's why everyone wants me to do their makeup. I'm good with makeup." She swallows hard. "He said—he wanted to talk to Mitch."

"Did he reject the idea of his brother beating you?" Reese asks.

She scoffs. "No. He didn't even blink, but he insisted on talking to Mitch. I begged him not to. He said he would not."

"Did he talk to Mitch?" Reese asks.

"He says he didn't. I believe he did."

"Why?" Reese asks.

"Because that night I was lectured on keeping our life private."

"Lectured or beaten?" Reese asks.

"He broke my arm," she states matter-of-factly.

"The medical records are in the file," I interject, tapping the folder still in front of him. "There are five separate incidents that required she see a doctor. All of which she called accidents."

"Did the brother," he glances at me and I supply, "Jim," before he continues with, "Did Jim know about your broken arm?"

"Yes," she says. "He told me that he didn't tell his brother. That he knows Mitch is crazy. He told me to be careful and that Mitch's first wife had an 'accident' and died."

"She fell while they were hiking in Colorado," I interject. "It was investigated and closed quickly, but the interesting thing is that her friends claim she was about to file for divorce."

Reese's lips press together and he glances at his watch and then at Delaney. "I have to go." He pauses and studies her two long beats before he asks. "Did your husband deserve to die?"

"It wasn't about him deserving to die. It was about me deserving to live. And that night it came down to me living or dying. I didn't make the decision to kill him. I made the decision to live."

He studies her for two more beats. "Do you deserve to go to jail?"

Her lashes lower and then lift. "I don't know. *I don't know.* I feel very confused."

He inclines his chin and then says, "I'll chat with Mia and we'll set-up another meeting. Do you want me to be involved with your defense?"

"I do," Delaney replies.

"And what do you hope that you'll get from my involvement?"

"Mia says you will help her, help me protect my daughter."

He considers that answer and then motions to the waitress and it's not long before Delaney leaves, and thankfully she has security in the lobby that I didn't know about until her departure.

She has just exited the restaurant when Reese holds up his phone. "I just got a text. We're delayed an hour for court." He motions to the table and we sit back down. "Her story is compelling and so is she. I'm on board if you both want me."

"We want you."

"Good. Now talk to me frankly. Because I don't even know why the hell she's being charged. What am I missing?"

"Nothing. She's suffering because the ADA was out to get Grayson and I'm an extension of him. It's unethical. It's wrong. I'd like to see him lose his job." I'm fired up now. "She shouldn't have been charged at all."

"Agreed."

"And for her benefit, rather than raising immediate hell over this, I'm hoping your name attached to her case will make this go away."

"And if we can't, what is your defense strategy?"

"That she was the murder weapon his brother used to kill him and inherit everything."

He arches a brow. "Come again?"

I lean in closer and lower my voice. "Friends of Mitch's first wife say Jim is the one that outed her divorce filing, knowing that Mitch was violent. Shortly after Jim did that, Mitch and the first wife went on a ski trip to a family wedding. That was where the accident happened. Mitch was misdiagnosed with cancer at that time. With her gone, Jim thought he was about to inherit."

"Jim does stand to inherit."

"Not just inherit. Inherit billions, Reese. We're talking Grayson's kind of bank account here. It's worth hiring Walker to investigate, and furthermore, Jim was whispering in Delaney's ear, scaring her. I believe he got rid of wife number one and when that didn't work, he needed wife number two to get rid of his brother. He used her as a murder weapon. He killed his brother. It's at least, reasonable doubt."

"It damn sure is," he says, approval lighting his eyes. "Let's start by me calling the ADA. If my involvement shuts this down, we celebrate tonight. If not, we look toward a trial and a win." He pulls out his phone and I listen to him greet the ADA. "Let's talk about Delaney Wittmore. I'm now on her legal team."

He listens a moment and then he says. "We both know she shouldn't have been charged. I don't care how many billions she inherits. She earned it." He grimaces at whatever is said and responds with, "I wonder if you could justify beating your wife, then? Or is it only okay if they get Chanel as an apology?" I don't know what the ADA says in reply, but Reese grimaces. "He hung up. He's unreasonable. There's more to this than you and Grayson. He wants a big win with a big name attached. I've seen this syndrome before and it's rotten. I have an idea, but before I share, I have to talk to Cat."

We stand up and he says, "For the record, Jim using her, a battered wife, as a murder weapon to inherit is a brilliant crime by a dangerous man. Furthermore," he adds, mimicking my earlier speech, "you catching onto it is brilliant lawyering."

"It's only brilliant if it works."

"The words of a winning lawyer unwilling to count her chickens until they hatch. I do believe we're going to be brilliant together."

I smile and I appreciate his compliments, but right now, I'm already thinking about how I will actually do that: winning for Delaney. I already have a million plans in my mind. I need to get to the office and start building a case against Jim.

I motion to Jacob where he sits at the bar and the three of us head outside. We've barely stepped out of the building when a tall man with a beard comes out of nowhere and rushes toward me. He's about ten seconds from grabbing me when Jacob grabs him.

I scream and Blake is suddenly there, pulling me forward and before I ever make it to the Escalade waiting at the curb, Grayson is out the door and running toward me.

Chapter Eighty-Two

Mia

I'm freaking out when Grayson all but drags me into the Escalade. I'm barely seated and he's cupping my face and staring down at me. "Did he hurt you?"

"No. Jacob was fast. I have no idea what that was or who that was. How did he even know I was here?" I lean around him to Reese. "Are you okay?"

"I'm used to reporters," he says. "They get crazy."

Grayson twists around to look at him. "Was it a reporter? Do we know that?"

"I recognize him," Reese confirms. "He is."

Jacob climbs into the front seat and turns to face me. "Is everyone okay?"

"Yes," I say, and despite Reese's claim that this man was a reporter, the Dungeon infiltrated our lives. They seem to be everywhere. I need to know if he's a reporter and one of them. "Tell me that wasn't the Dungeon," I say, needing to hear the words that tell me he wasn't. Needing that part of our lives to really be over.

The door beside Reese opens and Blake pokes his head in the door. "He's a reporter who swears he has a big scoop for you, Mia. We got rid of him and I have his card to verify his credentials."

"But is he with the Dungeon?" I press, not even considering a scoop for me. I'm not a reporter. That makes no sense.

"I don't believe that to be the case," Blake replies. "We'll check him out completely." He eyes Reese. "Make this damn deal with the Feds and get them some peace of mind."

"I'm going to call them at my lunch break," Reese promises, and Blake gives a nod. "All right then. Let me go handle this shit and let you all get Reese to the courthouse." He shuts the door.

"I need to move," Reese calls out to the front, and Smith immediately sets us in motion.

Reese leans forward to talk to us both. "Know this. The message I got from my conversation with Blake was that he believes the Dungeon threat is gone. He is not a man to make a statement like that lightly. He's not a false hope kind of guy, but I'll call you, Grayson, the minute I talk to the Feds. And once you sign an immunity agreement, you can do that interview you talked about with Cat or anyone you wish and shut down the press obsession with your stories." We've already made the walkable ride to the courthouse, which is swarming with protestors.

"Wonderful," Reese mumbles irritably. "This case has been a press nightmare."

Smith pulls us round to a side entrance, where the press is blocked off, parking right in front of a door for Reese's ease of escape into the building. Reese reaches for the door but hesitates, just a moment. "Don't get too happy when your press fades. It won't last. We're going to make headlines over Delaney." He exits the Escalade and shuts the door behind him.

Grayson arches a brow. "I take it that means you two are officially teaming up?"

"We are," I say. "Delaney won him over."

"And you had nothing to do with it?"

"I believe it was all Delaney, but Reese did try and call the ADA and got shut down hard and fast, just like I have." I frown. "It feels like there is more to this, doesn't it?"

"What are you thinking?"

"I don't know, but something is bothering me." I sink back into the seat and start beating up my mind, looking for an answer I can't quite reach, but it's there, wishing Grayson and I were alone so we could talk it out but we are not alone.

Grayson laces his fingers with my fingers. "It'll come to you," he says. "I know it will." He kisses my knuckles. That small little kiss sends goosebumps up my arm and warmth across my chest. This man loves me and when I think of the scandal around Mitch and his money, I'm really reminded of Grayson's trust issues. And he does have trust issues. Everyone is entranced by his money and power. He keeps a small circle around him. He's careful about who he lets close to him. He learned from his father to love hard, but to make sure the love is well-deserved and yet he didn't even want a prenup. He never once considered that I might be in this for his money. I'm so glad his father talked him into the prenup for more than one reason. As his father presented, of course, I want Grayson to know I don't want his money, but Grayson also needs to know that I won't stay for the money. The only way to do that is for the prenup to guarantee me money. That I wouldn't take of course, but that's not the point.

This man loves me.

And I am one lucky woman to have that love, but unlike the past, when I tended to see only my good fortune in this match, I now see his. He can trust me, and I love him passionately, with all my heart. *We* are lucky. Delaney was not. She was trapped in a diamond and Chanel-decorated prison and I haven't yet set her free.

Fifteen minutes later, we pull up to the Bennett building that is thankfully free of the press. Jacob walks us into the building and ensures I have his cellphone number. "Don't go anywhere without me."

I'm frowning when me and Grayson step onto the elevator. "So we aren't free of the Dungeon at all, are we?" I ask when the doors shut on us.

He turns to me, stroking hair behind my ear, his tenderness something that has always stolen my breath, and now is no different. "You have reporters hounding you left and right, baby. I've told them to keep you safe."

"Right. Of course. I'm just eager to have this over. I'm fortunate Walker was there when that man came at me. He could have been someone really dangerous."

"It's almost over."

Those words play in my mind the rest of the ride up: *almost over.* We're almost to the other side of our breakup because all of this is connected. Ri came at us and our relationship. Mitch came at Delaney, I think, shifting gears. Mitch's brother came at Delaney. I'll be okay. I have Grayson. Delaney is counting on me, and Reese, now. I have to come through for her.

We've just entered the Bennett executive offices and Eric and Davis are all but tackling Grayson. "We have the Feds' agreement," Eric informs him, both men in our path, halting us in the hallway. "We need to tear it apart."

Grayson kisses me. "Go solve your mystery. I'm going to go and read through this."

"Should I be there?"

"I can tell you that I know these two men. Two hours from now, it's not going to look the same. Spare yourself the twenty versions."

I'm torn, eager to work on the Delaney case, but nervous about this deal with the Feds. I eye Eric and Davis. "You feel good about it?"

Davis pipes in. "Cautiously—"

"Optimistic," I supply. "Okay, well, I'm getting used to that non-answer." I turn to Grayson. "I'll leave you three musketeers to your cautious optimism." I kiss Grayson's cheek and head into my office.

I've just sat down when my cellphone rings with a call from my father. "Hey, Dad."

"I just wanted to check on you, with all this mess going on. Are you still in the Hamptons with Grayson?"

"We're home now. I'm back at work at Bennett. And I have news. Are you up to a New Year's Eve wedding?"

"New Year's Eve?"

"Yes. New Year's Eve."

"That's fast, honey."

"It doesn't feel fast. It feels perfect."

We talk for a good twenty minutes and make plans for him to join us for the holidays. He struggles alone without my mother, and when we hang up, I wish for his happiness. I want him to find his partner in life.

My cellphone rings again and this time, it's Delaney. "I was just about to call you."

"I arrived home to being served." Her voice trembles. "You were right. Mitch's brother is suing me and my daughter for everything."

Of course, he is, I think. "That's good," I say.

"What? How is that good, Mia? This is not good."

"We need to talk about who the real killer is and it's not you. Jim used you to get rid of his brother and you, in one fatal swoop. He intends to inherit. Instead, we're going to make him pay. You have my word."

Chapter Eighty-Three

Grayson

T he immunity agreement is, as Blake said, a good deal.

I spend a good two hours with Eric and Davis, tearing apart the wording on the agreement sent to us by the Feds. All in all, we feel like we'll get to a place where this ends for me and Mia, and really, for the entire company. We're about to wrap up the meeting when Nancy hands me Reese's contract and Davis claims it for review. He heads to the conference room to have the quiet he needs to ensure he doesn't miss anything. Eric is about to leave as well, but I don't let that happen.

He's already at the door and I'm in front of my desk when I stop him. "Don't even think about it."

Eric's shoulders bunch but he turns around and shuts the door behind Davis. "If this is about—"

"It is," I assure him. "How much do I owe you?"

"You don't."

"Eric—"

"Grayson, damn it." He takes two steps toward me. "I don't want your money."

"Then I'll just make a very large deposit into your 401k. I'll estimate your generosity with my own."

"Damn it," he curses, scrubbing his jaw. "You know, if you weren't such a generous fuck, I wouldn't have done this. And now, because you are, you won't let me. For once, let someone do something for you."

"Here's what you need to understand, Eric. You did. You risked your life for me last night. And that was just last night. You and I are friends. I trust three people in this world. You, Mia, and Davis, though you and Davis are not on the same level, and you know it. We *are* brothers."

"Is that not what I'm showing you? Your money is not what we're about?"

"I have the money, Eric. You of all people know that it's a part of who I am. I was born into it. And I was taught to use it respectfully and thoughtfully and letting you pay to bail me out is not that."

"It's a gift."

"I don't need the money."

"And thanks to you, neither do I."

I inhale and exhale. "How much?"

"I estimated what Ri could afford based on his portfolio and finances, which Blake hacked for me."

"How much?"

"Five million, and I've made twenty times that working with you."

"How about a truce? Why don't we go half and half and do something good with the money?"

"Such as?"

I think of Delaney and the photos I'd seen in Mia's file. "Mia's client is an abused wife. Even with money, she was a prisoner in her own home. I can't imagine what it must be like for those who have no resources. I think we should help the battered women's shelter here locally."

"Considering my mother was a victim of my father in many ways, I'm all-in," Eric says.

There's a knock on the door and Nancy appears, entering and shutting the door behind her. "That new man, Kevin, that Mia hired is here. He says it's about Mia and urgent."

Eric and I exchange a concerned look. "Send him in," I say.

Nancy nods and hurries back to her desk, and Kevin appears in my office almost immediately. "This is Eric," I say. "You can speak freely around him."

"Hi Eric," he says, and looks between us. "I hope Mia forgives me for coming to you first, but she's been through a lot and I'm sensitive to that fact."

"What is this about?" I ask, trying not to sound impatient, but I am fucking impatient when it comes to Mia's safety.

"I went to the coffee shop and a man cornered me and handed me this." He indicates a folder. "He said it was a bombshell in the Delaney Wittmore case. I could have just walked it into Mia, but after the Ri stuff, I didn't want to risk handing her some threat or problem that I can't fully foresee. Especially since he knew I worked with Mia, and I've only been here a few days. That feels like a connection to Ri. Anyway, I thought you might want to be with her when she opened it." He moves forward and offers it to me. "It's sealed. I haven't looked inside. I wouldn't do that."

I accept the folder and study him intently, surprised by his level of loyalty and protection of Mia. He came to me to shelter her. Perhaps I've let the man in me misjudge him. Perhaps he really is just a good friend. "Thank you, Kevin. Your loyalty will not be forgotten."

"I'm not looking for good graces. Just trying to be a friend. Let me know if you need me." He turns and exits, shutting the door behind him.

Eric arches a brow. "What are you going to do?"

I stare at that envelope and fight my urge to rip it open, but I don't. I glance over at Eric. "In the past, I'd have opened it up and told her I did it to protect her. But I've learned my lesson. I'm going to respect my future wife and take this to her."

.

Chapter Eighty-Four

Mia

I've just hung up with Blake after he's confirmed the identity of the reporter who sideswiped me this morning when Grayson walks in. Just seeing him does funny things to my chest. The way he affects me just by entering a room never ceases to surprise me. Will that ever go away? I don't believe it will.

His eyes warm and I know he's read my reaction. The thing is, I don't even care. Yes, I swoon for Grayson, but we're mutually obsessed and in love, which is an amazing feeling that has me running a finger over my engagement band. "Hey," I say.

"Hey, baby." He shuts the door and my gaze slides to the envelope in his hand, my spine stiffening. "Is that the agreement?"

"No, but all is well on that end."

I frown, noting the edge to his presence I didn't initially see. "Something isn't good."

He rounds the desk and I stand up to meet him. "This," he says, "came to me from Kevin."

I blanch. "Kevin?"

"He was worried about you and thought I might want to give it to you. Note that I have not opened it despite a clawing need to do so."

I take the envelope. "What is this, Grayson?"

"A man confronted Kevin at the coffee shop and said this was a bombshell in the Wittmore case."

"And he cornered Kevin?"

"That's why Kevin thought it was strange. Whoever this reporter is knew he was here with you. He was afraid this was some kind of threat."

A realization hits me. "And you didn't open it?"

"No. Believe it or not, I used great restraint, however, if you should choose to hand it back to me and let me open it first, I'd be willing to trade you that little thing you like so much."

"That thing you do with your—"

"Exactly."

I laugh and hand him the envelope. "You win. Open it."

His gorgeous lips curve but he turns somber quickly, walking to the conference table and opening the envelope, while I wait anxiously. There's nothing that would be in that folder that would hurt Delaney. I know this. There is no part of me that fears otherwise, but God, I want to know what is in that envelope now.

"Huh," Grayson says, setting the documents on the table and motioning me forward. "Looks like financial transactions and photos of two men. Who are they?"

I pick up the first photo and my jaw drops. I indicate one of the men. "That's Delaney's brother-in-law, the one I believe used her as a weapon to kill Mitch, her husband. And that's the ADA who won't give her a deal."

"That looks shady," Grayson voices before I can.

"Yes, it does. What financial reports?" Grayson hands them to me and I glance through them. "I'm not sure what I'm looking at."

"Let me get our numbers man," Grayson says, walking to the desk to call him on the inner office phone.

"Wait," I say, before he has the chance to call Eric, scanning another sheet. "There are two sets of the same financial document. One shows large payments to an investment company to the initials NR. That matches the ADA's initials." I pass Grayson at the desk and dial Blake. "I need you to hack for me."

Grayson's eyes meet mine, pride in their depths. "I'll be in my office. Get him, baby."

"I will," I vow, and set out to do just that.

Blake agrees to hack for me, and when I can't locate any note or card in the envelope, I call him back. "I'm fast, but not that fast."

"I need you to text me the card for the reporter that cornered me this morning."

"You think this is him?"

"I do."

"I checked him out. He's legit, but be careful. I haven't had time to dig deeper. Check your messages now." He hangs up and the text is almost instant. "Robert Hall." My brows dip. Why does that name sound familiar? I google him and pull up his photo. He's a tall man with dark hair and glasses. His resume with a national news station is impressive. That has to be why he's familiar. Or rather, his name is familiar. His face is not.

I dial the cellphone on his card. He answers on the first ring. "Robert Hall."

"This is Mia Cavanaugh."

"You got it."

"I did. How did you get this?"

"I hired a PI."

"For a story? What's in this for you?"

"Mitch's first wife, his dead wife, was my sister."

The room spins around me. Now I know how I know his last name. The first wife. "And?"

"And I believe she was murdered."

"By who?"

"If you believe her journal. She feared him, but I found another journal recently. She was in an intimate relationship with Jim, Mitch's brother."

"You think he killed her?"

"I don't know who killed her, but she didn't fall down a cliff on her own. And I'm sure you know by now that Jim thought Mitch was dying at the time. And it sure seems like Jim is making a financial investment in Delaney being disinherited."

"Can I see the journals?"

"I left them at the security desk. I didn't want Kevin reading them."

"How did you know Kevin worked with me?"

"The PI was following Delaney's case. He told me where to find you and who to find you with."

"Will you testify to help Delaney?"

"I'll testify to help my sister, and if that means Delaney, yes. I will."

We disconnect and I dial Nancy. "Please can you go to the security desk downstairs and see if there is a package for me? It's urgent."

"Of course."

I stand up and start packing, thinking about my strategy, when an idea hits me. I return to my desk and dial Reese's office, and ask his secretary to have Cat call me ASAP. Right about the time Nancy hands me the package, my cellphone rings. "Thank you, Nancy. So much. This was important." I answer the line, "Cat?"

"Hi, Mia. I should have given you my number."

"I need a favor."

"Of course. I'm listening."

I tell her everything and then pitch her. "Would you agree to out the ADA in your column if I can't get the DA to drop the charges?"

"Heck yes. That's a big scoop."

"Thank you. Do you know the DA?"

"He's new. None of us have really interacted with him, but the word is he's not much better than his predecessor, who was shady. In other words, you were smart to use me. Do it. Use me and end this for that poor woman."

"Thanks, Cat." I have a thought.

I hang up and look up the DA's number. I dial his office and get his secretary. "I need to speak with DA Hendrix."

"He's out of the office."

"This is Mia Cavanaugh at the Bennett firm. I need to see him right away."

"Oh ah, okay. I'll let him know." She hangs up. She doesn't even get my number.

I dial Blake. He answers with, "Damn skippy, you're right. Jim Wittmore paid off the ADA. I have the proof."

My heart races. This is it. This is Delaney's salvation. "Can you email it to me?"

"You betcha. What else?"

"I need to have someone hand something to the DA once our immunity deal is signed. As in at home, where it will be more impactful. I know that's pushing limits but—can you make that happen?"

"Can we fucking make it happen? Are you serious? Ouch. Fuck. Kara, damn it. Okay. Mia. I meant, yes. I can."

I laugh and we disconnect.

A few minutes later, I've made copies of what I need for this meeting, and step to Grayson's door to find him behind his desk while Eric lounges on the edge. Eric stands up and crosses his arms. "I have to tell you," I admit. "I missed seeing you two powwowing like you are right now."

"Well then, you won't mind that I just invited myself to Thanksgiving dinner, now will you?" Eric asks.

This makes me smile inside. A family Thanksgiving, because that's what me, my father, Grayson, and Eric equal. And Delaney set free. Perfect.

"At the Hamptons house," I say. "Bring the peanut butter pie."

"I don't do peanut butter pie."

"You'd better start googling then."

Everyone laughs now and Grayson's eyes turn this wicked warm wonderful shade of green, a little bit lustful and a whole lot happy. "What's happening with Delaney?" he asks.

"I have a plan. A good one." And I realize then that I'm confident enough not to need to share it just yet. "Right now," I say. "I need to call the wedding planner." I grin, and with the satisfaction in Grayson's eyes, I head back to my office. I belong here and it feels good.

Chapter Eighty-Five

Mia

B efore our dinner with Reese and Cat, we gather in their kitchen, where we are introduced to their beautiful daughter, Heather, who is a blonde doppelganger for Cat. She's also a one-year-old daddy's girl. In between all the cuteness, Reese and I talk about Delaney and my plan to pressure the DA to clear Delaney's name. "I want to have the evidence delivered to him at his front door. That way it gets his attention. Blake said he'd make it happen. And Cat's willingness to write a tell-all helps immensely."

"Then let's clear a path for pressure on the DA," Reese says. He opens a drawer and slides a file onto the island. "I read the new agreement. The changes your team wanted are present, and honestly, they left me nothing to complain about. I'm feeling pretty overpriced right now, but bottom line, I'm going to advise you to sign it. Once you do, they have to clear any use of your business to catch the Dungeon through us. However, you do have to be reasonable, considering the full immunity clause." He glances at me. "And you don't need me after all. Go get the DA and make this right for Delaney. And now," he picks up Heather, "we're going to go put this little one to bed." He grabs a fancy Mont Blanc pen and sets it next to the folder. "Ink that and I'll scan that to the right people as soon as I get done reading Cinderella."

I smile and he and Cat head off with Heather. Grayson and I end up standing across from each other at their island.

"A little girl," Grayson says, his eyes tender as they meet mine. "I want a little Mia."

"I do believe you will be outnumbered if that happens."

"When that happens, I welcome that scenario. Did you call the wedding planner?"

"I did. And she said that a rush wedding, even small, was going to cost us a fortune."

"And?"

"And I set it up for New Year's Eve."

My reward is his devastatingly sexy smile. He grabs the pen on the counter and signs the agreement before sliding it in my direction. I sign as well: *Mia Cavanaugh.*

"Soon to be Mia Bennett," I say, casting him a shy smile.

"Not soon enough, baby."

Fifteen minutes later, we're on the balcony of Reese and Cat's apartment, with the fireplace sparked hot, a fall night breeze blowing cool, and expensive wine in our glasses. Reese has sent in the agreement, and I call Blake. "It's a go. Send him the file." I hang up and we touch glasses, toasting one win and another on the way. I sip my wine, which is delicious, but not a smart idea. We've been having a lot of unprotected sex. We want a baby. I end up pouring my wine into Grayson's glass. Cat arches an eyebrow, and as the men chat, she leans in closer. "Are you—"

"Not yet. Or I don't think so, but we want to be."

We start talking about pregnancy and Grayson clearly overhears because his hand settles on my leg, his fingers squeezing lightly. My hand covers his but I don't look at him. I'm shy and that is silly but true. A good kind of shy. The kind of shy that will be tender and warm and wonderful when we are alone.

For the next two hours, we enjoy conversation, food from the restaurant downstairs, and lots of legal discussion. It's clear that we have become fast friends with Reese and Cat. We are at the front door in the foyer of their apartment, just about to leave, when an unknown number rings my cell. I answer. "Mia Cavanaugh."

"Ms. Cavanaugh, this is the District Attorney."

My eyes go wide and I look between Grayson, Cat, and Reese. "Mr. Hendrix."

"I got your message. Loud and clear. Tell Mrs. Wittmore that I'm dismissing her case."

"And what of her brother-in-law?"

"I'll open an investigation."

"And the ADA?"

"Suspended immediately. He already knows. And yes, I'm opening an investigation. Unlike rumor would have it, I'm not my predecessor. I'm not dirty. It's handled. And Ms. Cavanaugh, try talking to me rather than threatening me in the future. I'm a Texas boy. You get further with me with sugar or queso, not the shit they make here in New York City, than you do with threats." He hangs up.

I have a silent scream because of Heather. "Oh my god. It's done. Case dismissed."

There is hugging and celebrating but I need this celebration to move. I turn to Grayson. "I need to see Delaney."

"Let's do it," he says.

Half an hour later, I call Delaney from her lobby and when we reach her front door, she opens it in pajamas. Her bottom lip trembles. "What's wrong?"

I tear up just telling her. "They dropped the charges."

She blanches and I pull out the photo of her beaten face. "They dropped the charges because you are not a killer."

She bursts into tears and I hug her. I know in that moment that I want to make a difference in other people's lives, just like I have for Delaney. I want to be the person in Grayson's life that helps him make a difference for other people.

Chapter Eighty-Six

Mia

Thanksgiving is chilly and rainy, but it's also wonderful. Me, Grayson, my father, and Eric put up a stunning silver tree. My father brings all of our old decorations over. We decorate with memories from Grayson's family and ours, and I'm sad when I learn that Eric has nothing of his mother left. As for his father, he wants nothing to do with him.

As for food, Grayson makes his dad's famous turkey, my dad and I make my mom's mac 'n' cheese, and Eric makes his mom's stuffing and potatoes. I don't get my peanut butter pie. I give Eric a hard time about it, too. I mean, I was really craving that pie. It's a special day that Grayson and I end with a chilly walk to our lighthouse.

Back at the office, come December first, I launch our charity division with the five million dollars Grayson donates in Eric's name before he adds another ten million himself. Delaney not only donates another ten million herself, she volunteers to help head up the program. By Christmas, we're already on our way to helping those in need, and I've come to believe that she and I were meant to cross paths for a higher purpose.

In between it all, the wedding planner keeps me on my toes, but so much of what Grayson and I wanted the first go-around hasn't changed. This is a small, intimate wedding, with only twenty guests invited. Memorable, not grandiose, is what we're looking for and it feels perfect. It's exactly what I want.

On Christmas Eve, I have a fitting for my dress. The stylist meets me at the apartment while Grayson runs last-minute holiday errands. I'm a bit shocked when my dress is snug, but the stylist assures me she can make adjustments, and promises the dress will arrive to the house the day after Christmas. I grab my phone and count the days since my last period and a smile touches my lips. I'm late. By the time we're loaded up to head to the Hamptons,

I've snuck out to buy a couple of tests, and picked up my gift to Grayson. We meet Eric and my father at the airport, and for the first time ever, the chopper ride makes me queasy. Somehow I hide it from Grayson. I have to hide it. I mean, what better Christmas gift than this? If it's even true. It might be wishful thinking.

Once we're at the house, I busy myself preparing for the holiday, but the minute the men are wrapped up in sports and drinking beer, I hide in the bedroom to wrap presents. I also can't find the pregnancy tests. In a panic, I hunt for them, because I don't want Grayson to find out from a box of untaken tests. That would ruin my surprise. They are nowhere to be found. I sneak to the store, buy a new one, along with cookies I don't need, just to have an excuse for going to the store. Grayson greets me at the door and we eat the cookies together.

The next morning, I wake to Grayson's mouth all over my body, and he does that thing with his tongue that I love. That thing in the most intimate part of me. It feels different, better, if that's even possible. I feel different. And when Grayson fixes me in those intense green eyes, he knows, too.

"What's different about you?"

"I'm about to be a married woman."

He settles the weight of his big perfect body over mine and presses inside me, burying himself deep before his lips brush mine, and he says, "Yes. You are."

He makes love to me, tender, beautiful love, and when we start our Christmas morning, I do so happier than I have been on a holiday since my mother died. Once Grayson heads to the kitchen to make coffee, I sneak into the bathroom to take my new test. The old ones are still missing. I pee on that little strip and then wait. It's one minute that feels like ten hours. And when it gives me a plus sign that means I'm pregnant, I cry happy tears.

I don't want to deny Grayson the chance to see the real test, because I know him—he'll want to see it. I wrap it all up in plastic and then place it in a box. I wrap it with silver paper and a huge bow. Once I'm dressed in my red Christmas sweater, I hunt down coffee. My father corners me in the kitchen. He looks younger today, happier. Even the wrinkles around his eyes seem to have lightened, despite the heavy salt and pepper in his hair and beard. He holds up a bag. The bag with my tests! I grab them. "Thank you. Did you tell anyone?"

"No, of course not. Are you?"

"Yes," I whisper. "I'm going to tell him today."

"Does he want a baby?"

"Oh yes. Yes, he does."

He pulls me into a bear hug and when he pulls back, he's tearing up. "I'm happy for you, for you both."

"Should I tell him for a wedding present or a Christmas present?"

"If you can manage to keep the secret, it's a part of starting your new life. Tell him on your wedding night."

"Yes. Yes, that feels right."

"Speaking of new lives," he says. "I met someone. She's away for the holiday. Her daughter is in Europe. I'd like you to meet her when she gets back."

I touch his face. "You look happy, Dad. I'd love to meet her. New beginnings."

"New beginnings."

It's Grayson, and I turn to find him standing in the kitchen, wearing a tan sweater with a high collar. "Hi."

"Hi, baby," he says, and when I walk to him he pulls me into his arms and kisses me. "How about a walk?"

"I'd love that."

We spend the next two hours walking, talking, and lounging in our lighthouse. When we return home, we cook. We eat. We exchange gifts. Eric gives me a peanut butter pie, which has us all laughing. And a beautiful butterfly necklace. "You're spreading your wings and flying, baby," he says about his thoughtful gift.

He gives Grayson a rare AC/DC vinyl record. "I thought you might add to your father's old collection."

My father gives us an album of photos he took the holiday before last of us. It's perfect and Grayson and I will spend way too much time looking through it later, for sure. Finally, it's our turn to give gifts.

For Eric, we gift him flight lessons. It seems that the one thing the inked SEAL, savant, attorney, and investor hasn't done is fly a plane. But I also give him an infinite number symbol statue. It's engraved with the words: *Forever friends.* Forever family. He doesn't tear up. That's not for savants and badass SEALs, but he hugs me so hard I almost choke. I'm not sure it's good for the baby.

For my father, Grayson and I give him a new car that Grayson has delivered to the house with a huge red bow on it. A Porsche. My father does cry. Like a baby. I give Grayson a ring for his right hand engraved with the words: *My best friend, my lover, my soulmate.*

He doesn't outwardly react, but he kisses me hard and deep, right there in front of everyone and the look in his eyes is pure love.

Next, he hands me his gift. A pretty red box with a silver bow. I open it and smile when I find a stunning bracelet with hearts and diamonds chasing the chain. A small charm dangles from it that reads: *No fear. Only love, All my love, Grayson.*

Now I'm tearing up at the message that speaks to our journey together. And our forever. I wrap my arms around him and he holds me close, his lips finding my ear. "Forever, Mia."

"Forever," I whisper.

Chapter Eighty-Seven

Mia

We sign all the legal paperwork, including our license, a few days before the wedding in the Hamptons. Afterward, bundled up in jeans and sweaters, with jackets over our clothes, we visit his parents' graves. Together we lay down flowers on each. At his mother's grave, Grayson kisses my hand and says, "She would have loved you and you her."

"And my mother would have loved you."

We leave the graveyard and stop at a Christmas shop where we choose an ornament for each of our parents and then go home and place them on the tree.

The eve of our wedding arrives and a crew with it to set-up for the wedding. Our living room furniture is moved and chairs are set-up in front of the tree. Little diamond ornaments are dangling from our ceiling to sparkle and shine like snowflakes twinkling in the moonlight.

It's ten when Grayson caves to my demand that he stay in a hotel. "It's bad luck to see the bride on the day of the wedding before the actual wedding."

We make it to the front door to say our goodnights, and he carries me back to our bed, where we end up naked. Somehow by 11:59, I get him out of the door. He calls me the minute he's in the hotel. "Tell me again why I'm not in bed with my future wife?"

"Bad luck."

"Hmmmm. Tell me what you're wearing."

I laugh. "You're bad."

"Right. Should I come home?"

"No."

"Mia—"

"No, Grayson."

He gives a heavy sigh. "Okay. But this is the only night for the rest of our lives that I'm sleeping anywhere without you."

"That's a hard vow to keep."

"Not hard at all. Goodnight, baby. I love you."

"I love you, too." We disconnect and I snuggle into his pillow and inhale that spicy, male scent of his, missing him. The way I missed him every day we were apart. The way I never want to miss him again.

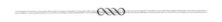

I wake alone and feel the emptiness of the house. My close friend, Courtney, has been traveling for work, and apparently married an Italian man in Italy. My mom is gone. Then Grayson sends me a text: *Almost mine.*

A smile spreads on my face and I type: *Already yours.*

Prove it, he replies. *Say I do. I love you, baby.*

I love you, too.

We've finished our exchange, and I've dressed in leggings, and clipped my hair on top of my head, when new friends come through for me. Cat calls me mid-morning with a surprise. "My brother is babysitting. Surprise. I just landed at the airport. Reese is here, too. He's going to see Grayson and the guys at the hotel."

Instantly, I'm smiling all over again. A few minutes later, she pulls up in a rental car. She exits with coffees in her hands, jeans and a pink sweater as her gear, and smiling her way past the front door. And somehow, some incredible somehow, the minute she's set her things down and really looked at me, she knows I'm pregnant. "Oh my God. Congratulations." She hugs me.

"How did you know?"

"You glow, Mia. It's such a beautiful glow. When are you telling him? Or does he know?"

"Tonight and if you know, maybe he knows."

"Oh he probably knows, but he doesn't know. Something just seems different to him. It did to Reese."

From there it's all girl talk and nerves for hours.

Late in the day, Cat helps me set-up a surprise for Grayson at the lighthouse. By the time we're back, not one but three stylists are waiting on me. Grayson clearly went overboard. At some point after my shower, Cat forces me to eat, but I don't even know what I eat. Banana bread, I think. Fruit, maybe. I'm just too nervous to know.

Someone, one of my stylists, tries to offer me champagne. Cat quickly takes the glass and downs it. "Thank you. That was delicious."

I laugh and she laughs, and I'm thankful for this new friend. Just before I put on my dress, Cat changes into a pretty floral dress. I'm raving over it, when Grayson's godmother, Leslie, rushes into the room. "Where is my new goddaughter?!"

I smile and hop to my feet, only to find myself in a big embrace. "I know you miss your mama just like Grayson does, but I'm right here, honey. I will be here as long as God lets me be here."

Leslie, who was best friend's with Grayson's mother, is a petite woman with long dark hair who vowed years ago to look after Grayson and she does. The idea of calling her my godmother squeezes my heart. "I'd like that."

Not long after Leslie arrives, Delaney joins us in the bedroom, and dressed in a pale pink dress, she looks lovely, but deep in her eyes shadows lurk and pain lingers.

"Hi," she says, sitting down in a chair next to the vanity where one of the stylists has been working her magic.

"I'm glad you made it."

She squeezes my hand. "I wanted to watch a real fairytale happen. So I know I can still find mine, too."

And she will, I decide. Otherwise, she wouldn't be here, looking beyond her own pain. She wouldn't be at our offices daily helping others look beyond their pain with our new charity program.

When finally, it's time to dress, my nerves go wild. I'm shaking, I think, as my hands won't steady. "I'm a mess."

"It's normal," Cat informs me. "I was a wreck when I married Reese."

Once I finally step into my gown, I stand in front of the mirror, my hair long and silky brown over my shoulders. The elegant white silk and the delicate floral designs are perfect. And it's not too tight anymore.

"Stunning," Cat says, as do all the stylists, in murmurs of approval.

One of the girls glosses my lips and then has me bend just enough to place my long, sheer floral veil. There's a knock on the door and my father pokes his head in. "It's time. Oh my." He steps through the door. "Stunning, baby girl. Just stunning. Wow. Your mother—oh god, your mother would be so proud."

I start to tear up and Cat points at me. "Do not cry and mess up your make-up."

I nod and eye my father's tuxedo. "You look pretty snazzy yourself, Dad."

He winks and the music, a violin right here in our house, begins to play, the beautiful sound lifting in the air. Nerves explode again and the room fades in and out. I barely know how I end up in the hallway, holding a bouquet of winter lilies, my mother's favorite flower. I'm holding my father's arm and when he urges me to walk, goosebumps rise on my skin.

This is it.

This is the moment Grayson and I have waited forever for, for years now. This is the moment we've been headed for since the very day I ran into him in the Bennett lobby. Somehow I'm walking, and as I bring a room full of close friends into view, I barely see them. I barely see the violinist playing near the tree. All I see is Grayson, standing by the tree with the preacher, the son of the man who'd married his parents. He looks stunning in his tuxedo. I hold tight to my father, my knees wobbling.

I clutch my flowers.

Grayson steps into my path, he waits for me, my knight in shining armor. Tall, dark, and so good-looking. My best friend. My hero. The father of my child. His eyes meet mine, and the world shines brighter, and my heart swells. My love grows broader and deeper. When finally I'm in front of him, he takes my hands, and it's like we're floating on a sea of forever.

"You look like a Christmas angel, baby. *Beautiful.*"

"Grayson," is all I manage for the emotion in my throat, and it's a whisper only he can hear.

"Mia," he replies, and we step in front of the preacher.

Our vows are simple. We wanted simple. The preacher begins to speak and we repeat the words he tells us to speak. When it comes time for the ring, Eric steps forward and offers Grayson my ring. He slides it onto my finger. "With this ring, I thee wed."

My father hands me Grayson's ring and with a shaky hand, I slide it onto his finger. "With this ring, I thee wed."

We're just staring at each other, when the preacher says, "Do you, Mia, take this man to be your lawfully wedded husband?"

"I do," I whisper, my voice cracking with emotion.

"Do you, Grayson, take Mia to be your lawfully wedded wife?"
"I do," he says, and he folds me close, his voice low and rough. "Forever, Mia."

"Forever," I repeat.

The preacher clears his throat. "I now pronounce you man and wife."

Epilogue

Mia

A long time later, with the new year fast approaching, I remove the long skirt to my dress to reveal a shorter one, pull on sneakers and a jacket, and Grayson and I leave our guests to ring in the new year at the house. We walk hand in hand to the lighthouse, the ocean crashing against the shore. I'm not nervous now about my surprise, the way I was about the wedding. I'm excited and every time Grayson and I peek at each other, I all but burst with my need to share our news.

Finally, we climb the steps to the lighthouse and I stop near the top. "You go first. I have a surprise for you."

His eyes light. "A surprise? Here?"

"Yes." I motion him forward. "I'm dying to share this surprise, so hurry up."

"Now I'm really curious." He walks ahead of me and I follow to the small outside space where he proposed that is now covered in pink and blue balloons.

Grayson glances over his shoulder at me with a curious look. "What is this?"

I step to his side and point to the lounge chairs we often sit in side by side. His holds his surprise. "Look in the box."

Now, he's more urgent with his curiosity, I wonder if some part of him knows what is coming. I mean the balloons are quite a hint. He sits down and the lid is off the box in seconds, and instantly emotions all but explode from me. Grayson pulls out the pregnancy test. He looks at it and then me. "Mia?" He sounds breathless, like he's not quite sure if this is real or a promise of the future.

"It's real, Grayson. We're pregnant."

He's on his feet in a blink, pulling me into his arms. And I swear it's the moment his lips touch mine that an explosion of fireworks hits the sky. It's officially a new year and we're the Bennetts. And our story is just getting started.

THE END

Don't miss the other Scandalous Billionaires!

https://www.lisareneejones.com/scandalous-billionaires.html

Want another KindleUnlimited read from me? Check out my Inside Out series! Grab the first few chapters plus exclusive bonus scenes here: https://bookhip.com/DHFRRLM

An **INSIDE OUT** Extra
and a sneak peek into CARELESS WHISPERS

How It All Started...

One day I was a high school teacher on summer break, leading a relatively uneventful but happy life. Or so I told myself. Later, I'd question that, as I would question pretty much everything I knew about me, my relationships, and my desires. It all began when my neighbor thrust a key to a storage unit at me. She'd bought it to make extra money after watching some storage auction show. Now she was on her way to the airport to elope with a man she barely knew, and she needed me to clear out the unit before the lease expired.

Soon, I was standing inside a small room that held the intimate details of another woman's life, feeling uncomfortable, as if I was invading her privacy. Why had she let these items so neatly packed, possessions that she clearly cared about deeply, be lost at an auction? Driven to find out by some unnamed force, I began to dig, to discover this woman's life, and yes, read her journals—dark, erotic journals that I had no business reading. Once I started, I couldn't stop. I read on obsessively, living out fantasies through her words that I'd never dare experience on my own, compelled by the three men in her life, none of whom had names. I read onward until the last terrifying dark entry left me certain that something had happened to this woman. I had to find her and be sure she was okay.

Before long, I was taking her job for the summer at the art gallery, living her life, and she was nowhere to be found. I was becoming someone I didn't know. I was becoming her.

The dark, passion it becomes...

Now, I am working at a prestigious gallery, where I have always dreamed of being, and I've been delivered to the doorstep of several men, all of which I envision as one I've read about in the journal. But there is one man that will call to me, that will awaken me in ways I never believed possible. That man is the ruggedly sexy artist, Chris Merit, who wants to paint me. He is rich and famous, and dark in ways I shouldn't find intriguing, but I do. I so do. I don't understand why his dark side appeals to me, but the attraction between us is rich with velvety promises of satisfaction. Chris is dark, and so are his desires, but I cannot turn away. He is damaged beneath his confident good looks and need for control, and in some way, I feel he needs me. I need him.

All I know for certain is that he knows me like I don't even know me, and he says I know him. Still, I keep asking myself — do I know him? Did he know her, the journal writer, and where is she? And why doesn't it seem to matter anymore? There is just him and me, and the burn for more.

Grab the first few chapters plus exclusive bonus scenes here:
https://bookhip.com/DHFRRLM

Also By Lisa Renee Jones

Surrender

Because I Can
When I Say Yes

THE TYLER & BELLA TRILOGY

Bastard Boss
Sweet Sinner
Dirty Little Vow

WALL STREET EMPIRE

Protégé King
Scorned Queen
Burned Dynasty

STANDALONE THRILLERS

You Look Beautiful Tonight (L.R. Jones)
A Perfect Lie
The Poet
The Wedding Party (L.R. Jones)

eBook only

About the Author

New York Times and *USA Today* bestselling author Lisa Renee Jones writes dark, edgy fiction including the highly acclaimed *Inside Out* series and the crime thriller *The Poet*. Suzanne Todd (producer of Alice in Wonderland and Bad Moms) on the *Inside Out* series: *Lisa has created a beautiful, complicated, and sensual world that is filled with intrigue and suspense.*

Prior to publishing, Lisa owned a multi-state staffing agency that was recognized many times by The Austin Business Journal and also praised by the Dallas Women's Magazine. In 1998 Lisa was listed as the #7 growing women-owned business in Entrepreneur Magazine. She lives in Colorado with her husband, a cat that talks too much, and a Golden Retriever who is afraid of trash bags.

Printed in Great Britain
by Amazon

43184470R00229